"Trumpeter, sou￼￼￼op-
ping her bow into the case. ￼￼￼out
high and brassy-sweet, and the Alliance horse sprang
forward with a single war-howl.

She tightened her grip on Hotblood, bracing her feet;
the Ri squealed, wind whipping his silver mane, and
even then horses on either side shied slightly. The consciousness of woman and Ri merged, a single mind
with two nodes. The shield slid off her back and her
left arm reached through the grips, the lance lifted out
of the scabbard; out of the corners of her eyes she could
see the others' long shafts slanting down. Under the
continuous trumpet note, hooves fell like muffled
thunder on the root-laced dirt.

Halfway there, and the Arkans were deployed. *Too
late, you should've sent out a half-troop to screen while you
got into line, shitheads,* Shkai'ra thought tightly, bringing
her lance around to point over Hotblood's head at the
man she had chosen. Their trumpet sang, and there
was a ripple of movement down the Imperial line as
the cavalrymen snapped down their visors, blank ovals
of scarlet steel with a slit for the eyes and a pattern of
holes over the mouth, emblazoned with a rayed sun in
gold. Another call, and they lowered their lances and
clapped heels to their mounts with a shout. The big
horses jumped off their haunches, slowly building
toward what would be an earth-shaking gallop.

Close enough now to see details, a hammered-out dint
in a shield's face, the dapple of a white's neck. A helmet
plumed with eagle feathers dyed red bending toward
her; a hint of blue eyes. *We're at full gallop, they're not
much more than standing . . .* Floating gallop, Hotblood's
pace smoother and more ground-hugging than a horse's.
She laughed, braced her feet and swung the point down.

The Fifth Millennium Series

The Cage by S.M. Stirling & Shirley Meier
Lion's Heart by Karen Wehrstein
Lion's Soul by Karen Wehrstein
Shadow's Daughter by Shirley Meier
Shadow's Son by Shirley Meier, S.M. Stirling &
  Karen Wehrstein
Snowbrother by S.M. Stirling (forthcoming)
Saber and Shadow by Shirley Meier and
  S.M. Stirling (forthcoming)

SHADOW'S SON

Shirley Meier
S.M. Stirling
Karen Wehrstein

BAEN
FANTASY

SHADOW'S SON

Copyright © 1991 by Shirley Meier, S.M. Stirling, and Karen Wehrstein

A Baen Books Original

Baen Publishing Enterprises
P.O. Box 1403
Riverdale, N.Y. 10471

ISBN: 0-671-72091-0

Cover art by Darrell Sweet

First printing, December 1991

Distributed by
SIMON & SCHUSTER
1230 Avenue of the Americas
New York, N.Y. 10020

Printed in the United States of America

Dedication

To Anne-Marie Meier,
Marjorie Stirling,
Olive Shaw (1926–1991),
and other mothers everywhere.

ACKNOWLEDGMENTS

Our first inclination is to thank each other, but we're all getting paid for this, so . . .

For critical help and support, thanks to the rest of the Bunch of Seven, who at the time were: Janet Stirling, Louise Hypher, Mandy Slater and Julie Czerneda. Also to Dave Edmund and Dave Kirby.

For letting us stay at the cottage in Muskoka, again: Margaret Layton and Dave Kirby.

For inspiration: Way Lem (who recently moved to Muskoka), Fred Foreman (who helped pioneer Muskoka), A. Pajitnov and V. Gerasimov (the creators of Tetris), Mike Oldfield, and the usual host of others.

For helping perfect strangers at the mere mention of the name Fred Foreman, in the spirit of Muskoka: Gail Dempsey.

And a particularly large second thank you to Janet Stirling, for doing the dishes and putting up with *three* oversensitive, compulsive/obsessive, cranky, caffeine-gulping writers instead of the usual one.

Book I: Summons

I

The address was written with an Arkan pen, leaving none of the sputters and blots a quill would leave. Megan Whitlock picked up the sealed envelope from the pile on her lap-desk. *News I've waited for?* No, probably more of the usual "prices of glass and luxury items have risen again, with the Arkan-Yeoli war drawn out so much longer than anyone expected . . ."—the usual information that came across the desk of the proprietor of a great merchant house.

She put the packet down, stretched, and strolled to the gallery that overlooked the atrium, its roof of glass and translucent agate letting in soft winter light, and leaned over the heavy oak railing. Megan was short, even for a Zak, a race shorter on average by a good head and a half than most others, with pale skin, a thin, faded white horizontal scar across the top of one cheek and the side of her nose. Her mid-calf-long hair was black with an ice-white streak at one temple, woven into elaborate braids which held the long mass neatly away from the heart-shaped face and out of her black eyes. The fingers of her hands tapped the honey-colored wood, her gray steel claws making a clicking sound.

She'd been working all day; time for a break. Below, Shkai'ra sword-danced, the drill that began with the Nine Cuts; beginning slow, her movements flowing into each other with a delicate grace incongruous in a woman her size. She was near six feet, in Zak measure 178 *schentiam*, a good two heads taller than most Zak. Her copper-blond hair was tied back in Kommanza warrior braids, bouncing on muscular shoulders slicked with sweat. The hawklike features too were unusual in F'talezon; now they wore a look of introspection, lips parted in a slight smile.

I married a woman from across the Lannic, Megan thought, smiling to herself as she breathed in the sweet cinnamon-scented oil burning in the lamps that hung from the iron strapping of the roof. *I'm used to how she looks, but I'm still not used to her being my wife; or Rilla; or Shyll being my husband either.*

Nearby Sova, now fourteen and already considerably taller than Megan, tumbled with the puppies on the flagstones, giggling, ash-blond hair pulling loose of its braids. Full-grown, the girl would be as tall as Shkai'ra, and not less muscular if the Kommanza had her way; now she was all feet and hands and tangled limbs, her breasts finally rounded. The pups, Dee and Dah, were bigger than the girl now, though not full-grown; greathounds not only outsized common dogs by double, but grew faster in their first months.

Megan had never expected to adopt a Thane, one of her people's oldest enemies; but then not much in her quest up the River Brezhan a year and a half before, to regain the Slaf Hikarmé from Habiku Smoothtongue, had gone as expected. Even the ending, not quite: in her rage at what he'd done to so many of her old shipmates, not to mention her, she'd planned to put him in a cage welded shut, and hang it up in this very atrium. That hadn't worked out. But every now and then, pacing in the gallery, she would imagine it was there, the room echoing with his screams, or perhaps mad laughter, instead of Sova's carefree noise, and know it would have been for the worse. For one thing, it would have made the house unfit for raising children.

Back to work. She ground a fist into the small of her back as she straightened; this sedentary life was making her stiff. Only a bit more, she promised herself as she went back to the packet on her desk. Examined closer, the writing seemed familiar. She broke the seal.

To MEGAN called Whitlock,
Slaf Hikarmé (House of the Sleeping Dragon)
F'talezon.
Third Iron-Cycle, Tenth Day, Year of the Lead
    Cat

My investigations regarding your expatriate son LIXAND, heretofore futile for the year that I have undertaken your contract, have suddenly borne substantial fruit. It seems very likely he is in Arko the City Itself. An agent of mine discovered a dancing boy owned by the AITZAS Family TEMONEN, of Fidelity Street, who fits his description perfectly: blond, black-eyed, small of build, about ten years old. Probing revealed that RASAS, as he is called there, was bought at the age of two in the slave-market of Arko, which matches well with the time he was abducted from you.

By all indications, he is healthy and well-fed, being prized as a lead performer in NUNINI-BAS TEMONEN's troupe of dancing boys. I made the utmost attempt to purchase him, but was refused absolutely; it seems he is also a favorite of the Lord.

I await your instructions.

Hoping you find this information of great value,

I am your faithful agent,

TIRPAS ORREN, *fessas*
37 Avenue Aven
Arko, the City Itself.

She read it three or four times, her hands shaking,
pulse pounding in her ears, barely believing. After eight
years, she knew where her son was. After eight years
wondering, then this last year, when it had finally become
possible, feverishly searching through a network of spies
hired in every major city in the Empire of Arko, there
was a house and a city to pin him to, circumstances to
imagine, a setting to make his life seem real to her. A
place to track him to, to find him, to buy or steal or
carve him free of . . . no, not buy. She'd stated clearly
from the start, the maximum price Tirpas was authorized
to offer: all she had, short of destituting the family. That
was rather a lot. Tirpas had obviously offered that and
been turned down. *How rich is this fish-gutted bastard,
that my son isn't worth that amount? Or how . . . besot-
ted . . .*

Steal or carve, then. She'd considered going into the
Empire personally before, despite the risk—foreigners
were accorded no right to freedom there, and slave-
catchers knew it—but had decided against. A hireling
who knew the ropes in Arko and didn't need to run and
hide had been a better bet, for such a needle-in-a-hay-
stack search.

But now the search was done. She ran back down the
stairs, and called into the atrium. "Shkai'ra! How soon
can you be ready to leave on a long trip?"

The Kommanza lowered her sword, wiped one forearm
across her face. "Two days, traveling light. Where to?
Business or pleasure?"

Rilla, Megan's second wife and cousin, came down the
steps with a basket of flower bulbs over her arm. She

was taller than Megan by almost a hand-width, mink brown hair trimmed short and sharp around her face, giving her an elfin look, making her dark amber eyes seem much bigger. "Dark Lord, Sova," she said. "We'll have to buy a warehouse of tunics; if you want to play with the dogs, wear an old one! Go change, now!"

Sova thumped on the ribs of the puppy who held her down, making a bang like a drum. "I want to hear about this trip."

"Arko," Megan said. "Business. Is Shyll home yet? I want to talk to everyone about this."

Rilla put the basket down. "No, he'll be back for the evening meal. Do you mean business *in* Arko, Meg? Nobody does that who isn't Arkan."

"My agent's found Lixand." Rilla froze, silent, then nodded.

Megan turned away up the stairs, the soft sigh of the door closing cutting off a question of Sova's, and walked back to her office. The setting sun shone red through the west window, touching the rim of the city over the Lake Quarter. She would come out when Shyll came home, she decided. She shuffled the papers with one hand, staring at the words without reading them, looking at the bloody light from the setting sun on her fingers, remembering.

Lixand, my son. She'd borne him at fourteen, on the old *Zingas Brezhani,* River Lady, docked in Bjornholm. *I swore you'd be my son, with nothing of him in you. Baby, born in blood and pain, I nearly gave my life for you. Too big for me, you were, my firstborn, ensuring you would be my last.* Soft blond hair under her fingers as he nursed, eyes that were blue like *his* at first, because *he* was an Arkan, but then turned dark like hers, *thank Koru,* blinking sleepily. . . .

Sarngeld, the captain, her owner. Atzathratzas was his real name, or part of it, *every Arkan tacks on all the formal-sounding titles he can dig up*—but no Zak could pronounce all those consonants. *Solas,* warrior caste. Nursing, she'd had too much of a woman's rounded shape to interest him. Ex-Arkan, ex-soldier. *May your soul freeze and burn at once in Halya.*

My son. The day you were weaned, how you were weaned. . . . He'd been two, both running and speaking, knew already to avoid the captain. *He* was on deck, dealing with another Arkan, in their clipped, snobbish tongue, hands hidden in gloves. The baby heard his tread before she did, looking away from the wood and string rattle she was dangling for him. She gathered him into her arms and stood up, big toddler though he was.

Sarngeld's face was twisted in a frozen sort of smile she couldn't read. "Come, girl." *I couldn't fight him anymore: for your sake, my son. You were his hold on me.* The wooden slave-links locked around her wrists, the chains, to the staple in the floor of the cabin, which he hadn't used for a year. . . .

Lixand had screamed a baby's bird-high shriek as Sarngeld tried to pull him from her chained-together arms. The black crash in her head as he hit her, the only way to make her let go. *My son. You couldn't know what he would do.*

"Sarngeld, master, leave me my baby, please don't drown him. Please, he's your son, don't kill him. Please, he's only a baby. Don't, please, master." She begged in a way she had never begged before. She'd never willingly called him master, got down on her knees, on her face. *My son. I would have done anything.*

"Kill the brat?" He laughed at her. "He's worth money!"

Maybe I knew what all that would mean, for the years ahead. She'd screamed and lunged to the end of her chain. All she could do was tear her fingers bloody on the wooden links, maddened, and scream her child's name as his father carried him on deck. To the other Arkan, just before the ship cast off for the day. *"Lixaaaaaaand!"* If she screamed it enough, maybe he would remember it.

Later that night, Katrana the healer had stolen his keys, freed Megan, got her knives. *I killed him, and took the ship. But that was too late to get you back. You were gone, into the Empire, where I couldn't go, sold Dark Lord knows where to Dark Lord knows whom.* Eight years ago.

The family sat down for dinner, in the atrium near the fountain, with candles floating over the flocks of eye-sized jewelfish. The big lamp overhead threw shadows from the plants over the tables and cushions. Gar-soup with dumplings, 'maranth bread, roast beef, vegetables and hot sauce, cloudberry tart. . . .

Megan pushed her food around her plate with her eating-pick. *I'd have killed for this much food, when I was eleven and on the street.* Shkai'ra was working on seconds, and another stein; she had been out on the estate with Hotblood yesterday. How she could stand riding a cross between a horse and a wolverine, that would sooner tear your head off than take a lick of salt from your hand, Megan had never understood. She herself had a bad enough time with ponies.

Shyll was picking at his food, too. Another naZak in the House of the Sleeping Dragon, first husband: an open-faced man with green eyes, wheat-blond hair cut shoulder length, but a build too slight and wiry for anyone to mistake him for a Thane. *I seem to have a taste for blonds, despite my past.*

Rilla stared, lost in thought, as she nursed little Ness, two iron-cycles old now; the baby's eyes were closed as she suckled. They were still baby-blue but with hazel flecks, more and more like her father Shyll's every day. *Your mother loves you, as my parents did me before they died,* Megan thought. Soft hair in the crook of her arm, she remembered, hungry lips tugging impatiently at a swollen breast; the milky smell of a clean baby. *Love, Lixand-mi, love* . . . She tore her mind away from that, looked down at the cold food on her plate, cleared her throat.

Shkai'ra finished her beer and wiped the foam off her lips with the back of a hand. "Well," she said; she spoke good Zak now, but with a rough accent she would probably never lose. "We'd best settle who's going, shouldn't we?" She looked sideways at Rilla and smiled a little crookedly. "Damn, I'd been looking forward to having one myself. Well, needs must when the demons drive; sooner started, sooner finished."

Dammit, Megan thought, *I should be used to her saying what I'm thinking by now. We've been together long enough.* "Rilla isn't going anywhere for now," Megan said. "Not with Ness on her arm." Her cousin looked up from the baby and nodded, the thought unspoken: *I could have another, or three more, if I liked. You'll only ever have one.* "Nor Shyll either."

"Wait a moment—"

"No, husband. Our family has a business to maintain. Can Rilla carry that alone, as well as the baby? Or would you have Shkai'ra look after the books?"

There was a general shudder around the table at that. Shkai'ra snorted and reached for another wedge of pie. "Better I'm at your back, Megan, or you'd come home to find us all sold off to pay the debts."

"What about me?" Sova; her pale brows, long enough almost to join in the middle, were even. She'd had two years of Shkai'ra's rigorous war-training now; at thirteen, she'd been blooded, against minions of Habiku on the river.

"No," said Megan. "You're well into this year's school and you're not wasting time gallivanting about with us."

"Wasting time? I thought *khyd-hird*"—she nodded her head towards Shkai'ra—"would want me to squire."

"*Ia,*" said the Kommanza. "It'd be good practice for her."

"No." Megan cut the air with her down-turned hand. *Play us off against each other, will you, girl?* "Sova isn't going to be away from school for the length of time it will take to find Lixand." To the Thane-girl: "I want to give you all the opportunity you can to learn more than how to sneak and kill. You're staying here and that's final."

Shkai'ra tilted her head on one side and visibly restrained herself from speaking. *We'll talk later*, Megan thought. Sova dug back into her dinner, face unchanged. *Showing no sign of what she wants to do, go or stay. I love her but she makes me angry sometimes. I suppose all children would at that age. I wasn't a child then; I never had time to be. Yet was I ever such a stranger to those who loved me, as she is to us sometimes?*

"It's damn risky," said Shyll.

"It'll be less so now than ever before, love. Look how the Arkans are getting cut up in Yeola-e. They've spread themselves so thin that patrols will be fewer, borders more weakly guarded; it'll be easier to move, and hide."

"From the news," said Shkai'ra, "the Yeolis were on their last legs only five months ago. How have they won back so far?"

Ivahn, the Benaiat of Saekrberk, had told of this in his letters to Megan. It was useful to have for a friend the one who was as close to a head of state as the freeport of Brahvniki could have; he knew everything in the known world.

"They apparently have a king who's hot. He came back out of captivity last summer, made alliances in the nick of time: Laka, Tor Ench, Hyerne, the Pirate Isles—he had friends all over, it seems. Even the Schvait blackshirts hired on their regiments. The way the Arkans broke the Compact and took Haiu Menshir was the last straw for many people. You know the World's Compact—everyone leaves the island alone, since it supplies the world with healers? It doesn't have an official name, actually, it's an unwritten law that's been followed for centuries, but people have started calling it that."

"Yes," Shkai'ra said, drawing it out into a thoughtful

hiss. "When I was younger I had no qualms about attacking pacifists. I think I've learned somewhat since then." Her pale brows furrowed. Trained in command as well as combat at home, and having wandered as a mercenary for six years, she had a feel for such things. "That's all the eastern powers turned against Arko, the Srian war still going on, the Kurkanians and the Roskati in revolt; and the tribes northwest of the Empire will start to move over the borders at the first chance. I'd be surprised if no one else invaded." She shook her head. "Stupid of Arko, like a peasant in a chicken coop trying to grab all the eggs at once. Opportunity, one way or the other. Quickly in, grab the child, quickly out. The quicker the better; *my* wanderlust is well and truly burned out."

Shyll stood, leaving half his meal untouched, and began pacing the flagstone path beside the fountain. Megan stood up and followed him, knowing what his silence meant. The two had been having more trouble in bed lately, more sudden pullings-away, breathless apologies, tears in the dark. *Always my fear,* she thought wearily, *from what happened when I was a child. Growing worse as I try harder to fight it; worse, not better. Will it ever end?* Under the rose tree, she put her hands on his face, keeping the steel of her claws well clear.

"Shyll, I'm not running away from you. I love you." She swallowed, dryly, struggling to say the difficult things, to be honest. "Sometimes I love you too much. I try too much, too fast." He held her as if she were made of spun glass, then turned away and went on pacing. His greathound Inu tried to heel without stepping on too many things until Rilla sent him back to his corner with the bitch Grey and her puppies.

"Promise me one thing," Shyll said softly. "That you'll both come back."

"I'll do what's necessary."

He stopped pacing and drew his hand through his blond hair. Rilla came over and hugged Megan in one arm, the other cradling the baby. Shyll forced a smile.

°   °   °

". . . pretty damn good when she's got her growth, Megan. She'd learn war-craft much faster practicing." Shkai'ra's voice wasn't raised, but carried clearly through the door to the corridor, where Sova was passing on the way to her room. The Thane-girl slowed, put up a hand to steady Fishhook, who lay across her shoulders purring, and pushed the wing-cat's buzzing nose out of her ear.

"I don't want to put her in the way of sharp steel again until she's of an age to choose." Megan's higher voice. "Two years is not too long to wait, and I'm sure there will be fights around here then if she wants them. She needs to learn other things that you don't on raids; you want her to end up knowing how to do nothing but creep around in the dark and bash heads?"

"Of course not, what do you think? You usually handle the bookish stuff, though, and you're going to be gone anyway . . ." A pause came, that made Sova worry about getting caught listening. The carpet was soft under her feet, like home used to be, but decorated in the severe Zak style rather than Thanish bright. *I miss the blue or red walls sometimes,* she thought, stepping forward; then she stopped again as Shkai'ra's voice continued. "*Kh'eeredo,* you're treading somewhat on her honor as a warrior."

A whisper of pacing feet: Megan, she could tell by the short steps. "No, I'm not. She has the *zight* of the house and her own behind her and all the pride and honor someone with her potential has. She'll be a warrior when she's of age, two years from now. Were *you* one at fourteen?"

"When I came back from my test I was considered one."

"Well," Megan said tartly, "I am hardly going to let you give her a knife and a rope and kick her out in the middle of winter—"

"Well, *Zoweitzum* on that!" Shkai'ra broke in.

"She's my daughter-of-choice and I don't want to see

her get her brains spattered on an Arkan warhammer by mischance or mistake."

A sigh. Sova could almost see the shrug. "Right. Right. It's your part of parenting. So she stays here, safe in school."

"It's because I love her, *akribhan*. Books and stability are what I think she needs—especially after what happened."

"Now, don't start that again—"

"All right, love. But dragging her all over the Midworld is a hurt I don't want to add to the others. The tea water must be boiling now."

Their footsteps faded into the kitchen. Fishhook mewed and launched off Sova's shoulder, gliding down the hall in front of her, to thump, a bit of orange fluff, in front of her chamber door. The girl followed slowly.

There was a stuffed bear, Sova thought. *His brown fur was worn mostly off on his rump, one of his bead eyes was missing. Franc said I chewed it off when I was a baby, but I think he was lying just to annoy me . . . well, I guess I might have. Babies do that sort of thing.* Yesterday little Ness had eaten a sow-bug, before anyone could stop her. Yesterday, just after *Zhymata* Megan and *Khyd-hird* Shkai'ra had left to seek Lixand.

Sova felt her blade whip through the air with easy ripping speed, saw her wrists, thickened with long daily practice, and a little veined, like *khyd-hird*'s or a man's. *To do as smooth a cut in sparring as I can going through the First Nine Cuts; that's the hard part.* When she looked in the mirror now, she saw cheekbones and a sharp chin where before there had once been round baby-fat. *I'm becoming a woman.* Those lumps on her chest, they were no longer pretenses, but breasts, proper breasts, shaped like a woman's. One day she had noticed her hips and legs were no longer the slightly-fleshed stick-bones of childhood, but flared and curved, as she'd imagined when trying to see herself grown-up in her old mother's big mirror.

But her arms and shoulders had bulges that had never been part of the mirror-picture; the arms and shoulders of a teenage boy, it seemed to her, somehow glued onto the trunk of a maiden.

The bear's name was Dof. Mooti wanted to throw him away. "My daughter shouldn't have such ragged old things! We'll get you a new bear." And they did, but he wasn't Dof. I hid him, and brought him out to cuddle when she wasn't looking.

"Keep your mind on what you're doing, girl!" Shyll called, watching her with the eyes he had in the back of his head, while he went through his own drill. While *khyd-hird* was gone, he'd taken over her war-training. "Are you going to daydream while you're in a fight? Then you mustn't *now*."

She allowed herself one last stray thought, before narrowing her concentration to the one steely path. *I wonder what happened to him, when the mob went through the house? Just an old stuffed bear, not worth anything, no one would want him—burned.*

Once I was naked, in front of a crowd of Zak. . . . No, don't think about that, she told herself. *Nothing undoes the past.* But somehow, if she woke in the dead of night before dawn—*why do I wake then? I never used to*— she couldn't make her thoughts go where she wanted them to, or not go where she didn't. Sometimes it came because she was half-dreaming, making things happen that weren't only horrible but strange; sometimes when she was fully awake, she couldn't control her thoughts, as if the dark of night leeched away her power over her own mind.

I won't remember. The day, blindingly sunny, the cold wind full of the smells of harbor, and sea beyond. The crowd that had gathered, having heard the news on the street or in inns; *they all hate us.* That was usual, but today it was unusually naked on the small Zak faces. Fater, Mooti, Francosz, her, the servants, all wore their festival best on the draped dais. *Fatted cattle;* in hindsight it looked that way.

She'd been twelve. All she had heard was that the Zak woman with the steel claws was a witch and an enemy, with no great regard for the life of anyone in her way; the other woman a plain savage. They'd race her father's proxies, three Schvait, the stakes—a bond, did that mean the witch and the barbarian would be her father's slaves, if they lost? In the house; she didn't think that was a good idea. She didn't like them, never wanted to see them again. *Their* stake was "a favor." She thought that meant some kind of errand.

Then came the barbarian's bow-shot, the gull with the arrow through it falling at their feet, her mother fainting. . . . *All anyone ever said was that her head sounded hollow when it hit the dais. Always laughing. No one ever asked whether she was hurt.*

She couldn't see most of the race, only knew by the hungry whooping of the crowd that her father's proxies had lost. Then Francosz was chasing the clown—Piatr, she'd find out his name was, later—around the dais with a knife, feeling somehow that he was somehow the source of all their troubles. The witch had hexed Franc, then turned him to stone until the judge called her off. But Franc had been right, it seemed; for as her "favor" the witch asked only the clown. *A friend of hers. He was bewitching us, too.*

I guess we go home now, she had thought then.

But instead the barbarian woman seized Francosz and her by the wrist. "That doubles my price," she'd said, when Fater had called her what she was: barbarian. *Else she wouldn't have taken me. Maybe. She's never really insulted when people call her that; it was just an excuse.* That face, so haughty, carved like stone in smug cruelty as if it could know no other expression, the harsh voice, deep for a woman's, the guttural accent; and the *smell,*

that no woman should have, no *human* should have, like
an unwashed arm-pit, or worse.

*I threw myself at Fater's feet. But there was nothing
he could do; if he'd clung she'd have torn me out of his
arms, and taken pleasure in doing it; worse for his* zight,
what was left of it. He was proud to the end. She began
to understand, when she saw the barbarian woman grab
Franc's hair, and draw her knife. The witch stopped it,
leaving him only slightly shorn, and said something about
an apprenticeship; but then the Zak turned her back, and
in the barbarian's face, and her word, *"Strip!"*, she saw
the truth.

She's claiming us. We're her slaves. She owns us. Yet
even as the truth sank in, a good part of her could not
believe this was happening at all. *It's all a dream, a make-
believe; Fater will rescue us and we'll go home.* A leer
on the big woman's face, the look, her mother had taught
her, that only a doxy, a whore, gets. Naked, the wind
touching her all over, the eyes of the crowd, laughing,
hating, while she put one tiny hand over the place
between her legs and the other forearm over her nipples,
not yet grown into breasts, as if that really hid anything,
Zak eyes seeing her as she truly was and pointing, laughing, seeing the tears she felt spill hot over her cheeks,
and laughing harder.

She'd learned enough trade-Zak to understand the barbarian's mocking words. *He's not my type and you're too
young.* But the eyes said different, running up and down
her, contemptuously measuring, like the hands of buyers
in the slave-market. *I'm too young,* she would think later.
*She wants to save me for sometime in the future. No. No,
this isn't happening. Fater . . .* Then the blows began, on
both of them, hand and belt and foot.

"The best you're likely to get is scutwork somewhere."
Choices; they were saying something about choices. That
was the Zak's doing, it turned out; she'd had words
with the barbarian. "Stay with us, and you'll have a berth
and enough to eat . . ." The Zak had said they weren't

slaves, that their answers weren't final, but hadn't asked again. In the meantime, they had to do whatever either woman said, and got beaten more than the household slaves.

The next weeks she remembered as a blur, of pain and exhaustion and shame, shame over and over again, more shame than she'd ever thought she could bear. She had to say sorry and ask forgiveness of Piatr, but no one ever said sorry to her, no matter what they did. *Ugly, ill-mannered, weak, ignorant . . .* They'd made Franc and her do their slave chores for them, hit them if they didn't want to, or when they didn't know how because they were highborn, hit them for that . . . She remembered Shkai'ra asking, exasperated, "Don't you have any will to survive?" just as she'd been thinking she'd be happier dead. *Even when I started to get stronger, even when she praised me, she always took it back by saying someone of her race two years younger could slice me to skunkbait or something like that.*

Trying to make me useful, she said. As if I was worth nothing before. The image had stayed, since someone on the ship had spoken off-hand of her being forged into steel: her on an anvil, Shkai'ra over her with the hammer. *No one ever asked the steel what shape it wants to be. It's made to be used.*

"I'm remembering again," she said aloud in the dark, to no one. She felt her own tears, and began the deep breathing to soothe them, a trick that Shkai'ra had taught her, which had, like everything Shkai'ra had taught her, been ground into her instincts by endless repetition, and showed up whether she wanted them to or not, like traitors. "I shouldn't remember. It doesn't do anything but hurt."

Then, being a child, she'd taken it all as part of life, however much the pain, knowing no other choice. Like everyone else on the ship, seeing what fates Megan's friends had suffered at the hands of Habiku Smooth-tongue, she'd got drawn into the feud up the river, even fought, risked her life for it, when Francosz had been in danger. *He* had *given* his, and been buried as a warrior—though not with more honor, Sova had not failed to notice, than Shkai'ra's cat. Grief had been black as Fehuund; like any brother and sister they'd had their spats, but he'd been all the family she had left. Without him she was alone.

At the end of it, Sova had accepted her and Megan, along with Rilla and Shyll, as her parents by adoption. Her blood-parents were dead or gone, run out of Brahvniki; she'd heard the mob cry, after the race, *"To Schotter's house! Bring torches!"* She'd also been dimly aware adoption gave her certain protections, at least on paper. *I didn't even know it in words then,* she thought, in the dark. *I was a child.* It had been instinct to cling to her only shelter, to not want to know what they'd do if she refused what they asked. *What would they have done?,* she wondered. *No one respectable in F'talezon or Brahvniki would have adopted me or taken me for an apprentice. An orphanage, maybe, getting trained how to do scutwork. Or they'd have kept me on as a servant. Or just thrown me on the street.*

She'd learned quickly not to complain; *never* to complain. Never to be anything but happy here, whatever they did. Never to be difficult in any but an innocent child's way, that they'd expect, in a spoiled child's way, that they could laugh at. When Shkai'ra hadn't been busy training her to cut off her tongue at the roots, as the Thanish saying went—"Oh, you evil adoptive parents, if you loved me you'd let me do what I want," she'd laugh, mocking, reducing it to that—Sova had trained herself, whenever her feelings weren't the grateful foundling's.

Now she was fourteen and a warrior, if a warrior was one who'd been in a real fight; she had begun to see it all with an adult's eyes. They were attached to her now; she knew that. Megan, the wicked witch, had never wanted to consider them slaves and was genuinely loving. Shkai'ra loved her in her own odd way, even if only because she'd been molded into one Shkai'ra could love by Shkai'ra herself. Whatever else the world might call her, no one could ever say she, Sova, blood daughter of zight-less Schotter Valders'sen, adopted daughter of the Slaf Hikarmé, didn't know where her bread was buttered.

But only a child need worry about that.

II

Matthas Bennas, fessas, resident of Brahvniki, he signed.

Spy, he didn't.

The paper was an invoice for sheet rubber from Karoseth, his home town, southwest of the City Itself, on the coast. Yeolis called the sea the Miyatara, Zak called it the Mitvald, both meaning Midworld. Arkans called it the Arkan Sea.

The rubber was only processed in Karoseth, actually, the raw material coming from further south. Matthas had not seen his birthplace for a decade, having lived here in Brahvniki; for a moment the memory came sharp. Marble and granite and pink brick, climbing in terraces from the city wall and the tarry mast-forest of the harbor. Orange groves outside the walls, fields of lavender, warm sun on the blue mountains rising northwards.

The servants had opened the windows again. *Brahvnikians,* he thought. *Arctic seals.* It was typical spring weather in the Brezhan delta; raw, damp and chill, to an Arkan. He went to the windows and latched them closed.

The panes were thick triangles of inferior local glass set in wood, appropriate for a merchant of his standing. They looked down from the third story of a tall narrow house of half-timbering, above a narrow cobbled street that smelled of fish and garbage and the river not far away. Rain started, beating at the glass, streaking his vision like tears.

He went to the door and quickly checked the corridor either way; there was no way someone could climb the stairs without making a loud creak, but it never hurt to be sure. He added a small shovelful of blackrock to the tile stove, settled himself at the homely clutter of his desk and unlocked the bottom drawer, with its secret compartment. From that he lifted a plain leather-bound account book, its pages studded with rag bookmarks.

This was his real work: for Irefas, the Secret Service of the Arkan Empire. As far as he was concerned, it was the best that one of his caste, *fessas,* artisan-professional, could get. *The merchant's life, that so many aspire to,* he thought. *The money's well and good, but the work's* so *boring.* Besides, more than one heroic spy in history had been elevated to *Aitzas,* noble. Another nice thing: in foreign countries there were no hair laws. His, blond like all Arkans' but silvering at the temples, was almost waist-long, as none but *Aitzas* were permitted, inside the Empire.

Item: prices. Mules and horses in the Aeniri towns upriver: up threefold since the spring herds had come in. Tool-grade F'talezonian and Rand steel: up *five*fold over the past six months. Significant increases in the prices of woolen cloth, grain, leather, oil, medical supplies and drugs, bronze; the armorers working overtime; the price of casual labor gone through the roof. *Thirty-two ships of fifty* tuin *or more have cleared the harbor already this season.* The bills of lading as fictional as *Marmori's Book of Children's Merry Tales.*

He looked at a copy his spy in the harbormaster's office had made. A seventy-five tuin two-master carrying braided horsehair—*catapult skeins*—dried fruit, neatsfoot oil—*for the maintenance of harness*—cured bullhide, glassfiber, resin—*shields, body armor*—miscellaneous metal goods. Shipping to Haiu Menshir. His spy had gotten a good look at the "metal goods"; spearheads, broadaxe-blades, brass-hilted swords from Rand. And Haians, as all the world knew, were absolute pacifists, under Arkan control. *If they're buying that, I'm the Queen of Hyerne.*

Arko's taking of Haiu Menshir made him uncomfortable, actually, as he was sure it made many Arkans. It was also a political blunder, to his mind; *no better way to turn all the world against the Empire,* he'd thought at the time. Now, plain as day, it was happening. What made it even worse was that the takeover had taken two tries. The first time, the greatest Empire in the world, attacking a small island populated entirely by pacifists, had been *defeated.* A ragtag band of sailors hiding behind bales and crates, led by a man who may now be proving himself one of the greatest generals of his time but then had been an accredited *lunatic* . . . he didn't like thinking about it.

In Yeola-e, Arko had taken all but those stubborn hedges of mountain in the north and southwest corners of the barbarian nation. Now—how had the *Pages* reports put it? "Strategic withdrawals and consolidation of our overall position." In other words, *the killer mountain boys are whipping our asses.* Last he'd heard, it was three-fifths taken back. Every major military power in the area had suddenly allied with the Yeolis, lending them troops or attacking on their own fronts.

And the non-military powers are lending them money. How else could a country all but conquered and broke half a year ago afford to buy all those war supplies? Or hire every cutthroat, sellsword, pirate and bar-brawler between Kreyen and Rand; he'd noticed evenings in the Knotted Worm had been more sedate recently. It didn't take a god's brains to figure out that Brahvnikian money was involved.

The Benai is probably acting as conduit for funds. The Benai Saekrberk was considerably more than the central abbey-temple of the Honey-Giving One—*only Brahvnikians would worship a bear, and a* fat *bear at that*—and the closest thing Brahvniki had to a government. It was also the largest deposit bank on this end of the Mitval— *Arkan* Sea, he reminded himself. Six months ago, Arko had had a powerful enough presence in Brahvniki to gain entrance to the Benai for inspection tours. The inspector, a military type from the Arkan embassy guard, had always come back three sheets to the wind on the Benai's famous distillate, cursing the Benaiat Ivahn as a senile dodderer and a crashing bore; but at least he'd got in. Then the Yeolis had taken back the nearest seaport, Selina, and now the Benai, politely but effectively, said no.

And Arko had done things to offend some of the most powerful private citizens of Brahvniki. Matthas had two reasons to curse Edremmas Forin, one of the two Arkans who'd worked their way onto the *Pretroi*, the Brahvnikian council of merchant princes, and also happened to be his, Matthas's, spy boss. *How could he be so stupid as to stand up in council and spout that verse of the Thanish goatherd song about diddling girl-children to Mikhail Farsight, considering how rich the little Zak bastard is, how Zak feel about kin, and how many daughters he has?* The whole city had heard about it, making Mikhail an enemy of Arko for life.

The other reason to curse Edremmas: he was dead. Not that the two were unrelated; he'd been killed on the street, in broad daylight, by an assassin good enough to cut him almost in half. Mikhail and all four daughters had just happened to be passing by, and the assassin had just happened to commit suicide while in the Benai's custody, so no one could ever prove who'd hired him. *And so I have to break in a new boss. A Mahid this time, Eforas Mahid, oh joy. Who because he got blown off course, but* mostly *because of those slow-as-constipation paper-shuffling donkeys in the Marble Palace, has taken six* fikken *months to get here. Not that I wasn't running things all right, but* fessas *riff-raff like me aren't qualified to request Imperial funding.* His payroll was half prom- ises, right now. *Thank Celestialis the rubber price went up. . . .*

Matthas pulled out the latest note from his agent in the Slaf Hikarmé. "Megan Whitlock and Shkai'ra Farshot will be arriving on the rebuilt *Zingas Vetri* soon after the spring breakup." Ice was still solid on the upper Brezhan; that meant a half-month hence, halfway between equinox and summer solstice. "This office was instructed to arrange for a draft of 1,500 silver Dragonclaws from the Benai Saekrberk to the liquid capital account." Not exactly tavern-wenching money—and yes, it *would* be wenching, for *those* two.

It had worried him for a while, that kinfolk of Mikhail and the like up the river in F'talezon had even greater resources. Involvement against Arko from that quarter, if it weren't in place already, would be disastrous. This Whitlock was thick as thieves with all the other Zak big fish here, and was known to have a grudge against Arko. She and her mate-in-the-ultimate-perversity Shkai'ra (who could even conceive what two women did in bed?) were the hands-on type, adventurers. *Ten-to-one they're the F'talezon connection, or at least part of it, or at least cognizant of it.*

Their coming was an opportunity, he saw. Out-of-town merchants were less well-protected than resident ones, and these two had a reputation for taking risks and keep- ing low company, even by local standards. Knotted Worm regulars, when here. He glanced with a smile at another of the objects in his secret drawer: a glass vial of clear liquid. How much the Empire had gained in its history, by the total honesty this Imperator of drugs elicited. *That's what I love about this job,* he thought. *I don't just have to ferret out information. I get intrigued.*

But this required aid from his superior, the Mahid.

Eforas, old boy, he thought that night, creeping by midnight to the embassy for his appointment, *you are about to have the pearls of my wisdom, thrown before you.*

All Mahid looked the same. It wasn't only that they were a clan or always wore black—onyxine, they called it, a glorified term for black—or had sworn the same oath, that of ultimate loyalty to the Imperator of Arko, whatever he asked. They all seemed to have the same mind, too. It was like the Press in Arko, the huge black rattling machine that spat out the *Pages* and other reading material: it worked when a lever was pulled one way, didn't work when it was pulled another way, always worked exactly the same way and produced the same product, over and over and over. You got the impression that if any part were jolted slightly out of line, the whole thing would come to a smoking halt.

It's the training, of course, Matthas thought, *their having to think no thoughts but the fifty Maxims and strangle dogs when they're kids and so forth.* One could feel sorry for them.

He wasn't sure which he disliked more, though: the young ones, with their boundless energy and their limitless hate, some still having the misfortune of being handsome; or the old ones with their faces of carven stone, who over the years had brought Mahidness to a fine art. Eforas, it turned out, had come out of the mold a middle age ago. It remained to be seen whether he'd combine the virtues of youth and age, or the vices.

Matthas vaguely wondered, as he seated himself in the back office of the Arkan embassy, what Mahid women were like. *All in onyxine aprons,* he thought. *With those same dead fish eyes, saying "Child, the will of the Imperator requires you to eat your turnips. . . ."*

Eforas had the usual Mahid bearing, straight and stiff as a rod, and a face incapable of expression. The two men nodded to each other. "Your report of activities since Edremmas's demise, *fessas*," the Mahid intoned. Typical of Mahid, to emphasize the inferior caste.

Matthas drew out his notes, and began. *I have to pretend I'm talking to a machine,* he thought, as even his most amusing and bizarre anecdotes passed one by one without bringing even a flicker of a smile to Eforas's deathly blue eyes. His deductions about Yeoli financing, which he'd thought were quite astute, actually, didn't bring even a nod of approval. *Machines don't laugh, or praise,* he reminded himself, *whether it's deserved or not.* He forged bravely ahead to his request: funding to secure the owner of the Slaf Hikarmé for truth-drugging.

"Fessas," the Mahid interrupted. "Did you say 'she'?"

"I did, sir," Matthas answered firmly. Mahid understood that syntax better than just yes, he'd learned.

"Then I am given to understand this Megan Whitlock is a woman?"

"She is, sir."

"Now how can you reconcile the ownership of said merchant house by said person, and the fact that she is a woman?"

Celestialis, this one doesn't know anything. By Arkan law, women could not hold property, being considered property themselves. But the first thing he'd learned in the Irefas academy was that laws and customs in other lands could take any form, no matter how unnatural.

"Zak and Brahvnikian law allows a woman to be a well-to-do merchant, as Whitlock is, sir." *Else I'd hardly be after her, would I, you bonehead.*

Somehow this seemed to get through into the cogs of the Mahid's mind; or else was brushed off and forgotten, Matthas couldn't tell. "Tell me more about this Shhh—skira Farshot, she's married to."

Matthas began. Two words in, Eforas interrupted. "Did you say 'she' again?"

"I did, sir."

For a moment the Mahid sat stock-still. *Oh-oh. Has some part been jolted slightly out of line?* "These barbarian cultures have some *very* perverse customs, honored Mahid," he continued smoothly.

"Explain entirely this Megan's marital status," Eforas commanded.

Oh, my little professional God, Matthas groaned inwardly. *Why did you have to ask that?* He'd been hoping just to have to tell about Shkai'ra.

"I hope you will forgive the bizarre complexity of the situation, honored Mahid, but in F'talezon, multiple marriages are quite accepted. The two are part of a foursome, with Rilla called Shadow'sShade, who is also Megan's cousin, and Shyll called Doglord, the one man. They were wed almost a year ago in F'talezon."

"Ah. A harem arrangement, with one woman owning the mercantile house in the master's name, or because she inherited it, since her father had no sons. That isn't so complicated, *fessas,* I've heard of such things in uncivilized lands. Why didn't you explain it that way from the beginning?"

Matthas remembered his classes in the Irefas training academy on dealing with alien cultures. *Yeola-e, Brahvniki, Tor Ench, Laka, they taught us how to adjust to; never Mahid.* "Because, if you please, sir, that's not how it is. The four, man and women alike, act as . . . equals, if you'll forgive me for explaining something so difficult to envision; the closest they have to a leader is Whitlock. In terms of love-bonds—" *Celestialis, why did I have to get into the sticky parts?* "—they're actually sort of two pairs, Megan and Shkai'ra in base depravity, and Rilla and Shyll, who have produced a child. Though there are apparently feelings between Megan and Shyll as well . . ."

Eforas sat looking, though Matthas had not thought that possible, even more like metal than he had before. Remembering seeing a Press servant, when one of the smaller devices broke down, curing it with a hefty whack with his fist, he suddenly imagined himself having to thump the Mahid on the skull, on which he would snap to life and begin talking sense, and maybe even smile.

"It is to purge this sort of cancer from the world that is Arko's sacred mission of civilization," Eforas said evenly.

"Exactly," Matthas answered smoothly. *Back to the matter at hand: whew.* "Which is why they must be way-laid and truth-drugged."

"Very well, *fessas,* I shall allocate funds for one embassy strong-arm, which day do you want him?"

"Er . . . Honored Mahid . . . You must forgive me for not enabling you to understand what we're up against here. By my estimation, it would take ten."

"Ten?" *My professional God, an expression. Disapproval and contempt, of course.* "You said they were both women, did you not? And one is a Zak, a race with an average height of some four feet?"

How do I explain four feet plus about forty knives, including ten where normal women have nails? Or the other one, six feet of solid muscle with breasts, her fighting skills of the calibre that elite forces would covet. He remembered the challenge archery and climbing race that had been the talk of the city a year and a half ago, Shkai'ra's show-off shot that had brought down a seagull from what had to be a hundred and fifty paces straight up.

And then the *manraug,* this magic thing, that Megan's people could do . . . no. He wasn't even going to try.

"These are . . . *unusual* women, Honored Mahid. Extraordinary, you might say. You of course know that many barbarian lands train their womenfolk in the fighting arts. These two were exceptional students, shall we say."

"It is among the worst excesses of savages to force the mothers and wives of their nations to be spear-fodder," Eforas pronounced. "No female is capable of performing the exercises or trials of proper war-training . . . and you claim you need ten men to restrain two women. Is there

some other operation you are planning without the permission of your superiors, *fessas*?"

"Most emphatically there is not, Honored Mahid." *I've
served Irefas totally loyally and faithfully for fifteen years
as you know damn well from your briefing, you onyxine
asshole; don't call me a fikken liar.* "I'll swear on my
hope of Celestialis if you wish. I'll submit to a dose of
truth-drug myself. These women are *dangerous*."

"I think I understand," the Mahid said. "It's an old
merchant's bargaining trick, to ask at first for an outrageous sum, isn't it, Matthas Bennas, *fessas*? Perhaps your
cover profession is more suitable to your true nature."

*They're erecting new hitching posts at the Kremlview
Inn,* Matthas thought, *perhaps you'd like to apply for the
job. Then again, perhaps I would.* Eforas wrote out the
papers allocating four men, Arkans attached to the
embassy. At least it was better than one. If they were
four *good* men, with a good enough plan . . .

"But you understand, *fessas*," Eforas added, as he
made the last signature required, his voice taking on a
pitch of claws on a chalk-board, "directing this many men
for such an operation, I am taking as a guarantee of
success. If by some implausible chance it fails, you will
be held personally responsible." The blank eyes fixed on
his, and their very emptiness suddenly became terrifying,
like a bottomless pit into which he was about to be
dropped, a cavern of Hayel void even of air, in which
sinners lived in the instant in which holding one's breath
becomes unbearable, stretched out to eternity. . . . He
felt a cold sweat break out on his back and neck. "You
had better not fail."

"I'm holding you personally responsible for this," the
Mahid said, toeing one of the corpses.

Throat torn out by steel fingernails, Matthas thought
helplessly, *poor bastard . . . she must have climbed up
him to do it.* He looked up, nauseated—from the sight

at his feet or Eforas's face? Both, he decided. He said nothing; there was nothing to to say.

"But I'll be merciful, *fessas*," Eforas said loftily. "You've been a useful servant to the Imperator, and perhaps will be unto death. You are hereby dismissed from your position *here*. But we will not abandon your little plan. These . . . *women* certainly acted with an alacrity suggestive of ill designs. You will act as an operative, reporting to me alone. You will truth-drug them. You will find what information they have. Since you've already wasted an extremely generous sum of Imperial resources on these four, three dead and the other deserted, you will be provided with no more. It is all one to me how you do it, whether you kill yourself, beggar yourself, have to swim all the way up the Brezhan after them clutching a vial of truth-drug in your mouth, but you will do it yourself, or you will not return. *Go!*"

III

Megan had promised Nikolakiaj she wouldn't wear any more grooves in his tables with her claws. She was drunk, and so was Shkai'ra, beautiful to Megan's eyes, relaxed, candlelight softening the sharp angles of her face, turning her copper hair a deep russet, sparking her nose-ring of thread-fine gold wire. She tossed bits of fish into the air for Fishhook to catch, velvet orange wings quivering and fluttering as the cat bounced, making impossibly loud crunching and smacking noises for such a tiny mouth over bits of fish with no bones.

The Knotted Worm was busy. Even the middle tables were full, though most people who drank here preferred to keep their backs to walls. The pair had their usual seat against one of the tile stoves; Megan leaned against the bee-hive shape and hitched her shoulders against the warm clay. "Pssst," Shkai'ra whispered in her ear at the top of her lungs. "Let's test the mattress, hey?" Probably it hadn't been such a good idea for the Kommanza to get so drunk, but they'd traveled hard down river, and then tonight's back-alley skirmish . . .

Megan shook her head. "Always want to fuck after you fight. I wonder who those Arkans were, anyway, and who sent them after us? They looked official. If you hadn't chopped up the last one, we might have found out."

"I thought you were going to save *your* last one, not claw out his throat," answered Shkai'ra, then added a cheery, "Oh well."

The tavern quieted; Nikolakiaj was on stage, holding up his hands, clearing his throat. It was Bard Night: that either promised crooning or threatened caterwauling; which, remained to be seen. "Let's have a good finger-snapping for Merikin Mara, of Selina," he announced, "who will regale us with song and news both."

The bard was Yeoli. There was the crystal, strung around his neck on a thong, and the curly hair—sure signs. Beyond that, he was flashy even for a bard, with flame-red hair in ringlets falling down long past his shoulders, a streak of white like Megan's on one side-lock, a streak of black on the other, a tunic of embroidered satin. On the stage he arranged himself, tuning a long curving harp with inlaid abalone in the soundbox, and grinning a big grin.

"Hello, gentle- and not-so-gentle-folk. *Nye'yingi.*" Yeoli for hello. She spotted two Arkan warriors sitting in a dark corner. Different from a few months ago; not swaggering. And wearing their swords peace-bonded; the Benai could enforce that with them again, now. *You dog-suckers will have lost a whole war,* she thought, *if Yeola-e's made it to their border.* She smiled. Many others in the bar looked as if they were going to enjoy this, too.

"As our dear friend Nikolakiaj says, I do indeed have news," the bard said happily. "Unexpected, indeed unprecedented news. News beyond your wildest conceptions, and you will see I do not exaggerate. Good Nikolakiaj said I would give news and song, as is customary. But this information so inspired me, dear listeners, that you will have the rare good fortune to hear both in one." Suddenly his face sobered and his voice dropped. "Tragic

and pathetic news, I bring. In fitting with its somber
nature, I must adopt a somber mien. . . ." Anticipatory
snickers echoed, including one from Shkai'ra. "My bal-
lad's title: A Lament for the Empire of Arko."

More snickers. Shkai'ra grinned like a wolf. Megan
peeked at the two Arkans, who looked as if they'd rather
not hear this, more inclined to hide behind their tan-
kards. The bard strummed a rich cord, and sang.

> *Pity the day when the Eagle of Arko*
> *First cast its eye on Yeola-e's plains.*
> *When battle is finished twixt Eagle and Circle,*
> *The world will count up the losses and gains.*
>
> *Long long ago, a great sage of Yeola-e*
> *prophesied gravely, that this century,*
> *His people, who'd lived so content in their borders*
> *The conquerors of a great nation would be.*
>
> *Now storming to Kaina, led hard by Chevenga,*
> *They'd won to the edge of the lands bought so dear.*
> *New risen from shackles, and calling for justice,*
> *They cried to each other, "Why should we stop here?*
>
> *"We know what it is, to be conquered by Arko.*
> *The world is not safe, while the Eagle still flies.*
> *Now that it runs, we should chase it down flaming*
> *For our land burned, our loves raped, our children's*
>   *death-cries."*
>
> *Debate raged like fire, all over Yeola-e*
> *Until in Assembly, a Servant asked this:*
> *"Our precious Chevenga, no one has worse suffered*
> *By Arkans than you have. What is it you wish?"*
>
> *"What wishes a demarch," he said, "does not matter."*
> *Refusing to answer, though uproar they made.*

E'en strode from Assembly, was dragged back and
     fin'ly
On pain of impeachment, replied, "To invade."

So chalk went the vote, to strike down the great Eagle.
Four ten-thousands heed the Invincible's call.
Eyes burning, the Circle comes threshing with
     longswords
To cut through the rot, and so Arko will fall.

Alas, oh, alas, for the Empire, and Kurkas,
Whose death-knell has tolled after so many years
The world's heart will bleed as the City falls crashing
So loud our lamenting, so soulful our tears. . . .

The bard struck the chord with one hand, and with
the other pulled out a large handkerchief of a scarlet
color strikingly similar to Arkan warships' sail-cloth, to
dab his cheek with a loud sniffle.

Pity the day when the Eagle of Arko
First cast its eye on Yeola-e's plains.
When the battle is finished twixt Eagle and Circle.
The world will count up the losses and gains.

Koru. Megan put her tankard down. No news had ever
sobered her so quickly. Not only had they made it to the
border, they'd decided to cross: Yeolis, who had a custom, held for centuries, against being the aggressor. This
hot king with all his alliances and mercenaries was
marching on Arko. "Sheepshit," Shkai'ra was yelling,
"Sh'our *chance!*"

Megan calculated. They had maybe forty thousand, by
Ivahn's last estimate, and the song's. The Arkans claimed
they could field a *rejin* of *rejins*, a million. But she
remembered a night at a river-port, Sarngeld speaking
with some Aenir, a mercenary by his words. "There
hasn't been a rejin of rejins for a good hundred years.

The story just sticks in people's heads. The Aans, Kurkas no less than his forebears, let things go, so now there's maybe five hundred rejins, spread out all over."

Five hundred thousand. How many were locked up fighting the Srians, the Kurkanians, guarding the northern border and patrolling the Mitvald, fighting the Lakans on *their* border, since King Astalaz of Laka had broken his peace-treaty with Arko, to ally with Yeola-e? There had been no word from Kurkania for a good two years, a good sign Arko was losing there. *Say forty thousand against, at most, one hundred thousand,* she thought. *A little better, but . . . Wait, I'm not counting those huge losses in the winter. Say forty thousand against sixty. And the forty thousand might not even be right anymore; Ivahn gave me that number a while back, and winning invading armies don't shrink, but grow.*

It was a chance. The eagle could be stung to death by the wasp, if the wasp flew quickly enough. If they had good generalling, *damn* good generalling, which supposedly they did.

Joyful stamping shook the floor. The bard had been lucky to be the first here with this; people were throwing him copper Claws. Everyone seemed happy except the Arkans, who looked like their dearest wish would be invisibility. One, a middle-aged fellow in Arkan issue armor that was obviously repainted, ground his face into the table in a most un-Arkan way.

People pelted the bard with questions as well as money. "What happened in the last battle?"

"It was a rout, what else?"

"How many did the Arkans lose?"

"Thousands. The rest scattered, or got thumbed."

"Had their sword-hand thumbs cut off," Megan explained to Shkai'ra. "A quaint Yeoli custom."

"What about Kranaj and Astalaz?" said someone else. "Are they going to invade too?"

"I haven't heard."

"So how big armies are they going to send?"

"I just told you, sparrow-brain, I haven't heard!"

"Kranazzh and Aztalazzh?" Shkai'ra hissed over the din.

"Kings of Laka and Tor Ench, respectively," Megan stage-whispered back.

"Are they still hiring mercenaries?" About ten people asked that, all at once, along with the rate of pay.

"Apply at the embassy," the bard said. "You'd have to move it to catch up with the army from here, though. This news is a few days old now, and with Chevenga, fast-march is fast-march." *That army's grown by about ten just here, tonight,* Megan thought.

"Zhv'ngh'kua," said Shkai'ra. "That's the hot Yeoli king, hmm?"

"Dah. Fourth Shchevenga." Ivahn's letters had mentioned the name, with the formal number tacked on front and the impossible-to-remember-let-alone-pronounce surname and titles behind, but Megan's eyes had skimmed over it.

Now it snagged her memory. "Wait a moment!" That name . . . it had been in older news that had come up the river. "He's *dead.*"

Fourth Chevenga was the Yeoli king who got captured by the Arkans, made to fight in their arena, and given some kind of circus execution, she thought. *Yes, dammit, I'm not remembering wrong, it was Fourth, Fourth Chevenga.* Fifty thousand people had witnessed his death.

"Fuckin' lively corpse," Shkai'ra said drily.

The Benai Saekrberk always made Megan feel calmer. Nobody ran or shouted or pushed her against the wall; the *Fraousra,* the monks, all looked as if they had something to do that made them, if not happy, at least at peace. There were more guard-monks down by the dock, though, five new galleys in the slipways, and she and Shkai'ra got an armed escort up to the hill. The *Fraousra* pruning the vines on the slopes stopped and waved; when they passed close, Megan heard them saying her name to each other, and pulled the floppy hat further down over her ears. The wind was from inland, full of marsh and plowed earth smells from the fields on the other side of the Benaiat, and a little salt from the Svartzee.

Ivahn's secretary, Stevahn, white-haired but young, and her attendants came out to meet them at the gate. Their robes were crimson against the blue walls of the abbey, with the white domes above. A small image of the Divine Bear hung at Stevahn's waist, clicking against the writing case next to it on her belt. "The Benaiat will meet you in the center court. He's a little tired." Her voice was low, as if the words were meant only for Megan.

They walked through the arcades to the courtyard gardens, simple stone and tile and fresh flowers; spring was well along here. Traveling south down the river was like leaving winter, cold and dark, to sail into summer; last time they had been here it had been fall, and they'd sailed into winter. Shkai'ra's eyes appraised all. *Still looking at everything as if she were about to sack and burn it,* Megan thought. *I'll train her out of that yet.*

Benaiat Ivahn was leaning on the edge of one of the lesser pools; looking up, he rose to meet them, smiling. *Stevahn's right,* Megan thought. *He is looking tired. Nonsense, he's looking the same as ever, three years older than the Goddess. Like a child when he smiles, except all wrinkles.* The other monks withdrew.

"Megan Whitlock," the old man said, clasping her hands, then Shkai'ra's. "It was a grief to me that I could not attend your wedding. Your other wife and your husband are not with you on this journey?" They strolled along the colonnade, the pair matching their pace to the old man's. He moved as smoothly as he ever did, but more slowly.

"No," she answered. "But we drank some of that case of Saekrberk liqueur you sent. In the glass loving-cups."

"They were beautiful," Shkai'ra said. "They reminded

me of this place." *Three years, we've been together,* Megan thought, *and she still surprises me.*

No doubt Ivahn was surprised, too; but he'd had a great deal of practice in hiding what he thought. They came to the door of his office, ancient oak, almost black, hinges silent as it swung open. Benaiats from time out of mind had used this office. *Strange to think of anyone but Ivahn being Benaiat; he has been since long before I was born.* He was three times Megan's age. Seventy-five. *What will I be like at that age? Stupid question. If I keep using the* manrauq *as much as I have lately, I won't die old. Shkai'ra isn't likely to die old either, unless we really do settle down after this.*

The office was in the outer part of the Benaiat; the view extended down to the docks and across the river to Brahvniki, back toward the woods and fields as well. The room was very plain, but not stark. Some monasteries of the Honey-Giving Bear seemed to worship austerity, but Ivahn had always said its purpose was to free one of distractions, not be held sacred for its own sake. He had bookshelves and desk and chairs, a row of large books on pegs; the symbol on the wall was his own handiwork, the colors still bright against whitewash. A warm breeze blew off the sea and in through the narrow windows. *This summer is going to be very hot, droughts in some places.*

As Megan and Ivahn gave each other the formal hug, she felt it: he was paper-thin, skin over ribs like tent-canvas, his grip more like a spider's than a bear's. He settled into his chair by the desk, sighing, motioned them to sit. His face had always been thin like a fox's; now the fox was a starving one, hollow-cheeked. Was he ill? But he smiled again, making it all seem imaginary.

A monk brought a tray with a bottle of Saekrberk and glasses, setting them out on the desk with a bow. "*Koru-kai,*" Ivahn said, lifting his tiny glass. "To your health," Megan said, hearing more meaning in it than she'd intended. He nodded, and the Saekrberk burned its way across her tongue.

"I share the salt," he said, the ritual words signalling it was time to get down to business; they were too close to take any longer with small-talk. "And I with you," she answered.

"Glad that's over with, it's stiff and stifling, like the robes," he said. "Well, Megan. Just what sort of advice did you want?"

Megan put down her cup, met his eyes. "We're considering joining the Yeoli army to get into Arko."

"The Yeoli army, to get into Arko." He didn't have to ask why. He steepled his fingers, lined brows creasing. "Hmm."

"We heard last night they crossed their border to march on Arko. What do you think of their chances?"

"Of conquering the Empire? Better than one would expect. Who would have thought they'd win back so far, when they had nothing left unoccupied but a few mountains? They have their alliances, with Astalaz of Laka, Kranaj of Tor Ench and Segiddis of Hyerne. When it becomes apparent, they'll have every mercenary, lootluster, and soul just plain angry at Arko that they care to join them. And they have Chevenga. When they advertise in town, it's for half the pay they offered at first, and goes down every day. Soon people will join them for nothing but a prospect of Arkan city plunder."

"It's not the money I care about."

"Oh, I didn't think so, *bylashka;* I'm only making the point of their perceived chances, of which the price is an indicator." *Bylashka,* she thought. *Well, I guess I am a child, to him.*

"'And they have Chevenga,' he said cryptically," she mimicked. "I am rapidly getting the impression this person's bottom is dipped in gold. You never praise anyone, Ivahn. All I knew before was, he was king of Yeola-e, and dead—"

"It's not king, it's *se-ma-na-kra-se-ye* . . . if you're going to deal with him, you ought to know that, they're touchy about it." A smile crept across the wrinkled face, wrinkled mostly with smiling. "He's alive."

She raised an eyebrow at him, as Shkai'ra chuckled. "I'd gathered that. But how good is he, really? Another Osgaerth, maybe, who the Thanish oligarchy kicked into war just to be rid of?"

"Somehow I can't imagine Fourth Chevenga being kicked anywhere," he said. "Though he has been. In all honesty, I should admit my bias: he's a friend. I first met him when he was fifteen. Just between the three of us, I got him drunk and we went to the Knotted Worm in disguise, to hear about ourselves. Poor lad, I had to give him a dose of extract of Halya to get him through all his official functions the next day. . . ."

"The Great Bear knows how little I know of war; I'm not much of a judge of fighters or commanders. But all who are seem to agree he is brilliant as both. He even has *manrauq*; a sense for weapons, which has stood him in very good stead. If he has any fault it's recklessness, but he's willing to learn from his mistakes, and is a quick study. A sample of the epithets his army has given him: the Invincible (that's the most common), the Immortal, the Infallible, the Imperturbable, another Curlion . . ."

"Another *Curlion*?" Megan said, brows shooting up.

"What's a Curlion?" asked Shkai'ra.

"Oh, just the man who carved out Iyesi, the first Empire after the Fire, merely the greatest general in history," Megan answered. "I guess this one's bottom really *is* dipped in gold."

"I've never seen it," Ivahn said, deadpan. "But to give you an idea, I can tell you what happened the first time Arko tried to take Haiu Menshir. They sent three ships, thinking an island of pacifists would be no trouble; *he* rousted a force up out of the harbor—where all the non-pacifists on Haiu Menshir stay, you understand—and defeated and captured the Arkan unit entire. With a handful of Yeoli elite, some Srian archers and a rabble

of knife-wielding sailors, none of whom got so much as
a scratch.

"In this war, the alliances, the hiring of mercenaries,
have all been his work. He has a genius for persuasion,
too. As soon as he was back in Yeola-e they stopped
losing and started winning. Those who say he turned the
tide single-handedly aren't far wrong."

"Hmmm," said Shkai'ra. "I'd like to meet this person."
And lecture him on cavalry tactics, probably, Megan
thought.

"Of course, there is the inherent danger," Ivahn
added, "of so much depending on one person. All would
change were he to come to grief. And, though he's managed to slip through them all so far—he has a tendency
to miraculous recoveries when he messes up, too, a good
thing in a leader—he takes great risks."

"Well, now this brings me back to a previous enigma,"
Megan said. "Six months ago my spies had it that he was
executed with a lot of fanfare in Arko."

The Benaiat smiled, and sipped his Saekrberk. "Being
one of your spies, I will report: like many things done in
Arko with a lot of fanfare, it was faked."

"The only thing Arko hasn't faked in a while, apparently, is losing," Shkai'ra snorted.

"They gave him what they said was poison, in front of
a sell-out crowd in the arena," Ivahn continued. "Actually
it was a drug that made him appear dead."

"He must have been rather surprised," Shkai'ra chortled, "when he woke up."

"He must carry a large grudge against Arko." Megan
ran a fingertip over the lock of one of the books on the
desk.

"Well," Ivahn answered, "they captured him treacherously—he was on a peace mission, carrying Kurkas's oath
of safe conduct, as I can attest, having a copy here—
invaded his homeland, killed his dearest friend in front
of his eyes and tortured him to madness—temporary
madness, I should add, that's why he was on Haiu Men-

shir. One *might* surmise he just *may* hold a *slight* grudge." Megan chuckled and nodded.

"I suppose he was able to make all those alliances that the Yeolis didn't make before, and get all those mercenaries, on the strength of his name?" asked Shkai'ra.

"And by renewing old friendships?" Megan added. "With people whose interests might be threatened by an Arkan conquest of Yeola-e, being near, and who have money in large enough amounts to pay for all those mercenaries he couldn't possibly afford himself?" She tilted her head and winked at Ivahn. "Wouldn't you say?"

His smile widened, good to see on that gaunt face. "Great trouble I should have, *bylashka*, were the Arkans as perspicacious as you. Yes, their conquering Yeola-e would—*did*—put their border a day and a night's sail from Brahvniki's very walls. And they've had ambitions against us for centuries. So yes, I did float Chevenga a very substantial loan. And I was not the only Brahvnikian who did; I think he raised at least double that again among prominent citizens who shall remain nameless. I will guarantee you one thing about him, which will explain at least in part all this. If you meet him, which I suspect you will, you'll like him, if not on first sight, on first word. Very few are those who don't."

Megan raised her eyebrows quizzically. "That's a rare talent, to say the least—to make *me* like you on sight."

"Oh, I know you better than that, *bylashka*," the old man chuckled. "At any rate, I think you will: you'll see."

Megan got up and paced along the windowed west wall, catching glimpses of the river and Brahvniki out of the corner of her eye. "Do you know how the Yeolis, in general, treat Zak? I've dealt with one or two, but one isn't likely to discuss pogrom over coffee."

"There are a number of Zak living in Yeola-e proper, mostly in and around Selina. They mind their own business, and the Yeolis mind theirs. The curly-hairs tend not to have the sort of atavistic beliefs about witchcraft that make people want to destroy and drive it out in terror; they'd put it down to some strange face of the God-in-Ourselves they haven't seen yet, not to demons or Halya-spawn or what-have-you. It's true that they tend to think of the rest of the world as a slow child that they earnestly and generously hope will improve enough to come around to their way some day, but underneath that they are fairly broadminded about spiritual things."

Shkai'ra snorted. "A slow child, hmmph. I've noticed people who favor mob rule tend to be that way. Not that I've ever seen it carried so far, as an entire race taking a vote over an invasion. Which brings me to a concern I had. The man's been given marching orders by his mob. And says he wants them. But from what we heard, it sounds like they had to all but pull his toenails out to get it out of him, grudge or no grudge. Is he *really* whole-hearted about this fight?"

"Oh, yes. It's a Yeoli thing. Any method, other than a vote, of deciding on an act so major—and so much against their customs; they've never done it before— Yeolis would consider unthinkable."

Megan nodded. She had been taught a little Yeoli politics—very little, it being seen as subversive by the Dragon'sNest—and remembered the main principle, "the people wills," in Yeoli, *semana kra,* hence *semanakraseye,* literally, "the-people-wills-one." Laws were initiated by citizens at large and enacted through plebiscites of various forms, sometimes complex, involving percentages and such; the *semanakraseye* existed only to oversee their administration, and to act quickly in case of war or emergency. Over the military, though, his power was absolute.

"And they are very jealous of their power; all sorts of ways they have, of clipping a *semanakraseye*'s wings. Including a forbiddance on his voicing his wishes regarding national policy. They made an exception this time, wanting to know as you do, Shkai'ra, whether he was whole-hearted."

"But he had to make a show of sticking to the rules," Megan said, "I understand."

"Oh, it was more than show. Chevenga is an adherent of mob rule, to the bone; he was bred that way from birth. Knowing him, he genuinely squirmed at having to say what he wanted, dreading to interfere with the vote. I know it's hard to believe. A sad irony, for him: no one *will* believe it, they'll think as you did that it was a show, that he pulled the strings all through, and he'll be pinned with having wreaked change on his people without their consent, when all he did in truth was act on their wishes. He just doesn't know how to do it any way but brilliantly, that's the trouble; with him as the sword in their hands, his people couldn't resist taking on the giant.

"And of course if he wins—well, he wouldn't leave Arko leaderless afterwards, to fall into chaos; he'd consider it a breach of responsibility. So he'll take over as Imperator. Arkans falling on their faces every time they enter his presence; imagine what Yeola-e will think of *that!* Poor Chevenga: he'll be the one who pays in the end, more than anyone else, I know, for he'll *arrange* it that way. Well, that's neither here nor there for you. You asked whether he's whole-hearted. I'd say he is."

Megan rubbed her hands thoughtfully up and down the sleeves of her shirt. "Well, it's good to know that an honest man stands a chance of becoming Imperator, anyway. Ivahn, thank you for being one I can count on for news."

He quirked an eyebrow at her. "That is almost like saying I'm a gossip, my friend." She crinkled the corners of her eyes at him. "Or an acerbic old fox."

Who in Halya told him I said that? He knows pissing everything. "Why don't we say . . . oh . . . a person with a great many sources of intelligence, instead?" She pushed herself away from the wall and held out her hands to him. "Thank you again for your advice. We'll be leaving as soon as we can."

"So be it," he said, taking her young hard hands in his gnarled gentle ones. "Good luck, Megan, Shkai'ra. When you find your son, will you bring him to visit?"

"I wouldn't dare not to. I hope you don't mind that I've called you an old fox."

"An acerbic old fox," he corrected. "Should I mind what is so apropos?"

"Not if it's meant affectionately, you acerbic old fox."

He laughed. "Zak imp. Honey-giving One be in your souls on your journey."

"Safe journey," Matthas's landlord wished him, as he handed over the big brass key. "Honey-giving One be with you, and may you sell lots of rubber and silk in Karoseth. An indefinite time, you say; I'll expect your letter, then."

"Thank you." *Thank Celestialis I did take this trade on as a cover*, he thought as he headed to harbor, a guard of two Brahvnikian hirelings in tow. *An established merchant can get a bank loan to finance a business journey.* The Benai had been amenable enough, despite his nationality, though they'd charged him hefty interest.

Now off to Selina, a quick change of nationality—he could convince Yeolis he was a Thane easily enough—put together the caravan and do what everyone else was doing: join Shefen-kas's army.

That was where the evil twosome had gone. For him, there was no other way to cross through Yeola-e than to say he meant to sell to the army. Their security wouldn't be too hard on a middle-aged merchant, obviously untrained in war—especially one who'd give good prices—and he'd be able to take his time once he'd got there. He didn't expect to be able to make an attempt to truth-drug them before that; he'd heard about Shkai'ra Farshot's mount and its night-senses. *What sort of person, let alone woman, would own a Ri?* Not a good idea to tangle with *that* in the dark. But in the army, there'd be more people around for camouflage, and the beast, because of its penchant for horsemeat, would have to be kept apart from the main camp. *Besides, I can make a little money from the army too, which I'm fikken well going to need. . . .*

IV

From the PAGES, *Machine-Scribed News-Chronicle of the City of Arko, 16th Day of the First Month Vernal, 55th to the Last Year of the Present Age (front page):*

MASSIVE LOSSES INFLICTED UPON
YEOLIS AGAIN

In a brilliantly executed fighting retreat, General Perisalas Kem, *Aitzas,* inflicted huge losses on Yeoli barbarians near the city of Tinga-e, at the tragic expense of his own life.

"We found it strategically advantageous to occupy higher ground outside the city after the battle," an aide of Perisalas stated. "In terms of casualties we were by far the victors. We are not certain how many of the enemy were slain, but the streets were ankle-deep in blood."

The conquest of Yeola-e has moved into its latter,

47

most difficult stages, sources say, requiring a strategy of "attrition rather than advancement": to wear the enemy down through inflicting losses. Hence the recent series of strategic withdrawals, which Generals Perisalas and Abatzas Kallen, *Aitzas,* now retired, have shown particular excellence in instigating.

Our hearts and prayers fight for our valiant heroes engaged in the divine work of conquering barbarism in all benighted lands.

"How long is it since the Yeolis took Tinga-e back?" Megan asked Tema, a local girl going into the market in town, and accompanying them, because she loved horses. *Brat,* Megan thought.

"Oh, tsaht was late last fall," she said in her bad Yeoli-accented Enchian. "Wassa complete rout. Blood ankle-deep, all over tseh city. Was *great.*"

Megan gathered the reins tighter and said, in her sweetest voice, "Quiet down, you sickly, vicious, stupid nasty-tempered walking pile of dog-food. Sooo, soooohhh, calm down, mash-for-brains." She tried to mimic Shkai'ra's tone. The beast swivelled its ears back and nodded forward, dragging the reins loose. It knew. It couldn't stand her, either.

She looked back at Shkai'ra on Hotblood, a few hundred paces behind. The Ri carried his wedge-shaped head lower than a horse would, silver-white forelock falling down between his green, forward-looking eyes, the eyes of a hunting carnivore. His black-on-black striped hide was glossy from having had to eat more cereals than he liked lately. He yawned, showing his tearing fangs. She hoped the wind wouldn't change; one whiff of the Ri and this herd of Aeniri horses would become totally uncontrollable. Instead of half uncontrollable, as they were now.

Fifty, they'd bought, which also meant finding six more people who both wanted to join the Yeoli army and herd on the way there for board, not to mention two herd-dogs. And Shkai'ra's mount's favorite meat happened to be horse, of which every horse from near Ri country with a sense of smell was aware. At least with all the mounts to switch, they could move fast. All armies were horse-hungry. It would finance the trip.

She dropped behind the herd and waited for Shkai'ra to catch up; her horse was Yeoli, didn't truly understand what a Ri was and so was only somewhat dangerously nervous near it. Against the sore places on her rear, dust had worked its way into the folds of cloth; her calves and thighs screamed. *If I could still grip with my legs, I'd be fine. As it is, those muscles just will not work.* Hotblood's paws hit the dust of the road with a *shduf-puff* sound, softer than a horse's hoof. *She makes riding look so fish-gutted easy.* . . . "You're not fooling anybody, *kh'eeredo*, least of all her," the Kommanza said blithely, flowing along with her mount, nodding at Megan's. Her eyes laughed. "Just *relax!*"

"I know." *Her and her Koru-forsaken beasts. Give me a good river-ship any day.* Megan risked sparing a hand to wipe dust out of her eyes and look ahead to Thara-e. Her animal suddenly decided to move sideways and dumped her on her behind in the road. *Coincidence, obviously. Shit.*

Shkai'ra leaned over Hotblood's withers, guffawing. Hotblood stretched his neck and hissed; she got the feeling he was laughing too. Her faithful mare trotted happily off to the herd ahead.

She heard Tema's shrill voice up ahead, talking to one of the others. "Cahn I try riding? Just forrh a bit? Cahn I, cahn I, pleeeeeease?"

Guttersnipe. Megan brushed off her pants and started walking.

"Come up, pillion." It was Shkai'ra, leaning over in the saddle and extending a hand down to her; Megan bit back the thought that the Kommanza was being patroniz-ing and accepted a pull up. "We should be closing up soon; bathe, set up the tent, and I'll give you a rub with liniment." Hotblood rolled an eye back at her. "Carrion-breath here says he still thinks we're being followed."

Megan leaned against Shkai'ra's arm, side-saddle, try-ing to find a position that didn't rub any aching spots, sneezing at Hotblood's odor. "It's probably that caravan that's a ways behind. He thought the same thing a while ago and it was just them. Koru, I'd kill for a bath."

They were in the ruins of Thara-e already, it seemed; Megan wasn't used to cities with no definite boundaries like walls. The Yeolis had thought this one was far enough inland not to need them. It had been wood. Sacked and burned last year, snowed and rained on since. At least there'd been no battle to liberate it; apparently Chevenga had sent ahead a small force to catch the Arkan governor sneaking out of the city with the war-chest, killed him, then bribed five thousand of the Arkan soldiers into deserting and the general into sur-rendering. With their own gold—the merchant in Megan snickered.

"They've been diligent, for the numbers of hands they have left," she said to Shkai'ra.

"*Ia.*" The Kommanza nodded at the new wood and Arkan-brick houses ahead. "Roads smoothed out, fields cleaned up . . ."

"Those fields are being tended by everyone who can walk." Oldsters sat and weeded or turned the earth by hand as far as they could reach, because the horses and oxen were gone with the army, or eaten; toddlers worked, directed by their parents. They knew they'd have to farm to eat, war or no war.

"*Ia,*" Shkai'ra said again, with the distracted look on her face that meant she was mind-talking to Hotblood. *Probably going over another order not to kill anything or anybody until she tells him.* The buildings nearer the center of the town were Arkan-built, during the occupa-tion, it seemed. People looked up as they passed; some waved, some didn't.

∘   ∘   ∘

Once they had the herd corralled and Hotblood stabled for the night, they went into town, to the first place always open after war went through, if it ever closed: the inn. It was an old stone place, a rarity here, obviously rebuilt after the fire: the walls were soot-stained, the rafters new.

"Morrre passers through," the serving-boy said in a pleasantly accented Enchian. "From Brahvniki? I hate to say, we hahve no beerrrh." Yeolis tended to like wine better, and so had more. It was good; *from being stored in cellars for longer than expected,* Megan thought, *because there's fewer Yeolis to drink it.*

"You have baths?" Megan asked.

The boy made a face. "Tseh neighbo'hood baths *were* three buildings down." A heap of rubble, they'd seen: the process of picking the stones up and mortaring them back together again had just recently begun. "But we cahn heat water ahn' bring a wooden tub to you' chamber."

"Please," Megan said fervently, lowering herself to the seat of a corner table with a wince. *I should be fishgutted used to this by now. Of course,* she inwardly added to comfort herself, *Shkai'ra still gets seasick.*

"May I join you, friend allies?" It was a Yeoli man, dressed roughish, looking too able-bodied to be here, not with He Whose Bottom Is Dipped in Gold; that was the running joke, now, whenever they mentioned Chevenga. Shkai'ra looked the Yeoli up and down, appraising on several levels at once, as usual; he didn't look like one who carried hidden knives, though, and the place was full, so Megan said, "Certainly." They all swapped names, and she forgot his immediately.

"You are going to join the army, I guess," he said, ordering wine. His Enchian was crisp and accentless. "Spirit infuse you."

"Thank you." Megan leaned back. "Where are they now?"

"Coming up fast on Roskat was the last I heard."

Shkai'ra whistled through her teeth. "At that rate, they'll be halfway to Arko before we catch them. He moves, that king of yours. We'll have to stop lolling about and *really* ride."

As Megan moaned, the Yeoli grinned, and made the hand-sign: palm up, *itai*, their word for chalk, meaning yes. They'd already gone through the old joke, *How do you gag a Yeoli? Tie his hands behind his back.* "He always does things fast." Almost religiously he added, "It's not king, though. It's *semanakraseye.*" *The-people-wills-one.* Every Yeoli, without exception, would make that correction; one was almost tempted to say "king" just to get a rise out of them.

They'd heard no Invincible or Immortal, though; his own people's only nickname for him was *amiyaseye*: beloved. Mostly they just called him Chevenga, as if they knew him personally.

"You are fighters by trade?" he asked.

"Shkai'ra here could say yes to that," Megan answered, "but I am a merchant. I own the Slaf Hikarmé, F'talezon. And for now: horse-dealers. My aching calves—server! More painkiller."

"My craft is one that didn't exist here two years ago," the Yeoli said, somewhat proudly. "Brickmaker."

The sleeve of his brown cotton shirt caught on the table and slid up slightly, showing a wrist scarred in a way Megan knew: from a manacle.

"Yes . . . I learned it under *their* whips. They made us work so hard people died, broke their backs, their hearts . . . there's not just sweat mixed into what this city's built out of, but blood too, lots of blood. The mark Arkans leave on a land, wherever they go. A year, it was. They wanted to make me an overseer, but I said I'd die first. I ended up a sort of manager.

"When the city was liberated, the warriors broke our chains. We were so happy, we decided we would torch the works. Smoky black torture-chamber, where we lost so many friends. . . . But the warriors said no, there were orders, no sacking was allowed. We began arguing, someone got the flat of a blade on the head that cut him somehow, and next thing we knew it was a fight, bricks flying everywhere, Yeoli against Yeoli. When there hadn't even been a fight for the city . . . so senseless. I guess being treated like a beast makes you think like one.

"Then there are warriors among us, talking calm, getting between people, and we hear this hoarse voice in the middle of it. 'Chen! Stop! You lunatics, what are you child-raping doing? Where's the God-in-you? Yeoli, you want to hit a Yeoli with a brick, hit *me*!' Everything goes quiet all of a sudden. Everyone who doesn't know his face knows the official collar. Or just—well, there's just something about him that says he's *him*. Aiigh, did we feel like idiots!

"He jumps up on a stack of bricks, calling for his herald. We all want to explain ourselves, I guess, so the chant starts, 'Burn the works! Burn the works!' He holds up his arms for silence, yells, whistles war-codes, nothing works. Finally he pulls one brick out of the stack, and underhands it high up into the sky over us; everyone gets a little quieter then, trying to see where that brick is going to come down. 'Listen!' he yells in the meantime. 'You are slaves no longer! You're a workfast, if you want to be!

"'You can work the time you want to,' says he, when we shut up, 'set up the place your way, sell at your price and the profit's all yours. No one will ever crack the whip on you again. There's nothing wrong with these things; they're made of good Yeoli clay and straw, the Arkans just have a good trick for building that they've generously passed on to us. And you are the only ones who know it.'

"'But it's torture to work in there!' someone cuts in.

"'Are you *awake*?' he says. 'Haven't you noticed, you're free? You can *change* that, make it good! Or walk away and do something else. But think of all the rebuilding that needs to be done all over the plains, where there's not much stone or wood. Whoever stays is going to be making money hand over fist.'

"We all look at each other. We hadn't thought of it that way. In chains, you forget how to be free. He sees the seed is planted, so he says, 'Now everyone who isn't hurt take care of someone who is,' and goes off.

"The next day, those of us who wanted to stay tore all the locks off the doors and the chain-bolts out of the floors, cut more windows in the walls, did this and that to make the place safer, and chose a manager . . . ahem. Thara-e Brick-fast, established last month, building materials of premier quality at reasonable prices—we make them better for Yeola-e than we ever did for Arko! I seem to recall you saying you were a merchant, *kere* Megan . . ."

Her mind was cast back ten years. The staple in the cabin floor of the *Zingas Brezhana:* tearing it out, flinging it and the oak chain overboard. Metal, she should have sold it; but it was just too good to see that black bar sink down and disappear into the blue Brezhan, a sight to remember for the rest of her life. It was the same for this Yeoli, every Yeoli here. The fighters were with the army; everyone else had been slaves of Arko.

There was only one way to answer him. "Unfortunately we have pressing business that occupies us at the moment: in Arko." He chuckled. "And my house deals mostly in luxury goods and metals such as sword-blanks, horseshoes, iron ingots and so forth. Still . . ." Shkai'ra's face buried itself behind the wine-goblet as they swapped pitches; she was always bored to yawning by such talk. *She's never been denied it*, Megan thought, as they took the names of each other's agents.

It had been raining since last night; they had broken camp in a downpour and marched all day in a steady cold drizzle. Water soaked through Megan's raw-wool cloak, into her breeches and tunic and loincloth, making

the cloth swell and chafe. The horses plodded with dragging hooves, their heads down and wet manes plastered
to their necks. The sky overhead was flat grey, dulling
the green of the fields on either side of the broad road
of Imperial poured-stone. On the abandoned furrows the
crops were spring-young; off to one side she could see
the black snags of a burnt farmhouse, with the bloated
forms of dead cattle lying in the yard.

They were past the border, and through newly-freed
Roskat; today they'd catch up with the army and He
Whose Bottom Was Dipped in Gold, *se-ma-na-kra-se-ye*,
Che-, not Shche-, but *Che*-ven-ga (they'd been practic-
ing). Here the local people did call him Invincible and
Immortal and such; in Yeola-e it was a matter of principle
not to, they'd realized, in case it swelled his head.

Shkai'ra shook her head, drops flying from the drooping brim of her leather hat. "Could be worse," she said.
"Could be winter. Amazing. No stragglers, just the odd
foundered horse. Discipline like iron." Hotblood was a
little bloated.

"Keep talking so loud we'll have a good late freeze
from the gods," Megan snarled. "I can do without ice
crystals in my underclothes. And I thought that rich merchants didn't have to deal with this shit."

The cavalry pickets had already looked them over; now
they could hear the rumble of marching boots and wheels
from the rearguard. Pike-points glistened through the
curtains of falling mist, and lilting Yeoli voices sang a
marching song—in Enchian, oddly enough. *"Underneath
the lamplight . . ."*

"I'll bet the officers have a bitch of a time not letting
the celebrations get out of hand, if they'll sing in *this*
stuff," Megan said. "Hah. No one's ever beaten Arko
before."

A mounted scout dropped back to challenge them.
Megan cleared her throat, twisted in the saddle to ease
her aches. "Speak Enchian? My Yeoli is lousy," she said,
making an effort to keep her tone polite.

" *'Tai,"* the sentry said, in a thick Yeoli accent. *Yes*—the shortened form of *itai.* "You got horse f'sale?"

"And mercenaries to join. Then, we want a hot cider."

The rider was young; her teeth grinned under the wet greased iron of her helmet, like a sudden bright crack in stone. "*Ayo,* you join ahn' sell us horrse, some plunder we haven't drunk yet. Horsse-master farrh up, paymahster furtser; so late in tseh day, you wait till we make cahmp, *seya?"* She looked Megan up and down, the familiar what-are-you look of someone who'd never seen a Zak before. *Wait till she sees Hotblood.* "Where you from?"

"F'talezon and Brahvniki an—" No, Megan decided, she'd never believe where Shkai'ra was from.

"Brahvnikians. I escorrt you." She whistled a single-tune and was answered from three different places.

"Wait, sentry—" All through Megan's explanation of how Hotblood mustn't get near horses from up the Brezhan, the woman's eyes and the set of her lips kept saying the same thing over and over: "Highly irrehgularrh." They ended up between the supply train and the rear-guard; the carts were for supplies and the wounded, it appeared. The last was a six wheeler double-teamed, probably carrying heavy stuff, with a phalanx of Yeolis, the rearguard, marching behind it. The pikers had their cloaks draped over their packs, and the archers' weapons were snug in their waxed-leather cases.

The foot soldiers seemed glad of something interesting to look at; one who knew Enchian made conversation, somewhat boorishly, boasting loudly to Shkai'ra about her sexual prowess. Someone on the cart tried to haggle with Megan for a horse, but someone else argued with him, with much Yeoli arm-waving, making it clear all horse sales were supposed to go through the Horse-master. Not wanting her first impression to be under the table dealing, she politely declined. And they all walked and rode on, cold to the bones, wet clothing slapping shockingly against marginally warmer skin, cloth catching and pulling, breathing wet air that stank of wet horse, wet human, and worst of all, wet Hotblood. Curled in Shkai'ra's hood, Fishhook kept up a continual low growling complaint, both audibly and in Megan's mind; *wetnastywetwetlick-notthirstywetwet*—hisss—*wet*.

Through the drizzle the light dimmed, grey-silver darkening to steel grey, clouds seeming to touch the ground. "Trees ahead," someone called between songs. Then a cry came all down the line that had a ritual sound to it; the day's march was over, set camp here. The column flowed slowly into a fork between two rivers, breaking up into organized chaos that spread beyond sight in the falling rain.

It was the usual sort of horse deal: "You want *how much* for those plugs?"—"You're asking me to *give* away these children of my heart, sons and daughters of the wind?" Megan resisted the urge to be too dishonest in exaggerating their quality; she'd be sticking around. Shkai'ra waited patiently through the haggling, picking her teeth with her thumbnail, holding Hotblood by the forelock to keep him from trying to eat the people around him.

"For that price, these beautiful, high-bred, loyal creatures are yours," Megan said. She left the smelly, bad-tempered brutes with them, wiped her face clear of rain with one hand. The herdsmen from Brahvniki had been given their final pay that morning; now they went their way. *If I were comfortable, I'd feel more human. And more valuable.* "Done. Ready to sell yourself?"

Shkai'ra took off her hat and shook out her damp braids, dropping a kiss on Megan's head. "*Ia.* I'm easy but not cheap, so you do the haggling while I look menacing, love."

The two women walked east, leading their mounts and packbeasts. The camp bustled wetly, soldiers and camp-followers splashing through sodden turf rapidly turning to liquid mud; pitching camp, scavenging for deadwood and stones to build fires, putting up spits. Somebody had obviously stolen a herd of pigs, for she could see the wagons dropping off carcasses. It smelled—there was no way to concentrate this many people and animals without a stink—but it was somewhat better than most of the thousand war-camps the Kommanza had seen.

"These must be the mercenaries, by the road," she said. "I've never seen such a collection of odds and sods." Megan just grunted. She hailed an Aenir with an axe across his shoulder. "Hai, where's the paymaster?"

The Aenir looked, looked again when he saw Hotblood. "The bell-tent." That was in the middle of an infantry regiment; mercenaries with mixed equipment, pikes, spears, axes, swords, bows.

"Shit, there are a bunch over there with threshing flails and stone-headed hammers, Baiwun pound me flat," Shkai'ra said.

"You Peraila Shae-Keril?" Megan asked in Enchian; that name she'd made sure to remember. The man who answered was strong-looking, middle-aged but moving smoothly; a curly-haired badger with a sort of bronze-brown look that said, "Don't mess with me and we'll get along fine." He looked up from the desk set under the tent-flap to keep the wet off the papers.

"Yes," he answered in the same language, closing the book.

Talkative curly-hair, Megan thought. He looked at the Ri, curious rather than nervous, then at both of them, with the long considering glance of a man who knew fighters.

"We'd like to hire on," Megan said coolly, ignoring the water running down her face. He beckoned them under the flap, but didn't offer a seat. Hotblood leaned his head on Shkai'ra's shoulder; she slapped his muzzle away. His breath tended to take on the fragrance of rotten horsemeat. "Answer me one question firrst," said Peraila. "What is *tsaht?*"

"It's a Ri," Shkai'ra replied. "It runs, fights, eats and

fucks; since there aren't any female Ri around here, it
fights a lot. It'll do what I tell it."

Peraila leaned back in his chair, unsmiling. "When—
if—we sign you up," he said, "you will call someone of
higher *rahnk kras*. Short fo' *kraseye*." *So that's how to
say "sir" in Yeoli*, Megan thought. *I've always wanted to
know.* He demonstrated the salute, one finger to the
temple. "You may *prahctice* on me, if you wish. Or
naht—till you signed up. Well, *hyere* I *ahm* . . . convince
me you worth *whaht* you *think* you *arrre*."

Megan made the formal introduction. "Shkai'ra is the
cavalry officer and her mount is very good at night hunting. They work as a team as well."

"Mounted archer, lance, mounted swordwork, sword-
and-shield on foot. Sneak-up-and-slit-their-throats. In
descending order," Shkai'ra said.

Megan turned her hand over, nails curled in. "I work
in the dark as well. I'm good with knives and . . . other
things. Have you heard of Zak?"

" *Tai*." His eyebrows took on an expression of intrigue,
though it was only slight. *Truly blasé*, Megan wondered,
or just feigning it? "We've never *hahd* one of *you* join
beforrhe." He looked around at the people bustling here
and there despite the rain, stood up, and, once reassured
Hotblood would stay where he was, beckoned them to
the open flap of his tent.

They hung sodden coats on a peg inside. There were
papers everywhere, but no sign of money; the treasury
was closer to the center of camp, it seemed, and better
guarded. They all knelt on the mat.

"*Arrhe* you good with *otser* things," he asked Megan,
"besides knives?"

"A few." Megan's hands were on her legs, fingers
pointing in. She took a deep breath and drew on the
manrauq, outlining her hands in yellow light. Once set,
the spell needed minimal attention, letting her talk. "This
sort of thing."

Now there was a reaction on that reactionless face.

The eyes widened. "Stop right *tsere*," he said. She snapped the spell in two, the light dying with it. "Show me no morrhe . . . I think you two arrhe special cases. You'll hahve to unde'go truth-drugging—strictly ahs precaution, you unde'stahnd."

Shit, Megan thought. An Arkan technique, truth-drug for anything suspicious, truth-drug scraping—asking you what it was you least wanted them to know, while you were under the drug—if they thought you were a spy. Seemed the heroes had picked up a few of the villains' tricks. Megan blinked once then nodded. "We've got nothing to hide." *Do we?* A quick mental inventory. *No, we really don't this time.*

The paymaster summoned a squire in fluid Yeoli, sent him ahead, rattled off an order to a clerkish-looking type near by, and rose. "Come with me. You cahn leave you' baggage hyere, my people will guarrd it, but bring tseh . . . ahnimal."

With Hotblood at Shkai'ra's side they went deeper into the camp, towards the center; soon there was no language in the air but Yeoli, flowing like water, full of unpronounceable sounds. Somehow the Yeolis managed to gesticulate even with both hands full. Every eye seemed to strain, puzzling out the nature of Hotblood. They passed a crowd of tiny tents of an odd grey-green color, the people in and around them dark, some almost black. *In the middle of the Yeoli camp*, Megan thought, *not with the other mercenaries?* "Teik Paymaster," she asked, "who are they?"

"A-niah." *That tells me a lot.* But Peraila didn't say more.

All the Yeoli tents were the same. He came to one that had an administrative sort of look. From several nondescript people, he chose a mouse-haired woman, conferring with her in whispers. He told her their names, Megan heard, but didn't tell them hers; nor did she introduce herself, or say what part of the army she was with. The sort of person the eye would miss in a crowd, unnoticeable against a blank wall. *Groups of them together*

give me chicken-skin on my soul, Megan thought; they
looked eerily wrong, because unlike a *normal* crowd, no
one stood out. *I don't know why I'm surprised. I guess
it's because Yeolis always seem so open and above board.*
She reminded herself of the name their secret service
went under: Ikal.

I wonder how Peraila strips, Shkai'ra thought. *Jaiwun
damn, traveling by horse puts Megan out of the mood
and me in . . . More sword-hand marriage for me tonight.*

"Come inside," the nameless woman said in perfect
Enchian, with a polite smile. "But leave all your weapons
outside." It was almost apologetic. Casting a glance at
Shkai'ra's: "Don't worry, they'll be well-guarded."

"Hope so. I lugged them right across the Lannic."

"Tseh *Lahnnic?*" Peraila shot her that fast horse-
merchant glance; it seemed he'd be in on this
questioning.

"From Almerkun. Other side of the big water outside
the Mitvald. Big, and godsdamned wet."

"No shit." He seemed to believe right off; of course,
he would have an easy way of finding out whether she
was telling the truth, very soon. *Probably doesn't think
I'd lie under those circumstances*, Shkai'ra thought, *and
he's right.* "You know, tseh morrhe I know of you two,
tseh morrhe interesting you get."

Beside the tent was a small table under a canopy,
spread with white linen, that the women gestured
towards. For the weapons; *Yeolis have a feel for them*,
Shkai'ra thought, as she laid her two daggers, sabre and
wheelbow on it. Megan would take longer. Needle sword,
wrist knives, back knives, boot knives, thigh, upper-arm,
belt-buckle, hair-hidden knife . . . It didn't help, Shkai'ra
knew, that doing this always made the Zak feel naked.
Several Yeoli faces watched, bemused, increasingly amazed.
Finally the Zak completed the pile with her hair-comb.

This was a tent where no one slept, bare to the walls
but for a rug, the one candle bright. The wet sky was

finally darkening, and the smell of roasting pork filled the air. Inside, two more nondescript people came alive from a stock-still stance and left, though not before carefully arranging a pair of pillows side by side on an open space of the mat, as Megan and Shkai'ra followed Peraila and the woman in. They all sat.

"You understand," the woman said, "this is in sworn confidence, Second Fire come if I lie, Kahara be witness"— she clasped her crystal, the Yeoli swearing-gesture, as she rattled off the highest oath, known in all nations, something she obviously did every day—"and no questions of a personal nature unless relevant to our cause will be asked."

"I understand," Megan said, looked to Shkai'ra for her nod. The woman opened a small box, lifted the needle in thin deft hands. "I'll do you both at once," she said, her tone like a healer's, as she filled its chamber out of a small glass vial. "When it takes effect, which won't be for a while, you'll have to lie down," she said, motioning towards the pillows.

And she didn't say a word to the minions who put them there, Shkai'ra thought. *If they do everything this smoothly in this army, no wonder they're winning.*

Shit. She rolled up a sleeve of her sodden shirt and presented her arm. *I hate needles.* The woman's touch was soft, cool and gentle, the liquid she touched to the inside of the crook of the elbow with a bit of lint was cold; no surprise, she found the vein on the first try, firmly sliding the point in. It didn't hurt, but made her skin creep. No strange feelings immediately. She wondered if Megan was all right; helplessness always struck her at least a flesh wound, inwardly. "Would you like some tea?" the woman said amicably, once it was done, as if she'd invited them over for an afternoon chat. *Ezethra,* Yeolis called the weak green stuff they drank; the grease that kept the wheels of Yeoli social life turning. But a little different here, she noticed, as another spook with a pot and four cups wordlessly appeared and disappeared as if summoned by *manrauq*.

They're so polite, Shkai'ra thought. *The woman's being tender as if she can tell Megan's afraid. Poor kh'eeredo, she wouldn't like that to be showing. But they're more than polite, they're kind, they're so gentle and warm. Wait a moment—Baiwun. None of these thoughts sound like my thoughts; they're too nice. It's the drug.*

A while later, a hand gently pressed Shkai'ra's shoulder. Yeolis were not a shy race about touching. It was time to lie down; yes, as she moved, the world about her wasn't moving quite in the usual way. They stretched out on the rugs, side by side, as if bedding down; on a whim she winked and flashed her tongue at Megan, who sent back a dirty look. "You know, you're gorgeous," she said. It was true; the candlelight in this tent showed new angles and new meanings in her wife's face that she'd somehow never seen before. "I adore you beyond words. I want to slide my hands all over you, throw my arms around you and run my tongue up inside you until you come like a plum bursting all over the—"

"Shut *up!*" Megan's sharp voice seemed almost to come from inside Shkai'ra's own skull; somehow she found it impossible to disobey. "Ah," Peraila was saying, his voice carrying the same impossibly deep resonance, "one who truth-drug makes talkahtive."

Gradually Shkai'ra's thoughts slowed down, then stopped, like the moment before falling asleep, without the drowsiness, unearthly quiet. Everything went very clear, like on a high mountain with bright sun; she looked at the ceiling of the tent, hearing herself breathe, and her heart beat like a slow drum, noticing the clear weaving of the canvas and each single thread. A great web; she floated in the midst of a sea of threads, each one with an answer on the other end. Far away from the world, and yet closer than ever before, she felt, and entirely safe.

What's your name? The words filled her head, as if a

god were speaking to her soul, bypassing her will. Her mouth answered; not speaking, but the words resonating in the web. *Shkai'ra Mek Kermak's kin, Senior in Stonefort.*

Known as . . .

Shkai'ra. Her tongue left out the click and the 'ghhh' sound foreigners couldn't pronounce.

Are you really from across the Lannic? Peraila. As her tongue answered, the sliver of her that could still think thought, *It must be like the fires of Zoweitzum if you lied the first time, or if it's enemies who have you and you're carrying secrets. . .*

Do you come to us meaning truly to fight for us and with us, loyal in action and will to us, to our cause, to our enmity against Arko, without connections or loyalties to Arko or to anyone who might wish us ill? The ritual question, quick and practiced; yet every word dropped down into her soul like warm oil into an aching ear.

Yes. Hate those glove-wearing sheep-raping fat-assed children of diseased donkeys anyway. A chuckle, deep as the ocean, from Peraila. *Why?* He was curious. *We had trouble with them. I'd like this war even if Megan didn't want to get in on the kill. Rich, they are too. Good looting.*

Well, that's it, then. The woman. *It'll wear off in a while.* They went on to Megan, soft words soothing. *Have you ever been truth-drugged before? —Nyata. —Answer in Enchian, so I can understand you. —All right. No. — How do you feel?*

Naked without my knives. Free of self-control. There is nothing that hurts here. Shkai'ra saw the woman's smile, limitlessly beneficient, a goddess's; no need to struggle, just surrender, as they had. This would go worse with Megan when she came out of it than it would for her, Shkai'ra knew; the Zak was more attached to her tension.

Free to be honest, the woman said, *as we all could be, without drugs, in a kinder world.* That was the greatest and deepest truth in the world, Shkai'ra knew, with utter certainty. When she was herself, she knew with equal certainty, it would seem fucking banal.

They had many more questions for Megan: whether she did assassin-work, and thief-work, about her claws, whether her powers were sufficient to be useful in the war, what causes she had used and would use her skills for, why she'd joined. Finally the ritual question with its precise wording came again. *Yes*, Megan's high rich voice answered. *With my heart*.

As they waited for it to wear off, Peraila and the woman spoke for a bit in fast Yeoli, then he was gone, and she dug into some paperwork, every now and then sparing a glance. Time parted like thick honey as Shkai'ra's mind swam up out of the drug-silence; she felt Megan's shoulder against her arm tighten, tension creeping back like a thief through an alley door. *Release can never last long enough, can it, kh'eeredo . . .* When she could, she gripped Megan's tiny steel-clawed hand in hers. She knew all was well when, as she wistfully murmured, "I could bed that paymaster," the little hand gave her big one a sharp slap. As they sat up, the Ikal woman offered them tea.

As Peraila led them through camp, Megan sheathed the last knife and shook off the last mistiness of the drug; very soon she would be bargaining. It had stopped drizzling; it was pouring. They passed cook-fire after cook-fire, a hundred carcasses turning on spits. *Can't we just make the deal now,* she thought, *and meet the next mucky-muck, Ikal or Special Forces or whatever, tomorrow?* "I'm hungry," Shkai'ra said. "And I'm tired and my bones hurt where the breaks've healed, and I want something hot, meat with potatoes and garlic and a drink and then just snuggle down with you and go to sleep."

"*You're* complaining?" Megan said snidely. "I thought you could ignore *anything*."

"It's catching," Shkai'ra said. *Nastywetcoldfurheavy-*

cavewarmsnooze, Hotblood joined in. *Softdrywarmarms,* Fishhook demanded. Megan held back a snarl.

They approached a tent, large for a Yeoli one, with a double guard in front of its canopy; near the feet of one of them a young man knelt, Yeoli warrior-style, apparently meditating, as athletic Yeolis did. He was wearing only a Yeoli kilt, his arms, chest and legs bare, but was outside the shelter of the canopy, seeming quite happy with the cold rain pouring down over his skin and slicking his dark hair into tendrils, eyes closed, head back, mouth slightly grinning. Just the sight made Megan pull her head deeper into her collar, grumbling inwardly. *Looped,* she thought at him, emphatically.

In a moment she was glad she hadn't said it out loud, for it was him who rose and greeted Peraila, saluting, then turned to them with a smile that flashed gold; two of his front teeth were capped with it. "Megan, you must be, and Shkai'ra." His Enchian was only slightly touched with the Yeoli lilt. "And your creatures. Nye'yingi. Come in out of the rain. Your *big* creature, we'll have to leave outside, as long as he can be unobtrusive; it's dry under the flap. Quite the evening, isn't it?"

"Dah, the gods are certainly pissing tonight," Megan answered.

"All over you," Shkai'ra added, to Megan's knife-sharp nudge; but the man just laughed.

Leaving the Ri with the order to lie still, they followed the Yeoli in. *The occupation didn't sit well with some of them,* Megan thought. His back was crossed with the distinctive scars of the Arkan ten-beaded whip; in fact his ropily muscular body was scarred to a gruesome extent all over, some of them obviously from fights, some ritual, and some plainly left by tortures; the Arkan initials A.M. had been written on his lower chest, it seemed, with a branding-iron. Around his neck, along with the obligatory crystal, he wore a human tooth as a pendant—another quaint Yeoli custom, keeping the teeth of dead kin.

The front room of the tent was an office, with a folding

desk covered messily with papers under an Arkan pole-lamp, with the flame glassed in, a file cabinet and a set of foldable traveling bookshelves. The only titles Megan could catch in an unobtrusive glance were, to her surprise, Arkan: *Laws of War and Empire, Elements of Tactical Excellence, Great Generals of History: Ilesias, Ankammas, Nenissas and Kurkas* . . .

The Yeoli towelled himself dry, and with a gesture invited them to sit on the rug. "Tea?" *The mucky-muck's out,* Megan thought, *so the lackey has to entertain us until he gets back. Koru, I'm hungry, how long is this going to take?* At least he had a warmth about him, gracefully authoritative without being superior, and pleasant to be near; he was handsome, too, even with his cheek scarred clear across, the scar bending with his smile.

Just as he was pouring, Fishhook decided to be friendly, launching herself in a gliding leap from Shkai'ra's shoulder to his, slipping and beating one wing in his face until she was steady. "Forgive me, Teik," Megan said quickly, reaching; wing-cat claws made no distinction between bare skin and branches. Peraila reached fast as well, strangely protective, Megan noticed, for the badger he looked like. *Lovers?* The dark-haired Yeoli just chuckled, managing to pet the cat with one hand and pour tea with the other. "No, no, no, I like wing-cats, he—she?—can stay there. Oh, yes, you're a nice one, aren't you? *A-e,* pretty puss puss puss . . ." In a moment of scratching her under the chin, he earned a sonorous purr. "Well," he said, handing out steaming cups, "I share the salt."

Wait a moment, Megan thought, even as she answered by sheer habit, "And I with you." *He's the mucky-muck? Nobody tells me anything, I just want to work here. And since when did Yeolis know about sharing the salt?* He went blithely on. "I'd like to know more about your gifts, Megan, and your beast, Shkai'ra, not to mention the

other services you're offering . . . as soon as *someone* gets
a loud nose out of my ear."

"Excuse me, Teik," Megan said politely. "Or should I
say, *kras*. You don't seem to be one of those nice people
who for professional reasons don't introduce themselves—"

"You know," Shkai'ra interjected helpfully. "Spooks."

Megan pretended Shkai'ra wasn't there. "May we
know your name?"

"*I'm* sorrrhy!" Peraila said, more obsequiously than
she'd thought he had in him. Was that an effect of the
candlelight, or was his face actually reddening? "I'm *terr-
rrhibly* sorrhy, I guess no one . . ." He trailed off lamely,
with a bleak look at the other.

"No matter," said the dark-haired Yeoli, shrugging,
and extended his hands with another warm smile. "It's
Fourth Chevenga Shae-Arano-e, *semanakraseye na
chakrachaseye*."

V

The Glory of Arko.
Cat-step, cat-step, back-stretch, twirl . . .
Give all the gentlemen a good long look at your rear,
there's a good boy, Tikas would tell him. Bigger tips that
way. *I love you, Tikas,* he thought. *You are so tall and
handsome and wise. You tell me everything I need to
know and teach me so well. I want to be like you some
day. Pirouette, stretch, lead with the elbow, nice taut
silhouette, and now the hand-spring . . .*

He wasn't going to be nervous, just because the governor of Korsardiana was going to be here tonight. That
was baby-stuff. He was a big boy. Lead. Leads didn't get
nervous. Some day he was going to be famous, he'd
decided: a Famous Performer. Famous Performers didn't
get nervous.

Tikas was making the other boys practice passing
oysters from their mouths to the guests. "No, no, you
have to throw your head back more, sweetheart. And bat
your eyes; that's it. So beautiful you are. Know it. Then
all the world will see it too." Tikas knew everything,
because he was so old: sixteen.

The boy leaned to the left and drew his hand in front of his face, fingers spread. Gold and black lace gloves, so elegant . . . *Ninth measure.* He knew the Glory of Arko really well now. "That's very graceful, Rasas, dear." Tikas had noticed, was smiling, proud. The boy felt as if everything in the whole wide world were good. *One day I'll be that tall and beautiful*, he thought, *have a voice that deep and manly.*

Tikas turned to Ardas, Rasas's best friend. "Present the wine-cup from the left to be unobtrusive. If the gentleman wants more, tilt your head sideways, darling, to show off your lovely, smooth neck. Remember, delicacy! No great, gauche moves—what's that I see on your face? A grimace? Wipe that off. A lord is a lord, and even his farts are noble. As if what you feel matters—get that out of your head, or do you want to feel more of the whip?"

It was a big party. The *Aitzas* all wore sword-belts around their paunches, and their gloved fingers were full of rings, like crusted filigree, their golden hair streaked with silver. Concubines leaned on the arms of their chairs, so tall and graceful, their lips so shiny red. Some got to wear satin draped over their smooth shoulders, being past Third Threshold, twenty-one. Everyone had yellow rose-petals in their hair and falling off their clothes, from the panels in the ceiling of the Garden Room, painted like clouds, that open up releasing a rain of flowers.

Tikas made them work hard, even beat them sometimes, but it was worth it. They had it good, compared to most slaves, getting fed more, wearing nice things. *Look at me, I'm strong and limber and graceful and clean, I smell good.* Patchouli went well on him, Tikas said. His body could do amazing things, things he hadn't thought possible until Tikas had showed him. Good to be small, for a dancer.

The beat-sticks rang in time, the chorus's voices climbed higher and higher. He shook his hair, cut like a horse's mane, from side to side, felt it wisp and hit his shoulders. Most slaves didn't get to keep any hair. Through the lace gloves his hands felt the sticky-powdery rosin on the dance-floor in front of the fountain. *Spin, spin* . . . Marble pillars winking, blur of torchlight, people; now the hard part. But he could do it perfectly. *Cat-step, spin, back-leap,* feeling the music . . . . Tikas said always feel the music, but never forget the audience. Feel their eyes, too. Don't let them see the sweat, the rosin, the aches. Make them see grace, beauty, love . . . *Back-leap, faster* . . . Make love to them through their eyes. Seduce them. No one in the world knows better than a boy your age . . . *Hands, feet, hands* . . . Now the climax, the most dramatic part, though not the hardest as people thought, he saw the mark on the floor, spin, fall—*slide.* The musicians' strings pulled him, stop. *Beat-sticks ticking, throw back the head, let the hair trail gracefully on the marble floor.* Silence.

He knew he'd done it the best he'd ever done it.

They got up to bow, and now he was allowed to have his head up, he saw the audience. The governor of Korsardiana was sitting in the chair of honor, next to Master Nuninibas. Tikas knelt at his feet. Rasas smiled, in pride, in triumph, in the joy of skill.

"Rasas." Tikas's voice. Called, he cast his eyes down at the green marble of the dais, the edge of the Master's sandals and his toes, Tikas's blue silk loincloth. He stepped gracefully. He was sweaty, but must not show it . . . *Oh no.* The fringe of his loin-cloth was stuck to his legs, the satin pulling, not hanging elegantly. *Celestialis . . . What'll the governor think? Maybe he and Master won't notice. But if I twitch it free they will for sure. But maybe if I do it real sneakily . . . no, they'll notice, what do I do?* He kept walking towards them, he had to. *My humble Slave God,* he prayed, *keep Master from noticing, so he won't mention it to Tikas, and I won't get whipped. Temonen household boys must be perfect. If only Tikas sees, I'll just get scolded.* He was there; he knelt, and then the loincloth didn't matter. He bowed all the way to the floor, first to Master, then to his honored guest. The governor's sandals were gilded, the nails on his toes thick and knobbly.

Now, he was allowed to look at the governor's face, being a pleasure-boy. The face was bread-loaf-shaped, eyes like grey glass beads with blue around the edges, set in folded pink dough. His hands were big and fat in white gloves. He was ugly. Rasas smiled and batted his eyes.

The governor looked him up and down, the eyes not changing, like beads. *I think that's another sign of nobility,* Rasas thought, *glass eyes that don't look at your face.* He nodded and turned away talking about grown-up noble things to another lord.

"Time to shower, dear," Tikas whispered. He had to be clean.

In the little room the boy stood in front of the governor, who lay in the scented cushions. The boy dimmed the lamp, took his gloves off, knelt and unlaced the sandals, massaging away the marks on the man's toes. Calluses were scratchy. The man's stomach hung over his belt in a big fold; he'd been sweating a lot in the cracks. The boy unbuckled the man's kilt, ermine-fur soft on his fingers. He smelled of old perfume and sour wine, oysters on his breath. *Pull the gloves off one finger at a time. Draw it out, tease him as long as he lets you. They enjoy it more that way in the end.* His bread-loaf face smiled, except for his bead-eyes, though they were brighter. His palms were wet.

He pulled the boy into his arms, rubbed against him for a while, then pushed down his head. *If he's ugly,* Tikas said, *pretend it's me. Even though I'm not there, I'll feel it, I will, wherever I am. It's for me you're doing it.* Rasas did it for Tikas. It was hard though; Tikas at least bathed twice a day.

Then the Governor yanked him up, a grin stretching his doughy face, and clamped a wide hand over his mouth and nose. *Give them what they want, always,* Tikas would say, *even if it is your death-throes; die gracefully* . . .

He'd get through this. He had before. It wasn't as bad as it had been; when he'd been little, he hadn't known it would end. Now he was big enough, the governor wouldn't tear him, or if he did, he'd heal again. He knew how to tell himself he wasn't really there, his body was just a lump of meat, that he'd leave behind when he went to Celestrinlis. He liked being nearly grown up, ten years old—things didn't hurt anymore. He knew how to think of something else, to look ahead. He never cried anymore.

Tikas would take care of him afterwards, put salve on his bruises and kiss him and rock him in long warm arms until he fell asleep. *I'll be all right.*

It was dark in the boys' barracks. He could hear Ardas, his best friend who he played pretend brothers with, breathing sleeping breaths in the next pallet.

After Tikas had held him for a while, he'd pretended he was sleeping so Tikas wouldn't worry about leaving him. Tikas was busy.

He shouldn't be awake, he knew. He needed his beauty sleep. But he couldn't sleep. He shouldn't think what he was thinking, but the memory kept pushing its hands into his head and hanging on like claws.

He'd thought after it happened he would be happy for the rest of his life. Now he knew it was something too good to happen more than once in forever. It was a long time ago.

I was afraid of him, when Master lent me to him. A barbarian, with long straggly writhing hair the color of dark red earth, and not even dyed: born that way. He was a famous gladiator that Master had invited to the party. He didn't wear gloves, and had dark hair on his knuckles like pig's bristles. He was called the Wolf, Mannas the Wolf. Rasas was afraid the Wolf would tear him up with his teeth and eat him.

Mannas came into the little room, and Rasas wanted

to back up against the wall, but he stayed where he was, sitting gracefully. The barbarian's head nearly reached the ceiling, or so it seemed, and his bare hands were gnarly, sword-callused from fighting, from killing other gladiators. He had so many victory-chains around his neck they were a wreath of gold that sparkled like glitter every time he moved; on his sword-arm, just above the elbow, he wore a black arm-ring, ebony. He sat down. *Always give them what they want, even if it kills you.* Though Rasas wanted to run crying, he started to do what he was supposed to. The barbarian stopped him. Looking straight at him, which showed how base-born he was.

"I'm a Yeoli," he said, in his strange accent. "I don't lust ahfter little boys. I only said yes to give you tseh night off." Rasas didn't understand. "No, no, no," the barbarian said, pulling the small hands off his dark-hairy chest. His big brown-bristled ones were gentle and strong at the same time, stronger than anyone else's that Rasas had ever felt, even though they did nothing to hurt. *He's displeased. What am I doing wrong?* "You don't hahve to," Mannas said, kept saying. "It'll be ourrh secret, just between you ahn' me, so you won't get in any trouble. I won't tell. I promise. I *swearrh.*" He held the bright clear glass thing dangling around his neck and said some strange words Rasas didn't understand. Then: "Second Firrhe come. You know no one breaks *tsaht* oath, Arkahn *orrh* Yeoli."

Rasas didn't know what to do, but Mannas said, "Let's just talk," and started. They talked about fighting and the Mezem and grown-ups, and Mannas showed Rasas all his scars and told him all sorts of war stories, about fighting the Lakans and how he'd had to save his best friend when one of the wood-cutters they were raiding pulled out a hidden bow. When Rasas told his stories, Mannas took him under his arm, just to hug him. The barbarian's arm was as warm as Tikas's, but thicker and harder. Though he didn't want to cry in front of Mannas because he was a famous gladiator even if he was base-born, Mannas said he didn't mind and wouldn't think any less of

Rasas for it; so Rasas did, and felt better after than he
ever had before in his life that he could remember.

Then Mannas said, "Where you from?"

"Arko," Rasas answered.

"No, you naht."

"Yes, I am." All the time they'd talked the barbarian
hadn't minded him talking back, but just argued as if he
was a grown-up too, so he felt safe contradicting him.

"You cahn't be," Mannas said. "Arkahns all hahve blue
eyes. *Yourrhs* are blahck."

Nowadays, he couldn't remember what they'd said
after that. It was a blur, of things about . . . when he'd
been little, all his made-up stories and places and the
made-up dream-tongue that he'd got in trouble for long
ago. Every time he'd talked in it or mentioned it they
beat him, until he'd stopped, except in his head. Gradually he'd forgotten the words.

No, he thought. *I mustn't think about it. It's too good.
It hurts too much. He never came back. He won fifty
fights, and went away to Yeoli-land. I'm going to cry.*

Tikas . . .

No. I can't call him. He's got important things to do.
The matron was asleep. He tried to push Mannas's smile
away out of his head with the governor's smothering
hand. *Mannas had dark eyes too, and I thought . . . but
I was never his son like I liked to pretend, or else he
would've taken me away with him, to live with his wife
and my brothers and sisters—Ardas, he would have taken
Ardas too—in his big house in Yeoli-land.* He saw the
governor open his mouth instead, his glass eyes creasing,
at the highest instant of his Noble Passion.

VI

Megan felt all blood drain out of her face as she gripped his hands.

No gold, no simpering attendants, no priceless furnishings . . . that lamp was an expensive item, actually; she'd thought it was plunder. "Oh, shit," Shkai'ra muttered under her breath, in Fehinnan. Fishhook just purred louder, and rubbed her head into his cheek.

Chevenga, Megan thought. *We've been talking to fucking Chevenga. The Invincible. The Immortal. Just sitting with us like a bar-friend. And I'm holding his hands.* Semanakraseye na . . . *that other word must be his military title, First General First. He Whose Bottom Is . . . oh my Goddess, no. It's not funny.*

Now, she saw the seal-ring on his finger, even that not particularly fancy, carved out of white stone, nephrite. *Everyone thought someone else told us* . . . His hands, naZak big, buried hers, hard, weapon-callused, but the grip much gentler than she would have expected. They let go to take Shkai'ra's next, then scratched Fishhook behind the ears.

At least stop doing your best imitation of a brook trout, Megan, she told herself, and cleared her throat. "Um, my profoundest apologies, for impertinence, Woyvode— ah, I should say, *Se-ma-na-k—*" *Shit! I fucking blew it. After all that practice . . . No, dammit, try again.* "*Se- ma-na-kra-se-ye.* We meant no lack of respect." She offered him her best bow, from kneeling. If it wasn't enough, they'd find out damn soon. *Stop acting like a first on board,* she told herself tartly. *The man has to take his pants down to shit like everyone else.*

"No, no, not at all," the semanakraseye said, smiling. "I didn't think you did. No offense taken. I'm not one for ceremony, more than the bare necessities of it." He answered Megan's bow with a finger-touch to his temple, as if they were two sentries changing places.

Shkai'ra sat back on her heels. "Well, that's a relief. Places I've been, you had to wiggle forward like a lizard to the throne, beating your head on the ground, or else die horribly."

"Like where I come from," Megan added.

"Ah. I understand." He was soft-spoken, so much so that sometimes she had to concentrate to catch all his words; very strange, in a politician. "You're Zak. And . . . Kommanz? You came by way of Brahvniki."

"Chevenga . . ." A man stuck his head in the door, and rattled off a question in rapid-fire Yeoli, with rapid-fire gestures. *Does everyone call him by his name to his face, too?* The *semanakraseye* answered in the same fast Yeoli, words and hands, and the man saluted and was gone, the first of a stream of people.

"By way of Brahvniki, yes," said Megan, using the hand-sign to be polite; that earned a smile. "We stopped there to get news out of the Benai, and horses for your army."

"Why do you want to join?" He didn't ask particularly sternly; at the same time his eyes, deep-set and large and dark brown, looked at her in a way she wouldn't have wanted to lie to.

"Because as far as I could see, you have a good chance of reaching the City Itself. Good enough for the Benaiat Ivahn to lend you money. I trust his judgment."

"Benaiat Ivahn? Lend me *money?*" Chevenga's eyes creased, confused. "He never did that. Where did you hear it?"

What? Megan ran back over the memory; yes, Ivahn had told her, plain. *Wait one fish-gutted minute. Someone's trying to spread cow-manure here, and I don't think it's Ivahn.*

It's for Ivahn's sake. She remembered how it had been in strictest confidence. *He's figuring I might be a loose-lipped type who's heard a rumor, and doesn't want to give anything away.* She'd never seen confusion faked so well.

She raised one eyebrow, lowered her voice to a whisper. "I have considerable financial dealings with the Benaiat, and we are also dear friends. We spoke of other things too, for instance a *certain* fifteen-year-old visitor to the city who had to be administered the remedy to a *certain* affliction contracted the night before in a *certain* establishment whose name is suggestive of a *certain* small long-bodied creature, entangled . . ."

Chevenga broke out laughing, his two gold teeth, no, three, there was another on the lowers, flashing. "He told you *that?* Did he tell you what happened when we were there?—no, never mind, I don't want to know. He certainly must trust *your* judgment. I should tell you, he didn't lend money to *me*—Yeoli law forbids me to own anything—just to my people, agented by me. So when I said he didn't, I spoke truth." *Tricky,* Megan thought, nodding. *But most wouldn't bother to explain it afterwards.* Every now and then, she'd noticed, he'd fall into an ancient-school Yeoli style of speaking, even in Enchian, almost ritually formal about matters of truth and choice.

"So what do you want to get into Arko for?" He must

have a report from Ikal, she knew, and was asking for answers he already knew, wanting to hear them drugless.

"My son. He was sold into slavery, and I've recently discovered he is there. I thought I'd have a better chance of finding him in the forefront rather than the aftermath."

"Aftermath? Of what?" The puzzlement in his eyes seemed utterly genuine.

"The sack of Arko."

Another interruption came then, giving Megan time to worry. *Maybe after the business is over, he trusts me and I'm signed on, I can make friends with him. I'd like to. Koru, Ivahn was right, I did like him right off. But it's too soon. Careful of your mouth, Megan.*

The interruption ended. "I mean to conquer Arko," Chevenga said casually. "I don't mean to sack it."

He doesn't mean to sack Arko, she thought. *No embellishments, no explanations, just "I don't mean to sack it," those big brown eyes shining with sincerity. Alllll right. They tortured him, he won't sack them. And I'm the queen of Shamballah. Either that, or he's more principled than I have ever known any one human to be . . . if he even can control this motley host when they get to the City.* The standing order, apparently, was no looting, all spoils to be divided in an orderly and fair fashion; she'd heard the tale on the way here, that he'd had people executed for stealing as little as a skin of wine. And yet that might also mean that the army, having been held back for so long, would feel all the more that destroying the City Itself was its just reward.

Yet maybe he could finesse it somehow; if he was so decided, he must have a plan. If so, she wouldn't have to outstrip a plundering, raping and burning army to find Lixand: there'd be margin for error. She worked her dry mouth, took a sip of scalding-hot tea.

Chevenga called an order in Yeoli to outside, and the interruptions stopped. "Before I go on, tell me, did the truth-drugging go all right? I've got rules about it: they should have sworn silence beforehand, told you they'd ask you nothing personal that wasn't relevant, and stuck to that."

Checking up on the underlings. "Yes, they did all that," Megan answered. "May I ask why you're being so careful? I didn't think you'd have to, the position you're in now."

"To set . . . an example. Because of this war, my people have discovered truth-drug. You'll see it all through our courts, in two or three years; I'm trying to demonstrate ways of being careful with its power. I suffered myself, by the way Arkans use it; when I was there they'd haul me in every month or so for Yeola-e's military secrets. I always prided myself on keeping things, even details, in my head."

Megan recoiled inwardly, her own memory of the drug so recent. *To hear what's going to cause your country's enslavement, kill your people by the thousand, coming out of your own mouth that way. . . .* It would be as bad as anything on a Mahid table, or worse. His torture scars, she realized, he'd got in Arko, not occupied Yeola-e.

"So. You offer more services than your knife-arm, Megan, I understand. What can you do, that might be useful to us? I want to see the trick with light."

Shkai'ra began a laugh, hid it with a cough and one hand; he flashed her a bemused glance. "Tricks, you haven't *seen* tricks until you move to F'talezon," she said. "Show him, love."

Pull in to the center, look inside me and reach for the manrauq. She took hold of the brightness she saw in her mind and brought it out with her, watching it bloom golden between her hands, pulling her palms apart slowly so that the light thinned to a twisting coil writhing between them. She held it for a second only, to save her strength. The next "trick" would be a lot harder.

The *semanakraseye* blinked and shook his head as if to get water out of his eyes, then leaned forward, elbows on knees; the gaze she'd thought intense before was nothing to this. *Hah*, she thought, catching her breath by the tail; the mental exertion of *manrauq* was as hard as any physical. *I, Megan Whitlock, have impressed the Invincible, Infallible, Imperturbable Fourth Chevenga.*

"Can you cast it? How far? How much can you make? Is it hot? I forgot to feel. Can you do other things?" Like Fehinnan crossbow bolts the questions flew. Suddenly, under the studied calm of command, she could imagine him on the edge of a circus ring, a boy with huge brown thrilled eyes.

"The light I can only throw when it's tied to something, like a knife," she said, forcing torn-cloth raggedness out of her voice. "Especially if I've touched it. My own knives are sensitive to me and would glow. It's not hot. I have to be seeing them to maintain it. And yes, I can do other things." He took it all in like a briefing on an armed unit's strengths.

"You said you can do assassin and thief-work: I take it that means you are good at moving unseen in the dark?" By the glint in his eyes, he was already making plans. She chortled inwardly. "What other things can you do?"

Breathe deep, calm. You've done it before. "Something a bit more elaborate. I can make people see what I imagine."

"Anything?"

"Within reason."

"Could you make someone see—a *dimas*?" *A quick study, Ivahn said that* ... "A large, ugly, hairy, scaly, blood-thirsty *dimas*. From an Arkan's nightmares. As horrible as you can imagine!"

You don't know how horrible I can imagine. She centered again. *My hands are shaking—wrong thought. Think of power flowing, a sea breaking on you as if you were the shore, hear the sound of the wind in your veins* ... She pulled in, crushing outside thought and stretching as if she could soak up the power-sea through her skin. She put one hand on the ground in front of her, then the other, and saw in her mind the boar's bristles sprout from her skin as it changed to a greenish, leathery hide; heard the crack as her back ripped open, muscles tearing free. Her lower jaw creaked as the bone stretched and grew, extending foot-long fangs as she raised her head to the ceiling, and grew, and grew. She could feel the steel quills rattle and quiver on her back as her tail coiled around behind her, barbed end twitching. Her talons scraped the floor, black and silver; her greenish hide wept tears of blood. From her throat, the silvery laughter of a child, under eyes gone yellow corner to corner. . . . *The demon I am is very female.* She strained to rise, hold the image, the sound, the thought. It shimmered, tottered like a tower built too high, and collapsed as she did, face in her hands, shaking. *How long did I hold it? A breath? Maybe two? I have to learn to sustain it longer.* Megan blinked back tears of pain.

But the Invincible, the Imperturbable, was leaning back on his arms, his eyes showing white all around.

"That was . . . that was . . ." He took a deep breath, shook his head hard, curls dancing. *"Fabulous!"*

Shkai'ra gave a laugh, half shudder. "She tried it out on *me* once. I woke up, stretched, turned over to kiss her good morning and . . . that . . . *thing* was on the pillow beside me. I swear, I didn't touch the ground until I was ten meters out of the tent, running bare-ass into a rainstorm with the horses running in front of me—and I was *catching up.*"

"How long could you make it last," Chevenga said, eyes gleaming, "in ideal conditions?"

"About two very slow breaths, perhaps a count of twenty, especially if the image is less complex," Megan swallowed a couple of times and controlled her shaking hands, feeling pale. *Don't throw up.* Her vision was greying. *Don't pass out.*

"Not that a moment of that couldn't do wonders, in the dark, with people already nervous . . . Megan, are you all right?"

Megan used the Yeoli gesture so she wouldn't have to nod, felt Shkai'ra's arm around her shoulders. "Yes. Just don't ask me to run any broken-field races. It costs, that's all. Like anything worth doing." The headache was there, but she expected that.

"Yes." His smile flashed, approving. "Maybe you should lie down for a bit, just rest. You needn't demonstrate more." She stayed sitting. "Those *nails* of yours . . . how did you come by them?"

How does he know it isn't just silver paint? It hadn't been mentioned in the truth-drugging. Then she remembered: his *manrauq*, the sense for weapons. "They're steel: I had them transmuted, by a fellow Zak. So I'd never be unarmed, you see. Not without price: I have to drink a fish-gutted *big* cup of fish-oil every day to keep me healthy."

"Tell me: how much are you two asking?"

Ah. The magic words. Megan opened her mouth to charge him all the market would bear, and heard herself say, "I really don't care. The standard will do." *Fik the money, it's not important.* The merchant in her screeched. "As long as I get a chance to find my son." Shkai'ra stared at her in mock surprise, winked as Megan gave her a corner-of-the-eye glare.

"It's for him you are in it," Chevenga said. "And you've got money elsewhere." Neither of these were questions. "I understand." His thinking look, that she could already recognize, came, with the slight cocking of the head. "You said your son was in the City Itself?"

"Dah."

"What does he look like? I used to live there, I might have seen him. Do you know who he'd be with?"

"I used to live there," he says, as if he just moved in because he preferred the climate. "He'd be nine, almost ten, eyes like mine, pale blond hair, though that might have darkened—more likely shaved, as a slave. *Aitzas* family Temonen. Their estate is on Fidelity Street, which is in the south end of the noble quarter, near the Fountain of Infinity."

"Temonen." He studied her eyes. "Temonen. What was the lord's first name?"

"Nuninibas."

"Nuninibas Temonen, yes. I got invited to his parties, but never went, though I had a friend who did." He was wearing an ebony arm-ring on his right arm; now he absently touched it with one tender finger. "The family's prospering; they were notorious parties. Which means at least they won't have sold him off to pay debts."

Megan closed her eyes for a second, thinking of how long it had taken to get all her information by proxy. "I'm sorry," he said gently. "I wish I could tell you more. If they have sold him, you can track him starting from there. It may also be that Nuninibas will see the writing on the wall and get his household out before we even arrive." *Before we arrive, not if,* she thought. *He's certain of himself as a Ryadn; that's why the rest of the army is.* "Even so there are ways to track him. I'll lend you help, if it comes to that." *So many mercenary employers say farewell and to Halya with you the moment the fight's over,* she thought, *your problem if you didn't get what you came for. No wonder people are loyal to him.* Then: *or else he's trying to get more out of us with promises.*

"Well. On to your bigger half." Shkai'ra had been watching, cat-smiling, working her fingers and wrists; she'd let the loose sleeves of her coat fall back, to show the tendons rippling in her forearms.

"My part is a little more difficult to demonstrate," she said. "Leading cavalry is what I was raised to do. I had five thousand lances under me in the Minztan War, before I was exiled and outlawed in Stonefort." She smiled reminiscently. "We won, too. Hmmm. You're getting a lot of odds-and-sods without unit organization? I've fought in a lot of mercenary armies, some of which had as much discipline to start with as a pack of jackals around a dead sheep. As to personal skills—"

A damselfly had been flitting around the lantern; Fishhook made a tentative snap at it from Chevenga's shoulder, and the insect darted for the door. Shkai'ra, resting her hands on her thighs, let it zip past her ear before she moved. Rising, drawing, the saber moving in a blurring slash that left a dazzling streak of silver in the air, the ripping-silk sound of it parting mingling with the slight *huff* of her breath. Turning in the same motion, kneeling again, the saber sheathed with a *snap* while the severed body of the damselfly was still fluttering toward the earth, not two heartbeats from her hand's first motion toward swordhilt.

"Good, very good," he said, with the same smile, but evenly. "I want to see what you can do against another warrior, though, and what you and that beast of yours can do together. That'll have to wait till morning, early, before we move out." *So much for enough sleep,* Megan grumbled inwardly. "We can haggle now—I'm willing to risk a guess—or after that, whichever you prefer. You want to know what standard joiner's rate is, these days? Board, and an equal share of the spoils. We don't even have to equip them, and they *still* join in droves . . .

"But what you have, I'd never take for so little. Not asking as much of you as I plan to. Here's my offer: for Megan, board, mercenary's share of spoils, and thirty *ankaryel* a month; for Shkai'ra, board, mount-board—you understand providing Hotblood's keep is going to be difficult, since I understand he eats horse and human meat—and twenty *ankaryel* a month, raised commensurate with promotion."

Starting low, Megan thought, translating the amounts into Dragonclaws, the haggling-mind locking in. *Damn low. Hard bargainer; I wouldn't have thought it. But he's full of surprises.* "It seems we *should* wait till Shkai'ra shows more," she said, coldly polite. "Your average Schvait mercenary earns one *ankarye* a day, or thirty or so a month. Your *average*"—she drew the word out and let it hang in the air for a beat—"*Schvait.*"

"No, no," Chevenga said. "That's silver *ankaryel*. I should have specified, sorry: gold."

Megan blinked before she could stop herself. Gold was ten times silver, for Yeoli *ankaryel*. *Koru, we're haggling, but it's the wrong way round.* With a slight motion Shkai'ra dug a sharp elbow into her ribs. *No, we shouldn't wait till tomorrow. That's what she's thinking, too. He might come to his senses and change his mind.* "Done," she said.

"I'll send word to Peraila," he said. "Megan, you'll work under me, no one else; and not a soul's to know anything of your gift. You Zak are used to that anyhow, aren't you?"

"*Dah.* Understood, *kras.*"

He held out his hands again, outlining the oath for going on the strength. *Swear by our own faiths,* Megan inwardly repeated his words. *Yes, he knows how to run an allied army.*

Shkai'ra drew a dagger, pricked her thumb and let a drop fall on the steel. "By Zaik Victory-Begetter and World-Devourer, by Baiwun and Jaiwun and the Steel Spirit and the souls of the Ancestors, my will is yours, Fourth Zh'ven'ghkua, may the Refought Godwar burn the world and the Ztrateke ahKommanz spurn me if I forswear."

Megan shielded her eyes as if from a bright light. "By the Lady and the Lord's Shadow, may I freeze and roast in Halya, Great Bear devour my soul if I swear false."

Chevenga gripped his crystal. *What, he's swearing an oath too? That's different.* "All-spirit hear me: I shall not fail or hold cheap the lives and good of those who have relinquished their wills to me, Megan Whitlock and Shkai'ra Mek Kermak's Kin, Second Fire come if I lie."

Then he flashed a grin like a boy who'd just sworn a friendship oath. "Right. Beer?"

"Zilk, linen, azorted other useful zupplies. Highest k-vality, *very* reasonable price. I understand you haf much need of rubber here—spring-black? Substance dat stretch, bounce? Never mind, I talk to storemaster. Sorry

I zo late, vanted to make it in tonight because owf deh rain, here's deh inventory, you read Enshian?"

The sentry didn't. Matthas had to go down the whole list with him, in his best Thanish accent, using his mantle to shield it from the rain driving down out of a pitch-black midnight sky, while letting in enough light from the man's torch-hook to see without setting the mantle on fire. "Dere iss name, Goonter Frahnzsson, of Neu-bonn, dat's, in Enshian, high g-o-o-n-t ..." He spoke in a non-stop monotone. "Neubonn, dat's Neubonn, high n-e-u, you've never heard owf? Vere you from? Never mind, no offense, high n-e-u-b-o-n-n, iss off Vechaslaf, tributary owf Brezhan ..." Soon enough the man cleared him, giving him the storemaster's name. "Yo-oh! For-vard!" The caravan lumbered into the section on the edge of the allied camp designated for hucksters.

Und now I vind dose two—Celestialis, I'm fikken thinking in it. To the better, really, that he thought and felt his part as well as spoke it; he'd more likely react in character in a crisis. *But it's damned irritating after this long.* Almost a month, to catch the fikken Yeolis and their allies, now stabbing deep into the Empire along the Eastern Wing highway; long enough both to get used to going without gloves and acquire a fair tan on the backs of his hands. Like eating mutton instead of beef, so he didn't smell Arkan; they hadn't thought of teaching that in spy-school, but to his mind it was a basic precaution.

The trip had been happily uneventful, the one rough spot coming when one of the hirelings had turned out to be Thanish of all things, her face lighting up when she'd found out, or thought she'd found out, his national-ity. Her tongue had launched into a great long string of fast non-stop Thanish, of which he could understand not a syllable. "Ve not speak dat in de new country, only in olt," he snapped back. She'd bought it, but for a time his heart had beat at a speed he really was too old for. From then on he'd avoided her.

And I find those two, he continued his thought. *And*

do what I have to. Whatever it takes. Next order of business, make some contact with the Arkan army, if he could find one, that opposed this circus of sixty-thousand, for a source of aid and an escape route already paved in case of trouble. Hopefully he could find someone of high-rank who wasn't a complete moron, though the Yeolis had been cutting the smart ones down—*one of his favorite tactics, that brilliant lunatic ex-gladiator barbarian whoreson, because he knows damn well smart Arkan generals are rare.* They wouldn't know he was out of favor with his superior, with orders to work alone; one thing he'd learned to count on, dealing with the Empire's lumbering mastodon of an administration, was that the left hand never knew what the right hand was doing unless it read it in the *Pages*, which would solemnly report that it had eight fingers.

VII

Megan woke up with Fishhook hopping over her face, velvet wings flapping. She pulled the blanket up and tried to ignore the fact that she wasn't asleep anymore. She never slept well anyway while they were on the road; Shkai'ra snored. *Fish-guts—it's still dark.*

The Kommanza wiggled out of the covers and got up. It was still overcast out, though it had stopped raining. Megan told herself she must be asleep, because she'd heard Sova. *I must be drea—*

"ZAIK DAMNED YOUR MAGGOT-EATEN SOUL, YOU SHEEPRAPING STEERFUCKING LITTLE BITCHCOLT, WHAT THE ZOWEITZUM ARE YOU DOING HERE? I'M GOING TO KICK YOUR UNPADDED ASS ALL THE WAY BACK HOME THEN WALLOP IT UNTIL YOU RIDE STANDING THE REST OF YOUR LIFE!"

Oh. Sova is here. Resignedly Megan threw back the covers and clambered out. *Nobody's going to get any sleep around here now.* From other tents all around, she could hear angry mutters, curses and yells to shut up.

Fishhook yawned *sleepsleep* and crawled under the pillow.

Shkai'ra spoke in something more like words. "And how *did* you get here?"

Megan slid out of the tent in time to hear the Thane-girl answer, "I followed you, *khyd-hird. Zhymata* said I could sail on any ship of the house, so I did and waited until you came down to Brahvniki. I knew you'd go to the Worm. I borrowed some of the money from the petty-cash box and left a note for Shyll, and came with a caravan to be safe."

Shkai'ra reacted calmly, burying her hands in her hair and trying to tear out pieces. "Sheepshit, girl, that's nearly a thousand *kylickz* overland—you could have been raped, robbed, killed, skinned and eaten fifteen times. We said it was too risky *with* us and you did it *by yourself?*"

Sova stood straight, hands on hips. "Yep."

Shkai'ra stopped, as if she were hearing her own words. "Hai, you *did* do it. You all right, girl?"

"*Yes,* I am all right. *You* said you were thrown out into the snow with nothing but a bow and a knife at fourteen; I had money and things, and something almost happened once, but I only had to break his elbow and then he left me alone and I made it here and I'm fine."

"Baiwun hammer me flat, you did." Suddenly Shkai'ra started laughing, dropping down into a crouch. "Megan, look who's here: our daughter." She laughed harder and pushed herself up with her hands on her knees. "Gods witness, I'm glad you did, daughter."

"Sova—" Megan started, then closed her mouth. What was there to say? She touched the girl's shoulder, then hugged her, hard, thinking of all that could have happened. *So much easier going into danger yourself, than watching someone you love do it.* She'd noticed that, over and over, since she'd let herself love again.

"Sova." Shkai'ra stood with her hands on her hips. "Three things. This—" she grabbed her and gave her a hug "—is congratulations for making it here. That took guts and smarts. I'll show you how to make warrior braids tomorrow. This—" she hugged her again and planted a smacking kiss on her forehead "—is because I'm so fucking relieved you're all right, and because I missed you. And *this*—" she turned the girl around and kicked her behind, medium hard, enough to make her jump "—is for disobeying orders and frightening the shit out of your mothers!"

She was grinning when Sova turned around. "Your turn, co-mother."

The Thane-girl seemed more apprehensive facing Megan. *She knows who was in favor of her being here and who wasn't.* "Come on," said the Zak. "I'll talk to you while we get a fire going and breakfast started." Shkai'ra rolled her eyes with that "here comes the lecture" look, then shrugged and rooted into the tent for a pan. Just then reveille sounded, the gong-beat and the call relayed over the camp in fluid Yeoli, *"Rise and wi-i-i-in!"*

"I'll get some water," Shkai'ra said. "Back in a minute."

"You know what could have happened?" Megan said. Sova nodded, shrugging, just like Shkai'ra. *She doesn't; thank Koru, she didn't find out.* "You understand why we're both angry?"

"I figured you would be," the girl said, shrugging again.

"Do you *understand* why?" Megan leaned forward, fixing her with a stare. "We thought you'd be better off at home. What would Shyll and Rilla have told us when we came back, if you'd disappeared somewhere on the way here? It would be worse than what happened to my son; at least I knew where to start looking. We might never have known what happened to you, whether you were dead, alive or in chains somewhere, some pederast's slave . . ."

Sova drew up, with a hardness Megan had never seen before; the girl had acquired it, it seemed, on this trip.

"It would have been my choice. You're angry because you don't like me making my own choices. Besides, nothing *did* happen to me. I did far riskier things to help you in the fight up the river, and you didn't mind."

Megan closed her lips on a sharp answer. "Your choice to risk your life and health, when I and your other parents have before law agreed to protect you to the best of our ability till your age of adulthood?" she said levelly. "I could hit you, but that wouldn't be fair. I'd be hitting you because I was scared and angry. But I want you to promise me something."

"What's that?" Sova said, more amenably. Shkai'ra came back with a bucket and plunked it down next to their hearthrocks, took out her tinderbox and struck sparks on the shavings, listening.

"Think of what might happen. No one can stop you if you really decide to do something, but if you get into trouble, I'd like to be in a position to help you."

"All right," Sova said breezily.

"And first thing, you are going to write a letter home to Rilla and Shyll, apologizing. I'll put it in the packet I'm sending home."

"I already wrote, I told you. I wrote, 'Sorry but it's something I have to do.'"

Megan pursed her lips. "All right. But you're going to write to them saying you got here safely." To that the girl agreed. "Come on then, there's work to do before we march. Whatever possessed you to come at this hour?"

"I only heard where you were when Sinanayi came in. She was on duty until now and I didn't want to have to try and find you on the march."

"Good enough," said Megan, wondering who in Halya Sinanayi was. Shkai'ra had dug out the frying pan, a filch of smoked bacon, some eggs they'd bought from a farmer yesterday but hadn't had time to cook; most of them were unbroken. Another disciplined thing in this army: no stripping the country if you could pay.

She started blowing at the kindling, then looked up.

"Two hours to dawn," she said, then looked at Sova. "Megan said it better than I could," she said. "Nobody your age thinks they can get hurt until they do. A burned hand teaches more caution than a thousand words. You're going to see war here, look carefully."

She shoved the stone a little closer to the fire, putting the pan across their surface, dropped in some lard from the jar and began slicing onions into it. "The way you managed was part luck, Sova; you only get so much good luck, don't use it when you don't have to. I want you to outlive me, and to see your children before I die. This is a war-camp, under discipline. If you break orders again, I *will* hit you, perhaps even flog you; that's the customary punishment here. For the same reason I've walloped you at weapons drill now and then, because you'll die if you don't learn. Understand *that?*"

"You've only told me a thousand times, *khyd-hird*, about armies. I knew I was coming to one. And you hitting me is no big news." Sova smiled, tapped the edge of the pan with a nail. "The onions are burning."

"Shit!" Shkai'ra stirred them with her knife. "Go get your gear, colt; I want it all here and laid out in half an hour. Jump!" The girl ran off.

Megan slid into her tunic from yesterday. *Well, another to worry about*. Shkai'ra, Sova, Hotblood, Fishhook . . . They might as well be a circus.

"Gods-damned gang of strolling players, aren't we," Shkai'ra said, yawning and scratching as she stirred the bacon strips into the onions.

"Just what I was thinking." Megan started rolling the bedding. "So, what did you think of the Gold-dipped Wonder?"

Shkai'ra winked. "Well, at first I was nervous. But then I said to myself, 'He's just another conquering hero-king. So what? *Fuck* Zh'ven'gkua,' I said to myself."

"Intending to be a woman of your word, too, no doubt—pass the knife?"

"We'll see." Shkai'ra smiled wickedly and reached the

cooking knife to her. _Dull. Weapons always ready to split hairs, and her camp knife can't spread butter_, Megan thought.

"Well, we'd best not be late for your little demonstration, even if the army isn't marching today."

"_Ia_. I think he's more interested in what Hotblood can do to the Arkans than my tits—damnitall."

"Ivahn was certainly right, that _you'd_ like him on sight," Megan said snidely. Shkai'ra snorted.

Last shot. The shield set up as a target on the other end of the cleared practice-ground receded as Hotblood galloped flat out away from it. Shkai'ra twisted and drew, the pulleys of the wheelbow silent as oil, aimed, angled to arch the shot. All around was motion, the Ri's surging body, the grass blurring beneath his feet, the rushing wind, the distance to the target, changing every moment; but the one point of her intent, guiding eyes, head, breath and hands, as her body flowed to the Ri's, was as still as a motionless pond, a moment frozen in time like glass.

Loose. The arrow was too fast to be visible, the first sign of it a flash of sunlight caught on the shaft, at the top of its three-hundred metre arch; then it was invisible again, until it appeared, sunk halfway into the shield and the wood pell under it, the deep _thump_ seeming an afterthought. The spectators, a solid rank of them all around, whistled and clashed wristlets.

It was the final trial all Kommanzas had to perform, to become full warriors, requiring many apparently impossible shots and maneuvers, including picking up a kerchief from the ground in her teeth, at a full gallop. The deal was done, but Chevenga had wanted to see what she could do. It couldn't hurt, to give him, and everyone else here, soon to be comrades-in-arms, or underlings, her measure.

On her silent command Hotblood wheeled, carrying her towards where the _semanakraseye_'s desk was set up under his tent-flap, at the edge of the ground. The misty early-morning light had started the grass steaming dry; sun struggled through thinning clouds. He was wearing a black satin shirt, bordered with white, the collar square with a "v" cut into it, just under his throat. The effect was dashingly official, making the scar on his cheek, clearer in sunlight, seem out-of-place. She dismounted with a graceful leap, Hotblood frisking and blowing.

"Very good," Chevenga said, grinning. She put a hand to Hotblood's mouth; he lipped her fingers, making her glad she was wearing gloves. "Tell me, how far apart can the two of you be, and still . . . think to each other?"

"About two . . . kylickz . . . kilometers, you say. Fades out to general feelings beyond that, then thins to nothing. We can tell each other's direction from much further away; say a hundred, two hundred kilometers. And whether the other is getting closer or farther."

"That could be useful . . . he *smells* like a meat-eater. Does he eat anything else?"

"Milk, cheese, grain, grass and leaves, if he can't get struggling meat. It makes him moody, though."

"Arkans?"

"Two-legs are his favorite after horses; and though he's not normally picky about nationalities, I've told him to be, in this case. Ri are like weasels: kill-crazy. I can keep him under control unless he's attacked. And I've told him that if I bite it, the yellow-haired red-armored ones are to blame, and he should rip up only them." That had been difficult; Hotblood didn't think in words, what-if a concept at the bare limit of his comprehension. On top of that he'd greeted the thought of her death with a monumental sulk.

Without warning, the Ri padded up to the desk, stretched his neck to lean his wedge-shaped face within a handspan of Chevenga's. *Scareyouhehehehe. Oh, shit . . . HERDSTALLION*, Shkai'ra thought frantically. Now, Hotblood chose to blithely ignore her, baring his fangs instead.

You're in trouble, Gold-bottom, if there's any fear in you now, whether you show it or not. . . . The Ri could smell it. Whether the *semanakraseye* sensed this or not, she couldn't tell; but he didn't move, his dark gaze, not so much hard as open, like a cat's hunting-stare, faintly smiling, if anything, back into the Ri's. They stared at each other frozen for a time. *The only two around here who aren't a little tense,* Shkai'ra thought. Some Yeolis had their hands on their sword-hilts, or knuckles white on spears. Chevenga raised a hand, signing them to do nothing. With a shrug of his mane, Hotblood turned away. *Noscare boring.*

"I'm telling him that you're herd stallion around here," said Shkai'ra, sending the thought as she spoke. "And a greater killer than I am, even. He believes me."

Chevenga shrugged and smiled. "Maybe it isn't true." He gave out some order, stripped off his shirt and took up a shield and a pair of wooden practice-swords that had been leaning on his desk. "Come."

Oh, good, Shkai'ra thought. *How good is he, his own self?* He offered and she chose, picking out the sword of white oak, and swung it to get the balance while they brought up a horse for him. *Not bad:* a big black Lakan gelding, about seventeen hands, definitely a destrier, not too showy but looking very strong and reasonably fast. Brave too; it just rolled the white of its eye at Hotblood, though they were upwind. The crowd around the ground suddenly thickened, munching on pieces of cold roast pork from last night; war-camps were as bad as cities for people with nothing to do but watch.

DO NOT BITE OR CLAW THIS HORSE, she thought to Hotblood. *Herdstallion and I are going to play.*

Gripinpushpushpush? he hoped.

Bastard peeping tom keeps listening in when I fuck. Of Hotblood's bad habits, that was the worst, at least in Shkai'ra's opinion. *No. Playfight.*

Oh. He looked at the horse speculatively. *Fight horse?*

DO NOT BITE OR CLAW THIS HORSE, she thought again.

Sigh. Sheep?

"He's being real good; do you have any spare sheep?"

"Oh, I think we could find one somewhere," Chevenga said, with a musing smile. He mounted, and the Lakan black stamped and sidled, not happy. He gentled it down but it sweated anyway, as he wheeled away to take position. Shkai'ra mounted, did likewise at the opposite ends of the field.

They saluted, then charged, Shkai'ra giving the Kommanza war-cry.

The *semanakraseye* was a little slower off the mark, his Lakan destrier needing greater time to build up speed. *Careful, it outweighs Hotblood by a third.* She leaned forward along his neck, blade out and wrist locked; Chevenga was sitting straight with his butt against the high cantle, sword back for a chopping stroke. Closer—but his horse swerved, and they passed just out of sword's reach.

"Shit!" Shkai'ra cursed.

Hehe, Hotblood commented.

Shut up!

They wheeled; he was speaking to his horse, patting its neck. The whites of its eyes showed; foam blew off its neck on muscles standing out like iron. She could see the strain in his forearms, from reining. "Is that a warhorse, *kras,* or a racer?" she called, grinning.

"Warhorse!" he called back. "Steady as stone, unfailing as a Haian's oath. Except today, when he's decided to be a racer...." She saw the flash of gold teeth, as he grinned. "As many an Arkan destrier will, too."

Hotblood darted forward before Shkai'ra could stop him; thought-giggling *hehehe,* he stretched his neck and hissed in the Lakan black's face, making it jump, all four feet in the air. *I wish he hadn't been eating so much horsemeat.* Chevenga barely managed to stay in the saddle and kept gentling. Between its urge to be elsewhere and his direction, the Lakan turned in a U, circling. The watchers laughed, shouting Yeoli, making chicken-clucks. He yelled something in Yeoli back to them, turning his head away from her. In the moment's relaxation she allowed herself then, a dark shadow with wooden sword was blurring above her.

Shit. She rolled out of the saddle, crouching down. *I should have expected it: horse being a hindrance, not a help—leave it. And off one leg while looking the other way, perfectly misleading clues, beautiful.* He twisted midair and landed on her leg, pinning her to the saddle, now giving *his* war-cry, hoarse and deafening. *Shield down, stop him chopping at the leg; Baiwun he's fast. Block, shield, sword, shield . . .*

Whump. Hotblood's head came around and back; she heard and felt the thump against Chevenga's back. He flew over her head, his scarred face passing by hers with an expression almost casual, eyes fixed carefully on the ground where he was headed, to land rolling fluidly onto his feet. She cantered off, flicking herself back upright in the saddle. His horse was long gone; she could see a gap in the spectators, and a bobbing black thing trailing a tent.

"Nice try!" she yelled from ten yards. *Sheepshit, that was close.* He just beckoned her to him with his sword, standing upright in a natural stance.

This says something. At least three hundred people were watching, enough to make whatever happened here common knowledge in camp in a day. A shrugging matter if he beat her—but if *she* beat *him*, the Invincible, on whom all their hopes rested. . . . *He's smart enough not to underestimate me, and to know I'm not going to hold back in one sinew for one instant. Yet he was doing this, and with a grin. So confident in your own skill, Gold-bottom?* She remembered Ivahn's words: "He takes great risks."

"*Eeeeeeiiiiiiii!*" Hotblood sprang into charge. Saber back and up for a forward-sweep cut, mount's shoulder into the footman and the blade chops with all the weight behind it *but pull it, we're sparring* . . .

As if he was going to stay there—damn. In the last instant Chevenga spun out of line somehow, *jumped, this one's a fucking jackrabbit he's over the line of my cut.* She flipped the saber into the overhand guard down her spine, but he kicked in midair, sandalled foot whipping out flicker-fast. The heel rapped her shoulder, just hard enough to make her reel in the saddle.

He should have gone for my head or neck; a miss, or intentional? She'd seen his face at the apex of the jump, measuring carefully like before. *Give him the benefit of the doubt, at least half of it.* She rolled out of the saddle on the other side, landing on her feet. Hotblood circled, then lay down and sulked when she told him to stay out. This was *not* a scream and leap situation.

Ex-gladiator, she thought. *Used to duels, in front of crowds.* She stood, shield up under her eyes, saber laid flat along her spine. Now he was rushing her, the hoarse cry again, cut low straight from the run, blurring fast. She leaped over it, milked the hilt as she slashed down, onto his shield. *Thud.* The shock jarred her arm.

Blocked his sight, hah!—she punched out the wood sabre in a lunge at his midriff, to be turned perfectly by his, almost delicately, just enough motion to send it offline. . . . *Shit, can the steer-raper see through leather?* Then he attacked, high cut, low cut, thrust at eyes, elbow . . . She remembered: *manrauq. He has weapon-man-rauq.* She kept the shield in front of her, on the defensive, the blows rocking back into her shoulders, *Baiwun, he's strong for his size,* slightly shorter than her. She yielded ground, stop-thrust to make him guard, bounded backward. *Thrust again while I'm outside his fighting range; keep him there and I can peck at him.*

No, he understood how to fight like one smaller, getting inside and moving quick; besides he had long arms for his height, deceptive. The brown eyes were even more wide-open now, concentrating, pupils big. She and

he moved together, like dancing, like sex, each placing
of hands and feet and bodies in concert, in amber honey.
Once their gaze caught, and his lips parted in a small
quiet smile.

His wooden sword quartered down from the left, neck-
cut. Shield up like the wing of a soaring gull, around to
stop the blow, her sword stabbing low. His shield locked
against the guard of her sword, and they stood locked
corps-a-corps for an instant, no open flesh to kick; he
pushed, and his sword-hand and shield-hand were like
the halves of a giant vise.

She waited till her arms *must* give way, part of a second, used his strength to throw herself back. She could
hear the crowd behind, distant, half yelling for him, half
good-naturedly, to her amazement, for her. *They're so
fucking confident, too, that they want to make it harder
for him.* She'd moved twenty yards back in three pas-
sages; that had to stop. The sun, out fully now, shone in
his eyes but didn't slow his responses. *If there were sand
I might try to kick some into his face;* but they were on
thick sod. *And it might do no good anyway.*

If you can't win, cheat. A trick she'd learned from a
Senlaw street-bravo, impossible to block. She attacked
hard, faster than she could maintain, pushing herself past
the reserve against extremity; he defended, waiting for
her last strength to wear out. *Beautiful, beautiful, nothing
wasted.* All her strikes were high-line, advancing a series
of running fleches to the throat, long-lunge. He parried
against the tip of the sword, stopping her movement with
the threat of running herself onto his point. Once she
tried to hit his wrist, but the steel band of his wristlet
glanced her point. *Bad luck*—but the exchange distracted
him from her shield.

She'd been working her arm out of the grips. One last
high-line, the point stabbing down with the hilt above
her head, and she snapped it at his shins, like a giant
discus, threw herself forward on one hand, body level
with the ground and sword extended.

Impossible to block—but he quartered, out of the way, switching stance so fast she didn't see his feet move. The shield flew by him, and his came down to pin her blade. On the back of her neck, she felt a light tap, barely a touch, of wood.

"Shit," she said. "That usually works."

"I can see it would," Chevenga answered breathlessly, grinning, reaching out a hand to help her up. She could barely hear him for cheers and a rush of metal clankings, those wrist-sheaths being banged together, the Yeoli way of applauding. "I'm honored to spar you, thank you," he said, too sincerely to be a pure formality. "I may again soon, I hope? And all my Elite? And everyone else you've got time for? You have tricks I've never seen—from across the water, I guess?"

"*Ia, kras,* what's mine is yours," she said. She felt her face flushed, with exhilaration as well as effort; his was the same. "It's been a long time since I met someone better than me with a sword. I needed to be stretched again, if I'm going to keep learning."

"Well, I'm hardly going to pretend *you* didn't stretch *me*," he answered. "Or teach me."

No harm in praise, either to swell a head or be taken as flattery, she thought, *if it's spoken true. Besides he wouldn't take it wrong;* by the harmony sparring could bring between two souls, she knew that. "The warrior's philosophy—skill uses least effort for greatest effect— I've rarely seen applied so well," she said. "I see why they call you Invincible."

"Eh. Philosophy, shmilosophy," he answered. Somehow it was suddenly strange, almost unimaginable, that he spoke Enchian, not Kommanzanu like a child of the same kin-fast, and in fact didn't even know it, to think in it. *Things of the body are deeper than language.* "I just plain *can't.*" He gestured to his scars. "Too much of this. Last summer I keeled over from exhaustion, and ever since then I'm sworn off using more strength than I have to—healer's orders." A squire who looked like his little sister brought a flask of water. Shkai'ra took a sip; it was ice-cold. "I don't call myself Invincible. Though I hardly need say that to you."

"The Warmasters who taught me always said you had to start replacing the physical with the mental if you wanted to live much past thirty," she said. He made the palm-up sign for *yes*, chuckling at something he did not say. Their eyes caught, understanding sparking between them again. *If I could tell you my joke*, his said clearly, *I know you'd get it*.

"Agh, my poor Akaznakir . . ." A Lakan name; the destrier. "I hope he'll forgive me. Well, what say we slake our thirst with something stronger?" She clapped him on the back.

Hah. She got beaten, thought Sova. *My unbeatable khyd-hird got beaten. Of course she'd probably say that it would all be different if it were real . . . still. Coming all this way would almost be worth it just for that.*

The journey had been uneventful; she'd made sure not to swagger down streets or through bars, worn her sword discretely, strapped her money to several different places on her body. The ship's crew had known whose daughter she was, and so—once she'd convinced them she was supposed to be there simply by making no excuses for it, along with an effective combination of superiority and cheery willingness to help—they'd asked no questions. The caravaneer she'd hired on with as able hand—for bed and board, all she wanted—had seemed a little crooked and furtive, but no more so than most; if anything, he'd avoided her.

Now, as she lay in her little pup-tent beside Shkai'ra's, face-down, buttocks sore, she wondered why she'd done this. The obvious reasons didn't seem enough, for the compulsion she had felt, to be near, to see, Megan and Shkai'ra. *So I was mad because they wouldn't let me; so what? That's happened before. Prove myself as a warrior? Sounds like the dumb things boys do. You'd think*

I couldn't bear them being away, she thought. *They'll probably think that themselves.*

Why did *I do this?* Stunned, she realized that she'd disobeyed her parents, borne the hardships of travel all the way down the Brezhan, risked, at least to some degree, her freedom and her life, all without truly knowing the reason. *I just itched, that's all. I got all restless, I wanted something that I could only get here. I had to come. So I did.*

In time, she shrugged it off. *Who cares why, now; I'm here.* It would work itself out, she felt, vaguely. Besides, she couldn't exactly turn around and go back. They wouldn't let her, for one thing, but more importantly, she'd look like a complete idiot.

VIII

Shkai'ra looked over the bunch of scruffy hired killers she'd been assigned to whip into shape, a half-kylick away from the road, so that no one else could watch this mess of shambolic quasi-soldiery, yet.

Eight tens and five, all had horses and the horses were all alive; that was as much as you could say. They didn't seem to be impressed with her. *Tough shit.* But some of them showed promise. *If that one over there gives the Arkans as much trouble as I think he's going to give me, the war's won . . . well, that much pay, I should have to earn it.*

She was in full kit, on her destrier, armored head to toe in black steel forged in F'talezon. Fantastically expensive: but that depended on how much you valued your life. All they could see of her was the mouth and her eyes on either side of the nasal bar. She could feel Hotblood sulking because she'd left him out. Sova was behind her on her pony.

"All right—dress ranks!" she shouted in Enchian.

They jostled around, horses shouldering and nipping.

104

Some of the weirder-looking ones were asking their neighbors what she'd said.

Fucking joy. They managed to get into something resembling a line, and she cantered down in front of them. The horses were all bigger than ponies. Everyone seemed to have a sword or axe, at least, lances, too, from manheight to twice that. All of them had metal helmets, leather shields. Nobody was without a boiled-leather breastplate, minimum; most with bone or horn scales on the leather, a few with iron or bronze; a few with chain-mail shirts. About a third had saddle-bows, mostly Aenir horn-backed types. *Better than nothing.* The tall skinny black one had a bucket of javelins on either side of his saddle. About six-in-ten were men, four women, the usual for this part of the Mitvald lands.

"Who doesn't speak Enchian?" she yelled. There was a moment of running translation, and about a dozen hands went up. "You beside them—you, you, you—teach them the command-words."

"First—dismount!" One fell on his backside. *Shit.* Shkai'ra vaulted to the ground, waiting till they sorted themselves out.

It's best to get things started by showing who's the toughest, meanest and craziest of all. That dark one in the long chain shirt, a Lakan, looked like a good candidate to her. He had a good enough sneer, some missing teeth, an earring showing under his peaked helmet; standing tall, thumbs in his belt, shoulders back. He was taller than she was, heavy shoulders and slightly bowed muscular legs with a sword-callus around the thumb and forefinger of his right hand.

"You, your name and rank," she said, pointing.

"Bukangkt," he answered, after an insultingly long pause. She didn't know much about Lakans, except that their country was south and west of Yeola-e, and they were in the war. This one must be an exile to be here and not with his king. He didn't add *"kras"* or any other

word of respect. Probably top-chicken with this bunch so
far, and he'd push it.

She stepped closer, stuck her face toward his. *He
smells like stale wine; too early. Younger than I thought,
not more than twenty-two.*

"You call me *kras*, Bukangkt," she said, slow and just
loud enough for the others to hear. "I call you whatever
I want. Right now I call you stupid. What were you exiled
for, raping pigs?"

She turned her back on him, walked away. *How stupid
is he?* Very stupid; she heard steel rasping free of leather
and the jingle of mail-rings as he lunged after her, and
Sova's warning cry, *"Khyd-hird!"*

Getting a fix by his shadow ahead of her, the Kommanza wheeled on one foot, fast, kicked as he went by.
He was quick, had got closer than she liked—maybe she
was starting to lose her speed. . . . Her boot heel hit right
behind his elbow. The sword was a long straight double-
edged type with a simple bar guard, grey steel; it flew
ahead of him and buried itself in the turf—*shunk*.

The Lakan turned, clutching his arm, shouting something in his own language. *Brave as a boar, at least.* She
kept her hands on her hips; showy, but necessary on this
sort of occasion. High-kick to the face with her right
boot; the Zak-made armor was marvelously flexible and
well-jointed. He blocked with crossed forearms, tried to
grab her foot. His unarmed work was all learned catch-
as-can in brawls, she could see that from the way he
moved.

Her foot snapped down; it had been a feint. The
motion of driving her right leg down scythed her left up
between his legs; he was standing in the straddled stance
of a sword-and-shield man with a chopping style and
her greave hit his loinguard—*smack*. It was leather that
buckled under the blow and he backed, wheezing, fighting not to puke, but keeping his eyes on her. *Knows how
to override pain, at least.* Good. His deep brown face

had turned grey under the helmet that almost matched his mail.

"That was stupid, Bukangkt," she said, advancing on him. Wheel-kick, heel struck him on the shoulder. Solid, even through the chain and the padding underneath, and the arm dropped limp. "I could kill you now, Bukangkt." She put her hands down, up on one foot; vulture-stork stance. Snap-kick once, twice to the stomach and chest, pulling at that last instant. He *oofed* back, the thick strong legs shaking. "Couldn't I, Bukangkt? *Speak.*"

"Yes," he wheezed. The others craned their necks to see, but didn't break line.

"Yes *what,* Bukangkt?"

"*Yes, kras!*" he gasped. She straightened up and smiled.

"That was what I was waiting to hear," she said.

Someone laughed. She wheeled, stabbing out a finger. "You with the jackass laugh, do *you* want to fight him? Now? Tomorrow?" Silence, except for unnerved horses. She turned back to Bukangkt, keeping her eyes on him as she bent to pull his sword from the turf, flipped it and offered it over her forearm.

"Think you could lead a section, Bukangkt?" she snapped, grinning at him. He was blinking at her. She could see the thought seeping through whatever he put between his ears.

He took the sword, weighed it in his hand and stepped back; she didn't tense, but her arm felt the way to her hilt without moving. He brought the sword up in salute. She could see what it cost him to straighten.

"Yes, *kras.*"

She called Hotblood out of the woods, as Sova took hold of her destrier's reins to keep him from bolting. The other horses in the line started shifting and stamping.

"Resume your station. Decurion." She went to stand by Hotblood, rested a hand on the pommel and vaulted up one-handed. The troop were just now noticing; like most people, they tended to see what they expected, and you expected to see a horse under a saddle. It was not an easy vault with half her weight of armor on; her knees felt as if they had sand in them.

"I am Centurion Shkai'ra Mek Kermak's-kin," she told them. "I command this troop. Decurion Bukangkt is provisional second." *And I'm provisional Centurion, but let's not get fancy.* "This is Squire Sova Shkai'ra's-daughter Far-Traveller, my aide. Further appointments will be made according to merit." The pony pranced, feeling Sova shift at her new use-name. Well, it fit as well as "Can't-take-your-eyes-off-her-for-a-moment" or "Disobedient Little Bitch."

She scanned the line. "At present, all you have is an appointment with the corpse-robbers!" She let the words sink in. "This is the most undisciplined, shabby, illassorted, uncoordinated excuse for a cavalry troop it's ever been my misfortune to see, let alone try to command! Steel Spirit weep, the thought of leading you up against Arkan regulars, I don't know whether to laugh, puke, or run!" She hammered a fist on her saddlebow. "*You will keep up with line of march, and you will drill at maneuver every minute of it.* You will take care of your horses before your gear, and your gear before yourselves; you will make a camp the Demarchic Guard would be proud of, and then you will do weapons-drill until you drop, and then, maybe, you can eat and sleep."

She let her scowl relax into a smile. "And when we meet the Arkans, we will kick their well-reamed assholes so hard their teeth march off to Kurkas like little wooden soldiers on parade, and we will skin them of loot right down to their bones.

"Mount!" That wiped out the grins. She drew her sword and took the file-leader's position, forward and to the right. "Form column of squads, from the left. Walk-march, *trot.*"

Zaik saw them try. Zaik wept, or maybe laughed. She sighed, and hoped the next battle would be delayed a long, long time.

● ○ ○

I'm never going to be done riding stupid horses, Megan thought sourly. Shkai'ra and Sova were off doing what cavalry did; Megan kept an eye as well as her rear on the revolting creature she was riding, while mentally reviewing the technique for using a wire garrote. She'd learned it quite a while ago and hadn't had much occasion to use one since. *Learn the flip/snap till you can do it falling on someone, Megan,* her old master had said, *since you're not likely to be able to reach up to a naZak's neck anyway.* So true, that had turned out to be. She'd brought one in her collar, thinking she might need it. The dust cloud was broadening; trot, walk, trot now rather than just walk.

She was near the head of the main column; far ahead was the vanguard, then a long stretch of open road curving slightly through rolling hills, then the mounted Elite Demarchic Guard at the head of the main column, under the great standard of Yeola-e, green mountains, blue sky with seven stars. *And I, here with the odds and sods, as Shkai'ra would say,* Megan thought sourly, all the bits and pieces attached to headquarters. Behind them the A-niah marching on foot, double-bitted axes over their shoulders; behind *that,* the endless column of troops and baggage.

The countryside around them was strange, hotly alien to F'talezonian eyes: terraced hills with vineyards, olives, apricot trees, oranges, figs, strips of yellowing barley and wheat. The stone cottages were deserted, no movement off across the hills except an occasional dust-cloud or twinkle of steel from the outriders. A manor house on a hill was burning, sending a dun club of black smoke and sparks up into the air. The road lanced across the hills, massive cuttings and embankments; there were poplars along either side, and the passing strips of shade were more than welcome. Megan took a sip of lukewarm canvas-tasting water from her canteen and spat.

Lixand. Son of my body. We're closer. Her pony

sneezed at the dust. *Lixand. I won't think of what your life is like.* The implications of the words in the agent's letter, ". . . he is a favorite of the Lord," tore at her like Hotblood's fangs tearing horsemeat.

Plans. What good suggestions could she come up with for scaring Arkans? Visions of Halya; Hayel, their Halya, didn't have air. *Hmmm. Could I make someone think there was no air?*

One of the squires came whipping back on a pony. "Megan called Whitlock?" She nodded. "You're commanded forward. To the *semanakraseye*." She thanked him and he went off. *Looks like I'll finally get to be useful. If I can get this beast to trot. . . .*

At the column-head, surrounded by his staff and gallopers, she found Chevenga riding on his Lakan black, carrying the great mountain-and-stars on his shoulder. *Symbolic. He believes in that.* His armor matched, the trim blue and green and, here and there, flashes of gold: it was segmented plate of the highest quality Yeolis made, as good as Zak. His helmet and gauntlets were off, hooked to his saddle; on his head he wore only a green bandanna. As she came up alongside him, he handed the standard off, and wheeled with a smile to her and a beckoning gesture. A little way back was a small covered cart; passing their horses' leads to a squire, he gave her a hand up, and they climbed in.

Inside was spare, reminding her of his tent. It was a rolling office: the folding desk was set up, and an old white-haired woman he introduced as Chinisa somebody, his scribe, sat behind it busy with some paperwork, glancing up with a polite smile. The same locking file cabinet was there too, and a small pallet with blankets neatly made up; beside it was a large sand-timer, the type with a switch-valve between the glass chambers so it could be shut off without being turned on its side. *Who sleeps here?* He and the scribe spoke back and forth in Yeoli; all Megan caught of Chinisa's words were "*semanakraseye*," and that only because he corrected her, clearly saying "No, it's just Chevenga." —"*Amiyaseye*," the scribe said then, teasingly. He said something with a peeved look, and she was gone, grinning. *Does it bother him to be called that?* Megan remembered how it had made her squirm, to learn of her own fame. *Still, I wasn't born and trained into a position. . . .*

Chevenga wrung out his bandanna, tucked it in a dagger-strap, and offered her a cushion, sitting himself on the one opposite, and running a hand through sweat-sodden curls. "Cider, unfermented, or tea?"

"Cider, please, *kras*," she answered. He called out the door; in barely a moment, the jar, sweating in the heat, came.

"Well," he said, as he poured, "I've been thinking about it some. I hope you've been thinking about it more; you understand what you can do better than I. We're going to have an Arkan camp within reach tonight, though, and probably fight tomorrow.

"Back inside Yeola-e, we were trying to convince them we had Hayel-demons on our side. The first time, I promised their general, the famous Abatzas Kallen, that is, that Hayel would visit their camp if they didn't march forthwith; he laughed, of course, and that night Hayel visited their camp. I won't say how, but we had them convinced enough." He didn't need to say more; she'd heard tales of the rout.

"We kept that sort of thing up, all across Yeola-e; I didn't know we were going to cross the border then, before my people took their decision. Now . . . Arko will be happier feeling we're winning by the grace of Celestialis, not Hayel."

What do you care, how they feel? But Ivahn's words came back: *He wouldn't leave Arko leaderless afterwards; he'd consider it a breach of responsibility. So he'll take over as Imperator.* She studied his eyes, trying to find ambition underneath that brown ingenuousness, not believing, despite Ivahn, that it couldn't be in there somewhere. No sign showed. "So I've retired the demons," he went on. "And yet terror at night still has its uses. You get the idea?"

"Hmm." Megan took her cider, wrapping her hands around the cup's coolness, and thought. "You want . . . portents of divine favor, for Yeola-e, perhaps."

"You've got a good feel for this," he said.

"And yet fearful . . . hmm. They're afraid of *you*, aren't they?" He made the "yes" gesture, wordlessly. *An understatement if I ever saw one*, she thought. *Hey, if you've got it, flaunt it.* "You sauntering around in their camp would cause something of a stir, wouldn't it?"

He chuckled, almost shyly, a boyish sound. "I think so."

"I can do that."

"All right: do it. We'll go over passwords and how their camp's set up and all that now, and again tonight. What else do you need to know?"

She hesitated, decided to leave it till after everything else. How he could have a map of the Arkan camp with such detail was beyond her, but there it was, apparently accurate; she committed the main features to memory. In half an hour— "Take your time, don't hurry for my sake, take care," he kept saying—she knew all she needed to except one thing; the time had come. *I have to.* She swallowed an internal balking.

"I need to put my hands on your face and arms, *kras*." She forced sheepishness out of her voice. "To get a good idea of *you* to make the image real."

He just said "Right," and sat still while she did it. Not even any jokes about how he could hardly protest the touch of a beautiful woman; yet he didn't get tense about it either, just sat, until she started to feel one or the other would make her more comfortable.

The warm feel of his skin, muscles hard underneath, she took in, the shape and angle of his jaw and ears, trying to ingrave it in memory, to concentrate on doing it. . . . *Stop feeling* that, *Megan*, she told herself sternly. *This is business, however attractive he is. He's a man.*

He's a king, whatever name Yeolis put on it, who can probably smell on me, under the Clawprince, the river-quarter scum. . . .

She finished. "I feel as if I've had my portrait done by an artist," he said. "Well, I guess I have."

"Thank you," she answered, curtly without shortness, and went back to her cushion. *He reminds me of an old friend.* She hadn't thought of her first love, Serkai, in years. *Always up front about everything; that was a lot of why I loved him. Dah, and those pushups he was always doing, wanting to be the best Palace guard there was. I wonder where he is now?*

"Come to my tent at around midnight," Chevenga said. "I'll send for you. We'll go over the same again. Until then."

"Kras." They exchanged salutes, and she climbed down out of the cart. Trotting back to her place in the column, Megan found herself wishing it had been longer, and that their meeting would come sooner. Fiercely, she shook off the feeling. *It's the famous Chevenga charm working on me. I'll make friends with him, in time. Or I won't. If he looks down on me, his friendship isn't worth a green copper anyway. Either way, Gold-bottom, is fine by me.*

Megan rubbed her hands together, blowing on the fingers. That was one problem with having steel claws; if it got cold the steel drew it into her fingertips, even just the difference between night and day. At home she had to be careful of frost-bite in the winter, something she hadn't thought of when she'd got them.

She swung her leg over the branch and climbed down the hemlock. *One of the trees I know the name for. I prefer doing this sort of thing in a nice orderly city where the streets don't rustle, squish maybe, but not rustle,* and began crawling through the brush into the Arkan camp. It wasn't the full trench and palisade of a more permanent camp, but the sort of camp that they threw up every night when they marched, with a dug trench of only four feet and a fence-wall of about the same—Arkan _solas_ were all required to carry three stakes with their kit for that wall.

She crouched in the shadow of the wall, looking down so her eyes wouldn't shine, fishing for the pebbles in her pouch, smiling to herself, careful not to let her teeth flash in her blackened face. She'd spent a whole day's march in a half-trance concentrating on the six small pebbles to sensitize them to her mind, till she knew the feel of each stone inside and out; then an entire evening building up an image, a Chevenga for each of them to carry. She'd found herself dwelling on the feel of his skin, fine hairs and all, had to snap herself back to the image with a jolt. _First thing I do is set it up so I have to lay hands on him,_ she thought. _It was so forward—_ though Shkai'ra would laugh at that idea—_he probably thinks I'm after him, like every other woman in this army with heart and loins._

Six pebbles. The first one rolled along the walkway and clicked against the palisade. A sentry wheeled, leveling his javelin at the dark. "Friend or foe?" No surprise, after everything else in this war, the Arkans were jumpy.

Megan crept away from the pebble to the limit her mind could reach. _Warm yellow line from my mind to the stone, glowing with the residue of my thought. The memory of his face under my hands, planes and angles under my palms. Chevenga. The_ semanakraseye _leaning nonchalantly against the palisade, smiling, his gold teeth flashing in the light of the sentry's torch. . . ._ Down the line came a hoarse yell and the thud of the javelin driving itself into the wood. The image frowned at the spear vibrating through it, then up at the sentry who stood there for an instant and turned and ran, as Chevenga seemed to step toward him. She let the spell fade, carefully in control, grinning. Even if it broke, she'd set it up so the snapping of the spell wouldn't lash back straight through her head.

The pounding of feet as the sentry's backup came running . . . *He'll have to explain what he saw.*

Further along the wall she climbed over and drifted along the outer row of tents. It was just as the map had described. There was a camp dog sniffing around a midden pit that she avoided. Near the command tents she rolled a second pebble into the light; it rolled to a stop, clicking against the armored boot of a deputy-general's guard. She'd forgotten the name; he was a high muckymuck, that was all that mattered. The guard looked down, then out, stepped forward, glancing around.

His partner covered his back. Megan concentrated; there was Chevenga, strolling between them. They froze, shouted and lunged, narrowly missing skewering each other; the image grinned and ambled into the tent. A portly man—the deputy-general, it had to be—plunged out, sword in hand, almost into his guard's javelins, shouting, "What's going on?"

She left the uproar behind her, heading to the darker portions of the camp. Four more pebbles, four more disturbances to arrange. The Arkans weren't going to be in good spirits for the battle tomorrow. . . .

"Slow march," Shkai'ra commanded.

The white dust of the road was still soft and heavy under the horses' hooves, lain by the dew that left a crisp taste in the air. To the east, light lay like a band of salmon-pink along the horizon, fading through purple-blue to a darkness where a few stars glittered around a moon huge and pale and translucent as if painted on backlit glass. The cavalry passed through the last of the village's whitewashed cottages, out among fields that rolled in long quiet swells like a gentle sea. The wheat was early-summer-high and bronze, rippling in swells starred with red cornflowers; in the woodlots scattered among the grain fields, the deep green crowns of oaks caught dawn light like a flash on metal. Purple gentian and wild white rose starred the long silky grass by the side of the road, their scent overwhelmingly sweet; a flight of quail started up at the muffled pounding of the hooves, skimming like flung stones over water before they went to ground, disappearing beneath the yellow waves.

Sova's eyes followed them, watching through a screen of bush head-high as she rode by, through a spiderweb starred with blue-white jewel beads of moisture. "Beautiful," she whispered, to no one in particular. "It doesn't seem quite real. Like we were looking at everything through diamonds."

Shkai'ra laughed softly to herself, chanting in a half-whisper:

> _Morning red, morning red_
> _Will you shine upon me dead?_
> _Soon the trumpets will be blowing_
> _Then must I to death be going_
> _I and many merry friends._

The girl patted her mount's neck, was answered with a quiet whicker. "Even the horses feel it, don't they, _khyd-hird_?" The world seemed to pause, waiting between breaths.

"They smell fate on a wind from tomorrow," Shkai'ra said. She turned, looking critically to where the column behind them climbed the low rise; eight hundred lances swayed like a bed of metal-tipped reeds, blades the smooth color of salt.

She still normally commanded a hundred; but today she'd been sent to lead this mission. _In other armies I could name,_ she thought, _I'd know it was because my superior didn't feel like getting out of bed this early. In this one . . . it's a test._

"Trumpeter," she said; her voice was not much louder, but she pitched it an octave higher. "Sound _deploy into column._"

The column split, the horses stepping higher as they

plunged and heaved through the breast-high wheat, trampling paths that lay tumbled and chaotic through the grain. Their coats and the chest-guards of metal and leather most wore glistened with moisture; they tossed their heads, nostrils flared into red pits and eyes rolling as they chewed at the bits. The standard-bearer rode up beside Shkai'ra and Sova, and the trumpeter on the other side.

"*Bows out. Walk-march—trot.*"

They crested the rise, birds and gold-bodied bees swarming up from the stalks beneath their hooves. A thousand meters down the slope from them the long column of Arkan infantry were marching from right to left across their front on a road that ran along the banks of a tree-fringed stream whose bed shone silver with mist.

"Gods-damned if I know how the Yeolis knew they'd be here, unless they're using magic scouts," Shkai'ra gritted happily. "But this is one flanking column that isn't going to arrive on the battlefield in time. If at all." She'd questioned it, in fact, when given the orders, though that carried risk of punishment. "Chevenga said they'd be there, so they'll be there," the cavalry-general had answered patiently. "You'll see—*and not question again.*"

Arkans, Sova thought. *The enemy.* She'd seen their camp before—a distant, indistinct mass. She'd even borrowed the far-lookers, fascinated to see, to measure. Scarlet lacquered breast-plates and greaves, blond braids, light eyes, the usual expressions, same as in the Alliance camp; but through the lenses they were still abstract, still far away in the summer haze. Now—she could smell them, sweat, dust from their booted feet, gritty in the crystal dawn air. Now—she would ride up to them, close with them, have them within her reach, be within theirs. . . .

Is that why the world seems so clear? On the river last year, there'd been fights, skirmishes in the dark, without warning; but never like this, hundreds against hundreds on a field in the cold light of day after thinking ahead to it all night.

Am I afraid? she asked herself. *No.* She wasn't, somehow, to her own amazement. *It's too beautiful a morning,* she concluded, *to be afraid.*

An officer's mount among the Arkans threw up its head and neighed a challenge. Shkai'ra's arm swept up, then chopped down, and the trumpet sang.

A roar broke out. Through and over it ran the screams of the cavalry and the gathering thunder of their hooves, pounding out palm-sized chunks of turf as they flung the tonne-weights of steel and armor and flesh forward.

The infantry—two thousand of them, or a little less— halted, turning in knots and clumps as the officers' voices screamed at them to deploy, too late. Pikes bristled and crossed in huge X shapes as they tried to face about, and crossbowmen and javelineers tried to force their way forward. Then they were suddenly close, arrows *thupping* out from the hornbows, men falling; some of them had no room to fall, clots of them toppling back off the road embankment and falling down towards the mud. Faces were close, shouting, screaming, mouths wide and red.

Sova crowded in behind Shkai'ra's right stirrup as the Kommanza dropped her bow into the case and swung down her lance. The Thane-girl's lance seemed suddenly light, and the motion of the gallop was like the swoop of birds. *I'm not afraid. I'm not—how can I not be afraid?* Then it was time to close, and she had no more time to wonder.

Thunk. Not like the sound of lances hitting practice dummies. Heavier. A shock like her horse stumbling at speed, it was jumping and there was a twisting body on the crushed rock surface of the road with her lance, broken, through his chest. A sound like one united scream, of massed human death-cries, so loud her ears felt pain, the sound of hurt horses even louder. They were stopped and Hotblood had an Arkan pikeman by the face and he was whipping his head back and forth and it *ripped* away and the man went running. . . . Then they were wheeling and turning and driving both ways up and down the road. She followed Shkai'ra, drawing her sword. An Arkan drove a halberd at her from the side, and her arm came over with the sword point-down, training moving it without thought; her foot lashed out and the stirrup-iron hit him in the mouth; she stabbed and the point went in over his breastplate. That jerked up her wrist; she could see his blue eyes flare wide, his face not two years older than hers, as he fell away and the steel dragged free with a sucking reluctance.

No enemy within reach. She didn't know what to do, and so followed Shkai'ra. *How do commanders know what to do?* She tried to see it with an officer's eyes, orderly, spotting signs suggesting courses of action, saw nothing but chaos.

"Don't let them rally!" Shkai'ra screamed. The Arkans were running away, out into the fields, up and down the road. "By platoons, pursuit!" *Of course,* Sova thought. *Don't let them rally, what else?*

She followed Shkai'ra as she spurred her horse out into the wheat; it was all trampled now, bodies lying or crawling, one right in their way with his hands over his head. Sova heard the hooves thumping into dirt and then into his body, a different sound. A knot of men beyond, an officer trying to get them to face about: he waited for Shkai'ra with his knees slightly bent, blade and shield up, eyes on her but mouth yelling for his soldiers. Hotblood twisted aside and her shield darted down to cover her calf; she stabbed over her mount's neck and the officer went down. The others ran, one right in front of Sova, then almost under her horse's nose, sobbing as he lumbered along, not even noticing her. His helmet was off and his *okas* crop was thin and white-blond. Sova raised the sword until the blade lay along her back.

Milk the hilt. Shkai'ra's voice said in her head. *Loose until it's three-quarters of the way along, think of the edge as a line you're drawing through the head from the*

*crown to nose. Then clench your gut and push your feet
into the stirrups. It's called the "pear-splitting cut."*

She did it, the movement exactly like the hundreds of
times in training, the feeling as the sword struck different. Bone split, and blood and brains burst out in a great
fan of red. Wet splashed across her face and into her
open mouth; it tasted of salt and iron. She spat, wanted
to wipe her mouth, couldn't, hands full. *It worked.* The
body ran two steps before it fell under her mount's
hooves. *Gotthumml, did it work. . . .*

Pursuit, the command rang again in her mind. She
looked around, saw no Arkans who weren't down or
going down or chased by someone else or on the other
side of a mill, too far to chase. She looked around; all
seemed confusion, and she didn't know what to do again.
Then the trumpet sounded rally. She looked for the banner and rejoined Shkai'ra.

The Kommanza's eyes scanned all around, a thin-
lipped grin on her hawk-face. "That was easy," she
drawled. "Very easy. They weren't expecting us." On the
faces of her motley cavalry, shit-eating grins were suddenly wiped away, replaced by businesslike attention.
"Help our wounded, gather our dead, strip theirs."

Why is there cold on my face? The blood-tang in
Sova's mouth reminded her. She pulled off a gauntlet,
wiped the back of her hand across her chin; it came away
soaked red. Her throat was parched, though she hadn't
noticed it getting that way; by will she slowed her breathing, and rinsed out her mouth with a swig from her
canteen. A flash of memory of the *okas*'s head splitting,
and suddenly her throat and the back of her mouth went
tight and sour, watering, her stomach— *No. I won't
throw up. Not in front of everyone. Think of breathing.
Now,* she was afraid. In a little time the nausea eased,
but it didn't go away completely. None of the wonderfully valuable Arkan breast-plates would fit her—a problem all women warriors in the Alliance had—but she got
a good pair of shoulder-guards that could be adjusted,

and a new dagger. The rose glow of dawn had changed to the harsh gold of full day, showing with wordless clarity the sleepy country landscape littered with corpses, darkened with blood.

"Word is, we've done our duty for the day," Shkai'ra told the unit, once she'd got Sova to read the letter of orders. "We get the battle off. And we're duly commended, signed Brigadier-General First Maka-unpronounceable." That brought a laugh, and shouted corrections from Yeolis in the unit.

She'd vaguely been hoping for the signature to be Chevenga's, actually. *That really would have smelled like promotion. I guess it's too much to expect for a mission of spearing fish in a barrel. Oh, well.*

Brigadier-General First, as the Yeolis called it, was the position Shkai'ra aspired to, being the highest she could hope for; it was directly under the First General First and meant membership in the privy Command Council. And a name in history, if she helped keep this war going as it was. *Maybe, as time goes by and Gold-bottom gets more trustful of foreigners,* she thought, *I won't have to be a Yeoli to get it.*

"This doesn't mean *you* get to relax," she said to Sova, once she'd dismissed the troop. "We're going to watch from the most convenient hilltop and see if you can't learn a thing or two about commanding from Gold-bottom himself."

On a rise over the plain, they settled, with a motley crowd of other watchers, walking wounded, camp followers and so forth. Reclining catlike on a blanket while Megan and Sova prepared the picnic, Shkai'ra scanned the field, where, wide and distant as a painting, the two armies were deployed.

"Well, there you have it, apprentice. Plain ground, two armies straight on, everything wide open—a strategist's fight. You know *our* number, or at least what the rumors say, since it keeps getting bigger." Sova had heard anything from sixty-five to seventy-two thousand in the last little while. "About sixty-odd on the field today, nine-thousand cavalry. What would you say, from a look, is *theirs*?"

Sova tried to estimate with a professional eye. "Uhhh . . . about the same? Maybe a little less?"

"Look closer," Shkai'ra barked.

"Ummm . . . less . . . uhhh . . ." The Kommanza's fingers drummed her knee significantly. "Oh, ya! Arkan close order isn't as close as ours, so it makes them look like more—fifty thousand." She tried to make it sound authoritative. "Would've been fifty-*two* thousand if it hadn't been for us this morning—heh, heh . . . ahem. Judging by the number of cavalry they have, too. Yep. Fifty-thousand. I think."

"Good enough for our purposes," Shkai'ra sniffed. "All right. Tell me who's making the first mistake."

Sova surveyed the field through Shkai'ra's far-lookers, then squinted without them. "Nobody's moved yet. I want to say the Arkans, but that's assuming. I don't think that the way he's got them ranked is that smart—"

"Commanders say things clearly, girl. He who, Zh'ven'-gka or the strawhair?"

"The strawhair. I'd say him anyway because his center can't really move without plowing over everyone else."

"You've gotten much too complicated, girl," the Kommanza chided. "From looking through those things, probably . . . you should be able to see it at a glance."

"Uhh . . ." Sova blinked a few times, looked, squinted, gazed helplessly at Shkai'ra. "*Khyd-hird* . . . I don't."

The Kommanza heaved a long-suffering sigh. "Well, I guess you aren't doing any worse than the strawhair—he doesn't see it, either. And he's an accredited strategist, trained and all. Or maybe he got orders and had no choice."

"But they're all just standing still!"

"You think the planning doesn't start before the ranks

are *drawn,* girl? Hurry up and figure it out before the fight starts and we have to watch for the *difficult* points."

"But—I thought you wanted me to look for the way they were ranked and that's what I answered!"

"I didn't say anything about how they were ranked, just who was making the first mistake."

"But all I can see that's different is—" She slapped herself on the cheek. "Oh, *duhhh!* The *numbers!*"

"Exactly," said Shkai'ra. "Here's this Arkan, of no particular genius anyone here has ever heard of, outnumbered, against He Whose Bottom Is Dipped in Gold. He, or whoever's commanding him, is *nuts* to fight here like this—they're going to get their asses kicked from here to Illizbuah. Maybe they're just being set up as sacrifice, to incur losses; stupid, when they've seen so many times that he knows how to win without great cost. . . ."

"Maybe," she amended her own prediction, heavily. "There are those who'd argue that it isn't particularly smart for Gold-Arse to fight sixty-thousand on fifty, on plain ground, if he wants to keep advancing through hostile territory. The numbers aren't *that* lopsided. But then, he's won with less advantage than this. All right. What else do you know that touches what's going to happen?"

"*They* haven't had much sleep," Megan said drily. Sova snickered.

"Ummm . . ."

"About either side. *Anything.*"

"*We're* in good morale. *They're* not."

"All right, what else?"

"The Arkan's commanding troops he's not familiar with. And a good chunk of them—" Shkai'ra gave her a withering look. "Uhh, about seven thousand are tired from marching here."

"What else? Sova, pretend I just came here from the moon. That I know nothing, and you have to tell me *everything.*"

"Uhh . . . despite being tired, the fresh troops are overconfident?"

"How do you know that?"

"Because they're *Arkan*. And they think they've never lost."

"You're assuming. They aren't blind; they can see how far into their Empire the invaders are."

"Oh." Sova cast her eyes downwards. *Gott, I feel stupid.*

Shkai'ra sat up sharply. "Zaikdammit, you're slow today, girl. Here."

Oh, no. Sova sidled to her side. She couldn't see the fist raised behind her head, but felt it there, waiting. "So. What else?"

"Ahhh—" Sova thought fast. "The fresh troops—their horses are tired. They must have outrun their supply lines and I *heard* there was a raid to cut them off but they've outrun them anyway. They don't have Haians, but that's standard—" *That was dumb, oh no . . .* She flinched, though without showing it, but the hand didn't come down. "Ummm . . ."

"You're missing half," said Shkai'ra. "At least mostly. *Which* half?"

One of those questions that had to be answered instantly, or else. "Half? Oh, Gotthumml, *our* half!" The fist, starting to come down, stopped. "Us, umm, all right. We've had a good night's sleep, we aren't tired, new mercenaries have joined up, we have Haians, and we have Che—"

Whap. Hard knuckles drove into the top of Sova's head. *Oww.* "You're just repeating the opposite of *them*," the Kommanza snapped. "Don't you know anything about us that you don't about them? We have Zh'vengh-kua, you said. So what?"

"Well, we don't only have him but his reputation—that makes them shit their pants. Excuse my la—"

"Yes, all right, though you mostly covered that before, under morale. What else does it mean? What does he habitually *do?*"

She hates giving hints, Sova thought. *So she's more*

likely to hit after she does. "Uhh ... leaves them a way out. To retreat."

"How do you know that?"

"Everyone—I mean, I heard it. It's common knowledge."

"What does that mean?"

"What—that it's common knowledge?"

She sensed Shkai'ra's hand wind up slightly, then hold off. *"Ia."*

"Uhh ... well ... I guess ... they'd know it, too! So they won't fight as hard as they would if they were cornered."

"Yes." Shkai'ra's voice actually sounded somewhat pleased, but she didn't go so far as to say "Good." "What else does he do, habitually? Can you think of anything?"

I haven't watched any battles before, how am I supposed to know? Sova racked her brain for anything else she'd heard, and came up with nothing. "Umm ... ahhh ..."

Too slow; the knuckles rang her skull. "Don't tell me what you think in your flea-sized brain I want to hear, Baiwundammit! Tell me the *zteafakaz* truth!"

"I don't know!" Sova said helplessly, trying to brace herself for another blow without flinching too obviously. Sometimes Shkai'ra would hit her just for flinching. *Think something will happen,* she'd say, *and it will!* "I can't think of anything, I haven't heard anything else, not that I can remember!"

"Good!" Sova felt her eyes widen with astonishment. Megan chuckled. "All right—what does *that* mean, that you've heard nothing?"

"Uhhh ... he keeps his habits secret? I guess he wouldn't want the Arkans—" *Whap. My poor head,* thought Sova. *It'll never be the same.*

"On the field we're all naked, as from the womb," Shkai'ra snapped. "Words might hide, but actions always reveal. Anything habitual enough to be called a habit, he can hide from no one."

"His habit is—he doesn't *have* any habits!"

"Ex-*act*-ly. Not that anyone's spotted yet, anyway."

"Oh," said Sova. Everything she'd read in strategy books about how your own habits could be used against you, and therefore how it was good to have none, came back to mind . . . *now,* too late.

"Actually, he does have another habit. He's doing it now." Sova waited for Shkai'ra to ask what, half-praying she wouldn't, because she couldn't think of the answer. Instead the Kommanza began muttering, eyes slitted: "Ah. Mm. Ah-hah. Oh." On the field, movement had begun; soon the wind brought the sounds, of shouted orders, war-cries, clashing of weapons, yells of agony.

The Kommanza dropped her hand and leaned forward. "Look at that," she muttered. To Sova it wasn't clear at all, making as much logical sense as swirls of powdered chocolate being mixed into white dough. Shkai'ra pointed. "Look there. That one unit is supporting all the others around it, the Arkan's trying to get at it, but he should be paying attention to that flank." *It's like chess,* Sova thought. *Not like this morning at all. That was simple.* "Those archers cover there, which means . . ." The Kommanza's eyes flicked back and forth across the battlefield. "Nicely done, nicely done, everything fits beautifully . . . not that the Arkan is doing too badly, he's no slouch. Apprentice, what would you say about the battle-plan, so far?"

Sova jerked as if Shkai'ra had rapped her, scrambled for an answer, the first thing that fell into her open mouth. "It's . . . ah . . . it's, ah, complicated?" She winced her eyes shut.

"*Ia!* Good." Shkai'ra clapped her hands together sharply on the word. "Remember the drawbacks of complicated, though. It's easy to get confused and make mistakes." Sova drew a deep breath, relieved. "So why is he able to even try it?" Her relief died.

"Uhhh . . . because he's smart?"

"That's why he can *think* of it—not why he can trust us to carry it out."

"Well, we've got good communications." She'd heard that. "We're well-organized." She'd heard that from the horse's mouth, as it were: *khyd-hird* herself.

She had to turn to see Shkai'ra's nod, the Kommanza's attention elsewhere. "See? Every unit is supporting every other unit, even as it moves. Damned difficult thing to do on the field. Except for those Enchians, there, they seem to be vulnerable but ..." She wasn't addressing Sova anymore, her voice going thoughtful. "Sheepshit, he can't think the Arkan's *that* stupid, the man's no Abatzas. Yeolis traditionally don't have a clue what to do with cavalry, but Gold-Arse ought to be smart enough to listen to his allies who do."

Sova finally managed to figure out that the Enchian infantry in question seemed to be advancing a bit too fast for their support, but Lakan cavalry on the flanks was ready to cut to ribbons anyone who tried to take advantage of that. It just didn't look as if the horsemen could get there. A trap? Lines dissolved into swirls again, order into chaos that her mind couldn't follow.

Shkai'ra went on following the action with occasional grunts and scattered comments such as, "Now why? Oh, I see, a diversion ... No, wait, *that's* the diversion, over *there* ... but they're really charging, and is that a ... a diversion *within* a diversion, oooh, nice. Look at that, Sova, he's got phalanxes and lines going this way and that way and weaving in and out of each other—hah, fished in, you straw-haired pig-fondlers! They're taking more losses but *we're* taking enough ... Maybe he's trying to *confuse* the strawhairs into submission, ha ha ... He must have a larger plan that's in too early a stage to see, let's see it play out."

Half an hour later: "So, Sova! I hope you've been following this!" The girl nodded enthusiastically—it was true, she had been following, though she'd been able to discern absolutely nothing, aside from a lot of movement

on both sides that didn't seem to be to any use but left
scattered corpses. "What do you think our Gold-
bottomed commander's doing, hmm?"

Sova looked through the far-lookers, gazed again without. The battle had raised enough dust that it was getting
hard to see anything. "Uhmmm. Ahhh." She glanced out
of the corner of her eye at Shkai'ra, felt a trickle of sweat
on her back. *Tell the truth.* There was only one thing
she could think of that was true. She hoped for a "Good"
and braced herself simultaneously as she answered, "I
don't know. I can't tell."

"Damn," said Shkai'ra. "I was hoping you'd see it,
because I don't." Sova stared, mouth open. *Whap.*
"Don't stare like a gaffed fish, it gives away what you're
thinking."

Another quarter-hour; then Shkai'ra pricked, and leapt
to her feet. "Hah! *Ay-galug,* he *does* listen to his cavaliers—look at that, do you see *that,* Sova?!" The girl
peered; everything looked much the same as a moment
ago. No one else near saw either, apparently, including
Megan; those around stared at Shkai'ra puzzled, saying,
"What? What?"

"Oh, beauty! Beauty! Strawhair's speared up the arse
again, ha ha! Look and weep, sheep-rapers. *Look, Sova*—
I'll tell you or you might miss it. See, there." One hand
on Sova's shoulder, she leaned over, pointing to let Sova
sight along her arm. "*There's* the strawhair's command
post. Their sword-shield infantry tied up with ours there,
there and *there,* archers *there,* cavalry; well, you can see
what's tied up with what. To defend his center he only
has spearmen and light horse, so if he gets pressed to
the left—which is about to happen, see?—he'll *have* to
shift that way. *And* call pikers to him. If he shifts . . . look
there." Her finger moved up and to the right. "What'll be
there and there?"

Sova followed the line of sight, her face closed with
concentration; her eyes flicked to Enchian light foot
seemingly caught in a crowd of Arkan foot. But the

Arkans, she realized, were out-of-ammunition archers. "The Lakan heavy horse, backed up by the Tor Enchian light horse—ya, the Princes' standards are moving, there they go, Gotthumml, you're right! He *has* to!"

"And if he calls the pikers?"

"They'll leave the whole center wide open and won't have time to get set anyway!"

"Well, maybe. Only if *we* don't do what we ought to quick enough. What's that?"

"Chase them! Seize the advantage!"

"Right. But with forces this size, Sova, things take so long that it's already too late—*unless it's already planned. Now look.* Look how things are arranged, stop seeing people and banners and spear-tips and lines, look at *patterns. Look what's forming.*" Confusion seemed to disappear like a fog burned away by sun, and the way every unit was placed sprang clear; a moment after she'd imagined it, it played out real, like a dream coming true.

Alliance formations that had been crossing or weaving, wheeling or standing pat were suddenly all moving together, one mile-wide axe-blow cutting into the sudden weak point in the Arkan line. Through the far-lookers, she watched pike-points bobbing backwards or wavering, then mown down as the great charge stabbed through. The Arkans were thrown into confusion, some running back and forth, some begging for orders from a command-post now lost under Lakan hooves, some breaking and fleeing, and some turning to fight alone or back to back, before the Alliance charge washed over, making none of it matter.

"Should you choose generalling," said Shkai'ra, "it will be twenty or thirty years, if ever, before you're in a position to try something like that, and twenty or thirty years before you *should.* But you've *seen* it, and you can never lose that learning. You saw it, probably about the same time the Arkan general did, and knew his pyre was lit . . . and he was a general.

"Well, the dance is over." Shkai'ra grinned. "Now

comes the kill. He always leaves them a way out; but tough luck if they can't run fast enough." In another quarter-hour, nothing was left that wasn't a clear Alliance rout. Sova witnessed the scene she'd lived that morning—*solas, okas* and *Aitzas* alike chased and cut down from behind—multiplied twenty-fold.

"Tonight we party, tomorrow we rest, the day after, we march," said Shkai'ra. "And so it will be, until Zh'veng-khua has hewn down this Empire, and someone else hews down him and his in his turn; and so on forever, until the time itself is hewn down, and spins dying into darkness." Her grin widened, teeth baring.

IX

Shkai'ra had been careful to eat a fair amount of bread, so the wine had not produced more than a sort of golden glow yet. Fires blazed high all over the Alliance camp, the roasting mostly done and the hearths piled high with wood for the celebrations. Everyone was happy; all except the injured and dead, of course, and there had been a gratifyingly small number of those on the Alliance side. The warm air smelled of drink, food, sweat and dust.

A nice, convincing victory, she thought happily, dropping out of Megan's dance-circle and heading for the rows of jugs sitting in buckets of water at the edge of the light. *And my load of outlaws, barn-burners, and horse-thieves did our part very nicely, even if it was before everyone else got up.* She hooked a finger in the jug's handle and pulled it out, resting it on the crook of an elbow as she worried the wax-sealed cork out of the neck. A stream poured down into her mouth when she raised it, white wine, cool and slightly tart; the wet outside of the pottery was pleasantly cool against the sweat-slick skin of her arm and bare torso.

Shkai'ra walked over to the circle.

"Megan!" she called. "I've got to go look in on my cutthroats!"

"Don't haul too many of them into the bushes, and come back before dawn!" Megan shouted back, without breaking stride in the intricate manoeuver.

Oh, good, she thought. *And I* will *be back.* The sentries around the inner camp were looking a little surly as they passed her through; this must be a punishment detail.

The celebration around the fires of Shkai'ra's Slaughterers, as the unit had begun calling itself—it sounded better in the dog-Enchian lingua franca of the army—was considerably more advanced. They were bivouacked next to a contingent of Hyerne light infantry, some of whom seemed to have joined the party. That southern kingdom was a matriarchy, and had sent the only all-female contingent to the army of the alliance against the Empire. There was a good deal of dancing here, too; some of the Hyerne were playing tabor-drum and long flutes, and two-score others were demonstrating a whirling spear-dance that ended with flying leaps across the fire. A few practical souls were still picking over the big pile of Imperial cavalry armor off to one side, stuffing pieces that fit into their equipment bags.

Shkai'ra did the rounds of those who weren't dancing or mattress-dancing, offering congratulations and condolences where deserved; she had been to the infirmary to see the seriously wounded earlier in the day. The jug was soon emptied, but there were others doing the rounds. At last she sat down on a coverlet to watch, firelight and moonlight glinting on oiled bodies and the edges of spearheads. One of the dancers finished with a leap and a yell and thrust her spear into the ground while she was still head-high in the air; then she grabbed the hand of an applauding Enchian trooper and led him over to Shkai'ra, smiling with a flash of white teeth against dark skin. The Hyerne spoke not one word either of them could understand, and the trooper an Enchian so pure it had nothing in common with the lingua franca. But there seemed little need for words, and less after they were all three naked.

No one in this army calls me Whitlock's Thane-brat or Kin-Slavey or Rokatzk-Spawn or Bugger-Bait, thought Sova happily.

Khyd-hird always thinks anyone with war-training doesn't hear things like that; but she can't read them written on the walls, she doesn't know about kid-packs who shout them from alleys they can run away into, she doesn't notice people too powerful for Zhymata to cross whispering them to me under silky smiles at soirées. . . .

Here, no one seemed to think about her race when they met her, aside from politely asking what it was, the unwritten convention of a polyglot army. They also had no way of knowing what family she'd come from and how she'd joined her present one, to laugh at that behind her back or to her face. For the most part they did what no one had done in her life on meeting her: took her as she was.

Another unwritten convention was sharing the wineskin. *I feel boneless,* she thought, stretching her legs out in the grass by the campfire, throwing on another log and watching pin-bright stars flicker where the stream of heat rippled them. Shkai'ra's Slaughterers (she couldn't imagine *khyd-hird* hadn't had at least a hand in conceiving the name—it had her stamp) sat around now with wine and pork-fat dribbling down chins bearded or naked, Provisional Second Bukangkt and some other Lakan playing a game with black and white stones, others dicing, others plain lazing. Then, bringing down her eyes to pass on the wine, she saw.

That cute Yeoli. He is looking at me. It really isn't chance, it's been too much for chance. He's looking at me.

He'd stood out from the start, his the freshest male face among the Slaughterers, flawless and too young for

a beard, framed by a curly halo of gold-brown hair that
was just long enough at the sides to form short ringlets.
A warrior, not a squire; he wore the wristlets. In the heat
he'd taken off his shirt, and she'd found herself all but
unable to take her eyes off the line of his youthfully lanky
but hard shoulders.

About a year before she'd suddenly found herself oddly
fascinated with boys, although she'd found them nothing
but distasteful before; in a household where such things
were spoken of freely, she'd soon learned why. But in
F'talezon, her origin known and her *zight* reckoned
accordingly, she'd found precious few friends, let alone
opportunities to admire boys in any way but from afar.
Such a handsome creature as this would never so much
as look at her, hard experience had taught, so she was
resigned to casting furtive, happy glances.

But now—he *was* looking at her.

O mine Gott, she thought. *Whaddoido?*

Blush. So it seemed, anyway; her face was determined
to do that, burningly, she found, whether she wanted it
to or not. Not only her face, but her neck, too, and lower.

OmineGott what do I look like? Instantly, she was horribly aware that she hadn't brushed her hair since before
she'd arrived here, the painful pimple beside her nose
was the size of a thumbnail and blood-red, her eyes were
too close together, her ears too big, her chin too weak,
and her arms and shoulders too thick. *What man would
ever look at a woman built like a greathound?* Of course,
the thought crept into her head, Yeoli women could be
fighters; their men must have nothing against muscular
curves. Her heart pounded like before a fight; but while
that was a sick fear, this was shivery, sparkly.

*Whaddoido? Act nonchalant, of course. Look every-
where but at him.* The stars, the fire, the trees, her left
foot; everywhere her eyes looked, the place where he sat
seemed to etch into her mind like an ember, an ember
with hawsers attached to her eyes, irresistibly pulling
them towards him. *I'll risk a glance. Just one glance. Just*

a moment. She did. He was looking straight at her. Their gaze collided. *OmineGottmineGott, he saw, mineGott . . . Can he see me blush? Dear Gott let it be too dark in the firelight.*

Maybe, she thought, *he's feeling all the same things I am. Could it be? Is it possible, outside a dream? Naaaahhh, don't be a fool. Thane-brat.* She glanced again; this time he smiled at her. Her heart felt as if it would burst out through her ribs and fly into his lap, dripping.

Calm. Collect yourself. What do I do? What would khyd-hird *do? Stomp up to him and say, "Let's fuck." No, I don't think that's quite my style. What am I saying, I don't have a style yet . . . but whatever it's going to be, it's not that. O Gotth-excuse my language-umml.*

The man next to the Yeoli nudged him with a loud, "Har har har." He answered so sharply she heard it, Yeoli words, one of them *"kyash,"* shit. *They're saying rude things to him, the stupid old insensitive assholes, how could they—poor oppressed prince—what could they be saying? He doesn't* deserve *it. OmineGott I'm staring at him. Nonchalant, nonchalant, nonchalant . . .*

Then the Yeoli got up, and was gone.

Oh, no. Where'd he go? Why now? Ohhhhhhh . . . Calm. He might just have gone off to the latrine. He'll be back in a moment. He was: right behind her. She nearly fell off her log. "Nye'yingi," he said.

"Uh . . . hi." *O Gott what a stupid thing to say. He must think I'm a complete imbecile. Is this really happening?* "Um . . . what are you doing here?" *O Gott I didn't think it was possible but I just said something even more stupid!*

"Slowerrr, if it you please?" he said, with an entrancing smile. In his musical Yeoli accent every word seemed the profoundest magic. "My Enchi-yahn naht so good."

"Um . . . what . . . are . . . you . . . doing . . . here?" *The stupidest thing in the world to say and I repeat it!*

"Oh . . . tsose *barayel,* how you say, stranchers, tsey naht good smell, I choose be ove' hyere. Isserrhe space?"

Oh, yes, make space on the log for someone who comes, that's polite, he shouldn't have had to ask—oh no, does he think I'm gauche?! She moved over, hastily enough to show politeness, but nonchalantly. As best she could, cramped on either side; she managed to make half a space, and that with people beside her grumbling. Then *khyd-hird* happened to get up, stretching, enabling everyone between them to move down one. *That was lucky. Now maybe if I'm really lucky, she'll go away.* "Well," said Shkai'ra, as if on cue, "I'm off to find my kh'eeredo." *If she tells me it's my bedtime . . .* but she didn't, just made her farewells and disappeared into the night.

The Yeoli squeezed in. His side, pressed against hers, was hard and warm; she smelled him, hot and musky-sweet with maleness. *Do I smell all right?* She couldn't sniff herself now. *I washed yesterday. Can he feel my heart thudding?*

"I Echera-e Lemana," he rattled off. "Whaht name yourrh?"

"Sova. Called Far-traveller." *What was that? Eshcher, Shcheryi, Cherry? Yeolis, you call them by their first names, don't you?* She hoped so; she'd forgotten the second. "I'm pleased to meet you."

"I you too." That beautiful wide smile again; Sova's heart felt like wax melting. He was missing a tooth. *Oh, poor prince; but you bear it so bravely. . . .* "I think you arrhe, how you say? Homely. No, no!—Comely, *comely,* I mean. I sorrhy. Mean cahmp . . . comp . . . say *nice* thing, I mean, I sorrhy."

"You know," said Sova, trying not to be too breathless, "you can practice your Enchian with me any time; I'll help you with it. And I should learn some Yeoli, really; would you help me?"

"*Ai itai,* yes," he said, the grin widening. "I *like* tsaht."

o   o   o

Shkai'ra walked down to the section of stream marked off for bathing; upstream of the horse watering point but down from the place where drinking water was drawn. It was a fair-sized little river, ten meters across with a bank of good sand as much again across on this bank, marking where it flowed at high-water. She dropped her clothes and swordbelt on a rock that thrust conveniently through the sand, and then walked in a careful straight line toward the water. *I feel good,* she thought. About three-quarters drunk, which was just right when you didn't want oblivion, and tingly all over.

But I whiff a little, she reflected, doing a front-hand-stand and flopping over on her back with a thud and a giggle. Not remarkable after a day in armor under the hot sun, and then fucking several hours away. *Megan's finicky. But soooo pretty; we'll tumble till dawn and sleep in.* The army was due a day of rest after the last three. There were a few other late bathers, but not many or close; it was about halfway between midnight and dawn, by the moon, which hung low in the east, casting a glittering trail on wavelets like rippled silver.

She took the water in a flat running dive and swam for a few minutes in a thrashing overarm stroke, before squatting in water that was waist-deep and scrubbing her body with handfuls of sand. The cool wet felt good on her flesh, stripping away the grease and oil. Unbinding her hair, she ducked her head into the flowing water and began to scrub at the roots. When she opened her eyes beneath the surface the strands floated in a dense mass; she gathered it in her hands and threw it back, raising her head above the surface . . .

. . . and made the beginnings of a turn, feeling the whistle of parting air behind her . . .

Black—

"Barefoot in the dark," Matthas sang to himself, his own version of the romantic song. "All goes well if you sneak barefoot in the dark . . ." Now, to take the great

huge barbarian woman, now a draped load in his arms
with wet hair trailing, fikken heavy for a woman, to a
private place.

The usual private place, where a man and a woman
would go. "Heh heh heh," some drunken sot of an
Enchian cavalryman greeted him hoarsely, with a significant look at the limp, shapely form. No suspicion; it
helped that Matthas was wearing this looted Arkan
knight's helmet, plume and all, the first thing show-off
savages would wear at victory celebrations, the last thing
an Arkan spy sneaking around would. "Heh heh heh,"
he agreed hoarsely, and passed on to Lovers' Bushes. In
a nest well away from others, he bound her wrists and
ankles and gagged her Irefas-style, prepared the needle
to be inserted in the standard part of the anatomy for
those Irefas didn't want to know they'd been truth-
drugged, and waited for her to wake up.

"Ohhhhh, *shit*," Shkai'ra mumbled; it was nearly dawn,
and she was *not* beside Megan.

She levered herself up on one elbow. There was someone beside her on the trampled grass, still unconscious;
with a three-day's beard, smelling bad enough to affect
her queasy stomach, snoring lips fluttering over a mouth
with only a few snags of tooth.

"Jaiwun Allmate, tell me I wasn't *that* drunk," she
muttered, climbing slowly to her feet and pushing erect
with her palms on her knee. The ache in her head was
as much like the aftermath of a warhammer as a hangover; the false dawn stabbed fingers of pain into her eyes
as she gathered up her clothes, and there was a particularly irritating prickle of discomfort inside the cheek of
one buttock. *What the fuck have I been doing?* The last
clear memory was walking—not staggering, walking—
toward the river to wash up. *I am definitely getting too
old for this shit.*

"I may never know," she said aloud, and regretted it,
wincing as she began walking very carefully through the

sleeping camp, buckling on her swordbelt and stepping into her boots but leaving the rest of the clothing over one shoulder. Her skin was clean, but the clothing was smelly and clammy to a degree that Megan had trained her out of tolerance for.

Normally there would be a fair amount of activity at this hour, but not after a major victory and a celebration like the one the night before. The fires had died down to ash and embers, and the tents were silent. From the figures sprawled about, you might have thought that it was the Alliance who had been slaughtered two days before. A company coming in from night patrol passed her, half Mogh-iur and half Royal Enchian. The Mogh-iur were in their usual motley of fur and leather and bits of metal; one wild-looking woman with hawk feathers in her black braids and a blue cape gave her a mock-smile and an *awwwwwww* of false sympathy. The Enchians were like some mural of ancient Iyesi; tall slender men in chain and graven steel on fine horses, armed with rapiers and lances and bows, which did not prevent them from catcalling amiably as they passed. "Fuck you very much too," Shkai'ra shouted back; the sexual words were pretty much the same as in trade-Enchian.

The guards around the Elite section were offensively sympathetic, and Shkai'ra passed them with a growl. That turned into a full-fledged scowl as she reached her tent and found Sova standing with the tall Yeoli boy she had been spending a lot of time with tonight, the two cuddling close beneath a single cloak and murmuring to each other in the light of the last pale stars. "Hmmmf," she grunted, dropping boots and clothing and racking her weapons and drinking from the water-bag beside the entrance before crawling in beside her wife. Megan stirred sleepily and muttered before settling down again.

At least we can sleep, Shkai'ra thought. The thought of a day's march was unbearable.

*   *   *

So. Matthas read through his notes again. *Some people get so loquacious as truth-drug takes effect.* The big fighting-wench had propositioned him, of all things. "Such a nicely turned bottom you have, ahhhhh . . ." A moment's image came of being in bed with her, in those gristly arms that were such perverse imitations of men's, and those massive tree-trunk thighs with the dank, dark nest of impurity between them. A touch of nausea came, too. *They don't wash. . . .*

He read the notes again. Megan's link with Mikhail Farsight and Brahvniki-Yeoli dealings was far more tenuous than he'd expected; well, all right, might as well say it out. Nonexistent. At least as far as the big woman knew; but he'd made sure to ask, "Does she hold you in entire confidence?" To which Shkai'ra had answered, "Yes." No, there was nothing so calculated. For Megan and Shkai'ra, this was not even a vendetta—surprising for them—but a family affair. Megan wanted to rescue a son, enslaved long ago, and for her there was no other way into Arko.

Shit, he thought. *And it was such a beautiful conspiracy theory, too. Am I losing my touch?* No, he realized, the conspiracy was happening, but elsewhere, through other agents; he'd chased a red herring and had no idea where to pick up the real trail. *All the way to Setzetra, smoothly infiltrating the Yeoli camp,* he thought, *all for a shennen bad lead. With Eforas making me personally responsible, and I can hardly pin it on him, can I, when it was my fikken theory. Maybe I am losing my touch. Shit shit shit.*

He paced his tent, kicked his lap-desk, and for a time wallowed in totally self-indulgent self-pity.

That's enough wallowing, he forcefully told himself after a while. *Discipline. On to the next step, of rational thought, planning and action.* Only one rational thought came: *Now the fuck what?*

Time passed. He read his notes ten times over again. He paced some more. He ran over his old principles of spy-craft, hoping to squeeze clues out of general inspiration. He ran over the principles he'd added to the list himself, from his experience in foreign lands: Brahvnikian intrigue and dealing techniques, Zak protocols of deception, Yeoli strategic philosophy with its elegantly naive, sweeping rules—perhaps not so naive, he reflected, as practiced by *these* Yeolis. *The path unconceived,* he thought—a Yeoli concept, that when faced with an impossible conundrum the general must find an answer outside of what appeared possible and was therefore conceivable. *Yes, that's what I need now.*

He catnapped on it. He slept properly on it. He drank a flask of wine on it. He turned it over and over in his head. *Some faceless Brahvnikian, Mikhail's hireling, money-bag runner. How in Hayel am I going to find him, in this obscene sprawl of a barbarian camp?* He fought off despair. *Celestialis, none of it matters.*

He woke in the night, tossed and turned, wanted a boy, an herb-pipe, another wine-flask, to grab and cling to. Outside wind flopped the canvas, near and far, on a thousand tents. Someone passing outside murmured in a barbarian tongue, Yeoli or Lakan or who knew what— a barbarian tongue on Arko's own sacred land, paid for with its blood, in the inviolate Empire. *Shefen-kas, son of a whore and a dog, is probably having no trouble sleeping right now,* he thought.

He woke again, before dawn; not even a paling showed through the tiny holes in the tent's seams. More rested now, his thoughts were not so tinged with jitters; his body felt warmer, and all did not seem lost. And then it came shining into his head.

Matthas crawled up and lit a lamp, chortling; following the original conception like the river after the first burst in the dam, the details filled themselves in. He drew a pigeon-paper out of the compartment in his lap-desk and uncapped his finest pen.

Patappas is in the City, down on his luck since he lost the arm, and Frenandias, compromised in that Srian matter so he'll never get trade work again, living off that fancy lover; there's Moras, too. They'd wrestle demons in Hayel for a tenth of the gold we'd get for this . . . *And what I'm asking is nothing, easy.* He chortled some more, and began to write. *That'll knock the heart out of this misbegotten barbarian host; they'll fall apart, into easy cuttings, in an eight-day. So much for the great threat; and Arko, despite itself, will be saved. The path unconceived* . . . *Hah! I found it.*

What would Kurkas give to its savior? The man who arranged what I'm going to? He paused to chortle louder, imagining the elevation ceremony, the mantle with the coat of arms he would be permitted to design, the deed to the estate, the speech ringing with words in his praise. No one had ever been elevated two rungs at once before, *fessas* to *Aitzas*; but for what he would do, it was not impossible, nor unreasonable to expect.

X

Didn't I get tired when I was fourteen? Megan thought, watching Sova's ash-blond braid bounce as she tossed bits of hardtack to a swooping Fishhook.

"Here kitty kitty kitty!" she chirped. "You actually *like* this stuff, so here you go!" The girl's set of manrauq-fused meshmail made a rustling chink as she moved, weapons and the helmet hooked to her belt clanked with each hop. She swung up onto her pony easily. Megan wiped sweat from her brow and cursed, kicking her feet free of her mount's stirrups and bringing her knees up to spare the calves. *I'm one of the only people I know who could be over-horsed on a fish-gutted* pony. Still, she'd got enough used to riding now that she could concentrate on other things. Especially on this old beast, that was like a living chaise longue—the most mild, sedate, half-asleep horse she'd ever dreamed could exist. She wondered where Shkai'ra had found it.

The Thane-girl's mood seemed to change as afternoon wore on; she stopped starting conversations, and her round face, flushed with heat, turned pensive and closed.

143

When Megan saw it, that was; more and more she found herself facing the braid. *After I made Shkai'ra give her a day off squiring so I could get re-acquainted*, she thought.

"*Ha-a-a-a-alt!*" The command came from the head herald, in tuneful Yeoli, and traveled away down the line behind them, relayed in mutiple languages until it faded away in the distance. Rest-break. They sat in the shade of an olive tree and passed the canteen of unfermented apple cider between them. Though all shade tended to get filled immediately with people, it was a small tree and they were alone. Megan propped her chin in a cupped hand, bracing her elbow on her knee.

"You prefer riding with Shkai'ra, Sovee? Or are you just tired?"

The girl blinked in surprise. "No, I'm not tired. And I don't . . . I mean, riding's easier than walking, but . . . I like being with you."

Megan leaned back against the tree, closing her eyes for a bit. "I always preferred walking, myself. I . . ." She hesitated, then opened her eyes, looking down from the bright stabs of sun. *I find myself looking into a face I've told myself I should know, then realizing that I've been assuming a Halya of a lot. I keep falling over those assumptions when we've been less than close.* "Something on your mind, then?"

The girl looked as if she were deciding how to answer, then said, "Ya." Education had smoothed Sova's Zak, but never rooted out the back-of-the-throat Thanish accent, something which had never stood her in good stead in F'talezon.

"I was just thinking about . . . the old place, that's all."

Home, she had once called Schotter's house in Brahv-niki, where she'd been born and raised by her natural parents until twelve, in the very rare times she'd mentioned it. She no longer did.

"I went riding then. I mean, nothing like how much I ride *now*, but that's where I first learned." The girl's hand fidgeted at her sword-hilt, one nail scratching one of the quillons, a nervous habit she'd acquired after the first fight she'd been in on the river. The hand looked awkward, a little too large for its arm, like a not-quite-grown-up puppy's paw. "I wonder sometimes . . . what happened to them."

Though she was careful not to show it, Megan flinched inwardly. It seldom came up, how Sova had been adopted. *Then, I just didn't care if Shkai'ra took both Thane-brats and drowned them. I forgot that they were human. I forgot what it was like to be sold off to a stranger when I was twelve.* Megan looked down at the rough skin around her claws where she'd bitten at the cuticles. *Until it was done; too late.*

"I can understand you wondering. If you like, when we get home, I can start inquiries—"

"*No!*" For a moment the girl's fresh young face flashed a flat anger too old for her age, before the eyes dropped and the words subsided into formal stiffness. "I mean . . . I wouldn't impose on your time, *zhymata.*"

Koru, how do I get through that? *Shkai'ra's taught her to hide behind that blank look.* Suddenly it came to her why the girl had refused, and that she'd been damned insensitive not to see it. "It *would* be more than impolite for me or Shkai'ra to try and find your parents, wouldn't it?"

The girl took time, putting it into words. "Well . . . Fater is a Thane. Even if you were as nice as Elder Brother to him, it's . . . it would almost be a worse insult to his *zight,* if he considers himself having any left. It would be like pity. As for *khyd-hird,* I wouldn't want her to get on the same side of the world as them. If they're alive, even."

"Ah, Sova . . ." Megan's sigh was barely that, a faint breath. "If you or a neutral party wanted to look, I could aid in that way."

"I do, and I will, when I can," the girl said. Her chin lifted slightly, firmed. "*Without* your help."

Megan shrugged. "It's up to you. Sova . . ." She heaved a sigh. *How to say what I've wanted to say?* Somehow there had always been other things in the way, other things on her mind, or Shkai'ra too busy with the girl. This hurt almost as much as thinking of her own old hates and troubles; but she nailed her feelings down like a slug under one of her claws. "To my mind I owe you. I can say it was Shkai'ra, not me, who took you, but I stood back; I *know*."

The girl's face stayed stony, but her hazel eyes blinked, as if through the eye-holes of a mask, the only part of her true face showing. "*You* owe *me?*"

"I owe you honest answers to how you feel, at least. If it hurts me, so be it; I pay for my own action, or lack of action."

"*Form u-u-u-up!*" From all around came muttered curses, as the army hauled itself to its feet. By the height of the sun, it was probably the last rest break of the day; next stop would be for camp, and bed. *War* . . . Always the demands of the many came first, before love, hate, hunger, fear, any need or wish of the one. They found their place on the road, and Megan massaged the insides of her thighs. "Forwa-a-a-a-ard *march!*"

The girl glanced forward and back as they heeled their ponies into a slow plodding walk, scanning for anyone who might understand Zak. Satisfied there was none, she asked, "Why did you stand back?"

Megan took a deep breath. "Some part of me hated you just for being Thanish. Another part of me saw what you'd done to a friend of mine, though it was your father, really. I was wound too tight into my own troubles to care. I wish I could go back and change things. But I can't, Sova." She looked at the backs of the warriors riding ahead of them.

"I know." The girl gazed down at the poured stone road.

"Anything more you want to say?" Megan said, as if it weren't as obvious as a painted nose.

The girl kicked a foot clear of the stirrup, crossing it over the pommel, to better face Megan. Another trick she'd picked up from Shkai'ra. "*Zhymata . . . you've* been nice to me. *You* say you're sorry." She gazed ahead, putting her foot back in the stirrup again. "But *she* never has. And never will, I know." *Shkai'ra*. "She *isn't* sorry; she thinks she did me and Francosz—Francosz and *me*, I mean—nothing but good. She doesn't care what I feel, just what she thinks. She doesn't care what *anyone* feels except herself and you. And not even you, sometimes."

How do I explain this without sounding carping? Megan thought for a minute. "I love Shkai'ra," she said finally, "but sometimes she pisses me off." Fishhook swooped low over Sova, earning a languid swat. "I don't know how she opened up enough to fall in love with me, because she is convinced that the world works exactly as it *should* . . . not necessarily as it *does*. She's trying to understand the way everyone else feels—but she hides so much hurt from herself that she can't bear to see anyone else's. That's my best guess. Someday she's going to have to understand these things if she wants to be a better warrior and a better person." Megan looked over at the girl. "She decided that what she did was right, period." *I'm not going to say that sometimes she's just a pigheaded idiot.*

"What's understanding those things got to do with being a better *warrior?*"

Koru, how do I get into these questions? "Well—the simplest answer is that if she doesn't understand, if she isn't sensitive to people, she'll treat them with contempt, underestimate someone and get killed; but that's only one. There are as many reasons as there are people. . . ." Megan stopped for a bit. "I know it all sounds mystical and airy, but a teacher of mine said that naZak who truly know themselves and thus, others, have a power aside from *manrauq*."

"Mmm." The girl's face stayed thoughtful for a while, as she mulled this over. "*Khyd-hird* doesn't really know herself. And she's trying to make me into someone else who doesn't really know myself. But I *want* to know myself, or how else will I know who I am? I mean . . ." She trailed off.

"You are right about what Shkai'ra's trying to teach you. And you're at an age when most people don't know themselves. *I* still don't know myself, but I'm still trying. It's almost more important than book learning." She looked sideways at Sova. "And you know how important *that* is." She smiled. "If I can help, feel free to ask."

"Thanks, *zhymata*." The round Thanish features lit in what was all too rare; a smile that was neither ironic nor childhood silliness.

"Thank you, Sovee." They were riding close enough to touch, the two ponies nipping at each other's necks. Megan laid her hand on the girl's mailed shoulder and smiled, a bare curving of the lips. "You've taught me how to love you. I do my best, hey, for an evil Zak witch that eats Thanish babies for breakfast?"

The girl didn't laugh; but after a little while, she said, "*Zhymata*, you taught me how to love you, too."

They rode on, through immaculate deserted farmland. Time passed, filled with the clopping of hooves, the click and creak of harness, a marching song from somewhere behind.

"*Zhymata*, I learned from you that all Zak are not bad, but some are nice, like any people. Am I—and was Francosz—teaching you that about Thanes?"

"You certainly are, and he did." Megan squinted up at the sun, at the distant silhouette of a soaring bird.

"I went to see the old place when I went through Brahvniki," Sova said, sometime later. Her voice was almost casual.

"Oh?" Megan said carefully, raising one eyebrow.

"I know it was on Syevyre Road, just north of the walls. And I remember Teik Anastosi's place, next door. But ours, I mean *theirs*, sorry, is all changed now. The house and the gate and even the trees are all gone, and someone else has built another one there. It's as if it never was."

Megan rode in silence thinking, at a loss for words. *I won't speak ill of her father, not to her face.* "Well as long as you remember it, it was. It's not a good thing to forget where you came from; that's where to start to understand yourself."

"But I thought everything I learned there was all wrong. I mean, I *know* some of it was, like being mean to Piatr and thinking women should be weak instead of strong and know nothing about month-bleeding. But everything else was, too. Thanish prejudices and my-father-was-a-cheating-coward and my-mother-was-a-fainting-cow and we lived too soft and didn't get beaten nearly enough, you know, the things *khyd-hird* says."

"Well, Shkai'ra lived too hard and got beaten too often and her opinion of your parents is decidedly biased by the fact that your father was my enemy," Megan said tartly. "The good things you learned there will ring most true to both old way of life and new." Her face softened as she thought of learning that herself. "Someone must have loved you there, or you wouldn't know how ... keep the best, toss everything that's bullshit out."

"All Thanes *don't* bugger their children, you know," Sova said, somewhat hotly. "Now I know what that means, so I can tell you. Mine didn't bugger me. So there."

Megan blinked. "I didn't think they did; you don't show signs of it. It's the same sort of crap that the races fling around to fuel ..." She waved at the army around them. "This. Most people don't think twice about saying 'Zak cannibal, Thanish child-raper, Arkan bastard' ... Her glance sharpened on Sova. "Has someone pointed that particular idea about Thanes and their children to you, ah, recently? Like Shkai'ra? When it comes to that, she's somehow particularly insensitive."

"Her and every Zak I've ever met except for you, now, and *Zhymata* Rilla," Sova said blithely.

Megan heaved a sigh. *She's exaggerating,* she thought. *But even so . . .* "Are you happier being away from F'talezon?" Megan had avoided letting anyone who was particularly intolerant associate with the Slaf Hikarmé, but she could only do so much.

"No," the girl said, but Megan got at least a vague impression she was just being polite. "I miss Rilla and Shyll and the baby and the house. And eating nice food. And not *marching,* Gotth—excuse me. But at least here strangers aren't any meaner to me than anyone else, or just being nice to me because I'm your daughter."

"Ha-a-a-a-alt!" They'd arrived at tonight's resting-place; time to fall out and set camp, and Sova should be with Shkai'ra. Megan answered the girl with an affirmative grunt, then reached up to hug her head. "That's good. We'll talk more. You know, you're outgrowing me, daughter." She smiled. "Go on with you."

"O my sons, my precious pooooor sonnnnns!"

As Dimae, the *solas* goddess, female counterpart to the Steel-Armed One, Megan put on her best *solas* accent, and overacted shamelessly. "Like flies you die, all in a doomed cause! Sweet innocent souls, deluded by fools, believing your Steel-armed God favors this cause after so many clear omens! O my babes, wasted, flung away, like dust, O woe, O woe, O wo-o-o-o-oe!"

Chevenga laughed so hard he fell off his cushion. *The only person in the world,* Megan thought, *who could maintain his dignity rolling on the floor of an office-cart.* She liked making him laugh. "Fabulous," he said. "Stunning. The prize of the play festival for you . . . we're planned then?"

She nodded. "We're planned, *kras.*"

"So fast, we've barely spoken two words." He swung back up to sitting. "Stay for a bit?"

She'd been hoping he'd let her linger this time, and had brought a suitable inducement; they knew each other well enough now that he wouldn't take it as trying to buy his favor, she knew. She hadn't expected an invitation. "Certainly. I understand—I've heard from one of the most comprehensive of sources—you have a taste for this." She drew out the small flask of Saekrberk. *Shkai'ra and I never got around to drinking it ourselves*, she'd thought, *so why not?*

"Well, yes . . ." His lips pursed, as if he were searching for a polite way to say something awkward. *Shit*, she thought. *Of course—security.* She held the flask up, showing him the waxen Benai Saekrberk seal affixing the cap. "It's been in our possession all the way from Brahvniki, my word and oath on it. Well and good in our possession, in a hip-pouch by day, in the bottom of our bedroll at night—we didn't want some scruff stealing it."

He grinned then, teeth flashing gold. "Good enough. The most comprehensive source first introduced me to that, as he told you. It's a little early . . . well, maybe not for just *one*. To toast . . . the gods of Arko, who are so just?"

Megan smiled. From the lowest drawer of the cabinet he drew two small cups, handing one to her; the jiggling of the cart made it unwise to put them down to pour. "To the gods of Arko, who are so just," they said together. "*Korukai.*" By ancient tradition, both emptied their cups in one draught.

The Saekrberk burned its familiar way across Megan's tongue; she licked the green sweetness off her lip. "I never thought I'd be a theater player. Truly, I'm not that . . . how would you say it . . . out-flung? No: outgoing."

"The audience will be too busy pissing themselves to give critical opinions," he said. "You keep to yourself; that's your way, or your nature, so be it."

"Tell me, *kras*: I'm only affecting a handful of people each time. Do you think it's making that much of a difference? It's the sort of information Arkan commanders would suppress."

"Would I send you out to risk your life doing it if I didn't think it made a difference? Suppress as hard as they can, they won't silence the rumor mill; it needs only one to start a rumor, a handful gives it greater credence. And Arkans are good rumor-mongers—because they know full well their commanders suppress information."

"Put it that way and it makes a lot more sense," Megan said. "Just one of my false-dawn snake-thoughts, that's all."

"I know, I have them too," said the Imperturbable.

Megan glanced at the bed. "You don't sleep well, then?"

"Shall we say, there are many other things I do better. I'm under healer's orders right now: six *aer* of sleep a night, no matter what. That's about five Arkan beads, it doesn't seem like much, I know, but I never slept long. He's very strict about it too, uses that sand-timer. I've got this bed here because if I haven't had my six *aer* by reveille, he makes me sleep on the march." Megan bit her lip to keep from laughing, not sure how he might take it.

"Strict Haian . . . Sometimes it pisse . . . ah . . . angers me when Shkai'ra can sleep anywhere, anytime . . . for no reason, I know, but I still feel it." Comfortable, sharing the trait with him . . . with a snap, she pulled herself to attention inwardly. *Shake off the liquor. He's still the Invincible. We aren't that close, yet.*

"Megan, you can say 'pisses me off.' We're in an *army*, you don't have to talk as if it were a diplomatic function . . . though I suppose it *is* a diplomatic function, after a fashion. . . ."

"I keep having to remind myself you're *semanakraseye. Kras.*" A little longer arm's length, she wanted to keep him, still.

"Call me Chevenga. Anyone who gives me Saekrberk is a friend of mine."

Megan threw up her hands. "Who am I to argue? *Kra-Shche . . . Shchevenga.*"

"My true use-name," he laughed. "Kraschevenga. Or with Yeolis, Semanachevenga. You know I've never asked you about your family, aside from the son you're seeking."

"Ah." She listed them off. *Nice to be with someone who isn't shocked at marriages of more than two,* she thought. Yeolis had the same custom, and he, it turned out, was in a three, planning to add a fourth. "They're all well," she said. "The hardest part right now, aside from missing Lixand, which is always, is getting to know what's going on in my daughter's head ... adopted daughter. You may have seen her, the Thanish girl squiring Shkai'ra? Round face, ash-blond hair?"

"Yes, I think I know her to see her. How old was she when you adopted her? They say that's everything, when it comes to adoption."

"It was last year; she was thirteen."

There was the faintest twitch of a knitting of his brows; in his eyes she could see him wavering on whether to pry or not. "That's rather old," he said finally.

Megan looked back at him steadily. "Let's just say it was necessary, to give her legal status in F'talezon. I've just lately been considering moving our household to Brahvniki, a more tolerant place."

"Because Thanes and Zak are enemies; that *would* be hard for her, in F'talezon. Good of you to consider, for her sake; no one's more helpless than a child without parents."

Megan winced inwardly. *There are about three meanings in that, and he only knows one of them. Yet nothing he said could even be called uncivil.* "Hmm." She didn't want to try to explain. "The other consideration is that both Shkai'ra and my husband Shyll are naZak."

"All standing out like Srians in a nursery; I understand. Tell me, did you have people at home objecting to you marrying all these foreigners?" *He wants to press the issue of Sova,* she thought, *but he's too polite.*

"No kin that matter. I think my aunt is still alive, but I don't particularly care."

"She betrayed you?" Megan drew back blinking; he

quickly added, "*If* you choose to make it my business. If not, so be it."

"She's the one who sold me . . . to Sarngeld. When I was twelve. His true name was At . . . Atza-trat . . . zas. As near as I can say it."

"Atzathratzas?" A Yeoli tongue was somehow more adapted to Arkan words. That too-open, too-perceptive, hunting-cat look fixed on her, trying to see inside. *Maybe I should cut this short and get out of here.* But then it was off her. She twined the ends of her hair in her fingers. "Your aunt *sold* you? To an Arkan? *Why?* I've seen what kinship means to Zak . . ."

"Most Zak. Not all. She was that way with my father. But me . . . I suppose she was tired of seeing his shade in me, my face, or she was tired of bothering. As far as I know, a drunken impulse. I've never cared to ask her why."

"That sounds like madness to me. Was she a drunkard?"

Megan studied the back of her one hand, held before her, for a moment. *Why not trust him? I've trusted him already with the knowledge of what I am, of the man-rauq. Her hands twisted together in her lap. Like a knife throw; risk it.*

"She was a three-flask drunk. One would get her ugly, two would get her mean and three would have her too fuzzy to aim, until she passed out. That was before she started brewing things out of her own herbs."

"Were your parents dead by then?"

Megan felt old pain twinge, like a pulled muscle tensed. "My father got executed for Avritha's birthday when I was ten, my mother died of fever when I was eleven."

Chevenga sat silent for a moment, entirely still. Then he said, "You've suffered as no one should." No sarcasm, no hesitation, just the thought itself, straightforward and real. *That's true. No one should.* She looked up at him. *Who else in all the world could say that as a bald state-*

ment and not have it sound puerile? "It does you credit
that you're even alive," he added.

"Well. It happened. It's past, or almost. Once I get
Lixand back that portion of my life will be truly done."
She smiled a twisted sort of smile. "Maybe I should thank
her; if she hadn't done that I would never have borne
him. Other children, but not him." She tried to keep it
light, suspected she wasn't succeeding. She looked up
through her eyelashes at his face.

There was understanding; she could almost see the
pieces fall into place in his mind, his eyes showing it
clear, a flicker of pain, then sorrow, for her. The breath
she let out was not as calm as she wanted to pretend.
She hadn't realized she was holding it.

"Atzathratzas was Lixand's father," he said, barely
louder than a whisper. It was only half-questioning. Then
he offered her his hand, palm up. Not reaching, but
leaving her the choice to take or not.

Careful not to scratch him, she laid her hand in his.
The ridge of his sword-callus lay warm under the soft
skin of her thumb, somehow comforting, like Shkai'ra's.
*These hands would never move anyone around like a
puppet, or a doll.*

"You said he was almost ten."

She cleared her throat, making a scratchy sound. "Dah.
He was born in the Year of the Iron Ri, summer—ten
now, he'd be."

"How old are you?"

"Twenty and four." She looked at her hand in his, the
scratches on her nails and the scrape on a knuckle, as if
they were the most important things in the world. Then
she raised her eyes to his, making them as calm as she
could.

He was looking beyond her, beyond the wall of the
cart, far away, eyebrows ridged black over narrowed eyes,
lips pressed into a thin line. Then the eyes came back,
and he mock-spat, hard, in the direction of Arko.

He's already closer than I let most people get, ever,

she thought. Another part of her thought: *that's the first bitterness I've ever seen from him, against them.*

Pain hung with claws from the inside of her ribs, drawn by his sympathy. She shrugged, casual like Shkai'ra, forced the words. "I lived." *Does he do this to everyone in this army? Even every special operative?* "I . . ." Her throat froze up, the worse since she'd told Shkai'ra, who hadn't made much of it, despite her efforts. "I can heal." Swallowing the hurt in her throat, she raised her eyes to his, forced them steady.

"Oh, yes," he said lightly, as if it were a given. "You can. You will. It's just difficult and takes a long time. I know."

I know. The word echoed in her ears, like a bell, significant, like a drop of blood in water. *He does.* It came to her: *he was a slave of Arko.*

Most of his scars were hidden under near-priceless armor, now, but she remembered them, the marks of the ten-beaded whip, the brand burns. *Why am I thinking he wouldn't have got the rest of the usual treatment? That sort of thing doesn't only happen to the poor; there are shits in every quarter. He just ran up against the richest shit of all, the Imperator.* A tale she had heard at a fire came hard back into her mind: that he'd suffered the worst tortures at the hands of Kurkas. Personally. *No one else would have had the nerve,* she thought. *Koru— what must it have felt like, while at the same time, he knew, the Arkan army was doing the same thing to his country?*

She hadn't thought much about his grudge; now she realized why. Off the field, he never showed it. Not so much as a snarl or a hiss or an icy-eyed stare; the worst he'd get was snide. He would just let drop stories of his sufferings there, now and then, understated and casual as if commenting on the weather, an instant's twinge on his face at the most.

And so, Megan thought, *you don't catch the full meaning until afterwards, perhaps lying in your tent at night, when the tale won't leave your head, like blood-taste in your mouth, but rattles around this way and that like a dagger in a bucket, while you try to sleep. And the only thing you can do is take it out onto the field next day, and carve out some Arkan's eyes with it.* Even his own pain, he turned to advantage.

"Megan." His soft voice called her back to now; those dark eyes with their sad lines were fixing hers, gentle, but firm with his "I mean this" look. His tone went old-school Yeoli again, almost ceremonial. "If there's anything you can think of that I could do to help, tell me, and I will do it."

Shkai'ra would have leaped at that offer. Her fingers were trembling still. *And dragged you into the nearest bed or bushes.* He looked puzzled; she must have shown something on her face, she knew. "And you will owe me nothing for it," he went on. "I wouldn't look for return." She picked at the cushion, with its bright-woven strands of wool; a twitch of her hand poked a hole into it. He just shrugged to her apology, saying, "It'll be fixed."

I'm avoiding the point. She looked up. "Thank you. Even though the merchant in me is cringing at that 'owe me nothing' part. Thank you. Some of my . . ." The word came hard. ". . . fears, I deal with every day. Some I've been trying to ignore. I would never ask you to help me with those."

"I said anything. I'm not known for not meaning what I say." Now his eyes were silk, with steel underneath.

"Koru!" She shook herself, as if out of a spell that had wrapped around her without her noticing, like a second skin. "What am I thinking? There's only one thing you could do, and I can't ask it. It would be too much of a risk, of clawing the *semanakraseye* into bloody shreds!" She held up her claws.

It occurred to her just as the words came out that they could be taken as a challenge. But he only shrugged and said, "I risk worse out on the field every battle. But I still go. When I was on Haiu Menshir . . ." Something

caught in his throat, and his voice went even more quiet,
hardly more than a whisper. "My healer found a woman,
to help me with *my* trouble. She asked no return. What
she gave, I would pass on. If you wish: in this I wish
what you wish."

Even Shyll had never told her that. *What I wish? I
had to take what I wanted for so long.* She felt uncomfortable, as if someone had handed her jewels: it would
be unmannerly to examine them to see if they were paste
and glass, however. Many people had given her that,
glass and cheap tin. But his eyes looked genuine, black
sapphires in the half-light of the office-cart.

"I will remember that," she said. "I will keep it in
mind. I won't say whether I will take you up on it." He
signed a plain chalk, yes. "Now I think I should stop
wasting your precious time so that your scribe can . . ."
*Keep it light; when it gets too serious, make it light again.
Will I ever grow out of that?*

"You know, *shemannn-Krazh* . . . whatever the fuck."

Chevenga had joined Shkai'ra, unannounced as usual,
at one of the Slaughterers' campfires.

"You're pretty," she went on. "Wanna fuck?"

His head turned to her; on his face, in the golden half-
light of the fire, partly shadowed by his thick side-curls,
she was sure she detected a little smile along with the
raised brows. Sova turned away to Echera-e, feeling her
face go red-hot, covering it with the coolness of her
hands. "I don't *know* her."

"Someone told you our custom," Chevenga said.

"Custom? What custom?"

Yeoli tradition, he explained, demanded that a *semanakraseye* leading an army must refuse no comers at a
campfire; they believed this bound the army as one.
Leading an alliance, he'd extended the favor to non-
Yeolis.

"Oh, *really?*"

From the distant woods: *Hehehehehe.*

"Hey!" She'd hardly heard him shout before, not even giving orders on the field; that was the task of the herald, or the gong. "Wait!" *About as heavy as I thought*, she thought. *Not overly*. His waist fit nicely, on her shoulder; his squirmings somehow didn't happen to overbalance him. "I don't know whether anyone else wants me!" The Slaughterers, howling with laughter so hard even some wine was spilled, made only encouragements, and the odd cry of "Me, later!" gesturing to the woods with a wide variety of suggestions and advice. "He-e-e-e-elp!" Chevenga rasped, thrashing and flailing dramatically. "Rape! Pillage! Wanton lust! I'm at the mercy of a ravishing barbarian! Wait, let me rephrase that . . . Ravening, I mean . . ." Sova just buried her head in her arms, as his mock protests faded into the trees.

The sheer effrontery of it sank in further. *She just carried off the Invincible*, Sova thought, *the Immortal, Imperturbable, Second Curlion . . . I mean, I know she thinks she's something, but . . . !*

Echera-e's hand touched hers. "You' shahdow-motser, he hahs—"

"*She* has."

"*Ayo*, she hahs . . . *rav'ye*, you know, naht cowarrd—"

"The nerve of a lake-quarter rat?"

" '*Tai*, yes. I like people like tsaht."

His hand feels like silk woven from threads of fire. Since that first night, the Yeoli youth had often happened to show up at whichever Slaughterer fire she was at. Like all Yeolis, he never felt he was speaking whole-heartedly to someone unless he was touching their hand or shoulder or knee (just as long as one hand was free to gesture); but that touch was unthinkingly casual, and though the first time his big palm had gently laid on the back of her hand had sent a lightning-bolt through her, she'd soon got used to it, though some part of her went on thinking it was vaguely perverse of him to do it, and her to not object. Then, somehow, their hands had stayed linked, even when he was just listening.

Is this love? She knew that whenever she saw his face come into the ring of firelight, she'd feel a lifting in her chest, a catch of her breath and her heart beating faster. When he didn't come, she'd feel the disappointment of denial sharper than she'd ever felt since what she counted as her childhood, the time before she'd been taken from her old home. *I want him here*, she thought. But she'd heard of something called infatuation too, and that it could feel no less passionate, often more, yet not be the true thing. She'd asked *zhymata* how she could tell: "Only time can say," was the answer.

He wants us to go into the bushes, she thought now, *like* khyd-hird *and Chevenga just did.* An old voice, her birth-mother's, grated in her ear. *Men only want one thing.*

If I just go into the bushes to be with him, does that make me a doxy? A slut? In her new home, she'd been taught the injustice of those terms, to be applied only to women, while men who did the same were to be admired.

He wants to ruin me. The old Thanish phrasing came easily. Behind those friendly light brown eyes, Fehuund lurked, too subtle to see, wrapping his evil temptation as always in hope and warmth and yearning. *But*, she thought, *I trust him.* And overlaid on the old were the ethics of her new home: go with him into the bushes, tumble, take some birth-herb, and do the same tomorrow night, untouched; it's just sex, how can it change you? Her older concerns she would never admit to *khyd-hird*, for fear of laughter or a sharp "Don't you know *anything?*" But that was no answer, to the touch of Echera-e's big tender hands, to the thought, that kept pressing into her imagination, of how they would feel touching her elsewhere, and to knowing that the pleasurable itch between her legs had something to do with it all.

The wineskin came around; she took a long draught. *I know what khyd-hird would do in this situation: what she just did. But that definitely is not my style, and besides he's probably too heavy. . . .*

Maybe I'm wrong, she thought, after a while. *Maybe he doesn't want to. After all, he hasn't tried anything, he hasn't carried me off or kissed me or even said anything.* He'd put his arm around her shoulder; but that was something friends could do. *He hasn't even looked at me that way. Yet he can't think I'm ugly, or he wouldn't keep holding my hand, or smiling, or saying I'm beautiful. What's he going to do?*

Nothing, it seemed; the night ground on, and her nervousness over what might happen in the bushes gave way for what might not. *I want to. Does that make me a doxy? I don't feel like someone bad. Francosz learned on the river, two years ago. He looked so happy after. It's not fair that girls shouldn't get to do what boys do. There's nothing wrong with sex, nothing evil about it, and I won't get pregnant as long as I take some birthherb. I won't be ruined, no decent Thanish family would marry me to their son anyway, and there's no such thing as being ruined by sex. Khyd-hird isn't a slut—she'd take off anyone's head who called her that—and look what she does. . . .*

Suddenly Echera-e excused himself to go to the latrine, and one of the Slaughterers, a man of about thirty or so who had seemed to be trying to catch the youth's eye, happened to get up at the same time. *I miss him,* she thought, *even when he's gone only a few steps. Is this normal? Is this what people mean when they say "lovesick"?* And why, she thought, sometime later, *have the two of them been gone so long?* Sudden terrors filled her, of traitors in disguise and knives in the dark; the thought of him dead was suddenly horrifyingly huge and unbearable. But then he was there, as if he'd never been gone.

"Hi." He looked embarrassed.

"What'd *he* want?"

"Oh . . . eh . . . to tell me a thing."

"Not my business?"

"*Ayo* . . . *ayo*, no. I mean, no, isn' *naht* yourrh business, meaning, I mean, it *is.*"

"Well, then, you've got to tell me."

"*Ayo*, yes. Sure. He say . . . he *said* he think maybe you ahn' me hahve mis . . . mis-naht-unde'stahnd. Ing. Of two differ country-*el.*"

"*Huh?* I mean, I beg your pardon? You mean misunderstanding, of two different countries?"

"'*Tai.*"

"Uh huh?"

"He say . . . maybe we both wait forrh *otser.* I mean . . ." He ran the hand that wasn't on her shoulder through his hair. *You're so beautiful when you're embarrassed,* she thought. "See, Sova, where *you* frahm, it, i's tseh *mahn* who, um, em, you know . . . *ayo*, who *ahsks.* In Yeola-e—i's tseh *woman.*"

Sova understood.

For a long time they gazed at each other, eyes shining, heads proud, in the joy of perfect understanding, as in a two-part song sung flawlessly. "So see," he added. "I thahnk him, 'cause if he naht say tsaht, we sit hyere ahn' hold hahnds ahn' naht do thing else forrh a *yearrrh.*"

As one they jumped up, arm in arm, and ran into the woods.

"You little scarrhy?" he whispered, in the darkness of the thicket. On a patch of soft earth they lay wrapped in each other's arms, and Sova wondered, *What should I be doing? Do we take off our clothes now or what? What do I do with my hands?* She was sure he wasn't a virgin; he had too sophisticated a look, and besides, she'd heard about Yeolis. Or heard them, in person; right now, in the next thicket over, two people, a man and another whose gender she couldn't tell by the voice, were moaning in rhythm and gibbering Yeoli sacred words as loudly and dramatically as grand show singers. *He'll think I'm a gauche child.*

"Ya, I'm a little scared," she whispered, then had to say it louder, for him to hear over the *"Mamaiyana, o mamaiyana, mahachao ayana, sekahara-a-a-ahh!"* from the other thicket. "Ya, I admit I'm a little scared! I'm sorry."

"No need sorrhy, Sovee. We ... *may* we kiss away scarrhy?"

Part of me thinks this is icky, she thought. *His mouth is wet. I guess because we both had the same dinner our mouths taste the same so that's why he doesn't taste different. But we did it under the trees before and it's so nice. I don't want to stop. How can it be both at the same time? Minegott it's the Fehuund. No it isn't. Don't be ridiculous. That's just atavistic Thane-bilge. Mmmmmmm ... I should be doing something with my hands to make him feel nice. Like he's running his hands gently over my back, I'll do that to him, too.* His back was wide and hard-ridged.

"May I ..." His whisper was throaty and deep in the darkness. "May I touch yourrh ... how you say, you know, um, I naht cahn think—" His words were drowned out by a throaty howl from the next thicket. "—little, drink, you know, two, *kyash!*" Frustration stopped up his words. *Why does he keep asking,* she thought. *It means I have to keep saying yes, like a slut, sluts don't know how to say no ... No! Stop thinking that! I'll just make myself miserable for no reason. I want him to touch me wherever he means.* So she just whispered "Yes," and felt his fingertips touch, with utter tenderness, one nipple, through the course cotton of her shirt. He wasn't a virgin, she knew with certainty, as feeling speared through her from the breasts downward; his touch was too knowledgeable of sensitivities she'd never dreamed of in her own body.

"Don't ask," she whispered, waited a moment until she could be heard again, continued. "You don't need to,

Echerry. You may touch me anywhere. Please." She heard her own throatiness, like *khyd-hird*'s and *zhyma-ta*'s in their darkened room, something she'd never thought to hear out of her own mouth. "I . . . I . . . give myself to you, Echerry. Please take me. Please."

Please take me away, it meant, and she suddenly knew it meant, *from all the fear and pain and anger. From the bleakness. I knew boredom, in the old time, and other bleakness, but now* . . . The hard view she'd learned in her new life, truth, they'd call it, intruded with its usual cold thoughts: *there is no escape, from the blows, the push-ups, the lung-tearing exhaustion, the aching limbs, the shame; the endless* endlessness.

But that was wrong: there was. He did take her away, at least for one soaring flight that seemed to last forever, and then another, and told her he would again as many times as she wanted. As he did, even the rising yowls from the other Yeolis were no longer brutish but magical, somehow joining with her own ecstasy to make it all the deeper. Each time was never long enough, so she *made* it last longer; there were ways, like fighting, using her mind.

Then she was done, she could tell: she felt truly bone-less, not just drunkenly so, but sated to the core, as if she had just eaten a full delicious meal with her soul as well as her body, if that were possible; and anything that was wrong in the world, her past or her doubts or even the war, were petty in truth, trivial flaws in the face of a vast peace.

He'd left the pain till after; it was nothing to feeling his pleasure, quick and needful and full of strength. Afterwards, as they lay basking in sweet breeze and moonlight, her head on his shoulder and his crystal clenched in her hand, she cried with joy, for having learned this was possible. "Echerry, I love you," she whispered.

He whispered back, "I love you, too."

o　　o　　o

Shkai'ra stretched and looked up at the stars, and an occasional spark from the fires whirling across the night. Both glittered through the limbs and leaves of apricot trees; the fruit glowed faint amber, nearly dropping-ripe. She picked one up from the silky grass, examined it critically and bit into it before offering it to Chevenga. *Perfect*. Some *Aitzas* was going to lose the rents from this plot, this year.

He lay warm beside her, as relaxed supine as a cat sleeping in summer, his head still arched slightly back. He'd been as passionate a lover as she'd expected, but far more sensitive, marvelously so, with a fragility that reminded her of Megan. *Of course he's had that kind of wounding too.* . . . But he'd thrown his arms wide when he came, as if to embrace something far greater than her, or himself, then lay so still that she'd nudged him, wondering whether he was all right. "Just enjoying the stillness within," he'd whispered.

"My food-taster," he said now. "You know the old story, about the emperor who trusts only fruit off the tree to be safe, so his mad wife injects poison into them?"

She laughed, then quoted in the snarling gutturals of her own tongue, translating:

> *When I was a warrior, the kettle-drums they beat*
> *The people scattered flowers before my horse's feet.*
> *Now I am a mighty king, the people dog my track*
> *Poison in the winecup, daggers at my back.*

He laughed. "You should see the precautions they take to protect Kurkas. I can't *wait* to live that way . . . if I live till then." She'd noticed that about him: while he always seemed certain of victory, he made no assumptions about his own life's length, Immortal or not.

"No more fucking in the grass *then*, eh? *Ia*, the problem with having everything is that everyone wants to take it away from you. I'll just settle for being rich, thank you; most of the perks a conquering king gets, and not so many competitors out for the job. Sitting alone on a mountaintop makes you a better target."

"I wouldn't know about being a ruler or rich," he said. At first she thought it was a deadpanned joke; then it came to her that, Yeoli political customs being what they were, he was sincere. "As for being a conqueror, it certainly beats losing. We did enough of that, thank you."

"*Nia*, of course you wouldn't know about ruling, O Invincible-Beloved-whose-orders-are-obeyed-with-quivering-eagerness, whether he likes it or not." That drew a laugh out of him, then a shrugging sigh. "When I was young and stupid," she added, "I'd have waded through fire to conquer a kingdom." She put a crone's quaver into her voice. "Now—once we've got Lixand— I'll just sit by the fire, heh, heh."

"Probably for the best," he said. "You care only for those close to you, and a ruler whose love doesn't spread to her people tends to bring suffering on them. But you're hardly *old;* you don't look any more venerable than somewhere between twenty . . . oh, seven, and thirty."

She frowned, holding up both hands and then glancing at her feet. "Twenty-and-nine . . . no. Thirty last moon. About your age, *nia?*"

"Not quite," he said, with a laugh that was actually, delightfully, shy. "I'm a cub, to you. Twenty-three."

She snorted. "Twenty-*three?* That *is* a cub. I thought I'd lived hard—you've got scars on scars." She traced a few of them, drawing happy sounds from deep in his throat. "And you've done all you've done . . . Baiwun, you're not even really in your *prime* yet."

"Early start, tight scheduling, and I only get to see my kids when the world feels like letting me—rarely, that is." That was rattled off, obviously practiced. "By the time my prime comes, I hope, there'll be peace and *I'll* be able to sit by the fire."

"Well, it's as I was saying," Shkai'ra said thoughtfully. "When I was nineteen, I'd ride a week's journey for a fight. But you grow out of it . . . if you live, true. Then, it's enough fighting just to sword the ones that run up to you with a mean look in their eyes. Fun enough when duty calls, and I'll listen to a bard lie about somebody *else's* adventures. Hero-king Zh'ven'ghka's, maybe."

"I hope the songs can do me enough credit without lies. Shefen-kas, J'vengka, Sievenka, Shchewenga, Tsefenga . . ." The mispronunciations of enemy and prominent allies alike he imitated perfectly, from long practice hearing them, it seemed. "You know, *I* have no trouble saying Chevenga correctly. I don't know *what's* wrong with everyone *else*."

She turned on her side and nuzzled his throat. "Repeat after me. *Shkai'ra*." She pronounced it proper Kommanzanu-style, exaggerating the throaty *hgggg* sound on the first syllable, and the clicking *tock* on the last.

"If you can pronounce *my* name right, I'll do yours," he shot back. A contest followed which sounded not unlike two drunken tigers arguing over a kill, and which they agreed afterwards they'd both lost. "Mmmm," she said then, feeling. "You *are* a man of tireless strength."

"Flatterer . . . ohhhh."

"Because you're such a cub, I guess. Shall we?"

"No. There are others. You're hogging me."

"Hmph. Kiss a little more then?"

"*Semana kra*-ahhhh, I *suppose* I could bear immph."

"Mmmm. This *is* even more fun than killing people. Learn from experience, *mmmmm* . . . Never thought I'd get sedate."

"Shkai'ra," he whispered after a while, "does it bring you pure pleasure, killing? No revulsion afterwards?"

She cuddled closer. "The pleasure isn't as much as it used to be. Sort of a hot thrill, but with an aftertaste, as you say, like bad liquor. Hard to decide what's the pleasure of fighting—the moves, you know, getting it right?"

"The pleasure of skill."

"*Ia*, and what's from killing itself. Been weaning myself off *zh'ivutrayzh*, murder-joy, for my wives and husband's sake; the Zak sort of frown on it, and I'm a settled married type now. Although," she added, "Ranion, the Drag-onLord back home"—it was odd to refer to F'talezon like that, but the Zak city was far more home than Stonefort in the Kommanz of Granfor, now—"pursues it with a pas-sion. These tyrants seem to like it; maybe it's a proof of their tyrant-ness, you know. 'Look, I can kill people nas-tily and get away with it.' Where Kurkas is a mural painter of tyranny, Ranion is a miniaturist. They'll need a bureaucracy to handle the queue, time comes to cut his throat."

"Sounds like it ought to be soon," Chevenga said, ris-ing to one elbow, his other hand absently tender on her middle. "Tell me; I've got an insider's sense of it from Megan; how does it look to a foreigner's eyes?" In a moment Shkai'ra regretted bringing politics up with a politician; grilling her, he stopped feather-stroking her. But soon enough he dropped the subject, and they lay silent in each other's warmth.

"Murder-joy," he said, after a while. "What an odd way of putting it. And so casual . . . A snake in the grass."

"What, where? I know of only one around here." She gripped, drawing a pleasure-yelp out of him.

"Yeoli saying. For something's being hidden under something else. You only gave it up for your spouses' sake, you say. Not your own—as if that were weakness. If the joy of the other's death comes of the continuation of one's own life, I doubt there is a warrior alive who's never felt it. You talk most casually speaking of the two most personal things there are between two people, did you know that?"

Shkai'ra shrugged. "Either casual or crying, *nia?* Life's too short to be *that* serious about anything, especially sex and dying."

He chuckled. "O Aged One, who knows all. Sex and fighting, I meant; dying doesn't have to be between two people. And there's the third one, I forgot, the mix of the first two, rape. Is there no way somewhere between casual and crying? Or must you be casual not only about your own death, but all others', to save yourself those tears?"

"Save myself tears? They're dead and I'm alive, and that's all that's important, *nia?* Rape—it's like a wound, you get over it." She laughed. "Alive, to do *this.*"

Chevenga refused to be distracted. *That's the trouble with these extraordinary people,* she thought. *They're so damnably single-minded.*

"Then you consider your own life precious, and spit on theirs?"

She shrugged. "Call me barbarian, if you want; many have. But I'm of a kind with most of the world, I think. Who doesn't care for their own life—or their love's— more than anyone else's?"

"Granted—though I've met some who don't. Haian healers spring to mind. Perhaps barbarism is a matter of how *much* less one cares about other lives than one's own, then. Shkai'ra, imagine this. You see a rockslide starting, that will grow big enough. to crush the town below where live ten thousand people—unless you throw yourself in its path and stop it now, at the cost of your own life. You have no obligation elsewhere except what anyone has, to family, friends and so forth. No punishment will come your way if you don't do it, nor accolades if you do, because no one will ever know. Those ten thousand people are neither friends nor enemies to you, just strangers; you've never even walked through the town. Would you do it?"

Shkai'ra propped herself up on both elbows, scratched between her breasts. "Do you lie awake at night thinking these things up?"

He chuckled, stroking her shoulder. "Not anymore. Debate training. Now I lie awake at night thinking up battle-plans." His eyes flicked up to hers, a single bright spot in each twinkling in the moonlight; the stroke turned snake-curvy as it continued down her upper arm.

Shkai'ra shrugged. "No. I wouldn't. Zaik take them. Megan and the family need me."

"And you wouldn't regret afterwards?"

"No. I do or I don't. Rogret is dithering."

"That's good. Perhaps. Would you tell Megan about it?"

She stared at him puzzled. "*Ia*—why not? *She'd* do the same. I hope."

"That's *very* good. Maybe. Wouldn't it bother you at all, having the blood of ten thousand people on your hands, even to save yourself?"

"*I* didn't kill them—a rockslide did. There's a difference between killing and not preventing death."

"Ah-hah—I knew we disagreed somewhere. You didn't *start* the rockslide, yes; but their blood is still on your hands, because you could have *stopped* it. You being too far away to reach the rockslide in time, hence having *no* choice, would be different again. In Yeoli the word for choice, *kra*, means power and responsibility both, because for a moment you held power over the town's fate, and hence responsibility. Whatever the cost to you; it's still power, and responsibility.

"Don't get me wrong: I don't necessarily think your choice is bad. Ten thousand people or better die somewhere every day anyway, and I can understand not wanting to commit suicide and bereave those you love for the sake of strangers. But it *is* wrong, to my mind, to pretend you *didn't* choose, that there was no forking path before you, no matter how unpleasant, no matter how unfair that one should be forced to take such a bitter choice. We all get stuck with them. I'd rather have the pain than delude myself."

Shkai'ra sat up. "Choose, don't choose, forking paths, this thread and that . . . I take this man into the bushes and fuck him until he's half passed-out with joy, and he starts giving me a Zaik-damned rhetoric course. Maybe I should carry you back."

Chevenga flicked her nipple with his tongue. "Don't tell me I didn't give as good as I got. But I have reason to raise these things, aside from being Yeoli—stop that and listen. I like to know my warriors, my officers most of all. You're all sworn to do whatever I command; but to my mind everything works best if I have people do as they are inclined. I know this about you, now: if I need someone to sacrifice to save many, you're a bad choice. If I need someone to do something that would be easy only for one who cares little for strangers, or can be casual about sex, fighting and rape—doing or being done to—you are."

Shkai'ra laughed. "Well, I can't protest that; I'm always delighted to do what I'm naturally inclined, mmm."

"Exactly." He pushed her hands away. "You cavaliers, you're all the same. Single-minded horse-mounters."

She fixed his eyes with hers. "Yet *you*, Zhven'ghka . . . I've heard much, but I can't believe you're so pure and noble that in all the fighting you've seen, you've never taken pleasure on a defeated enemy." She made the snake-gesture down his arm. "You asked truth out of me, hmm?"

His brows flew up, and his voice turned serious. "You doubt I would give it?"

He's touchy about that, she thought. "I didn't mean you'd *lie*."

"You just wouldn't believe me, if I said I never had, because you think it's impossible for anyone to forgo that. Are you trying to tell me we don't *choose* these things, then? Is human nature so limited? Suppose one had sworn an oath, or believed one would be punished by one's gods, or would corrupt oneself . . . or had suffered the same and didn't want to inflict it?"

Shkai'ra shrugged. "I suppose it's possible. Odd, though."

"Then you *will* believe me, if I say I haven't? I can't *make* you. If you won't believe me I won't bother answering."

"You have a name for honesty. All right, all right, I'll believe you."

"Well . . ." Chevenga laced his hands behind his head, a smile quirking his lips. "I *have*, actually. My people asked it of me. You recall the name Abatzas Kallen?"

Shkai'ra leaned forward on her elbows beside him.

"The Arkan general who was a great asset to an army—*yours.*"

"Yes," he chuckled. "That's the one. Well, at Siriha we captured him, and it was suggested to me I do the Arkan thing—do you know what I mean by that?"

What Arkans did to enemy leaders they captured, he meant. Sexual humiliation, in front of the assembled army and prisoners, if there were any. She'd never seen it; since she'd joined, Arko had never captured an enemy leader.

"My command council argued it was what my warriors wanted. I wasn't sure. So I called them to Assembly, and put it to a vote, which went very strongly chalk. So I did it."

"Don't tell me," Shkai'ra said drily. "You hated every moment."

He gave a sardonic chuckle. "Hardly. Else it wouldn't have been what they asked, would it? *Semana kra . . .* the people wills. And—before you accuse me of not telling the whole truth—the body will feel what it will feel."

"Of course. I've used that principle a time or two myself," she added, "when I was less civilized. It was my right, after all, as I thought then."

"I didn't feel it was my right. My people did, though. . . ." For a moment he seemed troubled, despite the stillness of his eyes; then he shrugged. "Well, it doesn't matter, as long as I remember not to let you loose among prisoners I *don't* want abused. I should go back to the fire. I seem to recall saying quite a while ago, that you were hogging me."

Shkai'ra mock-sighed and chuckled. "Right."

"They'll think you never put me down!" he giggled, as she heaved him up onto her shoulder.

Megan sat by the breakfast fire, listening to Shkai'ra's account of the night before, thinking of her own last time with Shyll. She'd got so sensitive he couldn't do more than just cuddle her. *Goddess, I'm tired of being over-sensitive.*

"You had him writhing on the moss?" The Zak raised an eyebrow. "Probably squeezed him dry." She smiled sweetly. "Going to have his baby?"

"Sheepshit—!" Shkai'ra started up counting on her fingers, then stuck out a bare foot to finish counting on her toes. "Don't scare me like that!" she said, rummaging in the saddlebags for the birth-herb and the special tea-pot, grimacing as she set the round brown clay by the fire, throwing in a double pinch of herb and adding the water. "Jaiwun, I hate the way this tastes. Better safe than sorry, though. Oh, well, men have to have *some* advantage to make up for being stiff and crotch-kick-able." She broke the eggs into the pan and stirred them around with a stick. "I'm getting too old for this sort of thing."

"News from the machine-scribed *Pages;* wrinkled granny takes advantage of young, good-looking com-mander . . ." Megan ducked the stick. "He *is* handsome." *I'm attracted and scared shitless all at the same time,* she thought, *as usual.*

Shkai'ra smiled more seriously. "Actually, I was think-ing of bearing one when we get back." She sighed. "I miss Shyll and Rilla and even the brat." She reached out to touch Megan on the cheek. "I never thought I'd say that about my family, my family were all—good Kom-manza, easy to hate." Her eyes were full of ghosts for a moment. "Glad you're here, love."

"Where else would I be?" *She's actually not that bad with a child,* Megan thought, *as long as it's in the walk-ing, talking phase and she can give it to someone else, and as long as someone reminds her not to tease too far.* "Love you, Shkai'ra."

"Love you, Megan." Softly. "More than my heart's blood. It'd be better for Sova if she were back home; better for the mission, more convenient all round. I'm still glad she's here; someone else we can trust. I must be going soft in my old age."

Reveille gongs sounded, and the call: *"Rise and shine*

and sma-a-a-a-ash Aa-a-a-a-a-ar-ko-o-o-o-o-oh!" Megan
frowned down at her cup of fish oil. *Sometimes these
claws are more trouble than they're worth.* "Shit," she
said, standing up. "Sova's not back yet."

"Yes, she is, there she comes." Shkai'ra pointed. "Jaiwun All-mate, I think . . . do you?"

"No, love, I don't think. I'm *sure.*"

The look on the girl's face was unmistakable.

Matthas had found a half-decent contact in the retreating
Arkan army: Manajas Sennen, an infantry commander
who was high enough to authorize what he needed. That
was as high as he cared to go. Manajas had been the
only one in the command awake when Matthas had come
in the first night, using overheard passwords to pass the
first barriers, stony looks and the bark of "Irefas" to get
through the deeper.

"Yes, Nerasas, old pal," Manajas had said sympatheti-
cally—no sense for Matthas to use his real name, let it
be thought a code name—when he gave a heavily edited
explanation of his plight. "I understand all too well; I've
received orders to buy the town and two copper chains
to do it with often enough myself. Cutbacks. Back in my
day it wasn't this way. . . . I'll help you out." A good egg,
his only fault having got too entwined in the vine. *Maybe
it was cutbacks killing off his soldiers that drove him to
drink.* Well, disadvantages were to turn into advantages;
Matthas had got Manajas to sign for a thing or two while
too sozzled to read.

Now they sat together, Matthas having decided to
allow himself a few as well. "Here's the answer, Manajas,
old pal, see? They've done it." The note was concise, as
pigeon-post required:

> Friend of our youth: mission accomplished as
> instructed. For best results mention the four
> moles on a square on the right shoulder-blade.
> —Entrepreneurs.

It had come nineteen days after his missive to which it was a reply.

"I know those old sods," he said laughing. "Dangle enough money in front of them and they'd storm Hayel itself. Same as everyone, I guess. All right, all right, *now* I'll tell you what it's all about. Heh, why not?"

He did, without mentioning any names, except one.

Manajas's guffawing burst out deafening in the quiet of the night.

"You're right! You're right, Nerashas, my friend, sh'worth it for *thish!* Yeh, yeh, all the pigeons and boxshes and that, sh'worth every ssshain-link! Here's to . . ."

They raised fancy pure-glass cups together. *"Shefen-kash in Hayel!"*

"Shefen-kash in Hayel!"

XI

Shkai'ra raised her binoculars, a good pair she had taken off an Arkan's corpse. She squinted a little; it was noon, the skirmishing had taken most of the day, with the enemy trying to break contact behind their cavalry screens, mercenary Mogh-iur horse-archers. Broad swatches had been trampled through nearly-ripe wheat that only birds and insects would harvest now. The bodies of humans and horses lay unmoving. *Cursed* good *horse-archers,* Shkai'ra thought. The Slaughterers had lost four, dead and wounded; the enemy a little less, probably.

There were hills to the west, gently rounded, with green pasture on the heights and a strip of dense oak-wood at their feet; the highway ran up the valley between cleared fields that were a lake of grain-gold, rising just enough to make an ox-team lean into the traces, through the forest, then zigzagging up through a notch in the hills, beautifully maintained. And there was a unit of Arkan infantry deployed where road met woods, a straight bar across the V of the woods, flanks securely anchored.

She turned the focusing screw, and the banner at the center of the formation sprang out; the Eagle clasping the sun at the head of the staff, a flag emblazoned with a wild boar below. The soldiers stood with pikes set in the ground, crossbowmen to each side with mostly single-shot crossbows, thank Zaik, not those nasty Fehinnan seven-round models that had been turning up lately. Not an elite unit, *okas*-caste soldiers under *solas* officers, but there was a stolid steadiness to their ranks.

"So, these have been to school," Shkai'ra said musingly to herself. To Sova: "Take a look at the edge of the woods, then that hillcrest. What do you see?"

"Well, there they are in the woods, without lances. They aren't going to have lances in the woods, get caught on the branches. Infantry. A small *rejin*. And there's more waiting over the hill . . . cavalry?"

"Excellent. Understanding your opponent's mind is the key to success in command. It's easier than understanding people generally, there's a . . . straightforwardness to it." She rapped her knuckles together. "You always know what the enemy wants.

"All right, here's why they're set up like this. They want that phalanx to block the road, right? So if any of *us* come up and engage, they've got light infantry in the woods—skirmishers, javelineers, those shitty barbed fuckers they like to use. The light infantry moves out quick and takes us in the flank. When we're nice and pinned, the lancers over the hillcrest come down through the woods—you can do that if you're careful—and roll us up. Remember, they're trying to win time to get away from us; the longer it takes to clear this roadblock, the better. Any questions?"

The girl stared at the scene for a time, scratching the quillons of her sword. "Uhhh . . . what do we do?"

Shkai'ra snorted. "That's the hard part. Take a note to Makalina Shae-Sorel, *rigaryekrachaseye*, Brigadier-General First." The Thane-girl pulled out a pad of paper sheets and licked the end of a writing stick. "From me, to her, the usual saddlesoap courtesies and the situation as I've just explained it." Sova's hand flew across the page. "Please send up, *firstly*, some good light foot to clear the forest, pikes, missile infantry, field artillery. A company or so of Lakan horse would be welcome. With all that, I estimate we could get this boy-buggering impediment off the road, many thanks, you'd better come up in person too, signed me."

"It's a good thing *I* can write, *khyd-hird*," Sova said amiably.

"Isn't it," Shkai'ra said, taking the pad and adding a sketch-map to the end. "Get it there, get an answer, get back, *fast.*"

Shkai'ra pushed her helmet back by the nasal, whistling tunelessly as she waited at the center of the three-rank formation of the Slaughterers. The sun was warm on her armor, this metal suit hotter than the lacquered leather on fiberglass she was accustomed to, if lighter. Sweat ran down her face into her coif.

At the sound of footfalls in unison behind her, she turned in the saddle. Sova was riding with her Yeoli boy at the head of the approaching column: three-hundred-odd women, dark chocolate brown, tall, wire-slender and loping at an easy pace that kept up with the horses' canter. Each carried two six-foot javelins with long iron heads in her left hand, along with a small wicker shield and another spear in her right, but was lightly equipped otherwise: a leather kirtle and jerkin, metal-strapped leather helmet with an ostrich-plume, long knife at the belt and one-handed axe across the backs. Warriors of the matriarchy of Hyerne, they were.

Against Arkans, she understood, who had just been rotated forward and so weren't used to fighting women yet; more prone to be shocked, insulted, ashamed or intimidated, and do stupid things, at least for a short time, which would be long enough. She wondered if this was Chevenga's idea; it had his stamp.

They were headed not by Peyepallo, the Hyerne high commander, but her second. *Who still outranks me,* Shkai'ra thought. But as the Hyerne arrived, giving Hotblood a wary glance, she said in pidgin-Enchian, "Makalina say you in command until main body comes up."

So, so. The smell of another promotion was in the air; somebody had noticed her sucker-punching that battalion of Arkan horse last week. Partly luck, but it always was, and she'd done something similar back in Senlaw, across the Lannic.

The Hyerne deployed to the left of Shkai'ra's cavalry, black and white plumes fluttering in the gusting breeze. Sova pulled up on her other side and saluted. The Yeoli boy was about seventeen . . . yes, it was the one the girl was bouncing the bedroll with. *Can't pronounce the name. Can't fault her taste, either.* "A regiment of Schvait, two springalds, three companies of Lakans, and *rigaryekrachaseye* Makalina Shae-Sorel are on the way, *khyd-hird,*" Sova said.

"Good," Shkai'ra replied. To the Hyerne: "The woods. I figure the skirmishers'll come out to meet you, since they don't want you taking the phalanx in the side. There's Arkan cavalry up on those hills; if they move down, we'll give three trumpet calls. You retreat sharpish, we'll handle them."

The Hyerne nodded and repeated back the orders to acknowledge. She had a jewelled Imperial longsword across her back, and a hastily repainted steel helmet that had obviously once protected some *Aitzas*.

"Sova, and you-with-the-unpronounceable-name-that-sounds-like-a-sneeze," Shkai'ra said, "stay here by the standard. If we engage, keep in the second rank. And *listen* for the commands, Sova: I'm expecting *you* to set an example."

The Hyerne ran ahead into position beside her standard, a dolphin leaping over a staff, and gave a long shrill cry. Her troops sprang up head-high from their crouch, howling in answer, slamming spears against shields three times, *whamp-whamp-whamp*. The thundercracks echoed across the fields towards the wood, and before the sound of the last died the Hyerne were charging at a bounding run through the waist-high wheat, plumes nodding, whetted spearheads glinting, cocked back over their right shoulders. Their shrieking war-cry was like files on metal, endless.

Scarlet and steel glinted along the edge of the woods as the Arkan skirmishers came forward to the edge of the undergrowth at the foot of the trees. The Hyerne infantry commander barked; the run of the first line changed to a sideways crab-step. Another shout: heavy javelins flew. Barbed Arkan darts answered, flying on a higher arch. The second line of Hyerne ran through the first, threw; the third did likewise, and the first were ready again. The next flight of Arkan spears was ragged, and men in scarlet tunics burst out of the brush to engage hand-to-hand.

"Stupid," Shkai'ra said, as their charging line staggered under a hail of spears. She handed Sova the binoculars. "See: the Hyerne had less shelter, but all their ranks could throw. The towhairs couldn't take the iron. They should have fallen back, where the Hyerne had to come to them on their own ground. At a guess I'd say their commander couldn't bear to run away from women. Asshole."

The Arkan light infantry had chainmail vests, small round shields faced with steel and double-edged short-swords; but the Hyerne were twice as numerous, and had a bounding agility the Imperials could not match. Through the glasses Sova saw an Arkan face spring out, teeth bared in a grin of tension as he backed before two black women whose spears licked out like the tongues of snakes, striking sparks from the surface of shield and sword . . . something flickered behind him, skin-brown and steel bright, his mouth and eyes popped open, stunned, and he was gone. For an instant all she could see were backs and three spearbutts jerking up and down. *Yeee-yeee-yeee*, the maddened battlecries came yipping across the distance. Shkai'ra giggled; that cut off as she took the glasses back and turned them to the heights above.

About a hundred, coming over the hill. Half her own numbers, but in full suits of articulated steel plate enameled in scarlet and gold, their harness almost as good as the Zak-made suit she'd had done up in F'talezon; big men on stocky white horses eighteen hands high, long lances in their right hands and kite-shaped shields with the eagle and sun on their left arms; longswords on their hips, axes or warhammers at their saddlebows. The Sunborn Elite, finest of the Empire's strike-cavalry. Even Arko couldn't equip and support all that many troops like this, but it was a *big* empire ... and even a hundred here-and-now was two kilometers of bad news.

"Ahh ... khyd-hird ... what do we do about *them?*"

"Run like hell, if we could." She turned to the trumpeter. "Sound off." The man put the long brass instrument to his lips and sounded three sharp blasts. "Again."

The Arkan cavalry was coming down the hill at a steady walk, no point in speeding up until they finished threading their way through the woods. What was left of their infantry had run for the woods; Shkai'ra could see the Hyerne officers calling, pushing or kicking them back from pursuit. The Arkans formed up, less about a score of dead and twice that of wounded, the fortunate being carried away on crossed spears between four comrades. The unfortunate were efficiently finished off by Hyerne.

"Bows forward!" Shkai'ra shouted. "Blunt wedge. Walk-march, *trot!*"

Ragged, ragged. She threw up her hand about two hundred meters from the woods; most of the Slaughterers swung to a halt, but here and there a horse kept going for a few paces. There were collisions, cursing, the outraged neighing of mounts shouldered in the haunch and the vengeful commands of sergeants promising punishment-drill.

"Dress line, you shitheads!" she yelled, and pulled her wheelbow out of its case. *I used to enjoy this sort of thing,* she thought, as her stomach muscles pulled tight; she clamped her knees against Hotblood's flanks. *funfunfun-fun,* the Ri thought. She let his exhilaration wake hers, skinning back her teeth as her arm remembered the twofold sensation of a saber-edge thudding home in meat and grating on the bone beneath.

"Sova. If those lobster-backs up there get time to build momentum, they'll hit us the way a sledgehammer hits a bowl of eggs," she said, conscious of the throaty tone of her voice. "We've got to either hit them before they can move, or peck at them from out of range. Watch."

The Hyerne were trotting by; Shkai'ra cast a sharp glance right, but the Arkan crossbowmen on the flank of the pike-hedge were keeping ranks, out of range and unlikely to break formation. On Hyerne spear-points were a few heads, including one belonging to an *Aitzas,* by the length of the fighting-braid, and many more sets of jiggling testicles. The Hyerne did *not* like the "purification" ritual of Arko, which involved slicing off every girl's clitoris at the age of seven.

"Nice work," Shkai'ra said, looking down. The Hyerne leader's brown skin glistened with sweat and blood, some of it from superficial cuts on her legs and right arm, mostly from the captured longsword that she twitched negligently back and forth.

"Want keep crop, kill the rats," she replied, grinning.

"Hold your troops in reserve. I'm going to try and stop them cold. Pile in if we do."

The Hyerne pulled her swordblade through a rag held in her left hand. "Pile in, yes."

"Even stalled, those lobster-shells have too much of an advantage," Shkai'ra muttered too low for the Hyerne to hear. She twisted in the saddle. "Sova, remember, do *not* break ranks. You, Sneeze-name," she continued to the Yeoli boy, shifting into an execrable pidgin of that language.

"Stay by her, behind me. Savvy?" He acknowledged with a stab of his hand, palm up, and a crisp "*Tai, kras!*"

The trampled bush along the edge of the woods shook as the big Arkan horses shouldered their way through, placing their feet with the nervous care horses took on uncertain ground. Their heads wore steel chamfrons, their chests, steel pectorals blazoned with the sun-clasping Eagle. Sunlight hammered back from scarlet and gold enamel, from the three razor-honed edges of each pyramidal lance-head, from a jewelled sword-hilt or silver-plated bridle.

"Five shafts, *shoot!*" Shkai'ra barked.

The bow slid up, pressing against her hand as she drew; the pressure of the string on her thumb-ring dropped off as the wheels flipped and levered against the weight of the stave. A flat snap, and the arrow twinkled, turned down at midpoint, and she could hear the head punch into the neck-armor of the Arkan she'd aimed for, wearing a fancy plumed helmet. Others fell; horses ran plunging as they were hit. But the steady movement out of the woods continued, the Imperial cavalry deploying in a two-deep formation.

"Trumpeter, sound *charge*," Shkai'ra called, dropping her bow back into the case. The note rang out high and brassy-sweet, and the Alliance horse sprang forward with a single war-howl.

She tightened her grip on Hotblood, bracing her feet; the Ri squealed, wind whipping his silver mane, and even then horses on either side shied slightly. The consciousness of woman and Ri merged, a single mind with two nodes. The shield slid off her back and her left arm reached through the grips, the lance lifted out of the scabbard; out of the corners of her eyes she could see the others' long shafts slanting down. Under the continuous trumpet note, hooves fell like muffled thunder on the root-laced dirt.

Halfway there, and the Arkans were deployed. *Too late, you should've sent out a half-troop to screen while you got into line, shitheads,* Shkai'ra thought tightly, bringing her lance around to point over Hotblood's head at the man she had chosen. Their trumpet sang, and there was a ripple of movement down the Imperial line as the cavalrymen snapped down their visors, blank ovals of scarlet steel with a slit for the eyes and a pattern of holes over the mouth, emblazoned with a rayed sun in gold. Another call, and they lowered their lances and clapped heels to their mounts with a shout. The big horses jumped off their haunches, slowly building toward what would be an earth-shaking gallop.

Horse noses came up on either side of Shkai'ra; Sova and her Yeoli. "Keep back, second rank, you don't fucking have lances!" she shouted. Target. Red-lacquered armor, chain and plate. Two-meter lance, oval shield. Close enough now to see details, a hammered-out dint in a shield's face, the dapple of a white's neck. A helmet plumed with eagle feathers dyed red bending toward her; a hint of blue eyes. *We're at full gallop, they're not much more than standing . . .* Floating gallop, Hotblood's pace smoother and more ground-hugging than a horse's. She laughed, braced her feet and swung the point down.

CRASH. All along the line, the heavy blacksmith sound of lances hitting steel, *tung-chung,* or the lighter shivering clang if the curved surfaces shed the blow. The Arkan's point banged off her shield, no force behind it. Hers took him on the gorget, *pink* and a hard feeling as it struck the metal, soft *punk* as the lancehead shoved the plate aside and he went over the crupper of his horse, impact slamming her back against the rear of the saddle and the stirrups. His horse twisted and went down, neighing as Hotblood shouldered it. Thrashing hooves. Crack, her lance snapped; she threw it aside and swept out her saber, keening the shrill Kommanz war-cry through her teeth.

Sova was at handstrokes with an Arkan, her arm jolting at the force of the blows from the long straight Imperial sword, her young face set with determination. Echera-e came up on Sova's other side and jabbed the Arkan under his armpit, and she struck the way Shkai'ra had taught her, up under the chin without hesitating. Then she sat there while his weight pulled him off the point, as if frozen in fascination with having killed.

"*Move*, girl!" Now another was at the Kommanza, boot to boot, hammering, sword, shield, sword. The Arkan's horse, an uncut stallion, bugled and reared to chop at Hotblood with ironshod hooves; the Ri twisted in, weasel-quick, and sank his fangs into the thick base of the neck. Shkai'ra locked shields and clinched, tilted her saber to let his longsword flow down it with an unmusical *shinnng;* then punched up under his visor with the eagle's-head pommel. Something broke, and he crumpled out of the saddle. The horse fell across him, kicking, lifeblood pumping out of a wound the size of two clenched fists. Hotblood's neck worked as he swallowed a huge lump of flesh, and belched.

The Arkan banner was beyond; the four Imperial troopers around it came for Shkai'ra, the forward pair with swords, the rear thrusting overarm with lances. Hotblood hissed and his head weaved like a striking snake's; the first two Arkans split unexpectedly as their horses shied—into perfect positions to take her from either side. A sword thundered on her shield, hard enough to numb her arm and cut the metal rim; another beat at her blade, and the Ri was too blood-drunk to back. Lance-points poised to take her life.

Shkai'ra saw them cock back, one man grinning as he saw her hands too full to stop it, and the knowledge of her own death ran through her as cold as steel. *Zaik dammit, Megan* needs *me!* she shouted in rage.

Something hissed past her ear, *shhhup* above the scrap-metal clamor of battle; a black Hyerne javelin-shaft stood stiff in the eye-slit of the Arkan before her, and he fell back limply off his horse. The other dropped his lance to draw sword and cut at the Hyerne woman who darted in to swing a hamstringing axe at his mount's hock. The long blade caught her in the neck and went halfway through the shoulder, catching in bone and nearly dragging the Arkan from the saddle. Shrieking, another leaped at him from the other side, *climbed* him, touching stirrup and knee and waist, wound her legs around his torso and jerked his chin back to slit his throat from ear to ear.

In the pause Shkai'ra glanced around. Arkans were going down all over. Charging, with the terrible weight of a mount under him, a horseman was a deadly weapon; standing, he was simply a soldier who couldn't turn around very quickly, atop a moving and very stupid object. Shkai'ra turned her shield like a giant disk, forcing the lance stuck in it out of the Imperial's hand; it fell loose from the plywood and leather to clatter to the ground. Just in time; the swordsman on the other side had nearly disarmed her. Hotblood caught the man's shield-arm in his fangs, and she gave him a solid overarm cut across one gauntlet. Minztan layer-forged steel cut the thin sheet metal, and he went over with a cry of despair.

She hammered free of the press and thrust her helmet back, standing in the stirrups. The Hyerne were going for the Arkan horses, hamstringing, slitting girths, stabbing bellies. But these Imperials had more going for them than weight and metal, no ox-witted *okas* conscripts here; dismounted, they still had superior weapons and armor, and were proving murderously quick and skilled at foot combat as well. Knots of them drew together, back-to-back, hacked their way toward the woods and flowed together to make bigger groups, locking shield to shield. Light-armed Hyerne were thrown back from shieldwalls and long swords.

It would cost too heavily to overwhelm them, and she had accomplished the mission; neither the Arkan skirmishers nor these lancers were going to support the pike-phalanx in the gap. Her trumpeter was still mounted. "Sound *retreat-and-rally*," she told him, thumping him on the shoulder to emphasize it.

The melee was a mess, twisting stamping horses, threshing swords above it, dust and bits of grass rising up and wounded humans and horses threshing or crawling on the ground, and Hotblood's unearthly squeal over it all, as he grabbed a wounded Arkan by the back of the neck and shook him like a rat; Shkai'ra could feel the quasi-sexual rush of pleasure he felt as the bone snap. No one was obeying fast enough. "Retreat, Zaikdammit!" she screamed. Bukangkt was there, a cut across one cheek of his half-Lakan face; between them they got the others to pull back.

The Hyerne went loping among the Slaughterers, some with enough energy left to whoop and leap, others hanging grimly onto stirrup-leathers or lowered hands. The wounded came draped over cavalry horses, some on spare Arkan mounts if a friend had had time to grab the reins; the Hyerne carried some on chair-hands, running despite their burdens. Anyone too badly hurt to get up or call for help was just out of luck. Suddenly there was time to notice the dryness in her mouth, the way her armor squeezed at her ribs . . . she forced her breathing slow and deep, hawked and spat.

The remnants of the Imperial horse were pulling back too, but she could see light infantry moving in the bush, sun twinkling on their barbed javelins. Sova and her Yeoli were too far back, a wounded rider between them, his feet dragging and their swordhands under his armpits. She reined in, swearing. *Good riding, though.* They handed him over to someone with an extra horse—and wheeled back for the bloodied field.

Shit . . . ! It looked safe, the Arkan cavalry were all gone; some friend of Sneeze-name was lying on the field, no doubt. *Nobody knows the difference between courage and stupidity at that age.* She stood in the stirrups and shouted at them—too far. Though not too far to hear the trumpeter blowing "retreat"; it wasn't just stupidity, but disobedience in the face of the enemy. Cold anger grew in her.

"Rally them a hundred meters further back," she said to Bukangkt, then spurred toward the two. Sova was going to hug the post for this, and Sneeze-name beside her . . . if they lived. *Zaik and Baiwun hear me,* she thought. *I'll keep her alive, if I have to kill her myself to do it.*

The pair had another body slung over Sova's horse, and cantered back towards the Alliance cavalry, glancing over their shoulders now and then, *zteafakaz* casual. Shkai'ra shouted and waved, seeing what they hadn't: the barbed javelin arching high from the woods, plunging down.

A horse sacrifice to you, Victory-Begetter, she prayed, helpless, as she rocked into a gallop toward them. "Heads up, *heads up!*" Zaik, or Glitch, godlet of mischance, heard her even if they didn't; the weapon plunged over Sova's shoulder and into Sneeze-name's horse, just behind the saddle. It gave a huge buck; he was thrown, landed badly, lay still.

And Sova actually started to dismount.

"*Keep moving—I'll get him!*" Shkai'ra shouted, close enough now to clout the girl on the side of the helmet. She passed at a gallop, down with one foot out of the stirrups, snatched the Yeoli's collar. "Uhnnn." *Heavy.* He was dead weight. She heaved him over her saddlehorn and Sova fell in beside her as they galloped back to the rest, face full of shock.

"Is he all right? *Khyd-hird,* is he all right?"

The Kommanza could see movement beyond her troop as it formed up, pike-points and helmets and dust. A Yeoli heavy-foot regiment, coming up at the double and deploying at the run. *Impressive.* Their pike-points came down with a long ripple, and the archers fanned out to either side. There was another regiment double-timing up behind them, Schvait in black armor and tunics, and a pair of springalds bumping along in the vanguard; light catapults with horizontal throwing-arms powered by skeins of twisted ox-sinew. The Alliance foot halted just out of crossbow range, staying motionless as Arkan points came down, the Imperials spitting on their hands and bracing their pikes. Waiting for the arrow-storm from longbows that outranged their own missile-troops' weapons.

Whack. A vicious sound, as the first of the springalds was swiveled around and cut loose. It threw a glass sphere that caught fire in mid-flight, then arched down to draw a streak of inextinguishable flame through the Arkan ranks. Clingfire, naphtha and tar, sulphur and phosphorus and pitch. *Whack:* the other springald fired, and trumpet and drums brayed from the group around the eagle-standard. The Arkans gave a deep guttural shout, loud enough to drown the screams of men being roasted alive in their armor, and charged.

The Yeolis charged to meet them, giving their war-cry, *"Ai-yae-ohhhhhh!"* The flat snap of crossbows resounded under the musical massed thrum-and-whistle of longbow fire, javelins rattling through the air, the Imperials screaming out *"Kellin, kellin."* The impact was a massive rolling sound, thudding in chest and stomach as eighteen-foot polearms struck with both sides at a dead run, thousands behind them. Both front ranks just disappeared, and the ripple threw warriors off their feet for scores of meters back into each formation; then they were locked, a giant tumbling street-brawl under the bristling pikes of the rear ranks. File-closers and decurions moved in with halberds and two-handed swords; warriors with shortswords and daggers clenched in their teeth crawled and rolled under the ranks too tightly locked to move, and stabbed and sliced from below.

Another Imperial rejin was moving down the road from where it had waited concealed, as the Schvait formed to deploy on the Yeoli's right flank. The springalds kept up their steady bucking *whack-whack,* clingfire globes making smoky tracks through the arching grey storm of missiles that sped both ways above the packed fight.

We're safe for the moment. Even Gold-bottom Chevenga wasn't going to be able to finesse a meeting engagement; this dance would last for a while. Those lancers weren't coming down to mix it in, either. Two many had lost their mounts, or their lives; the survivors would stay up on the hills, now, and keep the Yeoli foot from pursuing too hard when the Imperial infantry pulled back. *The Arkans are learning how to retreat,* I think. She had more immediate business.

"You insubordinate little shit!" She struck Sova across the side of the helmet again, harder, making a sound like a cracked bell; the girl kept her silence, and backed her horse out of reach. But her eyes went wide; now she realized what she'd done. *I've never campaigned with a child before, it's enough to turn your hair white.* "I *know* you're sheep-fucking brave, now show some brains. It's the trickster god's own *miracle* you weren't killed! Godsdammit, I want you at my funeral twenty years from now, not me at yours tomorrow!"

"Ve couldn't *leave* him, he's one of Echera-e's childhood friends!" The girl's Thanish accent always came out more, when she was excited. *Now she'll change the subject;* Shkai'ra was getting to know Sova well. "Khyd-hird, is he all right? Ve've got to get him to a Haian!"

Shkai'ra looked down at the Yeoli, still lying across her saddle. Bleeding from the nose, big graze across the side of his face, but probably no broken bones from the way his body moved. She peeled back an eyelid, then the other. The pupils reacted, but one was a little bigger than the other.

"Concussion," she said. "Not too bad." Her voice dropped, steady and just loud enough to carry a few feet over the enormous noise of combat from the road. She fixed the girl's eyes with hers. "What did I tell you when you arrived, about discipline?"

Sova's lips thinned. "I know. I'm under army law."

"Correct, military apprentice. And the punishment for disobeying a clear order in the face of the enemy is flogging. In this army, flogging up to falling at the discretion of the commander." Sova blinked; no doubt she'd heard tales of what that felt like, from Yeolis. Shkai'ra waited, expression bleak. "Given your youth, the circumstances and whatever, I'll commute it to fifteen strokes. Consider yourself on report, trooper. Now take that one—" she jerked a thumb at the casualty across Sova's saddlebow, the cause of the trouble "—and Sneeze-name doesn't-take-orders number two here back to the Haians. When he wakes up, you can decide whether you'd rather have your strokes right away or beside him when he's fit, because he's getting the same. Dismissed!"

Sova found her hands shaking, as she helped lift Echera-e, who was still limp, onto a litter. *He's so pale.* Suddenly she wanted to throw up. *Wake up, wake up, love . . .* The cool sense in her wondered why the fear. *He might die. I'm going to get flogged. He's going to get flogged if he doesn't die. I just fought* —the feeling was utterly divorced from thoughts or the truth of the present, that it was over and she was safe— *all of the above. Wake up, livling. If he dies I want to say I carried him,* she thought, and tried to keep her arms steady on the litter-grips. *No.* Khyd-hird *said it wasn't too bad.*

There was always a rolling infirmary near the head of the great column now, since the harassment had increased. She scanned for the cart with the double white-striped flag. A moan came from the litter. *"Mamaiyana, Tyizil . . ."* The name of his horse. "Sovee." The litter moved as his weight shifted; she looked over her shoulder to see him lean over its edge, and throw up onto the ground. *"Kyuzai,* escuse me, ohhhhhhhh . . ." He fell back.

"Keep still, Echerry," she said. "I'm here. You'll be all right and so will Ansena and we won and we're almost at the infirmary." She wondered how much he understood.

The Alliance army had a good hundred Haians, unheard of for a military force. *Because the Arkans broke the Compact and invaded them. This is their way of fighting for their freedom; if we take the Empire, Chev-*

enga will give Haiu Menshir back its independence. Gentle Haian hands lifted the two litters, quickly examined, touching necks, pressing wrists.

Ansena would need surgery; they took him straight into the cart. Echera-e they checked as Shkai'ra had, but more tenderly. "Concussion," the healer, a woman said. "Must stay lying; we put heem een cart and look efter heem today. He ken stay een hees own bed tonight, probebly, but should have someone weeth heem to keep heem still, end quiet. Come beck when we set camp."

"Their names and unit?" the Yeoli clerk with the waxboard said briskly, as the healer moved on, busy. Sova told him, and then opened her mouth, but he cut her off with a chop of his pen. "Healers and wounded only in the carts on march," he said, as if reading her mind. "They'll be fine, you've done what you can, off with you now." She wanted to argue, the pull on her heart like a claw to stay here, but the clerk looked annoyed. She'd be in more trouble if she disobeyed here, too.

I'm going to be in the infirmary next, she thought, dejectedly. At least the gut-fear of fighting was gone, faded while her mind had been on other things. *Fifteen strokes. I have to choose, now or later, with him ... later. I'm going to see him again before he's fit, so if I get it done now he'll know what he's in for.*

Now what? She'd been dismissed; no more fighting. *I don't want to any more today, anyway*, she thought. *Though there's no way I'll admit that to anyone.* She examined the feeling, turned it over in her mind. The memories came back, so fresh as to be barely memories, yet suddenly distant and changed, as if from a dream or another life: feeling through the grip of her sword the Arkan's throat muscles clamp on the blade; the wounded, clasping hands to bloody spots, knowing they were Arkans' meat if they weren't carried off, calling to her or screaming incoherently; Echera-e landing wrong as his horse threw him. ... *Does this mean I'm a coward? But I'm just fourteen. In Yeola-e people don't fight until they're sixteen. I'm not a coward, Shkai'ra said I'm sheep-fucking brave; I'm just young. I'll get tougher and it'll get easier.* She wheeled away from the cart to find the Elite section, and *zhymata.*

Well, thought Megan, as she prepared to bed down. *Clear ground, we march. Obstructed, we march through them.* She counted off days in her head as she unpinned her braids and brushed out her calf-long hair. *At the rate we're going, we'll be there in two and a half months or so.* Then, remembering the frequent fate of the best-laid plans: *at the rate we're going.* Many things could change that.

Shkai'ra was off partying with her unit; Sova was preparing her own bed. The Thane-girl had been silent and gaunt-eyed all evening as she did the chores, worrying about her Yeoli lover and being flogged.

"Good night, Sovee." She crouched to slip inside her tent. The girl answered the same quietly. *I hope Shkai'ra isn't too long . . . what in Halya is that?*

A patch of white clung to the inside of the tent-flap. Careful, mindful of plots and tricks, she looked before touching. A bit of paper, pinned to the canvas: holding it only with her claws, not the pads of her fingers, she unpinned and unfolded it.

The words were written in a tidy Arkan hand, superior-to-inferior inflection.

> Whitlock: Meet me in the copse downwind of the Enchian Elite latrine, tonight when the moon is straight above. I have your son, Lixand called Rasas, with the four moles in a square on his right shoulder-blade. His life and my cover are as twined vines, sworn upon my poison tooth. Let us chat.

Book II: Venture

XII

"Raise yeh full copper," said the one-armed man. "Hey, boy of gold! Put my bet in for me."

He must have a really good hand, Rasas thought, as he moved the copper chain from the man's pile to the center of the table, *if he isn't even willing to let go of it to put his money in himself. Still, I didn't think a hand where none of the cards look like any of the others either in numbers of spots or color was any good . . . maybe it's because I'm not good enough at telling the symbols.*

Rasas wasn't sure where exactly they were, except that it was the basement of a decrepit country house, the foundation-stones seeping water, and out-city. He was supposed to stay in the basement, but sometimes they let him come upstairs where it was dry and warm. He could even sleep there, as long as it was in one of their beds—and he'd peeked out a crack in a shutter. Huge wide fields, such as he'd never seen before in his life, except in his dreams.

"You know why we call you boy of gold?" one of the others said. There were five around the table, *solas* and

197

fessas gone to seed and fat, with uncombed beards and
stained jerkins. Watching them play, Rasas suspected
they'd never had other skills, though when he thought
about it he realized they must have. Patappas, for
instance, would still be fighting if he had two arms.

"Because you're going to make us all boys of gold!"
All five burst out into guffawing, their loudness enhanced
by the wine they were drinking. It was almost a ritual,
the joke. The first time they'd said it, he'd had the sudden image of five gilt statues; then he'd understood, they
meant _rich_.

He'd heard stories of kidnappings before, of a favorite
boy being snatched and held until his owner, pining for
him, coughed up a huge ransom. He'd always thought it
would be an adventure, imagining a handsome highwayman in satin and gold heaving him up over his noble
destrier and galloping off into the country. While they
were in hiding, the highwayman, struck by Rasas's plight,
would change his mind and refuse to return him to Nuninibas, even when the lord, desperate, offered a million
gold chains. The highwayman, who had dark eyes as well,
would adopt Rasas as his son, kidnap and adopt Ardas as
well so they really were brothers, and take them to his
secret estate in Kassabria or Korsardiana. He'd teach
them how to use a sword, and they'd raid evil _Aitzas_ and
give the money to poor _okas_, like the green-dressed gang
in the old story, and he'd be able to dress in suave satin
instead of pleasure boy's lace. No one would ever
smother him or Ardas again, and they'd live happily ever
after.

So he'd imagined it, at any rate. None of these men
quite fit the part; for one thing, they had no noble destrier, only a bow-backed old pony with a tangled ragged
mane. And they smelled, no surprise, since the house
didn't have a bath. They'd go off somewhere to bathe
only every few days, and he thought it must be in a river
or lake nearby, like the lowest of the poor. He only
bathed every few days too, when they brought him water,

which made his hair itch and him feel base and worthless, but at least he didn't have that rank grown-up smell.

Nor did they look about to refuse the ransom; rather, they slavered over the prospect of getting it, constantly. No matter; he'd just go home then and things would be as they'd been before. They hadn't hurt him much taking him. It had just been a big hand waking him up, torch-light in his eyes, and then arms hefting him up over a shoulder, though they had knocked out the dancing boys' quarters guards; he noticed them lying sprawled as he passed. He'd wanted to ask politely, "Sirs, will you take Ardas too, if you please? He doesn't weigh much, less than me," but they'd threaten to slit his throat if he said anything (part of the whole tradition of kidnapping, he knew), so he hadn't. They'd put him in a flour-sack to get him up the cliff-lift. "Give your oath you won't move or make a sound, or we'll sap you," they'd said, so he had given his oath, and then kept it as he felt the lift raise him smoothly up.

Now, he wasn't suffering unduly; they fed him enough that he wasn't hungry, played with him, taught him card tricks, and didn't make him serve them any more than Master's guests had; in fact, being lower-born, they were more gentle, never smothering him. The worst trouble he'd ever got into was when, standing behind Glikasonas at the card-table, he'd blurted, "Four cards that all have one spot, that's good, isn't it?", and there was good reason, he understood now, for that. He missed Ardas, sometimes desperately; but perhaps it was for the better, since, because the kidnappers weren't dashing high-waymen, the smaller boy might be frightened. *I'll see him again, and O my Humble Serving God, will I have a story, heh heh!* And these fellows would be rich; he didn't mind that, really. They all looked as if they'd been poor longer than anyone should have to be.

XIII

She read it four times, disbelieving.

The writer sounded sickeningly professional. *His life and my cover are as vines* ... Arkan tradecraft talk: it meant this person was sending a sign back to his accomplices putting a stop order on enacting the threat at regular times, to preserve himself; if he died, the stop order wouldn't go through, and the kidnappers would ... *Lixand-mi. Sworn upon my poison tooth* ... Arkan operatives usually had them—Mahid operatives, *always*—and would use them if captured. That meant if she tried to haul him off to Ikal for truth-drugging, he'd die, the stop order wouldn't go through, and ... *Lixand-mi* ...

Her mind ran through possibilities. *Did I ever mention to anyone, his moles?* There was no one she could remember. *A bluff? Even if it is, the* rokatzk *knows damn well I have to assume it isn't, just in case.*

The old feeling of chains came, *so far and no further, slamming against bounds someone else set. Invisible chains of being poor, oak links and cuffs stapled to a solid plank floor, tight-pack on a Fehinnan slaver* ... Her

eyes clenched shut as she tried to deny memories, feelings . . . *No*, she thought. *I'd left those behind, I'd almost
forgotten them.* Her eyes snapped open at the next
thought.

Whoever left the note might be watching. Her gaze
flicked from one nearby lounger to the next. *I won't give
him satisfaction. Him. It has to be a him, if it's an Arkan.*
She shook herself, as if shaking off all she was feeling,
ran a smooth hand over her hair. *Calm. Be calm. Be ice.
I've been that before. Lady Koru, hear me, help me.* She
leaned back stretching, and got up to saunter casually
over to the fire for another cup of chai, then back to the
tent.

Some part of her, the old, fearful Megan, longed to
shriek and run straight into Shkai'ra's arms, wanted desperately to leave this all to someone else. She held onto
the tentpole to steady herself. *Calm. That part of me I
know too well. I'll cry myself out when I have the luxury
to, once Lixand is safe.* Shkai'ra would be back before
midnight, since the army would march tomorrow, no
need to go running out to tell her.

She sat down and forced her breathing calm, trying to
reach for some of the *manrauq* exercises, cold, formal,
comfortingly empty of the emotions rushing through
her . . .

"Kh'eeredo? Megan, what's the matter?" Shkai'ra, far
earlier than she should have been here. Brought by a
hunch, or what was left of the linking of minds they'd
had on the ice last year, triggered by the Blue Mage's
manrauq-blast? Sometimes it came back, like the
memory-residue of a hallucinogen taken years before;
usually in moments of strong emotion. "I'm here,
kh'eeredo."

"Someone left me this note, pinned on the tent." She
translated in a whisper, looking up as the firelight painted
the planes of Shkai'ra's face, trying to be calm. "Somehow I don't think he wants to talk about the new taxes
in Brahvniki."

Shkai'ra's face didn't change. "Probably not," she said drily. "So, we'll have a little diversion. Glitch visits again ... Oh, well. This war was getting too easy anyway."

A smile forced itself onto Megan's lips. "You obviously haven't been sacrificing enough sheep."

Shkai'ra shrugged. "So. You get all the information you can from this ... *gentleman*, and we go from there."

Megan didn't answer immediately, listening to the fire crackle, the sound of a lap-harp drifting from the next campfire over. "Would you ..." She hesitated. "I'm feeling very cowardly about this." She flipped a hand, almost casually, claws flashing. "I feel as if I shouldn't be able to move this easily. It's almost obscene being this tied but free at the same time." She sighed, looking down at her spread fingers. "I'm not explaining this very well."

Shkai'ra's arms closed around her, pulled her in close. Megan resisted for a heartbeat, then let herself be drawn in. "I didn't get where I am by panicking," the Zak said quietly into Shkai'ra's shoulder.

"We've been in worse scrapes, love. Remember the alligators? To be eaten in such small bites ..." The Kommanza rubbed a knuckle along Megan's cheekbone.

"I know. I'll do what I have to." She looked up. "Careful: People will stop calling you a barbarian if you get this soft."

Shkai'ra chuckled. "But I am a barbarian—to anyone who deserves that shit."

Megan nodded. "So, I can't tear this pig-sucker into shreds ... *yet*."

It's you I smell, she thought, *not the latrine*. A tricky place for a clandestine meeting; no one would expect anyone to meet there. The copse was just far enough away from the privy itself to quietly talk without its many users hearing. Beeches, smooth-trunked with even branches; good climbing trees. She looked up, but saw no telltale dark shape. Wind pattered the leaves.

"As scheduled," a precise male voice said quietly, from

low, in Arkan. *The accent . . . Aitzas? Hardly, doing this work. He's faking it. Unless he's Mahid.* The robed figure had been sitting in the underbrush; now it rose, and leaned casually against a trunk. "You know, you're one person who is unmistakable, even in silhouette. Who else so short, with those curves . . . Well, never mind, we have business."

No. Not Mahid. They don't have a sense of humor. "I prefer to deal in Enchian," Megan said, in that language. "A more suitable tongue for business of any sort." *His face is in shadow, even if the moon came out clearer I wouldn't see it, here. He made sure of that. If I got truth-drugged again . . .*

"Indulge me, don't insult my nationality," the man said, still in Arkan, the inflection superior-to-inferior. The voice didn't even take on an edge. "I considered sending you one of the boy's fingers, but forbore, thinking you a subtle enough person that such brutality was unnecessary. Am I wrong? Are we communicating?"

"Quite," Megan said in Arkan, equal-to-equal. "And quite useless, since the last time I saw one of my son's fingers was eight years ago."

"Are you a fool? You couldn't know for sure it *wasn't* his. Not until you saw him again at any rate. Which is my intent."

The more I get him to say, the better chance I'll have of getting some scrap of information I can use. She took a step closer, sensed him tensing. "Having a poison tooth is one thing," she said. "*Using* it is quite another. I'm not sure you sound brave enough to do it."

"Eternal ecstasy in Celestialis receives the agent who gives himself in the moment he must," the voice answered without hesitation or apparent fear. "Eternal smothering in Hayel takes the one who fails to. Which would *you* choose?"

"You don't sound like a fanatic to me."

"Part pragmatic, part fanatic, that's what I've had to learn to be. Though I must admit nothing could impel me to be brave enough to do it more than the suggestion that I'm not . . . perhaps I'm not. And yet I might be. Rather a great uncertainty, I think, on which to stake the life of the only child you'll ever have, hmm?"

"Indeed." *I can't risk it. He's right. It's too much. You pig-sucker. You corpse-spawn* . . . She bit down on her rage, a teacher's voice echoing from a classroom in her memory: *Your emotions are cards to play, in negotiation; don't show your hand.* She forced calm out into trembling limbs.

"Not to be crass," she said. "But such a favor often calls for recompense, usually of similar worth."

"So crass . . . as usual with those who follow the merchant's profession." She detected a relaxing; natural, whether he had a poison tooth or not. "Actually, it's quite a bargain I offer you. How can it not be? Is there anything as important to you as your son's life? And freedom? I understand not . . . so how can it but be a sweet deal for you? You understand I offer not just his life but his freedom, and his delivery to yourself, too. It's all arranged, waiting only for a certain action from you."

"A certain action? Perhaps you'd deign to be more precise."

"You've been snippy," the Arkan said, a smile audible in his voice. "And got me in a contrary mood. *Guess.*"

Megan clenched her teeth. "Who do you want me to kill? There's no one I'm close to, I can think of, who Arko would want dead. Or is it just information?"

A quiet snicker cut the night air. "Perceptive . . . at least at first. You don't have and can't easily get information. But you have those claws, and those skills. And that determination; I've heard Megan Whitlock always finds a way."

"I'm out of practice murdering," she said, pretending boredom.

"Better brush up, then; a great shame it would be if you failed. I'll give you a hint, whom. One to whom you are not particularly attached. One to whom you are close enough to do it. One who trusts you." *I bet he enjoyed pulling the wings off flies when he was a boy*, thought Megan. *Who trusts me? They all do. I don't know that many . . . ohhhhhh shit.*

". . . and who absolutely *must die*."

As she breathed the name, she thought absurdly, *I'm pronouncing it right.* "Chevenga."

"Shefen-kas," he repeated. "Of course. Who else?" With the same amiable superior smoothness he'd affected all through, he added, "I'm not bothered about the difficulty of it. That's *your* problem. And one I have faith in your competence to solve. But I am not without patience, of course not. Consider it. I will get back to you."

I'm too old for this shit, Matthas thought. A good half-bead later, safe in his tent, in the section set apart for sellers, his hands were still shaking.

Once he *had* carried a poison tooth, in his early days in the field. *When I was young, fearless and expendable.* Now he had only a cavity filled with porcelain, de-venomed and fixed when he'd acquired too much experience to easily be thrown away, and a desk job. He remembered the first day without, the weight lifted of his shoulders bigger than he'd known, getting drunk, chewing nuts on *both* sides of his mouth . . .

But Megan Whitlock need not know he was no longer young, fearless and expendable. *Well, I am expendable, again. At least to Eforas.* That was all that counted. *Forget the humiliation*, he told himself, hard. *Forget that you don't deserve this, that you're only here through someone else's idiocy, against your own better judgment. Forget that it shouldn't be happening; that doesn't matter now. It is.*

As she had suspected, he wasn't sure he would be brave enough to use a poison tooth anymore. *Twenty years ago, it seemed so simple; I didn't fake my conviction, I didn't have to. Twenty years ago, before I knew all I know now.* Or was it just that as one got older, one got more attached to life since one had less of it left? He felt a certain relief that the matter was moot; all that was needful was that Whitlock believe him for long enough.

Which only means, he thought, watching his fingers tremble, and feeling the wet stickiness of his own armpit-sweat, *meeting in a place where she won't smell my fear, keeping my voice steady and my laugh light, never missing a comeback.* He laughed sickly. *Easy.*

"An Arkan looking to grow his hair down to his butt," Shkai'ra said drily. "Well, do you think he really does have a poison tooth? Or would use it?"

"Dammit, Shkai'ra, how the hell can I know? You think I wouldn't have told you if I had any inkling? Maybe he doesn't, I can't fish-gutted tell!" Megan bit back tears, took a deep breath, forced her voice down. "Love, I'm sorry." Shkai'ra squeezed her hand in wordless understanding. "He might not, but if he does . . . it's too much to risk." *If after everything I find out somehow he doesn't, I'll pull his testicles out through his mouth . . . over ten days . . .*

"So ambushing him and hauling him off to Gold-Dipped is out," said Shkai'ra. "And . . . well, oath or not, I'm somewhat disinclined to just go to *him* with it, too."

My thought again, love. She was thankful Shkai'ra had said it. If the Arkan's scheme were sophisticated enough that Chevenga's people—however many of them he was willing to call away from war missions—couldn't unravel it, he would sacrifice Lixand, whatever she said. *His country and himself, versus one child. He'd have no real choice.* "Yes," she said quietly. "I agree."

Shkai'ra sat with her back to the low-trimmed lantern at the inner end of the tent, eyes slitted in thought and her long fingers playing with the hilt of the sword across her lap. They had told Sova to absent herself for the night, which Megan had taken to suggesting now and then; she found the presence in the pup-tent an arm's length from theirs somewhat inhibiting. That and talking in Fehinnan, which nobody within a thousand kilometers knew, gave them fair security.

"I can't kill him, I can't capture him, I can't even bloody well *follow* him," Megan snarled, working her claws into the tentpost and making shavings of wood that patterned down on the canvas floor. "If I kill . . . if I do what he's asking me to . . . I can't trust him not to kill Lixand *anyway*, Lady Koru!"

We can't even be sure he hasn't already, Shkai'ra thought, but kept to herself; it would be throwing oil on the fire, pointlessly. *If he has* . . . Matthas might have been a little apprehensive if he could have seen her face then.

"Well, we have to proceed on the assumption that he will do as he promises," Megan said. "From what I've heard of Irefas, they generally do stick to their word for this kind of thing, so that they can keep doing it; he's got no particular reason *not* to. That we know of." She slammed a fist into the tent floor. "If he knows his business, there'll be watchers in hiding around the meeting place. What we need is a spy that can follow him invisibly. Or flying," she said ironically. "And even the most powerful witch I know can't fly. . . ." She trailed off, looking into the air over Shkai'ra's head as if she could see straight through the canvas, smiling. "*Fishhook* can."

The Kommanza's fierce concentration slackened in bewilderment for a moment, and then she smiled cruelly. "Who no Arkan would suspect of anything but being out looking for dinner. Can you control her that well?"

"Control her—a *cat*? No; I'd have to convince her he was worth following."

Megan pressed one hand to her middle, then pushed her fingers carefully through her loose hair. "I'm nervous. I want to be moving . . . I'll sit. We'll think this out." She sat down cross-legged and put her hands flat on her knees.

Shkai'ra leaned forward eagerly. "If you could get Fish-

hook to follow him—say, convince her he's got food—she'd
lurk around there of her own will. We'll have to be very
careful, one suspicion"—she made a gesture across her
throat. "But with luck, we could at least find his base."

Megan covered her eyes with the heels of her hands
and sat still for a while. "All right. *If* Fishhook comes up
with something. If not, then I'll have to consider . . ."

"Killing Gold-Arse. For your child. *Ia.* If you stalled
long enough before you did it, it wouldn't matter to the
war; it'll have enough of its own power without him, and
the world won't lose so much. I know things like that
bother you. Of course . . ." Her light-hearted grin faded
some. "It would mean breaking your strength-oath. Well,
we are anyway, by not telling."

It doesn't even cross her mind that he's a friend. She
shook off the feeling of Chevenga's face and shoulders
under her studying hands. *Only two iron-cycles ago, we
swore,* Megan thought. *Lady Koru, forgive me. I would
only do this for kin.* "We'll see what Fishhook finds."

The next note appeared on Megan's saddle-bags just
before the march began, two days later.

She crumpled it in her fist and thrust it into her pouch
to destroy later. *Why am I not surprised that he has an
affinity for meeting near latrines,* she thought sourly, and
swung the bags across her pony.

"Fishhook!" She offered her folded cloak as a sad-
dlepad in front of her. "Here, puss puss, here!" Orange
tabby bat-wings flipped and folded primly as the cat settled and started to wash. Megan yawned, wishing her
night forays left her with a bit more sleeping time.

"Form u-u-u-up!" The pony ambled over to its place,
rolling an eye. Megan stroked the wing-cat until she was
a sprawled bundle of purring fur, wing-tips bobbing gently to the pony's walk.

Playlater? She thought at Fishhook. The cat's mind
was fuzzy, half snoozing. *Finehunt, follow. Sneaky.* Fishhook shook her head, waking up from her snooze,

blinked. Megan desisted then, but took time several more times during the day to repeat the thought-threads to the wing-cat. *Have to get her to think it's her own idea.*

They camped. Shkai'ra asked no questions. Not that Megan showed anything but a closed face; but in the years that the Kommanza had lived with the Zak, she'd watched, with hope, Megan's habitual expression change from closed-in suspicion, a mask, to a more serene, open look. When this sort of thing happened, the mask came back. Megan kept Fishhook on her shoulder, one wing draped over her shoulder and tail wrapped firmly around one wrist, primarily through slipping her slivers of boneless pork.

"Meoew?" Fishhook pawed at Megan's cheek. *more-good nobonessmacklick?*

Later. A hard concept for the cat, future; she meowed peevishly. Megan refused wine, drinking only a swallow or two of the cider, her stomach knotting against food. She'd only taken meat to bribe the cat. She pressed a hand flat to her stomach. *I'll eat later, too, after I get back.*

When it was dark, she put on her full cloak and hid the wing-cat cradled in her arms. Fishhook was content enough to travel that way.

When she got close to the latrine, before she stepped out of shadow, she thought at the cat: *followman, goodmeat.* She could feel Fishhook sniffing. The cat sneezed— *I don't blame you, in this stink, beast*—and crawled out of the cloak, swooping in a low arc into the bushes. *I hope you want to follow. Koru, Goddess, make her want to follow him.*

She stepped out into a patch of starlight.

"So." The smooth whisper came from her left and in front of her. "Well?"

She sighed. "You leave me little choice."

"Who has choices in the face of duty? I must serve my Empire, you must retrieve your child. War makes barbarians of us all, and someone's life is always lost, ground between its wheels; this way we may ensure it is neither yours nor your child's nor mine. Hah! It should have been *his* sooner; it would have been far fewer others'."

Koru, a rokatzk *philosopher.* "I understand your point of view, Arkan," she said coldly, as though resigned. "I, of course, don't necessarily agree, having suffered enough at Arkan hands. It will take some time. I imagine you don't care how I do it; so I choose to be subtle. You understand the necessity, I'm sure. I wouldn't want to free my son to leave him an orphan moments later."

"Of course, of course, of course," he said, like an overly syrupy party host. "Though I am well-apprised of your superior capability in such matters; no one covers a getaway better than an illusionist. An illusionist—!"

For once the Arkan's smoothness was broken, interrupted, it seemed, by his own thought; but in a moment he'd put it aside or filed it away, and went on. "And you understand that while time may not be of the essence for you—an eight-day wouldn't come between you and your child—it is very much of the essence for *us*, with *him* rapidly coming between us and our future. How long did you have in mind?"

"An iron-cycle is roughly what I'll need," she said, sending a questing thought for Fishhook's mind. Nothing. "That should still give your army time to break the Alliance, if they're as good as they're supposed to be."

"My *dear*." His voice picked up a scolding edge. "First of all, stop the childish little stabs at my race. You don't want to try my patience unnecessarily, *believe me*. Second: all the rest of Arko may kid itself about how this war has gone, and will go. You and I are not such fools, so don't think to beguile me with *that*. And an iron-cycle is a damn long . . . what in Hayel is an iron-cycle?"

Whoops, thought Matthas. *Almost gave away I've lived on the Brezhan, there!*
An illusionist . . . the visions in camp . . .

* * *

"Thirty days." Megan pursed her lips. "Look, Arkan, how do I know you won't snuff my son just to clear up loose ends even if I do what you want? You ask me just to trust you, with no reassurances."

"If you won't trust me, there's no point in talking further; I shall just cease sending the order I'm sending, and never think of it again. But let me reassure you. First, I will swear the oath sacred to all: Second Fire come if I lie, I will deliver your son to you unharmed if you succeed at what I ask, kill him if you fail. Second, do I need to explain why it would be bad tradecraft to doublecross you?"

"No. I'm familiar with the principles. Fine, I'll trust you, but if you *do* betray me . . . I've gone a long way before, for revenge."

"As would be understandable and just."

"I need an iron-cycle to set things up properly."

"Thirty days. Why so long?"

"Do you think I carry subtle poisons with me?"

"Of course you do. What else would you be doing for Shefen-kas? You think I haven't done my homework on you? Besides, I don't *care how* you kill him, knife in the back or duel of honor, so long as you kill him *dead*, and *soon*."

"I already told you, I won't leave my child an orphan. An iron-cycle is what I need!"

"You're telling me it would take you thirty days to acquire a *poison?*"

"*And* establish my route home."

"That's just a matter of thinking it out! You aren't convincing me, Whitlock. I know you'd love to stall, to find some way to squirm out of this; you and I both know you have every reason to lie to me now. More than I to you."

Fishhook? she thought.

goodmeatnobonesman?, the cat's thought came back.

followman. "Look, Arkan, you can get messages to me.

Give me what time *you* think reasonable, and call me to account then, whether it's tomorrow or ten or twenty days from now. Is that reasonable enough?"

"Very reasonable. What say we meet again in an eight-day, and we'll take it from there?"

"All right." Her voice was resigned.

I hate you, I hate the ground you walk on and the air you breathe. I hate your guts and if I could curse you, I would. I hope my ill-wish gives you pox and dysentery and leprosy, and that you die a mass of painful sores.

She turned to walk away. "Good luck," he said. "I will pray for your success." *Everything you make me feel, you asshole, your people will feel, next time I go into the Arkan camp.*

The intrigue is intriguing, thought Matthas, as he slipped back to his tent. *But this trade has its pains. Like dealing with the likes of her, and having my honor, my integrity and my race shat on by same. After all these years, it shouldn't get under my skin, but somehow it still does; I guess at least I haven't had all my innocence burned out of me.*

Everyone thinks you're an asshole when you're a spy. At times in his career, mostly early in it, he'd wondered himself. He reassured himself by reviewing the ethic that required the work of him: *I had a gift for it, more than anything else. To do what you are best at is to serve your Empire, and the Gods, best.* Yet did he have that gift because he was in some way innately cruel, relishing the dirty work he so often had to do? (It was, he'd noticed, generally against people who relished dirty work more than he, as they plotted or wreaked harm on Arko. Such as Megan, most likely, and Shkai'ra, certainly.)

At the end of each bout of such doubts, he always came to the same conclusion, making him wonder every time why he bothered thinking these things at all. He had to do his duty, as best he could. That was virtue in itself, and—like it or not—what sort of person it showed him to be didn't matter. *When I am* Aitzas, he thought, *I'll have the luxury of moralizing.* He looked forward to that. Likelier now; it seemed she'd bought his story of the poison tooth. That made for much easier breathing.

Megan went back to the tent, lay down so none of her limbs would fall asleep on her, and in her mind stretched to find Fishhook.

In the distant silence she could hear the cat's thoughts, like meows muffled through two rooms and four heavy wooden doors.

goodmeat sheepsmell licklick groomtoes manmove??? slowslow swoop goodsheepmeat smellsneeze followfollow catchleaf chewholdkickkick play??? bitespit situplicklick meant that meant to whereman??? goodmeat follow huntsneak . . . bird! Slowdumb BIRD! The mental whisper faded.

Megan sat straight up. "Shit, shit, shit. The damn beast is off chasing birds! I'll wring her fool feline neck!"

"Don't worry, my heart," Shkai'ra said from the other bedroll where she'd settled down to let Megan track the wing-cat without disturbance. "Convince flutterbrain that the man gave her the bird and she'll find him. Or else she'll get interested in him again afterwards. She at least got the smell of him. We'll be able to find him, drop some snooze-drips in his water so he doesn't chomp himself dead, truth-drug him and then just keep sending his messages not to kill Lixand until the army gets to Arko." She was spouting every idea she could think of, to calm Megan down. "We'll do *something.*"

Megan lay back on her elbows, breathing hard. "All right. You're right, love, it was just an off chance." She smiled a twisted grin. "Worst comes to worst, I'll kill him and I'll learn to live with myself as a Halya-damned oathbreaker, friend-killer."

Shkai'ra gathered her up close in her arms, onto her lap. "Shhh, my heart, it's not that bad, not yet. You're letting the worst rule you. We'll find the guy, rescue Lixand, then scrag him."

Megan buried her face in Shkai'ra's neck. "I'm doing this all the time, aren't I?"

"Not too much. Too much and I'd scream at you."

The smile Megan gave this time was more sincere. "Why, thank you. That would help *immensely*." She stretched the kinks out of her muscles. "But you are right, in a number of ways. I love you, you great brute."

"I love you too, you *smallsnippydisagreeable*." Megan tried to smile at Shkai'ra's version of the Ri's name for her.

"You forgot *sharp*."

"Sorry. *Sharp*. *A-hia*, we'll work it out."

Zaik knows how, the Kommanza thought. *But somehow*.

Fifteen strokes, Sova thought. At least it wasn't to falling, the flogging that lasted as long as your strength, and one stroke longer. Fifteen strokes she'd be able to count. It was hardly as if she'd never been struck before.

The army was in the usual bustle and confusion of making camp; the flogging-posts were always among the first things set up, eighty thousand warriors, now, producing a good deal in the way of discipline problems. She'd watched before, as they were off-loaded from a wagon, work-crews standing in the bed of the vehicle to pound them in with stone-headed mauls: old oak posts with frayed tops, dark and stained. She'd expected not to get any closer acquainted. Those to be punished waited, some bound and under guard, most standing with knots of their friends, faces contrite and nervous. Dust made her sneeze, and there were the usual smells of dung and leather and sweat and greased iron.

She'd told Echera-e the first day he'd been up and around, two days after he'd been hurt; it was another two days now, and he'd been judged fit. "Fifteen stroke . . . we getting light 'cause she you' motser," he said. "Some *kras* outcahst, forrh tsaht. Most flahg to falling.

Bet she say us it tsaht, next time." Now he stood beside her, his rough-callused hand in hers; his friends were there, more subdued than usual. They seemed to agree with him that the sentence was on the light side of justice, though, if anything. Sova had felt it was harsh, until she thought about it. *If everyone ran around doing what they wanted, they'd cut through us like old cheese.*

The two hadn't been sure whether they'd get the choice, but each wanted to go first. They'd toyed with the idea of having the whip-wielder alternate strokes; but that, they realized, would make it last twice as long for both. The anticipation between, they both knew, was as bad as the pain. Sova swallowed; there was a fig orchard just north of the punishment field, and she could smell the over-sweet smell of the dropped fruit, hear the wasps buzzing about them.

Shkai'ra rode up on Hotblood with most of the Slaughterers behind her, and Megan, perched on her pony, worry lines on her face. "Attention to orders!" the Kommanza barked.

Echera-e and Sova looked at each other and straightened, stepped forward to stand before the commander; the Yeoli's eyes stopped for a moment on the man uncoiling the whip by the post, one of his own countryfolk. That was the rule, in this army, formed of nations that had in the past often been enemies, and were still sometimes touchy about perceived humiliations. Sova swallowed.

As one they exchanged the salute with Shkai'ra. Her voice continued in a tone like iron.

"Sova Far-Traveller, military apprentice, and Echera-e Lemana, common rank, did willfully disobey orders while in action and in the face of the enemy; specifically, did refuse to obey the signal to retreat although they heard and understood same, thereby endangering the mission and the good order and discipline of this army.

"Therefore, they are sentenced to punishment corporeal, for their own improvement and as example general.

In light of the fact that the offense was committed while attempting to rescue a wounded comrade with courage that would be commendable in other circumstances, and in view of their youth and previous clean records of both parties, sentence is commuted to fifteen strokes. I warn Military Apprentice Sova Far-Traveller, and am authorized by his own commander Makalina Shae-Sorel, *rigaryekrachaseye,* to so warn Echera-e Lemana, that the next such offense will be punished by flogging to falling. The sentenced may choose the order of punishment and whether they will be bound."

"Told you," whispered Echera-e.

"Stone, knife, and parchment?" They'd never come to a decision; there was no time to do it any other way now. They extended their fists. "One, two, three . . ." The first time both showed knife, and shared a nervous giggle; the second, Echera-e's knife beat Sova's parchment, and they gave each other a quick hug.

He peeled off his shirt and stepped up to the post, taking a firm grip on it, waving off the binding-rope. They'd both had an answer to that choice, without words. The whip-wielder had been warming his arm; the regulation Yeoli whip was too thick to crack, but could be made to whistle viciously through the air, as he was doing now. Echera-e spoke the ritual words, loud enough for everyone to hear and steadily, as tradition required. "So be it, I submit myself."

I can't turn away or shield my eyes or flinch, Sova thought, as the whip whistled around and thumped across his back for the first stroke, a sound like a hand-blow. *Not in front of all these people, when I'm next; it would look like cowardice. Shame him, too, who loves me.* It came to her that this was the sort of thought people had in war songs, and she'd thought it naturally, for the first time. *Because the songs . . . come out of truth.*

She kept her eyes on him, silently wishing, "Strength, livling." He didn't flinch himself, though she saw him tremble, and his head start to bow until he checked it.

"Five! . . . Six!" The count-herald's voice was clear and weighty. Echera-e's tanned back had come up brilliant pink in a broad stripe on the first stroke; now the stripes were enough to blend together into one huge patch. "Ten! . . . Eleven!" Pink grew brighter, angrier. *I should look at his head, not there. Strength, my love.* "Fourteen! . . . Fifteen!" The flesh of his back looked almost bloodied now, though it was unbroken.

Finished. And he'd managed not to cry out. He straightened, aching slow, kissed the whip-wielder's hand as Yeoli tradition required, and saluted Shkai'ra. His face was flushed red, but when his eyes turned to Sova he grinned.

The cruel sourness of fear had come up in her mouth of itself on his fourteenth stroke; now it watered, hard. *If I spit, everyone will know. My turn. I won't cry out. I mustn't cry out. But I don't know if I can keep myself from crying out, or stay still like he did.* She wanted to cry. His brave grin cut through the fear some, and she loved him for it, but it didn't cut through it all.

Everyone was looking at her. They wouldn't change whip-wielders; there weren't enough other Thanes in the army to find one for her. *Now. Only cowards hesitate.* She took off her shirt, trying not to let the cloth show the trembling of her hands, smelling the stink of her own fear-sweat while she pulled it over her head. They were waiting. Echera-e was with his friends; vaguely she saw him leaning on another youth's shoulder, and his hand make the first symbol to her, *strength*. Her own steps toward the post seemed jerky and wooden, like a puppet's; the arm that waved away the binding rope didn't seem her own.

It's just pain. I know what it's like to feel pain. She gripped the post, feeling the wood rough and splintery on her fingers. *Send the pain out of yourself,* the voice said inside her; Shkai'ra's. *Stare at a spot, send the pain into it. Control breathing, deep to the base of the lungs, slow.* Other people had given her the same hints for taking floggings. *Set your teeth, concentrate on not biting your lip.* She tried not to expect the first blow. *Why isn't he starting? It must be just because time seems like an eternity right now.* Then she remembered.

She cleared her throat, and forced her voice to be strong, and steady. "So be it." It sounded distant as a far-off sentry-call. *I hope it sounded better to everyone else than it did to me.* "I submit myself."

She set her teeth, and started the long slow breathing; then came the whistling of air, and the first blow.

I flinched. My face flinched, I didn't think of my face, shit! Next stroke, my face is rock, my face is stone. . . . She made her eyes bore through the spot on the post, worn grey wood-grain. *Breathing, I'm forgetting . . .* The second stroke came, before she was ready for it; she'd never be ready for it, but she managed not to flinch somehow. *It's not so bad. Not as bad as I feared.* She caught on, then, to the rhythm.

Lines she'd heard someone quote from an old strategy book came into her head, and somehow stayed there, the pain searing them in, in fluid Yeoli. *There is rhythm in all things. There is a season to everything.* She breathed, and burned into the spot with her gaze, and put all her soul into keeping still and silent. With all her soul she counted with the count-herald, to know and celebrate in her bones that it would only be eleven more, ten more, nine more, half over, to measure out her strength to last just as long as she needed. *It'll be over. It'll be over in a moment and then he'll hold me, and we'll stagger off to the healer together and get our backs salved.* "Ten!" She felt her face flinch again. *I almost yelled. Don't relax, yet. Only five more, I can make it, breathe in, and out, and in, and out . . . Eleven. I can make it. Twelve. I can make it. Just three more. Thirteen. Hardly anything left, I can make it. In, out . . . Fourteen. I've just about made it. Fifteen. It's over, O Gotthumml great god Nurse Zhymata it's over Echerry shit I'm still in front of everyone I'd better not fall over . . .*

Grey cleared from her eyes. Straightening was agony, walking all she could do. The whip-wielder was there, his face sympathetic; dully remembering what Echera-e had done, as if she hadn't known it before, she kissed the hand offered, and saluted *khyd-hird*, who sat impassive. Sensation returning, she realized she had tears in her eyes; but she was sweating so much as well, maybe no one had seen. In the ring of faces was only admiration. It occurred to her that they might never have seen a fourteen-year-old flogged before, since Yeolis under sixteen didn't get flogged. *I did it. I didn't cry out or fall over or faint or anything. I did it.* Echera-e's arms welcomed her, clasping her shoulders.

XIV

To: Slaf Hikarmé, Rilla called Shadow'sShade and Shyll called DogLord
From: Megan called Whitlock
Dated: Seventh Iron-Cycle, Sixth Day, Year of the Lead Cat

I greet you both, with love, from the middle of the largest gathering of naZak that I have ever seen in one place at one time. We are all well; Sova arrived with not so much as a scratch on her. She is doing well fighting in Shkai'ra's collection of "odds and sods" mercenaries and is associating with a very nice young Yeoli boy, Echera-e. Since she speaks not a word of his tongue and he very little Enchian, this is doing wonders for her Yeoli language lessons, among other things.

Shkai'ra is having a marvelous time doing what she does best, bashing heads. The command that they've given her was, at first, exactly how she described it, but has since improved. She has been awarded a Nephrite Flame, the decoration for "conspicuous presence of mind," which is high enough that she had it presented by the Yeoli king in front of the whole army. I'm glad; this might be her last chance for true glory. You know how she measures herself by kills made and battles won. Any other acknowledgements of merit seem rather hollow and toy-like, to her.

I have been having a wonderful time causing Arkans grief, usually losing sleep doing it but, as one says, "No party without the risk of headache." Rest assured, Shyll, that I am taking all the care I can, so I am not likely to get hurt.

All my love to you and to little Ness. I won't get started on business or this letter will be far too long. I hope that the assorted creatures aren't making an unreefable mess of the house. I pray for you, and think of you often, which is a great comfort. Stay well, please, till we get home safe with Lixand.

> Love, Meg

To: Same
From: Sova called Learned Scribe

Dear Zhymata Rilla and Zhypatr Shyll:

I guess Zhymata has said everything about the war and the army and all that. I'm learning so much I never dreamed of before. People are strange. But they're nice. Except for the Arkans that is. I've fought in a couple of battles and I don't think I did too badly, though khyd-hird had me flogged once, for insubordination (what else). I like it here.

Oh, the biggest news: I'M IN LOVE I'M IN
LOVE I'M IN LOVE!!!!! His name (I hope I'm
spelling it right) is Echerry Lemana, he's sixteen
and he used to be with his hometown infantry
until he got himself transferred to khyd-hird's
unit (wonder why that happened, hmmmm).
He's Yeoli and SOOOOO handsome, Rilla, you
wouldn't believe it. His accent is so romantic.

I've met Chevenga the *semanakraseye* (that's
Yeoli for king, and I know that's how you spell
it). He is very different from Ranion. He lets
you come up to him without wiping your face
along the floor, for instance, and he'll talk to
you just as if he were a normal person. He's
fantastically handsome too, but much too old for
me (ha ha).

Love to the animals, Ness, and you.

                                              Sova

From: Shkai'ra called Mek Kermak's Kin
To: Rilla called Shadow'sShade and Shyll called
DogLord
Scribed in entire and unerring accuracy as per
the Oath of the Scrivener by: Sova called Far-
Traveller
Spelling corrected by: Megan called Whitlock

Dear Rilla and Shyll:

Greetings. The usual nice stuff, Sova, you know,
how-de-do's and all that, but less formal, you
know, more familiar, since we're dealing with
family here and not some tight-assed woolly-
haired mucky-muck, got that? All right, uhhhhhh
. . . Everyone's fine so far, healthy, no wounds
or ills. So far. Emmmm . . . We're kicking Arko's
asshole all the way up into its heart . . . wait,

girl, maybe I shouldn't say it that way, Rilla might think I'm being crude again. Uuuu-uhhhhnn, all right, write this: we're scoring massive victories against Arko, and that should continue. Can't wait for the sack. Ummmm ... We miss you. Urp [belch]. Errrr ... Shit, I'm no good at this personal letter-writing thing, *kh'eeredo,* I've *said* everything already. Help?

[At this juncture, an interjection from aforementioned Megan: "*I've* written *my* letter, love. You're doing fine; just relax!"]

Well, what else is there to say? I mean—hey! I've stopped dictating and *you're* still *writing,* WHAT ARE YOU WRITING, GLITCH-TAKEN BRAT!? YOU'D BETTER WRITE WHAT I DICTATE, NO MORE, NO LESS, OR I'LL SKIN YOUR HIDE, YOU NO GOOD INSUBORDINATE LITTLE SHIT-KICKER! GOT THAT, OR DO YOU WANT TO BE PEELED FROM HOLE TO HOLE!? *Zoweitzum,* I've said enough anyway, they'll get the idea and there's the letters from *you two,* just say I love them and all that mushy spouse crap and fuck the rest.

As always, my heart brimming with tenderness,

SHKAI'RA
(her mark)

"You're telling me," said Manajas, studying the crystal wine cup he turned delicately in one gloved hand, "that a four-foot witch is sneaking into our camp and causing us to have visions?"

Matthas tried to keep from clutching his chair, strained not to seem tense. *I had to tell someone. I had to try.* "Could be, *could* be, that's all I said," he answered hastily. "I can't know for sure. I've just heard what strange

things have been going on in our camp, and I *know* what
this wo ... *person*'s capable of."

"Oh, just *could be*, I see." The foot-commander took a
heavy slug from his goblet. "Mm-hmm. You know, friend
Nerasas, *I* see visions too, sometimes. Gods, demons,
ghosties, ghoulies, myself getting promoted to Grand
Ultimate General of the Empire's Divine Forces ...
Drink some more, I've always found, and they eventually
go away." Matthas tried to keep from biting the inside
of his cheek.

"Be careful, heart of mine," Shkai'ra brushed her
knuckle on Megan's cheek in the familiar gesture of
affection. "I'm sending Hotblood to be your backup. Told
him I'd skin him alive if you didn't come back."

That was not in the plan—when Chevenga had called
her up to plot it that day, she'd found forcing all thoughts
of what the Arkan was demanding she do out of her
mind easier than she had feared it would be—but Hotblood was a good enough darkworker that no one would
ever know. Probably. Megan chuckled a little tiredly.
"Such precautions." She started pulling on a tight dusty
grayish black tunic. Clear black cloth was too visible,
even in the dark. They kissed for luck.

The moon was down; it was black under the forest
with only the soft brilliance of the summer stars for light.
The dry dust-smell of summer and the intense green
odor of the forest mixed in the night air. Megan sat easily
in the crook of an oak, looking out over the Arkan camp,
ignoring the damp chill of dew soaking into her clothes.
It was a *big* camp; even now the Empire did things in
style. Fifty or sixty thousand men, half that many horses.
It smelled worse than the Alliance camp, she found,
when the breeze turned for a moment. There was a
severely regular ditch and mound with a tree trunk palisade on top, this time; the Alliance had taught the Arkans
something about night attacks.

The campfires had been many and bright, the men

reluctant to turn in until the officers ordered it. Megan waited until the Arkans were as quiet as they would get, then dropped and ghosted over the cleared ground toward the palisade; pause, crawl, pause, pause, becoming a shadow every sentry round. No matter how thoroughly the troops scoured the perimeter there was always a little brush overlooked, left because it wouldn't hide a normal-sized person.

The wooden wall was unbarked logs, still studded with lopped-off stubs of branches, formidable to an armored soldier and easy as stairs for her. There was a rattle of armor above, bored Arkan voices with the *solas* accent exchanging the password.

Far too loudly, she thought. *They don't imagine anyone would dare come this close. Arrogant.*

She rolled over the sharpened points of the logs and dropped down in a soft crouch on the inside; there was a roadway around the interior of the wall, then regular rows of tents graded by rank, like every other Arkan camp. Megan was next to the officer's row of an infantry rejin; there were fires, one in front of every third tent, burned down to grey red pits of ash and embers. An hour before there had still been soldiers up, cleaning their armor, talking, singing; she had heard two younger *solas* working out the harmonies to "Under the Lamplight," same melody as in the Alliance camp, the Arkan words fitting just as well. *Some things get shared, across the field, somehow. Strange, war.*

In the still air now she could hear someone snoring, the sound echoing as if his head were still in his helmet. *His tent-mates and neighbors must love him,* she thought. *I'll fix that soon enough.*

She could almost walk through with her eyes closed the pattern was so regular. The high commanders' tents were near the center, the pickets off that way, upwind so the horses wouldn't smell her, the supply carts over there. On the other side of the neatly laid out section, past the privy trenches and facing toward the Yeolis, was the clump of camp followers and hangers-on, sleeping where they could.

No mercenaries attached to this camp, especially since that general, Abatzas Kallen, had tried to doublecross the Schvait and make them fight their own kin at Michere, back in Yeola-e. The story was well known. Three companies of blackshirts had deserted, coming out straight through the sleeping Arkan army—through, in every sense of the term. Arko was having trouble hiring anybody but scum nowadays; using them as sword-fodder in a losing campaign, they didn't have many left.

She froze again as the sentry paced by, torch half-burned. Her nose wrinkled at the strong odor of someone who ate beef more than three times a week, and was tense. Waiting for something frightening to happen . . . she cackled inwardly. Hotblood waited outside the palisade, wanting to come and eat a few more *blondprey,* as he had started calling them.

She stopped by the infirmary tent, near an ash tree. In this forest country it was too much trouble to clear a camp entirely by logging it. Megan reached inside for the *manrauq,* the pool of blue/violet behind her eyes. As she found it, she caught her breath, as if making a dive into cool water that tasted blue and sounded of vinegar. The more she practiced it the clearer and sharper it became, as addictive in its way as Dreamdust. *Using it kills you—the more power you use, the younger you die,* she reminded herself, riding the sensation of power like the swells of the sea, the voice of her mind the thin lost mew of a gull.

In the woods on the next hill a screech owl called. She reached for the sound, imagined it echoing through the rows of tents. *Quiet at first. Play them.* Then across the camp she imagined the sounds of armor, like pots being beaten on with sticks. *Men shouting.*

Men shouted, rousted out of bed as the alarm was given, torches flaring. *Stop.* She melded back further into the shadow of the infirmary tent, hearing the groan as someone inside, wounded, woke up to a pain he'd escaped in sleep; the smell of medical alcohol and the sweet stench of *thal*, poppy derived.

It took a good half-bead for the camp to settle down again. "*Fikken kaina*, we can't sleep. Yeoli bastard has the gods on his side ..." someone snarled, unbuckling by the sound. "Shut up, Jas, that's flogging if heard." — "Fik you." —"... and your mother, asshole."

It was quiet when Megan acted next, quiet enough that the *chhee-rup* of swifts in the night sky could be heard again, though there were many more men awake. She could almost feel them trying to sleep, their breathing refusing to even out, ears unconsciously straining for the next wrong sound.

She settled herself in such a way that she couldn't fall over. This was going to take all the power she had. Night wind raised gooseflesh on suddenly sweating skin.

Faintly. Softly. The sound of distant bells out of the sky. Flutes, metal flutes and the clashing of metal on metal, like swords dancing to the flute-notes, swelling louder and louder ... Sound was easier than images, even only affecting a handful of men. Her mind filled with *manrauq*-sound, she heard the questions and shouts and sounds of running feet like the buzzing of meadow flies.

Louder. A choir of men, hundreds, singing praises to the God of Solas, The Steel Armed One, chanting ARAS, ARAS, ARAS! Directionless sound from the sky. Stars falling into the Arkan camp falling to shape the figure of their God, taller than the trees. Sapphire stare pitiless under the edge of the helm, sword in gleaming steel fingers, and the other hand a clenched fist over their heads, outlined in the yellow glow of my power ... No more shouting; silence around her as those who saw the image froze.

"*YOU SIN.*" The voice was like the sound of a sword-blade breaking, the shriek of metal being sheared through, though soft, the rumble of a volcano about to erupt. *"YOU SIN."* Megan knew the *solas* accent in her bones, the images and words taken from books seized out of the libraries. A scream, then others, deep and unaccustomed from male throats. "The God! The God is here!" They threw themselves to their faces, cupping hands at their temples, even those who had not seen, believing those who had. The image faded but the voice from the sky went on. *"YOU FIGHT FOR A FALSE SON. I DISOWN HE WHO YOU CALL SON OF THE SUN AND RAISE A NEW SON. AND FOR YOUR SINS HE SHALL BE SEEN AS DARK. WOE UNTO YOU MISGUIDED, WOE—*

Then Megan tumbled, the image in her head snapping, the mighty voice gone like a snuffed candle, as a man running blindly in the dark fell over the guy-rope and landed on her.

His panting breath cut off. *"Yai!"* Here was something he understood; he leaped for the vague shape on the ground, shouting. *"Itzen!"* Their word for "alarm." "Assassins in the camp! *Itzen!*"

Megan flailed blindly at his face, the headache of being jolted out of the spell slamming her so hard she almost couldn't lift herself from the ground, retching. Her claws caught in something; he flinched back. *"Yaaaiiigh! Demon!"* And ran, thank Koru . . . She set her teeth, staggered to her feet and back behind the tent just as someone with a lit torch ran around the corner.

Shit, I'm leaving a blood-trail—his, thank Koru. She wrapped her hands around her head, trying to control the pain as she ran, dived behind a log that someone had thoughtfully left by a fire-pit. The alarm was spreading out, fighting with the panic left by her spell. More torches flared alight. *They'll cover this ground like starving pigs rooting for truffles. They catch me, I'm raped and smothered as a demon before their army* . . . She held down her gorge through sheer will. An officer, properly armored, pulled to a halt near her, with squires and bowmen. *Shit, more light.* Her strength was too spent to hide using *manrauq*.

"Namas, call your men to order!" The *Aitzas* spoke calmly. "Infiltrators in the camp will be apprehended. Demons, too; we have the Gods with us. Spread out and overlap with Laranas's and Simalanas's men on either side, *jump!*"

As they re-lit one torch doused by the wind, Megan used the shadow to crawl back to the edge of the infirmary tent. Her head was pounding as if her brain had turned into a giant heart, and she kept having to fight not to throw up. She eased one of the pegs out of the ground. Floor was sewn to the walls and enough slack ... she crept underneath, the weight of the musty canvas pressing her into the dirt like a hand covering her whole body, cutting off most of the noise of the search. The smell of moist dirt filled her nose. She lifted the canvas just a hair-thin crack to peek out.

The corridors between the tents were crawling with searching Arkans, combing the ground, kicking barrels, driving spears through bushes. *No trouble. They aren't going to think anyone could fit under here.* All she had to do was wait them out. *And at least I'm lying down.* She pressed her eyes shut, forced relaxation, wished this was an Alliance infirmary.

A dog barking. *Koru, no.* It got closer and more distressed, half whining, paws scratched the earth a hand-span from her face. Just a camp hound, finding something its senses knew was wrong. *Only a matter of time,* she thought dully, *before someone hears, wonders, and checks ... I'm so tired I can't even hear the son-of-a-bitch's thoughts ...* "Go lie down!" she hissed in Arkan, hoping that would send it away, but though it stopped barking it stayed. It sat down, still pawing at the dirt.

She inched along, worming her way through hoping nothing heavy was ... *shit.* It was either a folding table or a patient. At the motion of the floor he—a patient, *fish-guts*—shifted and groaned. She scanned, squirmed out into a too-small patch of shadow.

There was an Arkan at one corner with a light. The dog came at her, growling. She mustered all her strength, thought at it. *Skunk!* It fled yipping.

The Arkan turned, at a sound like something with claws scrambling up the ash-tree. He saw the dog running with its tail between its legs. He called without leaving his post. One of the commander's bowmen answered. "What?"

"Something climbing, sir. Might have been a racoon . . . but it sounded too big."

"Raise the light a bit."

"Begging forgiveness, sir, I'm at full stretch now."

"Fikket." The torchlight illuminated only the lower part of the trunk, sending flickering shadows up into the branches. "Did it sound like a man climbing?"

"If it were a man it . . . he had claws, sir."

A good body-length above the first spread of branches, five of her height above the ground, Megan clung to the trunk, frozen, barely breathing, hoping in the dark she looked like a burl. She didn't dare turn her head; in the gap between her armpit and the wood she could just see the edge of the torchlight below.

"Well, just on the chance . . ." The bowman. *Oh, shit.* She held tighter to the trunk, wood digging into her cheek. A spider scuttered over her ear. A creak of leather, the rattle of shafts, a pause. *Koru have mercy* . . . The snap of the bowstring and the blow came as one, through the back of her right thigh.

It didn't immediately hurt, just seemed to stun the muscle, and made her hands almost loosen; then the skin stung, and the full pain washed through her like a wave over a deck. Her hands spasmed tighter, claws digging into wood hard enough to make her fingerbones hurt. In her mind she screamed.

Hold on. Hold on. Don't move. Don't make a sound, don't breathe, you'll moan. Sweet Koru, Great Bear, don't take me now before I save my son . . . Involuntary tears squeezed out of her eyes. She tasted blood: she'd bitten the insides of her cheeks. *I'm not going to die yet.* In her head somewhere she could hear Hotblood, a mosquito buzz question that she ignored. *Don't pass out.*

"Must have been a racoon," said the bowman. "Well, better safe than sorry . . . Keep a good watch." The light went away.

Megan let her whole world narrow to holding on in silence, not letting her head tip back; she'd pass out and fall if she did. She heard a slow patter on the leaves below her, thought vaguely, "It's starting to rain, my face is wet, too." *Hang on. Hang on. Hang on. Hotblood.* In another half-bead, that to her seemed like forever, the camp was quiet again.

Sneaksneak. The mindvoice was below her. *Blondprey/ stupid/blind/nonose* A mild curiosity. *Smallsharpsnippy- disagreeable leaking? Dying?*

No. That was all she could manage; she didn't know if he could catch it.

Down, he thought. *Meclimb?* The idea of the horselike creature trying to climb almost pulled a hysterical laugh out of her. *Leaking . . . ? Oh, bleeding.* The patter on the leaves . . .

Down, he thought more insistently. *Noskinaliveme.* She had to force her hands loose, fearing she'd pass out just from moving. Pain and tingling counterpointed the sharp agony in her leg. The night was growing fuzzy gray and black blotches.

DOWNNOW. She put down one hand to try and support the wound, realized she couldn't, slid down to the branches below her, bark scraping her face and hands. Her heel glanced then slipped off a branch, which caught her in the crotch. *Hardly hurts, next to the arrow.* She was sliding sideways, almost strengthless, caught the branch with her knees and her hands, half hanging.

DOWN!

Shutup, weasel-ass. Falling would be faster . . . and probably kill her. She held on, trying to tighten the one leg, flexed the muscles in the other, couldn't move.

Something long and dark rose up beneath her, claws scraping the bark. Hotblood, rearing up no mistaking the gape and stink of his breath. He grabbed her by the back of the belt in his teeth, backed down to all fours, holding her like a rat he was about to shake, lowered her to the trampled grass.

Ground, Koru . . . Honey Giving One give me strength. She blinked away muzziness, took delicate hold of the slippery arrowshaft. *No. Leave it for the healer.* Hotblood lay down beside her. *ON.* She dragged herself onto his back, clinging to his mane. He stank even worse than usual, and his fur was wet everywhere. *Riversneaksneak.* The only way for him to get in unseen. *Stayon. Smallsharpsnippydisagreeable—*

Vision faded in and out. There were flashes; the flexing and rippling of Hotblood's body under hers, torchlight on his mane, an Arkan's face working as he stumbled back screaming, *"Dimas, dimas!", fierceterriblefleescream-falldowntrembleatME, hehehe!*

Like a mantra: *Hang on. Hang on. Hang on.*

Did I hear Yeoli words? Why isn't Hotblood moving? Hang on. A babble of voices—Shkai'ra, Yeoli, Haian— *Alliance camp. Safe.* She fainted.

Noise, loud noise. Megan tried to roll over in bed, pull the covers over . . . *oww.* The twist of pain in her leg woke her more thoroughly. A sharp stink of medications threaded its way into her nose. She tried to open her eyes, found that they were gummy and didn't want to obey her. The weight of blankets; someone hadn't cleared this tent ground as well as they could have, there was a small pebble under the mat, under her shoulder. Someone's hand, in hers. Early morning chorus of birds. She forced her eyes open and tried to blink them clear.

The further reaches of the big tent were a vague blur. Someone moaned a few beds down.

"Do not worry, you weel hev some trouble seeing et first. Eet will go ayway een a while." She blinked, managed to make the swimming brown blur resolve itself, at least for a moment, into a Haian face.

"I *did* make it back." Her voice was a croak. A momentary fear ... *No Haian would work for Arko—unless under duress.* She groped; no, the hand holding hers had no shackle on its wrist.

"Yiss. We hed to vein-leenk your weeth a donor, you lost so much blood, but you weel be all right." The Haian shifted to offer her a drink from the invalid's drip-bottle, that she suddenly realized she wanted desperately. "You've been aslip three *aer*"—hours, that meant—"end the arrow was removed just fine. You weel be up een three, four days."

"Th-thank you."

"Ees my work. I call your wife; she hes been risting."

Shkai'ra was wearing a sleeveless tunic and a gauze bandage across the inside of her right elbow. "Hello, love. Hotblood's pissed because we had to cut his mane to get you loose," she said, taking the Haian's stool and clasping Megan's hand. "They used me to top you up, after that poor squire gave out. How can somebody so small have room for so much blood?"

"I have this bad habit of spilling it." Shkai'ra snorted. "I wish I didn't feel this shitty."

Outside it was false dawn. Megan closed her eyes against even that, thankful for the pain-killers that soothed not only the wound, but her head. Shkai'ra leaned close and whispered in her ear, switching to Fehinnan. "Fishhook brought you a present that'll make you feel better."

"Oh, a dead mouse," Megan said sarcastically, in the same language. "It's as if Ten-knife were back. Just what I need now to keep my strength up."

Grinning, the Kommanza held out a tiny rectangle of

heavy-bond Arkan paper, written over in a minuscule hand. "Not a mouse . . . a pigeon." Megan blinked, puzzled. "A *messenger* pigeon."

"Oh, *great*," she groaned. "I bet this time Gold-Bottom finally decides the stupid beast should be strangled. We'll catch it fish-gutted good from whoever owned it . . ." Fishhook's passion for pigeon-meat was an ongoing problem, in an army whose command used messenger-pigeons all the time. Several times they'd had to sheepishly return a bloodied feathery corpse, minus head or part of breast but with leg-band and sealed paper left carefully intact, to the Yeoli command council scribe, at the cost of a chewing-out and a stiff fine.

"Hah!" Shkai'ra laughed. "Not unless he wants to blow his cover. Whatever piss that Haian put in your veins *has* got your wits, hasn't it?"

The Zak struggled up to her elbows, ignoring the pain and fuzziness. "You mean . . . not from our *rokatzk*! What does it say? What does it *say*?"

"My heart, I can barely read Zak!"

"Shit. Sorry. You bring my magnifying glass?"

Shkai'ra pulled it out of her pants pocket, out from among the half-eaten figs, bits of jerky, dirty sweat-rags. "You wouldn't have brought the cloth, too?" Shkai'ra handed it over with a smirk and Megan awkwardly polished the lens. She propped herself on one elbow, nausea rising.

"Here, don't be an idiot, lie down." The Haian's apprentice's protest echoed Shkai'ra's. She pushed a pillow behind Megan's back. "Sssa, love." The Zak fought down irritation: it was the Kommanza's horse-soothing voice. *My son. This might be the key to freeing Lixand and I can't focus my Koru-forsaken eyes on it!* She shook her head and peered through the glass at the scrap of paper, refusing to let the remnants of the headache distract her.

"It's in Arkan, sure enough," she whispered, and translated into Fehinnan. " 'Box 596 . . . Commercial enterprise . . . proceeding as planned. Do not liquidate investments . . .' Fish-guts, Shkai'ra, this is it, the stop action message! Oh Koru . . . Lixand-mi . . ."

"Easy, love. He can't be relying on just one pigeon to carry that message; he'll have it double or triple-covered, in case the pigeon happens into storms or predators. Like wing-cats."

"Of course, of course he would, all right." She read on. "'Food greasy, wish you were here.'" She put the glass down and laid her head back. "*Dah,* by Koru, I know that style, that's *him.* Dark Lord, I feel awful." She closed her eyes and rubbed them with her hands and thought. "But so what? This could only do us good if we had someone in Arko who could do something about it and the only one of us who could masquerade as an Arkan would be you."

"Shit," Shkai'ra said, wrinkling her nose. "Just when this war was getting interesting." *And I was in line for a cavalry brigade,* she added to herself. *My last chance at command. Oh, well.*

"Love—you aren't taking me *seriously,* are you?"

Shkai'ra held out one red-blond braid. "*Ia,* I am. Unless you think we could pull off a rescue through letters in wartime?"

"Shkai'ra . . . you don't know the language well enough. You don't move like an Arkan woman and never will. Arrgh—*oww.* I know you think Arkans are blind, but . . ."

"No, Megan," said the Kommanza, smiling. "Remember that time we were in one of those Thanish trade-towns . . . Vyksa, wasn't it? And it took that idiot Thanish chandler *ten minutes* to realize we were female. *Zoweit-zum,* I had my shirt unlaced almost to the bottom of my breastbone and he didn't notice! People see what they expect; Arkans are even more trained to see 'men' in pants and 'women' in skirts than Thanes, and city ones don't meet outsiders, like those Thanes would."

"As a man! You're *tall* enough . . . But you'd have to

go as a *solas* if you wanted to be armed, and they're fish-gutted *literate,* let alone fluent in their mother-tongue, in a certain accent, and knowing who to talk up and down to—not to mention the low voice! There'd be no reason for you to be in the City Itself unless you were wounded . . ." Her voice trailed off, thoughtfully. "Wounded on the *head*. The right sort, and you wouldn't be able to write much, or talk straight . . ."

She shook herself mentally. "No. Koru, what am I thinking? This isn't enough information for you to go haring off ahead of the army to chase Lixand—one scrap of paper with a box number on it. Besides, you can hardly walk up to You Know Who and say 'I need to leave your army for a few weeks to get my wife's son, or she'll have to kill you.'" She put a hand on Shkai'ra's knee. "Thank you anyway, love, for the thought."

"No," Shkai'ra said. "We were planning to think of a way to get you out of the choice, Lixand or Gold-bottom; this is it. Think about it when you're a little less wretched, after you've slept some. There's no *tearing* hurry, because you have a good excuse for delay to give the *rokatzk* now—you're wounded! And think about that message; Lixand's obviously *not* being held by Irefas proper, *nia*? If he were, that would be going to the Marble Palace, not a drop-off box."

"Maybe. Maybe not."

"Your *rokatzk* never said 'we have him in the Marble Palace dungeon'—just 'I have him.' He's freelancing, with a few other people, probably not more than half a dozen—easy work for me. Worth the attempt, at any rate." Her eyes closed for a second. "Rest now. We're going to win."

Megan chewed on her Arkan pen, looking at the neat columns of positives and negatives on the paper before her. She was propped up on pillows, the lap-desk on her lap; her bad leg hurt like a rotten tooth but bigger, the pain made worse by the lurching of the un-sprung

e thought, and began to back more quickly.
followed, hard and fast, cut-thrust-backhand
hrust-thrust, shield up and point keeping line
ar foot, stamping into each blow. Shkai'ra let
to the rhythm of parry and stop-thrust, then
nder the next, releasing the outer grip of her
her left hand, letting her knees relax and
y her down. Instinctively he slashed, dropping
o cover the exposed thigh; her legs shot out,
g behind his knee and the other around his
ling erect, braced on the man's leg, she
o-handed at his exposed shoulder. The heavy
of the *boka* thudded flat and heavy on the
ather of his armor, and the shield-arm went

eeeeee! she shrieked, a sound like a file on
attacked with a berserker flurry that banged
blade, helmet, shoulder, midriff, finishing
otsweep and a precisely controlled overhead
uld have sliced halfway down from his

ians get too fucking academic," she rasped,
he other defeated sparring partners who sat
bruises along the edge of the trampled
attle's more like a bar brawl than fencing
'armes, remember it. Dismissed from foot
your centurion for formation riding." She
ad. "Sova! Water!"

ought the wooden bucket to the edge of
er's tent. The sides were rolled up along
leaving an awning from the bright morning
unlaced her armor and the sweat-soaked
led her shirt off while the girl put the
its stand, drank thirstily and wiped herself
wet towel. She glanced around; nobody
ng she need do urgently for the next little

e said, pouring a final dipper over her

wounded-cart, even on roads this smooth. It was stuffy
in there, and people kept groaning. *Never thought I'd
wish I were riding.* But the Haians weren't going to let
her up yet; when she did try standing, just to see what
would happen, she instantly felt why they didn't—her
head going light, and her whole body insisting on lying
down again.

The only bright moment today had been when Chevenga had come into the cart, to squeeze hands, stroke
brows and present everyone with the decoration all
wounded got, the Saint Mother's Bloodstone, slipping it
under their pillows if they were sleeping. *Good thing
he can't read Zak,* she'd thought as they exchanged
pleasantries.

It was an old habit, laying out her thoughts on paper
to see in black and white whether an idea was viable.
Most times she had to burn the paper once the decision
was made, this time no exception.

Shkai'ra would have to count on the fact that no one
would challenge the wound—on both head and throat—
and her limited Arkan vocabulary could be garbled
enough that no one would notice the accent. Scribbled
in one corner of the list was the notation "Emmas Penaras, *solas*"; Shkai'ra could learn to write that. For the
rest, a few cards that Megan could easily forge, along
with travel papers ... If she could stall the *rokatzk* for
an iron-cycle, and Shkai'ra were both lucky and careful,
it was possible.

"I'll wrap my head in bandages stained with chicken
blood." Shkai'ra, lying back by the fire with one ankle
over her knee and fingers laced behind her head, grinned
raffishly. In two days, Megan had healed enough to be
let out of the wounded-cart at night. "Poor valiant ...
umm ... Emmas Penaras, *solas,* head-wounded fighting
the benighted barbarian invaders. Can't speak very well,
forgetful, lost his letters mostly, hands shaky anyway ...
it's perfect! We can get Imperial harness easily enough."

Megan appraised her. "You'll have to trim your hair some, dear. It's too long for a *solas*."

Shkai'ra winced. "My hair! I guess I couldn't pass for an *Aitzas* . . . Damn, I haven't done more than trim the ends since I got warrior-braids." She brought the plaits, shining in the lamplight, around in her hands. "Well, that should wait until I go missing, of course. So, love, think you could make a convincing widow?"

Megan scanned the dark tents around them, idly wondering if the blackmailer was near, or whether people were starting to wonder why she and her wife had started speaking Fehinnan so much. "Or at least the worried wife of someone gone missing in action," she answered. "I'll stall things for an iron-cycle, the length of time I told him first. I think I can do that."

"That should be enough time," Shkai'ra said.

"Then you bring Lixand back to the army . . . or if the army takes the City first, we'll meet on the steps of the Marble Palace. Or, barring that, the Temonen manor. At noon. And if the other's not there in, say, an eight-day after the army arrives, we'll know for sure." The Kommanza nodded wordlessly. "Hotblood would have to stay here."

"He will, if I tell him to, even though he doesn't like it," Shkai'ra said. "You can trust me, my heart. I'll win for both of us."

"*Three* of us," Megan corrected. "Lixand, too."

I trust you, love, she thought later, when sleep would not come. Shkai'ra snored peacefully. *Chevenga will have to as well, though he doesn't know it.* She tried to feel as determined as she could make her voice sound. *You always come through in the crunch. You're your best when things are worst.*

The next morning, well enough to walk a little, she was summoned to the office-cart. *Koru* . . . It couldn't be to plan; she was wounded. *Lady grant he doesn't suspect something. He can't, how can he know anything?* She swallowed back nervousness as the *semanakraseye* spot-

ted her, and handed off the smiling.

In the cart, a few words of the point. "However much o accolades," he said, "there's sented in privacy." His stern grin like a boy's, waiting to s face when he gave a presen pendant, a white one: Meg Serpent. Not quite the Inca spectacular results, but still there was, for actions of ste

She felt her face go burn *remember, I've forsworn m it, now.* "I was just doing w for," she sputtered. *I'm blu it's more than I would for j* rate me the other times."

"Look," he said, his dar "If you had fallen out of you had given up, they' taken all you *have* done killed you, and taken all getting it for. Now stop

"You'll win, Shkai'ra," limped back to the wo her belt-pouch. "Not fo

Shkai'ra backed care tice sword alternately own blade. The brow scuffed up around th Or a crop, before? The harsh sound of clack-*bang* of the fi dred sparring pairs that narrowed dow nasal of her helme

Now, sh The man cut-thrust- with his re him fall in *squatted* u shield with gravity carr his shield t one hookin ankle. Cur chopped tw curved oak steel and le limp.

Eeeeeeee stone, and off shield, him with a f cut that w shoulder.

"You Enc to him and t nursing their ground. "A in the *salle* drill: report t turned her he

The girl br the command the guy ropes, sun. Shkai'ra gambeson, pu equipment on down with a near, and nothi while.

"Thanks," sh

own head. "Come on in, I want to talk to you for a minute." The Thane-girl followed. The inside of the tent was bare of anything but a scroll-rack and some cushions; Shkai'ra sank to one, kneeling back and resting her chin on her sword-hilt.

"Sova," she said abruptly, after the girl had sat down. "Talking isn't my skill. Megan's better at it." Another silence. "But sometimes things must be said." Her copper brows knitted in a frown of concentration. "I never expected to ... have a child in my care before I came to Brahvniki last year." A faint smile. "I got out of the habit of thinking far ahead, after I left my homeland. Now that I've got family responsibilities, I've got to get it back. Zoweitzum, I might get killed tomorrow, and there'd be all sorts of things I couldn't say, dead."

Tomorrow. Little do you know. Zaik and Jaiwun, I'm not looking forward to sneaking into Arko. Give me a stand-up fight any day.

Her face settled and went a little distant. "Sova, I don't know how you feel about your birth-parents. It's ... private, eh?"

The girl's pale eyes peered up at her from under her brows. "My *birth-parents?*" Shkai'ra didn't make a habit of mentioning them, had never spoken of Sova's feelings about them. "With all due respect, *khyd-hird,*" she answered, after a time of thought, "what I feel about my birth-parents is none of your fucking business."

Shkai'ra gave a short bark of laughter. "Megan will scorch my ears for teaching you bad speech." Grimly. "Now, as my daughter—"

"I'm not your daughter."

"By adoption, legalist!"

"It's not the same."

Shkai'ra blinked. "Didn't say it was. Doesn't make a difference to my obligations; when you come of age in two years, you can tell us to fuck off."

"You said 'as my daughter.' But I'm not. And never will be."

Shkai'ra sighed. "You're my daughter under the law. And Megan's, Rilla's, and Shyll's. You'll inherit our property equally with any other child, we have to see to your education, we're responsible to the authorities for you. Savvy?"

"So say 'my daughter under the law.' It's not by blood." Sova lifted the dipper, took a long draught.

"Consider it understood," Shkai'ra said drily. "What I wanted to talk about was your further education. You're getting old enough to start thinking about what you want to spend effort on, and what you have talent for. We've been giving you a general training—you're going to be rich, after all, you don't need to know how to weave or hoe turnips—and we've had enough time to know your aptitudes, a little. Megan says you're doing well on the books, very well for a late start. I'd say, and I should know, that you've got exceptional promise as a warrior; as good as me, potentially—"

"As good as *you?*" The girl's ash-blond eyebrows flew up. "You're *joking.*"

"Potentially, I said. You've got the physical side, senses, stamina, reflexes, balance—which are important, no use in trying if they're lacking—it's the motivation, the drive I'm not certain about. You'd have to train long and hard, and there's no point in doing that unless you *want* it; and there's the training in command, as well. But I've been instructing you for a year, now; trust my judgment, why don't you? It's my skill, after all."

"I don't *not* trust your judgment," the girl said, blinking. "You've just never . . . said anything like that before. I mean . . . as good as *you?* I didn't think you thought *anyone* could be as good as *you.*"

Shkai'ra shrugged. "It's dangerous to praise too soon in training. I'd have waited until I got back, except for this war. Don't get complacent—you can still die, it's another four years or so till you reach your full growth." A wry smile. "Then a decade till you start losing the physical edge; I've got another couple of years at my best, no more. Though spirit can make up for a good deal of youthful pep."

"You always think people are being cocky," Sova said. "I'm not cocky, I'm just amazed."

"I was your age once, and thought I could whip my weight in tigers. Cockiness is a hazard of youth, especially in the genuinely talented. The problem is that in this business, it doesn't lead to learning, it mostly gets you dead. And I want you to live. Of course, sheer luck counts for a good deal, too."

A wink. "I'll let you in on a secret. Up at the top of the profession, who's the 'greatest warrior' as often as not depends on things like who slept better the night before, or who has a head-cold." Steadily: "Look, Sova, we'll teach you the basics anyway; everyone needs to know how to defend themselves. If you want, I can teach you to the point where you'll never have to back down from someone simply because they're better with a blade. It's a useful set of skills. The question is, what do you want?"

The girl thought for a moment, her nail scratching the edge of the handle of the dipper. "But . . . to *never* have to back down from someone because they're better means I'd have to be the greatest warrior in the world."

Shkai'ra made a weighing gesture. "Not really. If you're in the very top rank, the odds against running into someone much better are small; particularly if you don't make a career of following the drum—you weren't planning on being a mercenary, I hope? It's an overrated career."

"Well, I didn't think so. But what's the point of doing all the training to be that good if I'm *not* going to do it for a living?"

"You don't have to follow war for it to come to you. Stay in F'talezon and you'll see a good deal of fighting, will you nil you; anywhere else on the Brezhan, the same. And out on the Mitvald, once Arko's gone, there's going to be bloody chaos a generation, at least. I'd like to see you able to handle it wherever you go; there's more than one way—Megan knows others—but I can teach you only mine."

The girl sat thinking, the expression unreadable, but filled with some point she wasn't making aloud.

She will speak when she will, Shkai'ra thought. "You think on this, girl. Such a choice should not be left to whim or default. You're done here now, go."

"Yes, *khyd-hird,*" the girl said curtly.

The sound of the first morning gong rang out over the camp, mellow and too lovely for the business of war. Shkai'ra looked down at the dark head with its white streak in the crook of her arm.

"Goodbye for now," she whispered.

"Some part of me desperately wants to keep you here," Megan whispered back. "All the Gods be with you, love." She buried her head in Shkai'ra's neck, clinging. "I need you. I love you."

"The day we met was the luckiest of all my life," Shkai'ra said, "and will be if I live fourscore." She kissed the other on the top of the head. "Smile for good fortune, my heart: I love you, too."

"Come back to me."

"First, this army; second, Marble Palace steps; third, Temonen manor, at noon," the Kommanza said. Almost shyly Megan reached into the clothing hanging from the tentpole and pulled out a long lock of hair knotted at one end, mingled black and silver. "You'll be cutting yours for me, and my son."

"I will always come back to you, even if mountains and seas lie between," Shkai'ra said. She pulled her boot-knife from the footwear, and clipped a lock of her own. "Huh. This'll be the longest it gets for a while."

They lay for a moment, holding each other wordlessly, and then crawled out into the pale predawn light. It was important not to alter their routine, with enemy eyes possibly watching, friendly eyes, certainly. Shkai'ra went into her stretches as Megan shook out her kinks and braided her hair; Sova yawned out of her pup-tent, stoking up the fire and putting on water before helping Shkai'ra on with her armor. They'd told the girl nothing; the fewer knew the better.

"Sova," Shkai'ra said, "you're off with that Yeoli staff type today, aren't you?" To broaden her experience, they arranged such things.

"Yes, *khyd-hird*," the girl said sleepily.

"I'm trying out that Arkan sword," she said, buckling it on. It was loot, a plain straight longsword except for the silver wire on the pommel, and the best layer-forged blade she had seen on this side of the Lannic. "Look after this for me until this evening, wouldn't you?" She handed the girl her Minztan-made Kommanz saber. "By the way, in the unlikely event I'm ever killed," Shkai'ra added, with a wry grin, "don't put it on the pyre with me. Use it. You're the only one in the family who's going to have the heft and the training both."

Sova's pale eyes flicked up from the sword into Shkai'ra's, wide. The saber was legend even in steelmaking F'talezon, as great as an ancient-made or perfect Yeoli blade. "Yes, *khyd-hird*," she said, as Shkai'ra swung into Hotblood's saddle.

"Take care, love," Megan called, as she always did.

Sadsadmoanwhimper? the Ri thought; images of dead colts and snowstorms ran through his mind.

Sadsaddon'tshownowhimpersneak, Shkai'ra thought back. Aloud: "I will, my heart. You also. Go well, both of you."

"This I don't like, *kras*," Bukangkt said, as the column halted in the shade of the great trees. It had probably been some Arkan *Aitzas's* hunting preserve until recently, looked too manicured for wild wood.

"I think I can take care of myself for an hour or so, centurion," she said. Promotions had come thick and fast among Shkai'ra's Slaughterers, this past month; five hundred lances were under her command now, and doing

well enough some regulars from allied contingents had
tried slipping in as mercenaries. She waved to indicate
their surroundings. "I want that ravine about two klicks
west checked thoroughly, though."

The battalion Shkai'ra was commanding were on out-
rider screen today; the Arkans were backing again,
through an area that was mostly rolling plain. The wheat
had been reaped and carted but there were big cornfields
just tasseling out, and occasional copses of oak and beech
like this, many hectares in extent. Deceptive country, you
thought you could see as far as on a steppe, but there
was enough cover to hide substantial bodies of troops.
They had just passed a village; the locals were mostly
slaves and eager enough to help—the Alliance army was
trailing an enormous rabble of them now, armed with
whatever and making up for lack of training in blood-
thirsty enthusiasm—but here they'd known nothing useful except that a column of Imperial cavalry had passed
through a day before, burning or stealing the grain harvest. The local landowners had left a month ago.

"You command," Bukangkt said, saluting in Yeoli style.
His company fell in to the trumpet and formed column
of fours, trotting off into the waves of yellow stubble.

That left Shkai'ra with her standardbearer and a few
messengers; she spent the next several hours finding tasks
for them. Afternoon in high summer was no joke here
in the southlands, and the woman with the Slaughterer's
banner—a fanged skull impaled on a sword; Shkai'ra
thought it rather fetching, and had been surprised at the
odd looks—was an Aenir from the Brezhan, unaccustomed to such weather. Also unaccustomed to Arkan
steel sheet-armor, such as the whole unit was wearing
now; her round pink face shone and sweat dripped out
of the sodden sponge lining of her helmet, falling on the
breastplate with a *plink . . . plink* sound.

"Here," Shkai'ra said, offering one of the canteens at
her saddlebow; experienced troops always carried extra.
"Don't want you passing out from the heat."

"Tenk you, *kras*," the trooper replied, surprised. She had gotten the coveted position of standardbearer for conspicuous bravery. Her nickname of "Mad Cow" had been earned more recently, for a studied indifference to discipline remarkable even in one of her race, and she had been expecting to be broken to the ranks for weeks now.

Another half hour, and the Aenir woman was yawning and nodding, bringing her head up with a jerk every time the chin-guard went *clink* on the gorget.

"Unsaddle and sack out for a while," Shkai'ra said.

Mad Cow Zoltanova was probably the only soldier in the Slaughterers who would have obeyed that order with quite so much unthinking eagerness. Her commander took the banner, waiting until Zoltanova was snoring before kissing the victory ribbons and leaning the staff reverently against a tree. Then she took the leading reins of her two spare horses and cut the trooper's beast loose, half-grinning down at the sleeping form.

Flogging to falling was what I had planned for you after that last piece of ignorance, and it's what you're going to get, she thought, as she filled Zoltanova's canteen with the mixture of pure white *wadiki* and water from her own. It was pleasant not to have to do this to an undeserving soldier ... drunk and asleep, while the commander went into the woods to take a dump and never came back. Not *quite* enough for execution ... maybe. Now the plan: off into the woods a little, put her armor down a well, quick-change into the Imperial set she had packed on one of the mounts; *they* were both of the Arkan breed as well, runners, not destriers. Cut her arm a little, blood on Hotblood's saddle along with the point and broken-off shaft of a barbed Arkan javelin ...

NO, Hotblood thought. Shkai'ra groaned mentally.

YES

NO

YES!

NONONONONONONONONONO! smallsharpsnippydisagreeable—the Ri's thought-concept for Megan, colored with a mixture of dislike, respect and apprehension—
golook/search/smellcoltredmaneherdmarestaywithMEME
MEMEMEMEME!

YES! Shkai'ra threw her greatest overtone of domi-
nance into the thought, along with images of dismem-
bered bleeding Arkans in Megan's company.

Sulk.

She hesitated for a moment, looking at the banner.
"Sheepshit," she muttered to herself. The biggest war
she'd ever been involved in, a brigade command coming
up, and she had to *leave*, on a clandestine mission. That
was irony for you, sneaking around was Megan's special
skill . . . totally useless now, simply because of her size
and the color of her hair and eyes.

"Only for you, my love," she muttered, turning Hotblood's head into the woods. "Only for you." The Slaughterers would search energetically, of course, but evading
a search and running mounted ahead of a cavalry screen
were skills she had learned as soon as she could walk.
And the Alliance army had moved into the Empire like
a spear into flesh, a long narrow thrust down its eastern
highway; she would not have far to go to reach territory
more or less under Arkan control.

XV

The sunlight deepened from golden to orange, the slanting shadow of each rider growing longer; soon they'd halt and camp. Not soon enough; despite the leather riding-sling giving it support, Megan's leg hurt like Halya.

"*Zhymata?*" Sova had been deep in thought all day as she rode, the hazel eyes seeming full to bursting, but the lips tightly closed. Buckled to her saddle, in the place of honor, was Shkai'ra's saber. "I had a talk with *khyd-hird*. She said . . . she wants me to decide whether I wanted to train to be a great warrior and a commander, or just good enough to defend myself. She says she thinks I could be as good as *her*."

"From what I can see, she's right," Megan said. "You also show promise at mathematics; you could be a good merchant, if you wanted. You are a bit old to choose what you want to be, but you don't have to yet, because the family has money."

"I don't know what I want." The girl pursed her lips. "I used to: I wanted to marry a good Thane-man and live in a big house in Brahvniki. I know you think that's

249

wimpy, but that's what I wanted. But I can't do that *now*."

"So marry a good person of some *other* nationality and live in a big house in Brahvniki. If you're happy raising children and running the household, that's fine too." Megan scratched the back of her neck carefully, nervous, waiting for the news she knew was coming, feeling her stomach knot, but stopping her hand from pressing under her breastbone.

"*Zhymata*, do you really think anyone in Brahvniki, anyone who knows or would be warned what happened, and cares for his *zight*, would marry me?"

"If the person you want to marry cares more for their *zight* than for you, fik 'em. Find someone who doesn't give a shit for what your father or I did but cares only for you. Shyll is like that, and *I* hardly went looking for *him*." Sova didn't answer. "Does it matter to you that he's Thanish? It hasn't seemed to, when I think of a certain young Yeoli." The Thane-girl smiled helplessly.

"Megan! Megan called Whitlock!" The voice came from ahead, official sounding, but with a tinge of hidden panic.

Oh, Halya. Here it comes.

"Here!" Megan raised a hand, turned the pony out a step or two without stopping. The caller was a cavalrywoman, one of the Slaughterers, it looked like, breathless even though she was mounted.

"You've got to come forward! We need you! It's by authorization of Bukangkt . . . uh . . . Slaughterers' acting *kras*."

"Oh, shit, Bukangkt? Where's Shkai'ra? I'm coming." She kicked the pony hard enough that it jumped and crow-hopped in surprise before plunging forward. Megan didn't even notice that, clinging on. The cavalrywoman wheeled before Megan reached her and led the way.

"She's gone missing," the woman, whose nationality Megan couldn't tell, said once they were out of earshot of Sova. "The only one escorting her we found sleeping dead-drunk under a tree; and Hotblood came back . . ." She glanced over her shoulder, eyes seeming to measure how Megan was taking it. "With a javelin stuck in his saddle, and blood. Bukangkt said you had some way . . . of searching."

Megan set her face, thinning her lips, as if holding in emotion. For a moment she thought it might be real, not the faked missing in action, long enough to pale her face; she didn't answer, only nodded. The woman said nothing, only kicked her horse into a gallop, Megan doing likewise. They passed the head of the column.

Badfeelingaboutthis. badfeelingaboutthis. Hotblood's thoughts, not berserk; yes, Shkai'ra was intentionally gone, according to plan. *Redleadmareaway, miss, MISS!* The woman led her to a field where a knot of horses stood; the Ri she saw standing off, pacing, the javelinshaft standing up from his saddle visible even from here. *Ah, akribhan,* she thought. *Never moderation where excess will do.* Someone was on the ground, kneeling; she could hear the yelling from here.

Words in various accents came clear as she got closer. "Buk, why can't we scrag this fat *bitch* right now? Why the fuck not?"—"One fuck-up after another, and now Shkai'ra!" The female voice with the Aeniri lilt was almost screaming. "I swear, I fucking swear *Second Fire come* I did not put fucking wadiki in my water that was some other child of two pigs spiked it and I swear *Second Fire come* she said I could sleep!" A more even voice: "No, Buk, don't, what she's saying is possible, remember the rules: you can't execute someone without witnessed proof, you've got to get her truth-drugged." —"Ya, *ya!*" the Aenir woman shrieked. "Get me truth-drugged! Get me truth-drugged!"

I think I know who put wadiki in your water, Megan thought, hiding it behind a stony mask. Bukangkt—odd to see a brawny broken-nosed Lakan in Arkan plate— beckoned her. "I sent them searching," he said, in bad

Enchian. "But *kras* said if she ever went missing, you her kreedo best to find her. And do with Hotblood."

"I'll do my best. Spare an arm? I've got a leg-wound." He dismounted, and helped her off the pony, half-carrying her to where the Ri was pacing. *Wrongwrongwrong redfurleadmare gone GONE want want*. She called him both with her voice and thought. He turned to look at her. *Smallsnippysharpdisagreeable*, he acknowledged her, but turned his head with almost a snort of disdain. *Notimportant redfurmissMISS!*

LISTENWEASEL-ASS! Her fury tinged her thought red. He hissed at her. *Shkai'ra (redfur) wants this, NEEDS this. To rescue Lixand (blondcolt)*. She sent images of a Ri-mare—with red fur—defending her young.

Disagreeable, he thought but stopped pacing, turned and lowered her head to stare into her face, the eyes set for binocular vision strange in the horse's head, green with a hint of Shkai'ra's grey.

Listen. We'll take off the saddle. You pretend sneak-sneak to look for Shkai'ra. Hunt blondprey, follow, don't come back till I or Shkai'ra calls you.

—— He tossed his head, breaking eye contact. *Nonono—!*

Sulk. He sidled around so Bukangkt could reach the saddle-girths. Once it slid off into a heap the Ri sprang away from it and her, reared and loped off toward the woods.

! Megan thought at him. He stopped near the edge of the trees, sniffing the ground.

Sneaksneak find redfurleadmare. Then he disappeared in the underbrush.

"I'll go over there, if you don't mind," Megan said, "and try to find her in my own way. Don't touch or disturb me until I move again, you understand?" The Lakan nodded. "If the sun is down before I move, have someone come over and call me; I might need it by then."

"Column still march," Bukangkt said. "Flank-riders not

know, disturb you." More riders came in, having heard the dispute, breaking the pattern. *"Do you fuckheads or do you not fuckheads,"* he roared, *"have orders that not been changed?"* They dispersed again at a gallop, what little of their faces showed through their visors, reddening.

"All right, how long can you give me?" She translated hastily to the Arkan clock in her head. "A bead? With *one* person seeing that I'm not disturbed?"

"Sure, yes, *kras* kreedo." He called up one of the others, a Brahvnikian. More likely to understand a Zak; this Lakan wasn't stupid as she'd thought from Shkai'ra's first words of him. "And you, Mad Cow . . . you got reprieve. We get you truth-drugged, and *then* chop up your fucking fat ass!"

Megan settled herself with her back against a tree, her wounded leg straight out along the ground in front of her. *A bit of a show* . . . She drew a deep breath when there was only the one watcher sitting his horse. In the orange-pink light of the setting sun she imagined a faint shimmer of light around herself, heard the man gasp. *Right.* It flowed off her, over her head, formed itself into a heat-shimmer-like bird-shape that hovered a moment, sharp pointed beak shape apparently casting about, then darted in the direction the Ri had taken, and disappeared. The Brahvnikian pretended very hard not to see.

Another deep breath. Not too hard to do because it was faint. She sat absolutely still, breathing very slow, eyes almost closed so she could still see through the lashes. *Remember, when they call you, you're exhausted.*

She heard her Brahvnikian warn off the flankers, heard Bukangkt come back. The sun was almost down, sending shadows looming along the ground in front of her when the Brahvnikian walked his horse close, and called, "Whitlock." She didn't move. "Megan, called *Whitlock!*" Ahead, she imagined the bright spot of yellow light arrowing toward them, backed by the dark-edged fish-scale clouds. She imagined it flashing like a bolt of lightning, vaguely bird shaped, to angle down and strike her in the top of the head as if she were absorbing it. Then she stirred, made as if to get up, fell back, hands out to catch herself. She shook her head and squinted up at the Brahvnikian, who clearly didn't want to come close but felt he should help, hesitating on his horse. Behind him she could hear Bukangkt clearing his throat.

"Nothing," she said hoarsely. "I couldn't find her. Give me a minute, and a hand, and I'll ride back to report." *Witchcraft as a game of smoke and mirrors.*

He just said, "Shit. Shit shit *shit*."

"You don't think . . . anything worse could have happened to her than just . . . going missing, do you?"

The girl poked up the campfire with a stick, making the flaming logs crash together, and a shower of sparks fall upwards into the night sky.

"I hope not." Megan's shrug was slow, as if she were afraid she'd break. She pressed a hand to her middle, though her stomach wasn't acting up. "I have to hope that they'll offer ransom, if that's what happened. I just don't understand why *I* couldn't find her, even if I'm not blood-kin." Her folded hands clutched her sleeves. *I've always done my best to tell Sova the truth as I saw it. I hate having to lie to her.*

"I guess . . . we just have to wait, and hope she's all right. She . . . she wouldn't be easy for anyone to kill." The girl filled her voice with forced hope. "*That's* for sure." She poked the fire again. "I sure wouldn't want to be an Arkan or even ten Arkans, trying to kill *her*." The saber was leaning on the log, next to her; she hadn't let it out of her sight. Now Megan saw her look at it, her eyes widen with a thought and then go casual again, as she decided not to say it. *I know what she's thinking. She's thinking, "Maybe* khyd-hird *somehow knew. . . ."*

On the eighth day the note appeared, specifying which latrine. *Right on schedule,* she thought. *An efficient* rokatzk.

Well, some nice Arkan bowman had kindly given her the perfect excuse. Using the stick Sova had cut for her, she limped to the appointed copse at midnight.

Struggle. Play it for all it's worth. Pain, pain, pain . . . Putting all her weight on the stick to keep it off the leg entirely, she made an involuntary grunt. *Good.* It *did* start to hurt worse, aided by the pretense. *H'kuritz rokatzk.*

"You knew damn well I was wounded, and how badly," she hissed, when she heard the cool voice greet her. "Why did you still fish-gutted drag me here?"

"Why, to see if you were up to making it, of course," he answered cheerily. "That'll give me an idea of how long it'll take you to heal . . . you know, in case you decide to tell me any tales, exaggerating the recovery time or such; not that you *would*—of *course* not!—but just as a precaution, you understand."

Shit. Turns out today's one of those days in which I really should have stayed in bed. "I see." She bit back the desire to be sarcastic; it didn't help. *Any other tests? Like dancing a Zurke?* "Do you mind terribly if I sit down? I have to." All she let show in her voice was weariness and pain. The predictable answer came: "Of *course* not!"

She settled to the ground, her breath catching as she jarred the leg. "Look, Arkan, just give me time to heal up. Please? I'll do it for my son's sake, when I can. I swear."

"Good. But when *is* when you can? How many days? Let's be specific and not have any misunderstandings to leave you convenient outs."

She put her hand over her eyes. "An eight-day to heal up. An eight-day to do it. Sixteen days."

To her amazement, he said, "That's reasonable. Your oath's on it, then?"

"Yes," she gritted. *"Yes."*

"The best of luck to you, then." She could hear a smile

in his voice. His loose-clothed shape ghosted away into the night.

When she comes back—not if, but when—she comes back, I want to ask her something. Sova was squiring for Megan, now; in the secured section's pool of squares, she'd come up for firewood detail.

She's a great warrior. She wandered all over Almer-kun, being a great warrior, getting greater; like she says, the only real training is the real thing. Then she came over here, to be in a family. I'm going to ask her: where was she happier?

Once she'd happened to snap up the first split wood she could find for Megan's fire—that was the good part of firewood detail, eating first—she went back to the splitting place at the edge of the forest. The tang of trees laid open filled the air; a good ten axes were ringing. *I don't think I could do that,* she thought. *I'm too small, and probably too weak, even if I am trained.* Most of the people chopping had height and weight on her, though they were all squires, the warriors having orders to rest. *But I can't stand here watching, I have to do something.* She settled for helping a Yeoli, placing the logs on his chopping block so he wouldn't have to put down his axe.

"You want to learn how to do tsaht," a voice close behind her whispered. "Wahtch him, how *he* does it, closely, with tseh unthinking gaze, like you wahtch you' war-teacher show you a move."

She did for a while; then it occurred to her that she didn't know who the voice, cracked with age and broadly Yeoli-accented, belonged to, and perhaps she ought to turn around and check. Its tone had been so sincerely friendly and helpful that danger hadn't crossed her mind.

It was an old Yeoli man, grinning wrinkly at her with the same expression as his voice had held, bald but for a fringe of thick white curls, and stripped to the waist to show a thin chest stringy with muscle, and arms with veins standing up under loose age-lined skin, the whole marvelous network of them showing. By the sawdust sweat-pasted to his shoulders, he was obviously helping here; but she'd never seen a squire that old. His crystal was tight-tied, close to his neck, not dangling, as Yeoli warriors wore them, but he had no wristlets, and besides he was too old for that as well. "*Nye'yingi*," he said, sticking out gnarled ancient hands, and grinning wider, the grin going all the way up past piercing pale green-gold eyes, up into his thick-lined forehead. "I'm Azaila Shae-Chila."

"I'm Sova. Called Far-Traveler." She'd never taken the hands of someone so old before; they were hard and bony and dry, but had a warm grip.

"Good! Pleasedtomeetyou. Look at *tsaht*." She found her eyes back on the youth with the axe almost without knowing it. It seemed the most natural thing in the world to do what the old man said, stranger or not; he hadn't said it like a command, but more like a little boy calling a little girl's attention to something wondrously fascinating, with an enthusiasm too strong not to share. "You see how he's bending his knees when tseh ahxe comes down? Ahn' whipping his body, with his stomach? It's tseh same as anything, you put you' whole body into it, use tseh best form, it doesn't mahtter how small or weak you arrhe ... Well, you cahn't really learn without trying it yourself, ahn' all tseh ahxes are taken; we better do something before we get caught shirking. I need someone for tseh otser end of a saw, shall we?" As if he were a handsome swain gesturing to the dance-hall; she followed, entranced.

He took up the first unused saw to hand, a long arm-length of toothed steel with wooden handgrips at either end, and went to the first felled log whose branches had been hacked off enough to saw. *It's not much less wide than the saw is long,* she thought. *I don't know if I can do this, and what about* him, *so ancient?* But without a thought the oldster positioned the saw and looked at her, her hands went to the handle, and they started.

Don't get out of rhythm with him, she told herself. Easily enough she fell into it, then tried directing her strength at different angles and times in the stroke, until she found the one that made the saw-teeth chew through the wood fastest. Then she enjoyed it. Then her arms were tired; her exercises didn't include any that used exactly these muscles so steadily for so long. Then her arms were hurting, and sweat poured from her face; she wanted to let go to wipe her forehead, but Azaila kept going. In fact he hadn't even stopped grinning. *We're going to take a break soon, I hope . . . He's an old man, he's got to rest. Well, I'm not going to call a rest until he does.* He didn't; soon her arms felt near to breaking, and he didn't even slacken the pace. *He must've been a lumberjack all his life*, she thought, swallowing back tears of pain. *I'm not going to stop. We're not even halfway through . . . No, wrong thought, we're almost halfway through. It'll get easier after that.*

As they worked down to the narrowing bottom curve of the log, just knowing it would soon be finished eased the pain, and she found her second wind. Finally the saw broke through, and the section fell off with a satisfying thump. The old man stood up grinning. Sova straightened slowly, gingerly uncurling her fingers. "Good! Good! Now we take it to split." *Gotthumml, I have to lift half of that? Or else . . . no way. I'm an angel in dragonfly-wing pants if he can lift it himself.*

"I take one end?" she volunteered bleakly.

He waved the suggestion away. "Nah. Too hard. We do *tsis.*" The section had landed on its bark-covered side; giving it a hefty push with a sandalled foot he started it rolling along the new-trampled path towards the splitting place. "Shape like a wheel, why naht make it one, *seya?* A little heft hyere ahn' tsere over roots ahn' rocks, no problem! We small weak people, we hahve to try harder ahn' be smarter, *seya?* Might ahs well both do it, only one of us cahn't saw."

So they kicked and shoved and lifted the log along together.

Near where the trees thinned, brightening the near-dusk light, the old man started, and straightened up, gazing ahead. "Look at *tsaht!*" They were within sight of the splitting-place; Sova tried to notice what he had. There were only the people working; then she saw one who hadn't been there before, bare-chested so his scars showed, black hair sweat-tendriled, splitting wood like any commoner, except that he was using one hand, apparently effortlessly: Chevenga.

"He's *amazing*," she said gushingly.

"Tsaht's for sure!" said the old man, spitting. "Tseh strutting little cockerrrhel, he could do *tsaht* at eighteen, he only wants to show tseh world he's better with one hahnd tsahn everyone else with two. One string of good bahttles ahn' I tell you! *I'll* rub his face in tseh dirt of truth, yes, escuse me, *kere* Sova."

For a moment she missed his meaning; as he began to stride away, she understood. "But, but. . . ! He's the *semana . . .*"

"*Semanakraseye na chakrachaseye*," Azaila rattled off over one bony shoulder. "Exahctly."

"But, but . . . !" You couldn't . . . I mean, he's . . . I mean . . ." She remembered *khyd-hird* lying in the grass of the field when she and Chevenga had sparred, a wooden sword gently tapping the back of her neck; *khyd-hird*, whom she'd thought the best, bettered. They'd sparred several other times, and Chevenga won most. This old man would get flattened.

"Couldn't, *pfah*," the old voice snapped, receding. "I'm *going* to."

And he *did*.

He just walked up, waited until the *semanakraseye*'s axe was stuck in the log, and tapped him on the shoulder; then there was a flurry of motion too fast for her to follow, and both disappeared, downward. Kicking her log onto its flat side she jumped up on it, balancing on tiptoes, to see over the underbrush.

Chevenga was flat on the ground, face-down, with Azaila on his back, the old legs pinning the young arms, somehow, and the old veined hands ... yes, each gripping a fistful of black curls, indeed grinding that famous face in the dirt, back and forth, Chevenga's thrashing struggles only making it worse. He tried to squirm loose, looking for purchase for his feet, trying to draw his knees under himself; the old man just rode him like an unbroken horse, laughing, and shouting, "Yield, cockerrrrhel! Yield, Invincible! If you're so shit-hot you cahn one-hahnd ahxe, tsen get an ahxe twice as heavy ahn' cut *twice ahs much wood, dahmmit!*" All around the chopping had halted; people stood staring.

Suddenly both were still. "All right, all right, Azaila," the familiar soft voice, muffled, said. "I yield." The old man got to his feet, slapped the *semanakraseye* on the head and came back to Sova, leaving him wiping dirt from his cheeks and shaking it out of his hair.

Sova waited in horror, sickness starting in her guts, for Chevenga to call the guards, have the old man seized. *Maybe they'll execute him right here, Gotthumml, I hope not, I don't want to see it, it shouldn't happen at all.* But he just stood up, his reddened face making the scar on his cheek stand out white, grinned sheepishly, and said nothing.

She stood staring, blinking, as Azaila came beside her. "Well?" he said, grinning personably again. "Tsis log's *hyere*, should be *tsere*, what's keeping us? I wonder how it got ahn its end." As if nothing had happened, he reached down to turn the log on its side again; she rushed to help.

"Um ... most honorable *kras*," she said obsequiously, as they rolled the log. Such manners seemed the better part of valor.

"Tsaht's Azaila to you."

"Az ... aila. Um ... how did you do that?"

The old man made the brush-off sign. "Easy. It was his time to get thrahshed. Better I do it tsahn *tsem, seya?*" He gestured with his thumb in the direction of the Arkan camp. "People always preach a principle loudest just before tsey break it, show off most before tsey screw up. I had to stop him."

Sova blinked. "His time?"

"Some otser day, he would thrahsh me. So I don't do it *tsaht* day, heh heh heh!" *When he laughs,* she thought, *he really laughs loud, not caring what anyone thinks; even his eyes laugh.* "He doesn't *need* it tsen. Today, he thought he could defeat tseh world ... Wrong, wrong, wrong. He's young. You know, blows always hit you in the weak spot, you know tsaht? You hahve to *count* on it, be certain it will hahppen. Because tsey always come everywhere; you just *notice* tseh ones hit you in the weak spot."

Cocky, Sova thought. *Even Chevenga.* But still she half-disbelived what she'd seen. "But he's supposed to be the Invincible and Immortal and all that. I mean, if anyone had a right to be cocky ... And you ... how?"

"You already *felt* how," he said, a touch impatiently. "Today, did striving-miracle yourself; just don't know it. Maybe you'll notice when we saw next log ... how it got easier because of whaht you were *thinking.*"

She remembered. *Because I was thinking it was more than half-done.* "But that's not the same as ... !"

"Oh, yes it is! Exahctly tseh same! You got lots more logs to saw before you understahnd, tsough. You got time for a thousahnd thousahnd more before you *my* age. Anotser one waits."

"But ... how could you tell it was his time to get thrashed?"

"Easy! He was splitting wood with one hahnd!"

"But!" This was getting almost exasperating. *I can't say what I'm thinking. Well, yes I can. Why not?* "You're hiding something from me! You know more about him!"

The old man's grin went sheepish. "*Ayo, 'tai*, yes. You

caught me. I know his weak points like my own wrinkles. I only been trying to train him out of tsem for seventeen yearrhs, Spirit-infuse-me-for-tseh-sake-of-Yeola-e."

"You're his *war-teacher?*" Somehow Sova had never imagined an Invincible could have one.

"Yep." The log delivered, they turned back to the woods, and Azaila cast a glance over his shoulder, his light old eyes full of affection. Chevenga was holding a double-weight axe, with both hands. "Good lahd, heart of crystal. Love him like my own child. His kind you got to keep in line." The old man skipped ahead, like a boy. "Tsere's more wood, Sova Far-Traveller! A few more pieces like tsaht ahn' we'll hahve done our share, I think." Sova followed, numb.

He said nothing as they sawed the next log, and neither did she, her head bursting with thoughts, so many she hardly noticed the agony in her arms. Her old refrain rang over and over in her mind, cracked like a bell with doubt.

She'd first learned it from her father: *The strong eat the weak.* And it was true, the one common thing she'd learned from both homes, that ran like a song in her head: "Pa hits Mooti, Mooti hits 'Talia, Franc and I hit Piatr, *khyd-hird* hits *me!*" She'd learned it deeper and wider as she'd got older, found reason for her old questions. What had happened to her had nothing to do with fairness; it was only children who expected that, as *khyd-hird* kept saying. Her adopted mothers had just been better climbers and archers, that was all. *So they kicked us good,* and the world would now say that they were better people, the hardest kick. The strong wrote history, she'd learned that, too. She had another rhyme: "Arko kicks the rest of the world, one by one. But we gang up on Arko, and Arko's ass is done!"

Yet by the same principle, no one should be able to kick Chevenga, least of all a skinny old man who said, "We small weak people," meaning himself as well as her, who'd let her call him by his name and speak freely.

He's one of those legendary Yeoli masters who live up on mountains and can kill people with one finger and that kind of thing, she thought, as they rolled the next log to the splitting-place. *He must be, teaching the sema-nakraseye. Should I . . . Why not? People probably ask him things like this all the time.* "Azalia, sir," she'd said, as they rolled the fourth log. "I . . . I have to decide something. My *khyd-hird* says I could be a . . ." Out of modesty she chose against the word "great." ". . . a really good warrior."

"Yep," he said casually. "She right." *How does he know? He's never seen me spar . . . has he?* The thought was terrifying.

"But I'm learning other things, as well, for other trades. I have to choose which to do. How do I decide?"

She thought he'd think for a bit, but he just said, "Simple. Ahsk yourself two questions. One: does duty require it? Duty means, whaht's best for yourself ahn' tsose you love."

She remembered what Shkai'ra had said, that there would be fighting in F'talezon. She wasn't sure she was going to stay there, though, when she grew up. "I . . . don't know."

"Don't tell me, it's none of *my* business—think it out ahn' answer for yourself. Question two: do you *like* doing it?"

Stink and fear and pain and meanness; smooth clear motion, comrades as one, victory . . . She didn't know the answer to that one either. "Ahnswer tsose two questions, ahn' you will know," said Azaila. "Simple!"

"Ya," she said bleakly. "Simple." Azaila just grinned.

"You've never seen me pick up a blade," she said. It was starting to get dark, the work nearly done; she held down a pang of disappointment at the thought of saying good-bye to him. "How can you tell whether I'm any good?"

"Naht so!" he said grinning. "I did *so* see you pick up a blade. Half of one, anyway."

"Huh?" She blinked. "When?"

He chuckled. "A riddle for you. A lesson. You figure."

XVI

Images and sensations drifted through the Ri's word-
bereft but flicker-quick mind, inspired by his surroundings, his instincts, his hungers, happily ignorant of past
and future, knowing only *now*, as he crept noiselessly
towards the Arkan camp.

Night dark, sniffwind, wind come to me, me. Lie down,
downdown in bush. Night warm/safe/blackdark, mane-
tailsilver on bushes. Sniffwind; small life all around. Fur-
ryjumper, littlescurry, run, run, hide. Men; men, men,
men, men, horses, horses. Blondprey. Tallowsmell, dead-
cowsweat smell. Horses. Stallion, mares. Mareinheat, like-
Rinotlike. Bare fangs. Clawsgrip, down hill, sneaksneak
sneak. Menmeat. Bigherd, men, men. Blondprey in fields
alone. Stomp, stomp, loudclumsystupidhardfeet.

Steepplace, flatplace, bush, bush. Redmaneherdmare-
not here, nothere. Sadsadwhimpermoanhissss! Twoblond-
prey. Rottengrapesmell. Loudnoise, ba-ba-ba peoplemouth-
noise.

"*Fikken kaina marugh miniren,* Kemmas, where'd you
get that wine?"

"Fikken officer's baggage cart that turned over in the ditch today, where else? Celestialis's crapholes, we're still carrying their gear on our fikken backs, aren't we? Here, have some; no fikken barehanded *okas*-piss ration swill for *them*. Or for us, tonight, ha ha ha."

"Honest Laboring fikken God, that's good!"

"Strong stuff. Dinare wine. Fikken sheephairs've got it now, fikken officers get us all killed and then the killer mountain boys ream our assholes anyway."

Mysound. Makesound, clawrock.

"Shhh, thas' fikken flogging talk. Gimme. Ahhh ... Hey, Kem, you hear that?"

"Fikken kaina sergeant sneaking around again. Quick, under the fikken bush with it, Akinas."

Blondprey freeze, hide rottengrapesmellbad.

Hehehehe.

Mysound, turnrock. Blondprey stand, standstiff, pacepace. Sneak ... closeclose. Standquietquiet, openmouth.

"Akinas, I don't think that was the sergeant. Sounded more like an animal. God, what's that fikken *smell*? Like rotten horsemeat ..."

Hehehehe. Fearsweatsmell.

"Shit, it's dark."

Stepstepstep, rear, hissssssshriek! Grabblondprey. Stomachgrabripcloth. Screamscreamsfunfunfunfun. Gutpullouttwisttwist. Hehehehe. Tastegood. Yum. Dodgespear, pullgutlonglonglonglong.

"Help me, Akinas, don't nooooooooooooo—"

"Sergeant! It's got fikken Kemmas, the demon's got Kemmas! Oh, kaina marugh miniren, it's got Kemmas! Sergeant? Sergeant?"

Yum. Muzzleinbitelungstwistpullslurp. Blondpreyherd muchnoise. Go, sneaksneak. Hehehehe.

"Aaaaaaaaaaaaaaaaaaahhhhhhhhhhhhhhh!"

Burp.

Megan lay awake. No matter; Sova would wake her up anyway, either by coming to bed in good time, or by *not* coming to bed in good time. Past midnight, the faint cool brightness of the moon touched her tent-wall; shortly after came the sound of a greeting meow from the ridge-pole, and the Thane-girl trying to hiss silently, "Shh! Shut up you stupid animal you'll wake the dead not to mention *zhymata!*"

"It's all right, Sovee, I'm awake," Megan whispered. "How was your evening?"

The girl sat in the opening to pull off her boots. "Oh, good." Megan could hear her smile. "Hook, in." The wing-cat dropped onto the girl's knee with a brief flutter of wings, hopped inside and curled comfortably in the center of Sova's bedding, beginning a tick-tocking purr. "And yours, *zhymata?*" she said, as she pulled off her clothes and slid down under the blankets, shoving an annoyed wing-cat off from underneath.

"Not bad. I spent some of the evening thinking about you." Megan turned on her side, propping her head on her elbow. The half open tent-flap let in the night breeze with the odor of drowned fires, canvas and tramped grass.

"Uh-huh. C'mere, Hook." A long smooth arm pulled the more-or-less compliant cat, still purring, under it, and stroked the folded wings.

Wanting to talk as much as she wants latrine duty. Megan sighed. "Is there anything bothering you, Sovee?"

"No. I mean yes, well . . . I mean no, aside from how can't there be when *khyd-hird's* missing?"

"I just thought you seemed disinclined to talk to me much, and I wondered, that's all."

"Sorry, *zhymata*. No, nothing's bugging me. She'll come back. I mean, if she died, wouldn't you be able to . . . tell? With *manrauq?*"

"Not necessarily. My *manrauq* isn't that shape; we all shared minds on the ice last year only because of some-one else's *manrauq*. Sometimes it comes back, in extreme emotion; sometimes it doesn't. And she might be too far away."

The girl said nothing to that. There was nothing for

Megan to do but respect her right to keep her own counsel. "Koru hear you."

Megan lay still with her eyes closed, but even though she was dog-tired, sleep wouldn't come. The moon brightened; wind rustled the leaves of a nearby copse, and someone in the next tent over tossed and murmured. Her mind ran in circles; she was too tired to stop it.

"*Zhymata*," came a tiny whisper, after a long while. "You're still awake, aren't you?"

"Yes." The words had been pitched not to rouse her, were she asleep. *If she was planning to sneak out ...* "How could you tell?"

"Right after you fall asleep, you usually have the twitches for a while. Like, I should say *as if* something inside you was having a fight. But now you're lying still. You're worried about *khyd-hird*, aren't you?"

"Yes." It was true enough. *Worried about whether she can do it, and in time....*

"I'm sure she'll be all right and come back because she's too tough to get killed and Koru help her and I'd never mean her when I said this, but ... some people who go missing are never found, are they?"

"Some, yes."

"So their family never know whether they're dead or alive, do they?"

"It happens."

The girl was silent for a time, hard in thought. "That would be really terrible," she said finally.

"I'd rather know for sure she were dead than never know what happened," Megan said. She knew both. *Mourning is black, for a time. Uncertainty is grey-black, forever.*

"Me, too," the girl said gravely.

It's my tiredness, Megan thought. *She doesn't mean it that way.* But the flare of anger rose. She strangled it down. *She has a right to think what she thinks.* "Sovee ... some part of you would be glad if you knew she were dead, wouldn't it?" Megan said, as gently as she could.

She sensed the girl freezing. "*Glad? Zhymata*, whatever gave you *that* idea?"

Megan felt the chill she always felt, witnessing the telling of a bare-faced lie. *She feels she has to,* she thought. *For my sake. It's not as if she wished it wholeheartedly; just part of her does, and you can't blame her.* "Just a thought." Megan thumped her pillow and settled down again. "I'd be an idiot if I thought you loved us completely after what happened between your family and us, wouldn't I?"

"I don't think you're an idiot, *zhymata*," the girl said, stroking Fishhook with deliberate attention. "*Niiiiiice* Hook."

"Not many parents get to hear that, from adolescents," Megan said drily.

"Here, Hooky-hooky-hooky. *Niiiiice* kitty." Sova yawned conspicuously.

Megan let her anger snap into words. "Don't you dare ignore me!" She propped herself up on her elbows. "If you don't want to talk about it, *say so!*"

"I *can't* talk about it."

"Why not?"

"Because . . . because she's your akribhan."

Megan sighed. "I suppose that's reasonable. But since you don't have anyone else here to talk to, you can always ask whether I could hear you objectively."

"Could you?" The girl's whisper was full of suspicion. "You're not usually very objective."

Megan bit back a retort. "If I promised then I'd have to do my best. If I couldn't, I'd go away for a while to cool down, afterwards. So: I promise."

Sova drew up onto her elbows suddenly. "Vat if I told you I hated her? What if I told you I *did* vish she vass dead?" Excitement brought out her accent. "I'm not saying I do! But vat if I *did?*"

"I'd do my best to understand."

There was a long silence. Fishhook shifted, and carefully licked her wings. Finally Sova said, "*Khyd-hird* likes to hurt people who are already hurt. Even if she wasn't the one who defeated them. I don't think that's right."

"Yes. I was already in love with Shkai'ra before I found out that her people taught her that anyone helpless deserved to be kicked. She's trying to learn that the rest of the world doesn't think that, but it doesn't come easy to her to admit she has to learn anything. You can still love someone and yet disagree with them and the way they were brought up."

"How old are people when they stop being the way they were brought up, and start being the way they decide?"

Megan started to answer, stopped, thought. "When they decide to decide; at age ten or one hundred, or never. It takes work, though. The first step is seeing how." She grimaced in the dark. "Next there's the choice of what kind of person to be—and *then* you have to be strong enough to stick to a course that leads toward that."

"You've shown me all the problems with the way *I* was brought up," Sova said. "That women shouldn't be weak or stupid or illiterate or pacifistic . . ." She went on listing the Zak and Kommanz counter-prejudices to Thanish prejudices, by rote. "But *she* doesn't think there's anything wrong with the way she was brought up. Or why would she *brag* about it so much?"

"That's a way of hiding how much it hurts—the 'see-I'm-tough' ruse. She doesn't always know there are other ways to see the world. Saying, knowing in your guts, and acting are three different things. You can *say* women aren't weak, stupid and so on, but when it comes down to it, it's how you *feel*."

"I feel weak and stupid a lot when she's training me. I only feel strong when I'm somewhere else. I sometimes feel strong when I'm fighting; I'm getting used to it. I don't know whether I feel like *me* or not because I don't know who me is anymore." In the slight light, Megan could see the girl's face turned mask-like again; hiding emotion, like Shkai'ra.

"Everyone wonders who they are at fourteen. I was telling myself I wasn't 'the captain's slut.' I suppose you're imagining parallels between Shkai'ra and Sarngeld ..." Megan faltered for a moment, stopped short by the thought. "Sarngeld, who owned me, because she can be tyrannical, and maybe because of things I've said, though you *know* Shkai'ra would never abuse you. In that sense I can understand part of you being glad she's missing; perhaps dead."

She made the words sound sure; but felt her hands trembling. *Why? I know Shkai'ra. After all this time, there can't be anything I don't know, any hidden darkness in her I haven't seen . . . can there?*

Silence held for a while. Finally Sova said quietly, "It's not things *you* said. It's things *she* said."

"Oh?" The night suddenly got quieter, and hotter.

"You weren't there." The girl's voice was barely a whisper.

"What did she say?"

"She . . . she made us take off all our clothes. In front of the crowd. You didn't see; you were helping Piatr. And she . . . she said I was too young, but the way she looked at me . . . that was two years ago."

"Too young. Too young for *what?*" Megan felt the edge creep into her voice, the shrill of tension, roiling up out of the pit of her stomach. *No one knows anyone,* one of her teachers had once said. *Entirely.* She set her teeth, pressed her hands on her knees to stop their shaking.

"Too young for . . . you know! We were . . . we were *naked.* She said it was about time she got some of her own back. She says *that* happened to her all the time . . ."

"*Damn her.*" Megan heard her own voice: black, thick, Dark Lord-toned. The girl wasn't making it up to sow discord, she was sure. For one thing, she was too honest; for another, those things had Shkai'ra's stamp. "Damn her! When she gets back, I'm going to . . . Sova, why didn't you tell me?"

"She vass your *akribhan!* Besides . . . ven we came into the Kchnotet Vurm, ve were naked und had welts all over us. You saw dat! She only shows you her nice side, but you saw *dat!*"

Megan flinched, swallowed bile. "Shkai'ra's very careful with me. She never . . . she didn't . . . she loves me very much, and she's never seen me as weak. She eased up on you when she started seeing you as people, didn't she?"

"Ven ve could do fifty push-ups, more like. She doesn't really think anyone's a person unless they're a warrior."

"Sova. Did she ever carry through on that threat?"

"No. But I always figured it was because I was still too young. I kept wishing I wouldn't grow, or get breasts . . ."

The words fell dully into Megan's head, echoing. *I wouldn't grow. Get breasts.* For *her* it had been the other way round, hoping she *would* grow, *would* get breasts, so Sarngeld would be less interested. "No." Her voice was hoarse, almost a growl. "Never. You're her daughter, and *my* daughter. If she ever raised so much as a finger that way, I would divorce her so fast she wouldn't have time to grab her bowcase."

"You *vould?* I didn't think you'd leave her for *anything.*"

Megan's voice was dead calm, deadly even. "There are some things I will not forgive, and *that* is one of them. Adopted or blood-kin, it doesn't matter."

"You don't mind her *beating* me."

"I've never seen her raise more than bruises on your butt, and for good reason."

"There's things you don't see. The day she took us, we didn't do anything bad except not run faster than we could to where we didn't vant to go!"

"Well, there she was wrong."

"Vat about all dose times when I really *vass* trying as hard as I could in war-training and she'd hit me anyway? Zhymata, that all made me into a different person and I didn't want it and I'm not sure I *like* who it made me into!"

"Made you into a different *person?* Hardly." Megan faced Sova in the dark, fists on her knees. "In war-training, you found the steel in you. It was already there."

"I'm not talking about the steel. I'm talking about the *hate.*"

"You mean her trying to teach you to hate everyone and everything, or just her?"

"*Myself!*"

"Do you? Hate yourself?"

"Sometimes."

"Well, I don't think that's right, either. If you feel that way, why don't you talk to me about it more?"

"I know *you* don't think that's right. But she *does.* She thinks you have to, to be a warrior. She thinks I was mean and cruel before, it just needed polishing. But I . . . well, maybe I was mean to Piatr, I know I was. But . . . well, no one taught me it was wrong then, everyone else was doing it, he was just a nasty witch my Pa gave me to torment, that's all I knew, and I . . . I didn't know what was bothering me, so I took it out on him. I didn't *know* it was cruel; I didn't know what cruel *was,* den. I vass chust a stupid girl!" Suddenly tears muddied the clear young voice. "I vasn't *mean!* I was chust ignorant! I didn't know how much it hurt! *She* vould haf done *vorse!*" Cautiously, ready in case the girl recoiled, Megan touched her trembling shoulder, then pulled her into her arms. "*Khyd-hird* is *mean!* She's *really* mean! She knows vat she's doing!"

"Ah, Sovee, Sovee. She does as she was taught and does *not* know better either, though she's so much older than you are. She says crude and cruel things and doesn't see how she hurts Shyll or Rilla with her ignorance, even me sometimes. She doesn't think there's a problem, though she tries—stumbling, bruising souls, stepping on hearts." Megan hugged the girl, smoothing hair back off her face. "It helps if you think of her like the pups, all big feet and not knowing their own strength. Take what good she can give you and leave her hard-headed idiocies to me. I'll handle them as best I can."

"The pups are just dumb animals, they can't help it. They aren't my teachers, claiming to know everything. And *she* can't do anything to *you*, so you don't know how it feels!"

"Look," said Megan, taking Sova by the shoulders. "Talking to me isn't helping, that's clear enough. If she— *when* she—comes back, you are going to have to take it up with *her*. You are a warrior; you can speak up."

Even in the darkness, Megan could see the girl's lips thin and eyes widen. "But I'm not really a warrior, at least she doesn't think so, because she hasn't *said* I am and I'm only a warrior if she says I am, right? Besides I couldn't . . ." Her voice thinned and trailed off.

"Couldn't what?"

"Couldn't *take* her. She doesn't listen to anyone she doesn't think could . . . at least make a good account of demself. She doesn't think anyone who can't fight is any good, deserve anything but pissing on, or being made a slave of one who *can*.

This might crack my family right in half. My family that isn't yet complete. Maybe it never will be; if Shkai'ra doesn't come back, if Lixand dies. Megan controlled the shudders, so Sova wouldn't feel them. "Then tell her," she said hoarsely, "tell her I'm behind you on this and she'd better listen. She may surprise you and listen anyway because you're family."

"You're behind me? Against *her?*"

Megan felt as if a clawed hand had wrapped around one side of her heart, another clawed hand around the other, and they were pulling, tearing it in two. "For her *listening*. And paying some damned good attention."

She heard Sova's hands fidgeting, nails scratching the bedroll. "*If,*" the girl said quietly. "*If* she comes back."

* * *

Do you like doing it? Sova heard the voice of Azaila in her ears.

Not right now, she answered to herself.

The fight, with both armies full-pitched, had gone from before noon to sundown. After a while the dust had hid most of the foot-combat, a yellow-brown cloud twice a tall man's height; now and then an arrow would flick up out of it, or the head of a pike, and the continuous huge noise. The cavalry fight had been whirling chaos; after a while she'd been too bewildered to be afraid, she'd just concentrated and hoped she didn't make a mistake. After a while her whole body had screamed in protest at the thought of another jarring blow on her shield, another wrist-hurting swordstroke, every one of the enemy bigger and stronger than her. In a pause, sucking at the canteen so hard the water had come out of her nose, colored with the dust that choked her, she had said something to the trooper beside her, a Nellan, a stocky hook-nosed woman with a faint mustache. When she looked back, the Nellan was slumping sideways with a shocked look and an arrow through her gorget, spitting blood.

She hadn't thought it at the time, but now, visiting Echera-e in the infirmary, she did. *That could have been me. Just a puff of wind or a hand twitch . . .*

"Iss shaming," said Echera-e, from his cot in the infirmary tent. He gestured to the other patients, mostly Yeolis, in the infirmary, the beds in neat long white rows; here and there Haians leaned, peered closely, felt. There were a good ten just in her sight. "All wounded in fighting, forrh Yeola-e, forrh Beloved, brave . . . me, get sick . . . flowing sick, stink sick . . ."

"Dysentery," Sova said.

"Yes, dysentyere."

He was pale, like leeched-out soil. It had started two days before. The Haian had said he probably wasn't in danger of death, but it would be another five days before he was up, and perhaps a half-moon before he could fight. *Khyd-hird* had said the Alliance army was lucky,

with so many Haians and strong latrine-discipline. She'd
been in wars where dysentery killed five times more than
battle and wounds together. Only about a quarter of the
patients in the huge rectangular tent were in with fevers
of all kinds, which was almost miraculously good. Some
of the soldiers said it showed the Gods fought for
Chevenga.

"Hate dirrht," he said weakly. "Ahn' naht fight when
should."

"'Who's to know what would have happened, in a battle you missed,'" Sova quoted, and went on with her
account of it. "So, finally, they stopped standing-retreating
and *really* broke ranks. We chased them down for a
while, sticking them in the back, little fights with the
cavalry trying to cover the retreat. Their cavalry was
really thin today, actually, maybe they all had hoof-rot or
something. I'm so tired I hurt all over just from
tiredness."

She was still in her dusty armor, the quilted gambeson
underneath sodden with sweat; the chain sleeves were
sewn to the undergarment, and the one on her right arm
was clotted with blood. Guilt pricked at her, a little; the
manrauq-forged meshmail was fantastically expensive—
the more so as she would outgrow it soon. *I can only
visit him for an hour or two; I'll clean it after that.*

"Now," she said, "time to party. No, no, don't
move, *livling.* I'll raise both our cups, my wine and
your water . . ."

This was a horrible place, full of moaning, sometimes
screaming, unnatural chemical odors mixed with incense
and the worse bodily smells it was all trying to defeat,
and the sheer weight of pain in the air. *How can Haians
stand it all the time? But I'd still rather be here with
him than anywhere else,* she thought. *He needs me. If I
were here, I'd want him to come.* Every now and then
he would ask her to call the healer's apprentice for a bed
pan. Though he didn't ask her to, she'd look the other
way; the Yeoli incense burning by his bed did little to

hide the smell, then. But she stayed; feeling healthy and strong, even if tired. She held his cold hand, and tried to send her strength through it into him.

Last night, when she'd told *zhymata* about it, she'd answered, "That's love, Sovee." And for a moment she'd looked so sad it made her face twenty years older: thinking of Shkai'ra.

"I wish Chevenga hyere," Echera-e said now. After a battle, the *semanakraseye* always visited one of the infirmaries—the army was too big now, to have only one—to comfort the wounded. "Tsey say, he touch you, heal faster. Don't know if I believe tsaht . . . But nice if true. Arrrgh."

Just then, the noise started.

Hoofbeats, alarm cries, Arkan war-yells: *"Kellin! Aras! Imperium!"* But it's over, her mind thought vaguely, lazily. *Here? Here?* From then on, things happened so fast she had no time to think.

Horses—Arkan horses, in the infirmary, ripping through the tent-walls all over—white horses, *the Sunborn Elite.* Her mind tried to refuse what her eyes saw, Arkan horsemen joyfully whooping. *Why no warning?* An Imperial in light cavalry armor, breastplate and helmet and chainmail leggings all blackened, two buckets of javelins at his saddlebow, all of them with javelins, barbed heads cocked back over their shoulders or flaming torches in their hands, grins on their faces, blue eyes slitted. *The cavalry. The cavalry, who weren't there in the day* . . . An officer in a plumed helmet scanned, eyes snake-cold, shouted, "Shefen-kas! Shefen-kas! *Kellin!*" More Arkan, then Enchian with a thick, clipped Arkan accent: *"Ten thousand gold chains and Aitzas rank for his head—whichever side you're on!"*

Gotthumml. Gotthumml. Echerry. Everyone was screaming, it seemed, him, the healers, the wounded. *Get him out of here. I've got to get him out of here. He can't fight.* Haian healers were fearless, she'd heard; because of the World's Compact, because no one would ever hurt them.

A Haian tried to stand between an Arkan horseman and
a patient, his arms upraised, begging; the Imperial's arm
went back smoothly, his body bending with the curve
and the movement of his horse, the whetted edges flashing, then the barbed point sticking out of the back of the
healer's robe as he crashed down. *Gotthumml. A Haian.
He killed a Haian.* An Arkan slashed at a lantern, and it
spewed burning alcohol across half a dozen beds; a
patient covered in bandages from neck to knees ran
flaming into the night, screaming. Another Haian, not
having seen the first, perhaps, tried to stand between a
patient and an Arkan, and was struck down.

She grabbed Echera-e's arm, as he shouted something
in Yeoli. He pulled himself up on her arm as she'd
wanted, but then turned to the Arkans, advancing, stark
naked. *"You'll chust get cut down, you haf no armor!"*
she shrieked, grabbed him, spun him by the shoulder;
weak, he staggered. She seized his wrist to pull him away.
A javelin whistled by her ear. The Arkans were slashing
through the wounded, whether they stayed lying down,
flung themselves off their beds, or rose to fight. She saw
one Yeoli, a giant of a man with a wide bandage that was
turning freshly red on one leg, rear up lifting a cot, and
fling it at an Arkan, unhorsing him. But soon he was run
down. She saw another Arkan scan all around, javelin
cocked in his hand, find a fleeing Haian, aim and throw
. . . *They're going after them. They're going after Haians.*

"Echerry!" Get in front of him. He was still fighting
her, the closest Arkan within two horse-lengths. That one
twisted in the saddle, while his horse's legs knocked over
the bed two beds down with a crash, tearing a saline drip
loose from an arm. The weight of armor that had bowed
Sova's shoulders a moment before seemed weightless.
She drew her sword; it caught in the tent-rigging over
her head. The plated arm, scarlet-lacquered, whipped
forward; she began to move, no time, the edge of the
spear banged off the shoulder of her hauberk and
stunned her shield-arm—*Echerry*—she couldn't look

backward, just struck at the Arkan's thigh. He was moving too fast past her along the row, gone.

I'll cut through the tent-wall, she thought, dragging Echera-e by the wrist. He staggered, fell to kneeling, retching. *I'll carry him* . . . An Arkan *too close!* jumped his horse over a bed *struck at Echerry with a sword* blood-spurt *striking at me* she parried the blow *go for his legs* but he parried *Sunborn Elite oh Gotthumml* then was past and gone.

"Echerry! Echerry!" He was lying across a bed, trying feebly to pull himself up, his right foot from the upper calf down . . . *gone. Just gone.* Blood spurted out in rhythm. She grabbed him around the waist, clasping the wrist of her sword-hand with her shield-hand, dragged him back towards the tent-wall; he went rigid in her arms and yelped, then bit it back, bloodying his lips. *The cut-off part of his leg, on the ground* . . . She heaved him up higher. *I'm stronger than usual.* She knew it with a strange calm. "Sova." It was a weeping whisper. "Sova, I love you." *Smoke*—at the other end the roof of the tent and beds were in flames. No Arkans came at her, *thank you, Gotthumml,* she was at the tent-wall. "Hold on, I haf to put you down, I haf to put you down, love." She struck a long slit through the canvas, bent to take him over her back. He swore in Yeoli. "*Kyash, kyash, kyash,* I hahve to . . ."

Outside Alliance warriors were running in, faces full of rage and naked weapons shining in firelight, pushing past her, towards a roiling fight outside. *Get him away from here.* Darkness between two tents. *I need light.* First aid lessons crowded back into her mind. *Get his feet high. Tourniquet.* Then someone was helping her, telling her in some strange accent to bring him in here, hands guiding her shoulders, leading her into a tent with a soft glow of lamplight.

"He's got dysentery," she breathed, and heard how quivery and tearful her own voice was. "I sorrhy, I sorrrhy," he was moaning, "Need bed pahn, sorrhy, please . . ."

They had to clean him with cloths, then they tightened a strap around his leg-stump just under the knee until the blood slowed to a trickle, propped his legs high and covered him with blankets.

She slid close to him, took his head in her arms. "You'll be all right," she whispered. "You'll be well, you'll be fine ..." *Maybe he knows I'm just reassuring him because that's what you're supposed to do to keep someone from going into shock*, she thought, *and he won't believe me*. She kept reassuring. Outside the battlecries were fading. She watched Echera-e's face contort as the pain hit him. He set his teeth, but grunting moans forced their way out of him; it made no difference how hard she held him, how much she said, "I love you." There was no painkiller here, only in the infirmary.

His foot's gone, she thought then. *His foot's gone. He'll be on crutches, or a peg-leg, the rest of his life. He can't be a warrior anymore. And he just became one. Azaila ... I don't like it. I hate it. I hate it.*

In the morning, the army was called to post-battle assembly, on the field where it had fought. The host was far too big for anyone's voice to carry to its furthest edges; hearlds and interpreters were positioned among the host to relay the announcements outwards. But Megan, being in the special forces, and Sova, with her, were close to the front.

Chevenga usually spoke with a herald right beside him bellowing his words, so he didn't have to raise his voice; now, though, he stood alone on the dais. *No surprise*, thought Megan. *He wants to yell today.*

First came the usual commendation for yesterday's victory, the decorations, the armor-clashing applause. She had almost forgotten. There was less joy in it than usual, though, as the army waited to see which rumors of raids were true. "We will celebrate," Chevenga said, "when we feel like it; if that isn't until after the next time we thrash them, or the next five times, so be it." Then he raised his arms for silence, and spoke of the night before.

Not only the one infirmary, it seemed, but all eight in the camp, had been attacked. A desperation move, he called it, aimed to undermine morale. "Cheap," he spat, "as desperation moves are, and . . ." He laughed, a laugh with a knife-edge. "Of course when they saw me, they came after me. *That* part of the plan, as you can see, was futile." *Infirmaries*, Megan thought. *He always visits one—they knew that.* An old assassin's rule: use the target's habits. "Whether their bid to undermine morale was futile"—he reached his arms out to the army—"that, my warriors, is up to *you*." It was a while before the answering shout subsided enough for him to go on.

Some seven hundred Arkan cavalry had attacked; two or three hundred had got away, the rest killed or captured. The Alliance deaths were worse than a thousand. "Easy to kill," that rasping voice said, rising, building, "being already weak from wounds"; a good fifteen-hundred more were newly wounded. *Counting Sova's love*, Megan thought.

And the Haians . . . Megan had seen the *semanakras-eye* flushed with anger before, his cheeks bearing two bright points of red, though as often as not he seemed to be forcing it in his speeches; she'd never seen him livid, nor the anger so sincere. *He owes them much*, she thought, *and was pulled closer by saving them from Arko once.* Twenty-nine Haians had been struck down, fifteen of them dead, being armorless against heavy cavalry swords or lances. She felt sick. It grew worse, as Chevenga told his army what he had never told her, nor many others, clearly, since she had never heard it: when Arko had seized Haiu Menshir, they'd taken the Haians who'd healed him back to Kurkas. Not to ransom—no demand had been made—but to punish, for the crime of giving succor to one who needed it, as Haians would for all.

The army answered his rage, with howls and death-chants and weapons thrust into the air; beside her, Sova screamed in Thanish, waving a fist. When it subsided, he ended it by saying those Arkans who'd been taken alive would be impaled, then drawn and quartered, then beheaded, and what remained sent back to the Arkan camp. "Let them get a good long look," he said, "and remember that when they consider such a mission again. And *we* will save our anger, dedicate it to them, turn it on them next time. So we have suffered; only in dreams is even a winning war nothing but easy charges and triumphs and victory parties. It's the wrong Arko did that brought us all together in the first place; let it go on binding us as one now, to make us not weaker but stronger, so they bring on themselves the fate they deserve!"

She couldn't hear her own voice for the roar, like the great breakers of the Lannic, going on and on. Beside her Sova jumped up and down, sword in the air, cheeks soaked with tears.

He said what they'd do to the Arkans who were left, Sova thought, *but he didn't say where.*

She'd told *zhymata* she was going to see Echera-e, which was true; she would, after she'd watched *this* for a while. Until she'd seen enough to be satisfied, she decided. She found the place by the sound of male screams.

There was a crowd there already, Alliance-motley, laughing, jeering, making the sign of asses' ears that mocked the cupped hands at the temples, the Arkan prayer gesture, whenever one of the victims used it. The pole and the ground between the four draft horses were already blood-soaked; ringed in with spears on one side stood the shrinking clutch of naked men, their blond hair shorn; to the other lay the growing red and white heap, here and there blond, or innard-colors as she'd seen before, of torn-apart corpses, now and then settling of its own accord, as if something in it were still alive. She stayed upwind.

"Tsey're taking tseir time," said a Yeoli beside her. "Wouldn't want to wind tsose horses, no!" He burst out laughing. "Wahtch *tsis* child-raper try to take tseh pain silently . . . each one thinks *he's* gong to be the first one to mahnage it, ha ha ha! Shit-eaters, tsey don't know whaht pain *is*."

Hurt, you stinking bastard, she thought. *Hurt for Echera-e*.

The Arkan did, and she watched, and enjoyed, for her lover, lying in the infirmary one-footed. The sound of the man being ripped apart reminded her of when she tore the legs and wings off a chicken carcass for the stew, but so much bigger, the shoulder-bone popping out of the socket making a crack like a thick rotten branch breaking, but a little wetter. And he, unlike the chicken, was fighting it, the muscles in death-throes as they tore, the mouth screaming, sometimes screaming words . . . When they untied the ropes, lopped off the head, threw the body in parts onto the heap and turned to the next, she suddenly knew one was enough to see. She walked away, feeling satisfied and sick, both at once.

They'd refused to let her in this morning when she'd come to see Echera-e, saying he wasn't well enough, and things were too much a mess anyway, the infirmary being cleaned up and repaired. This time, though, they said " *'Tai*."

The healer's apprentice led her deep in. *This is where they keep the worst cases*, she thought, fear growing. None of the patients here spoke to each other or shifted, or even looked bored; they just lay utterly still, staring upwards, or with eyes closed like corpses already. Some softly moaned.

"Echera-e, bahd," the apprentice, who was Yeoli, whispered in thick Enchian. "Flux. Foot cut off also. Probably naht die. He naht know where is, now. We let in you, 'cause he call you' name."

The youth lay as still as the others—the patient in the bed next to him, a Haian—his face yellow-pale. As she knelt next to him, she remembered something she'd heard, that people who'd lost a limb felt its ghost, hurting as if the flesh were still there, so they sometimes refused to believe they'd lost it. *Does he know? I better not say anything.*

His lips moved, whispering in Yeoli. She leaned close to make it out. *"Boru."* No. *"Meparae ..."* *Don't take me to the slaughterhouse, not yet, not yet!* She slipped her hand under the Haian-pristine sheets, found his lying cold and limp, squeezed it. *He's delirious; maybe he won't hear me.* "Echerry. It's *me*. Shh, you're safe, no one's going to hurt you. I love you."

His head turned, eyes blinking slowly. "Sovee?"

"Ya. Hi." She leaned, kissed his forehead, his nose, his lips. "I love you." She looked, saw a weak smile on his face.

"I love you too. Miss you." She kissed him for a while, holding his shoulders through the sheets, ignoring the tang of medicines on him.

"A bunch of them got captured," she said. "Chevenga said 'draw and quarter them, for an example.' I saw them do it to the one who ..." *Cut your foot off*, she stopped herself from saying just in time. Not true, but, she figured, a good lie. " ... got you. They made it last nice and long, like putting him on the rack, and he hurt like the Fehuund, yelling and screaming his fool head off ... so to speak. . ."

The youth turned his head away, the knot of his throat shifting as he swallowed. *Maybe this isn't what he needs to hear right now*, she thought suddenly. "Well, you're avenged, anyway. Are the healers being good to you?"

"Ya," he whispered. "Tsere's a Haian next to me, see tsaht? He keep giving healer's orders, forrh how tsey should look ahfter *him*." His whisper got even quieter; Sova leaned close. "He dying anyway. Tsey take him to tseh ... *baityo* ... How you say?"

"Slaughterhouse?"

"Soon." It came to her: that was their word for the part of the infirmary where the hopeless cases were put, to wait for death. "A *Haian*. How tsey could . . ." *They killed fifteen of them, soon to be sixteen,* Sova thought, but this time kept her mouth shut.

The youth lay silent. She wasn't sure what to say; so she stroked his forehead, and now and then kissed him and said, "I love you," or "Heal, *livling*." So it went, with apprentices coming to check him or refill his water or help him use the bed pan, until darkness fell and one came to walk her to the door.

The next evening he looked better, even though he'd been in a wounded-cart all day, on the march. "Flux less," he said. "Look, Sovee." He pulled up the leather thong that held his crystal, showed the other jewel on it. "Chevenga gave me tsis." It was like Saint Mother's Bloodstone, with the same setting, steel-wrought as on all Yeoli decorations, of two enwrapping arms. But it was bigger, and the drop-shaped stone, polished smooth, was dark purple. "*Anchena d'mahachao ayana*," he said. *Saint Mother's Amethyst,* she thought. *The award they give to the ones whose wounds are crippling. He knows.*

Their eyes met. "I go home," he said.

Sova's stomach and chest suddenly went hollow and tight; then the feeling turned to pain, as if she were sick. She hadn't thought of this. He tightened his big hands around hers and said, "Warrh over, you go bahck through Yeola-e, we see again?"

Goodbye, she thought numbly. *This is goodbye.* "Wait— Echerry! When . . . when are you going home?"

"Nex' big caravahn going bahck. Tomorrow morning, army go fo' warrd, me bahck." He smiled; it was steady but she knew he was forcing it. "I tell my motser ahbout you. She never heard of Thanes."

"Well—" *What are we going to do?* she thought. *We never talked about the future. Does he—would he con-*

sider marrying me? A cruel thought wormed into her head, in *khyd-hird*'s voice. *You want to live with, and defend, when fights come, a cripple? A life-mate you were already sworn to, I can see—but someone you rolled with in a war-camp? You're a teenager, so of course he seems like the whole world to you. They all will.*

I've told him I love him, she answered inwardly. *I've said I love him.*

"I'll write," she said, then realized however much they'd learned how to speak to each other, they had no common written language. "I'll ... get it translated. From Enchian into Yeoli."

He smiled. *"Inchaya esan piyae." The die has no mercy.* A Yeoli saying: fate's whims, it meant, don't take into account the wishes of the heart. "Sovee. Whahtever, I always remember you. You, me?"

"I'll draw my last breath before I forget you," she said, and suddenly found tears coming too fast to swallow. "Echerry!" *I'll miss you* was too much to say. He sat up a little, pulled her into his arms, clung to her as she clung to him. *Look at me, snivelling; he's seventeen, he'll think I'm a baby.* But she felt wetness on her cheek; he was weeping, too. Yeoli men, she remembered, did.

In time, a healer came to send her away, since she'd ignored the apprentices. *Children,* the look on the middle-aged Haian face said clearly. "When we come back through Yeola-e I'll visit you," she said desperately. "Where ... ?" He'd mentioned the name of his hometown, but not often enough; it was long and unpronounceable. This time she'd write it down; she dug in her pouch for a wax tablet, spelled it as best she could. They clung kissing until the Haian laid his hand on her shoulder; then she backed all the way out waving, tears blurring her sight.

"Think of it this way," Megan said, as they sat together, the girl absently poking at the last coals of the fire with a stick. "There are far worse ways you and he could have parted. Or that he could have ended his days as a warrior." That was true, and a comfort. *He's far away, but I know he's alive and safe, even if he's on crutches.* Sova looked up at Megan. The Zak's small heart-shaped face was blood-red in ember-light, the dark eyes staring beneath hard, thin brows into nothing. *She's thinking about* khyd-hird. The Thane-girl remembered her own brother. *Ya, there are far worse ways. Quit moping.*

XVII

Shkai'ra's bandages itched.

It was a minor chore to find fresh linen gauze and fresh chicken blood, but they were an advantage otherwise; nobody wanted to get close to someone who looked and smelled quite so gruesome. Fun, in a way, making gargling noises as she slurped soup behind a hand, while everyone assumed she'd had her lips burnt off by clingfire.

The fake papers specified "detached duty" for Emmas Penaras, *solas*, of Marsae. A big port city in the far western provinces; she was unlikely to meet anyone from there and could always claim not to know them. The papers also mentioned "stress," the Arkan euphemism for someone whose mind was no longer quite topped up to the cork. That would account for minor gaucheries.

This empire is deeply fucked, Shkai'ra thought, smoothing her gloves and sucking fruit juice through the straw that pierced the bandages over her mouth.

The tavern was only a few kilometers outside the City Itself. Here in the central provinces the inns were a half-day's journey apart, on roads that made even the magnificent military highways on the frontiers look like goat-tracks. Each inn was lividly ornate with carved marble and terracotta, at least in the *solas* section, which was out on a terrace flung across a forested ravine, pleasant with the scent of pines and the sound of tinkling water. Half of the sleeping quarters had been commandeered for wounded.

The roads outside were full of refugees: *okas* women trudging bare-footed, raggedly gloved with their children at their heels and their belongings on their backs; *fessas* families with carts; half-veiled *solas* and *Aitzas* in carriages . . . and very few men. Males between sixteen and sixty were being taken out and herded off to makeshift training camps, by *solas* themselves past retirement age or with only fuzz on their cheeks, or wounds not quite bad enough to keep them bedbound or addled. Wagon trains rolled out of the City, as well, full of equipment that looked either brand new or as if it had rested in an armory for the better part of a century; every blacksmith shop she passed had been working overtime, with clumsy conscripted field-slaves doing routine chores to spare the skilled men. And there were columns of troops coming in from the west and south, with the lined faces of men force-marched beyond exhaustion.

Papers were checked and rechecked at roadblocks; this last time by regular scarlet-clad soldiers under the command of a mask-faced man in black armor. She had passed dozens of corpses hanging from trees with their severed heads tied between their ankles; the last hundred kilometers had rarely been out of the sight or stink of such. Signs on their chests; she couldn't read them but knew they must say, "deserter" or "defeatist" or "rumor-spreader."

They're finally getting their heads out of their asses, Shkai'ra thought. She had been on the losing side of enough wars to know the signs. *Good thing it's too late.*

The Empire had never managed to mobilize more than a fraction of its strength, and now it never would; like a crocodile killed with an arrow through the eye, the armor and fangs and smashing tail would go on twitching uselessly, without a directing mind. *Not that the mind was much to begin with.*

Press on. Even though she'd been at as brisk a pace as she could with two mounts, it had taken her eighteen days to get this far. The Empire was in dire enough straits, she'd caught on quickly, to commandeer the horses and armor of out of commission soldiers—though not swords, since they were often family heirlooms. She'd been able to take this lovely smooth road only at night and away from cities, towns, roadblocks, traveling army units, watch, or anyone else who stood a good chance of bringing her down alone. *Eighteen days ... and Megan asked the* rokatzk *for what, sixteen? She thinks he'll give her a month; I hope she's doing some* zteafakaz *good stalling.*

Shitshitshitshit.

The last roadblock was at the gate of the City Itself; Arko was built in a deep crater around a lake, and the only ways in were by a ramp-tunnel and the *lefaeti*, the winch-powered lifts. Shkai'ra had had to leave her horses stabled and her armor stored at the last tavern, buying expensive silence; they were no use in the City anyway. The road behind the in-line of the tunnel had been backed up for hours, and she could see why now. The commander of the troops checking those going in was a black; black cloth, this time, with only helmet and breastplate. He barely glanced at the papers, examining the people instead, with a slow methodical care and the meanest pair of eyes she had seen since leaving Stonefort, across the great ocean, more than a decade ago. They were as mean as her own mother's eyes. *Mahid ...* one of the Imperator's special clan of spies, secret police and dirty-tricks enforcers, trained since birth. This one for clandestine operations, obviously. *He uses his eyes for something more than separating his brows from his nose.*

"Kill him," he said in a flat uninflected voice, pointing to a plump *fessas* sweating before the soldiers. "He does not have the infirmities specified in his papers. Clerk, note the official who issued them; they conspire to thwart the will of the Imperator." The soldiers grabbed the *fessas* with swift obedience and professional skill, forcing him to his knees despite his protesting screams and thrashings, taking off his head with two strokes of a longsword.

The regular officer working under the Mahid's supervision took Shkai'ra's papers. She let her head loll slightly to one side, and mumbled without words. *Don't overact,* she thought.

The Mahid looked at her for an uncomfortably long time. Fear ran gelid into her belly, worse than anything on a battlefield. There she knew the risks and exactly what she was doing; too much depended on this—her life, Lixand, Megan's happiness—and this was *not* her best skill.

He made a small gesture with his sword-hand. *He's seen through my injury disguise, but the* detached duty *means some Arkan spook thing. Zaik Victory-Begetter, Mother of Death, be with me now,* she prayed. Not that she was very pious concerning the gods of her homeland anymore, but shit, it couldn't hurt. Her gloved hands she kept immobile, except for the slight tremors she'd seen in warriors with head injuries.

The Mahid nodded almost imperceptibly, as if congratulating her on her tradecraft, and signaled her through; the officer commanding the regulars handed her back her papers. Relief washed through her, stronger than an orgasm. All through the long corridor in the rock, she was barely conscious of her surroundings; alertness returned only when she came to the gate, slabs of cast steel from the forges of Temono seven man-heights wide and three high, raised out of the roadway by massive cables. She felt a slight prickle as she walked under them, one twenty meters back from the exit and one on the verge. The space between was lined with arrowslits and the muzzles of flamethrowers.

XVIII

Excerpt from a report by Irefas Agent code-name Jesas, "On the Device of Gliding in Use by the Sun-forsaken Enemy, submitted to General Farras Magofen":

"Unlike the machines of ancient times, or the living avian creatures on which it was perhaps patterned, the contraption provides no propulsion of its own, and has no means of gaining height except by skillful riding of upward-traveling winds. Getting one into the air is done by one of two methods: a) running or leaping off a suitable hill or cliff; or b) the use of a giant strap made of elastic material (rubber), by which the flyer is pulled back by some forty pullers and literally shot into the air, through the same principle as a slingstone . . .

. . . this would explain the enemy's massive purchases of silk—the only fabric light and strong enough to make the wings of these devices—and rubber, from caravaneers associated with the army, most prominently Goonter Frahnzsson of Neubonn, a Thane dealing through Brahvniki, and others . . ."

O Celestialis, he thought as he watched the no-longer-secret ritual. Two lines of sweaty black savages, bodies heaving, muscles rippling, rough barbaric voices chanting to a primitive drum-rhythm, hauled on the ropes attached to the monstrous black rubber strap, stretched between two tall tree-stumps on a gentle rise. In the pocket of the giant sling sat the flyer with her—yes, certain signs were unmistakable in any race, it was a *her*—masterfully-made silk and bamboo craft, like a huge sky-blue bird, but more fragile looking.

On a signal they all let go, and with an unearthly, deep, whistling *bwwwoing-g-g*, woman and wing shot into the sky, like a huge blue dart at first, then slowing and catching the wind, like a hovering eagle, high above.

Actually, he thought, as the next flyer stepped up and the whole process was begun again, *it looks like fun . . . Celestialis, what am I thinking!? No wonder the price of rubber went up. If home ever finds out, my privates are mince.*

It had been one and a half eight-days since he'd last spoken with Whitlock, and Shefen-kas was still horribly, unmercifully, disastrously alive. *That little cat-clawed bitch is stringing me along*, he thought. *We're past Kirliana, I don't have much more time . . . Arko doesn't have much more time . . . She's going to push it to the limit, and I haven't made the limit hard enough yet, because of that fikken arrow-wound. The next one's got to be it. Do, or he dies. All or nothing. Arko has nothing more to lose.*

The man's got the guts of a lake-quarter rat, Megan thought. *Either that, or he's just plain crazy.*

"It would add something to the illusion, wouldn't it," Chevenga was saying, "if *some* of the Chevengal—Chevengas, I mean—traipsing about the Arkan camp happened to be real, *seya?*"

She knew the stories. He'd assassinated a brilliant Lakan general by creeping through *their* camp at night, sneaked over the wall to open the gate of a city the Yeolis were besieging, at sixteen, and so on and on . . . On his collar he wore two Serpent Incarnadines, the only person in camp who could wear such openly. *So, he has a name. But he has a few other things now, too, that he didn't then. Like a position.* She'd heard rumors of arguments with his command council over his taking personal risks. *No matter how good you are, someday someone will catch you. . . .* She was very conscious of the ache in her leg, where the wound still twinged.

And yet . . . She kept her face as carefully neutral as if she were dealing with a Rand Jade Button, Third Rank. *Lixand. If he got killed I wouldn't have to kill him. If I could make that* rokatzk *believe I arranged it . . . I should argue, though, since it would be unlike me not to.*

She cocked her head. "With all due respect, *semana-kraseye: you* are First General First of this army, said to be one of the finest generals in the last century, and the only one capable of keeping this fractious bunch of nationalities together. That makes you a *little* more valuable than your average Ikal agent." She rubbed her wounded leg significantly.

Chevenga shrugged, shoulders lifting in the relaxed Yeoli way. "I know." In that impossibly-innocent-of-conceit tone; it could be irritating. "But this sort of thing *is* my worth. They've just brought reinforcements in who haven't seen our visions yet; we haven't won so far that I'm not going to keep using every advantage that comes even near my hands, not *yet.* If I may indulge in sounding immodest: for nearly ten years people have thought I was headstrong or over-confident because of what I would try. But I pulled it off often enough that people don't put it down to luck anymore. Did I or anyone ever mention, I have a gift? You'd call it *manrauq.*"

She tapped at the edge of the waxboard, thoughtfully. "Weapon-sense. Ivahn did."

"It makes darkness my advantage. In light the enemy and I each know where the other is; in the dark he doesn't know where I am but *I* know where *he* is ... well, I'll tell more later. So, I'm in the Arkan camp, sauntering around, looking like this" —he struck a casual pose, with a dark little smile— "vanishing, appearing, sometimes an illusion, sometimes real and carving out the guts of anyone who laughs at me for being an illusion."

"And sometimes in the Imperial regalia," said Megan, the thought coming out of nowhere.

The black eyebrows flashed up for a moment; then the scheming look with the dark grin came back. "Yes! Foreknowledge ... something to make them take it as foreknowledge. Inevitable destiny." He chortled. "You're a fiend; I'd hate to have you against me."

"I'd have to know what the regalia looks like," she said. "Do you know? Crown, scepter, royal sword or what?"

"Oh yes, I know. He always wears the seals, a bracelet attached by a chain to a ring, one on each hand, all gold but the four seals, the Eagle on the right bracelet, the Sun his talons are clasping on the left, on the right ring crossed Arkan swords, on the left, a wooden ship with a house-shaped cabin. Ceremonially he wears the robe, floor-length, jewels from collar to hem, sunbursts, swirls. Nothing on the head but hair long as it will grow." She conjured up a brief flash of image for him to correct. *I like the idea of a Yeoli Imperator*, she thought, tired, afterwards. *Arko would be less obnoxious.*

If they win, she thought. *If he doesn't get killed. If I don't kill him.*

"Those things," she found herself saying. "You've seen them far too close, too often, haven't you?" The moment the words were out she regretted them. *Familiar*, she thought, *as if he were a friend, not a* semanakraseye; *just because he knows my scars doesn't mean I can ask him about his.* "Excuse me, *kras,*" she added quickly. "Perhaps that's too prying."

'No, not at all. And that's Chevenga to you. Of all that passed in Arko, I have nothing to hide. Yes, I've seen it all close. The robe not so much as the seals." She raised an eyebrow, then nodded. *Hands.* Arkans considered them a private part, to be covered in public; obscene.

I've got to be crazy, too, she thought. He'd talked her into it.

It was pitch dark; so much the better. Megan parted the branches of low, scrubby—willow?—bush, whatever, with her hands. *I don't know what the Koru-forsaken thing is. I do this sort of thing a Halya of a lot better in a nice orderly city. This time I won't end up with an arrow in me. Careful. Gently over this rotten log.* There were sentries ahead, about twenty-five paces, almost close enough together to scratch each other's backs, as the Ikal report said they were, in pairs. She could hear them talking, some singing, trying to keep up their nerve. The dark was so thick it seemed as if it would bleed if you cut it. *Ouch. Damn thorn-bush.* She crawled under a deadfall.

Chevenga was ahead some ten paces, to her left, but she couldn't hear him move; she only knew by the bird calls they exchanged. *He* is *stinking good at creeping around in the dark, for a warrior,* she thought. *Especially a* semanakraseye. *It's one thing to take to the field with the army* ... He'd put on dark clothes, like a thief, quite happily, without any apparent thought for his dignity: a Yeoli thing.

Nightjars called. Through a hole in the canopy of trees, against a sky as black as the inside of a leather bag, she saw a flicker of soot momentarily snuff a star. *Maybe an owl; maybe a Niah.* She'd heard a rumor that the mysterious dark people, whose purpose no one knew, were secretly using flying machines for scouting, breaking sieges, and so on. Supposedly they'd kept the knowledge of how to make and fly the things from before the Fire, hiding it from all others for three millennia. "This army will go down in history just for the number of preposterous tales about it," she'd said jokingly to Chevenga during their planning session.

"Probably," he'd answered. "But *that* one's true. I'll show you a wing, later." *The Arkans would have a fit*, she thought now, chuckling inwardly, *if they knew that such a so-called primitive tribe had a flying machine*. She wished she could see them fly in daylight, learn how the thing was built, learn how to soar herself. *After this war I am going to learn how. Meantime it's Shae-Arano-e, Whitlock and A-niah—Nightmares to Order.*

If they caught her, they'd think she was a demon, and smother or burn her. *Easy*, she thought. *Just don't get caught.*

An owl-call, from Chevenga: "closer to me," that meant. He was some ten paces ahead, now, to her left. *To slip through the sentries and—*

Then there was an ungodly loud ssshhh-*spung*, followed by rustling and crackling of leaves and twigs so loud they were deafening in the silence of the night. High off the ground, halfway to the treetops, some ten paces ahead to her left.

The Arkans all went silent for a moment, then she heard their alarm call, "*Itzen!*" from several places, the nearest seeming within spitting distance.

"*Kyash.*" His soft voice: it had been too much to hope, she knew, that some other night-wanderer, animal or human, had made the noise. *O Koru. Why do I get the feeling the dung-cart is about to tip over?* Armor clanked, feet crashed through the brush; she heard an Arkan sword rasp out of a scabbard. An odd thing about the word he'd spoken—aside from the fact that he didn't swear easily—twinged awfully at her awareness. *Why did it seem to come from so high?*

She kept moving, to get a view, while the first blinding pin-pricks of Arkan torches through the trees appeared.

By a patch of the lesser black sky through velvet black leaves, she sensed a clearing and motion above, smooth like a pendulum's. She heard a sound she knew well from ships: the creak of a rope pulled taut. From far above came his hissing whisper: "I tripped a *kyashin* snare." The moving black shape resolved itself; Fourth Chevenga Shae-Arano-e, *semanakraseye*, the Invincible, the Immortal, the Infallible, was dangling upside-down by one ankle, twice her height off the ground.

Fish-guts. They'd never used traps before. *The price of their nervousness ... Goddess and little demons, why didn't we think of it? Why didn't he, who's so brilliant, think of it?*

"Stay hidden," he whispered, curling his body up to climb or cut the rope. "You can do more unseen ..." *What did you think I was going to do, dance around in the shrubbery waving flags?* But he wasn't Shkai'ra, didn't know her; she acknowledged and crouched low. The torches came in, faster than he could free himself. By wavering flamelight she saw him, twisting now to turn facing them, with the faint gleam of steel in his hands, short sword in his right, dagger in his left. A flash showed his face, still handsome-lined, even inverted: but the lips were stone-hard thin, and the eyes ... she'd heard tales of a stare that could stop a platoon of Arkans dead in its tracks with sheer fear, that had made one veteran officer fall over, dead, his heart stopped. *I'm a storyteller's daughter*, she'd thought at the time. Now all she could think was, *I'm glad that's on my side.* She'd never seen such a pure expression of not only anger—at himself, it must be, but turned on them—but will, utter will, inhuman certainty. Only when it vanished into shadow again did she remember he was swinging upside-down, mostly helpless; his eyes had burned that away while they were visible.

The Arkans, six, came in fast. A knife throw would never cut the rope, which was probably wet with dew, she knew; she'd more likely hit him. *Closer.* She drew her neck-sheath knife, twitched the two wrist-sheathed blades into her hands quick as thought. Her hands were sweating. He was going to have to fight fikken well. *Damn you, why didn't you listen to me? Why didn't you listen to your command council?*

Just don't be stupid, she said, to herself this time, *don't do anything dumb. I've got to get him out of this. It's up to me, and has been ever since he put his foot in it.*

Or . . . The thought came slowly, unfolding cold and pure and practical. *Or I could leave him. I could leave him for them to kill, tell the* rokatzk *I knew where the snare was from checking before and led him into it. And have Lixand.*

The Arkans rattled to a clash-kettle stop, just out of his reach. No one had run for an archer or to alert the camp, as far as she knew.

"Well, well, well." They relaxed, straightening, their crouching stances turning into swaggering. *As only Arkans can*, she thought. *Always so manly when your opponent is chained.* "Looks like we've caught ourselves an assassin. Why don't you just drop those sharp, dangerous objects, my boy, and we'll let you down. Hmm?"

Fish-guts—because he's not dripping with gold six chilioi *behind the line—where he should be—they don't recognize him.* The Arkan voice was young and haughty for a *solas*, some half-lordling getting his training; she saw him, beardless, nose high in the air. By habit she crouched with knife cocked, waiting for the first flash of Arkan flesh not covered with steel.

But Lixand . . . They'd truth-drug her if she came back without the *semanakraseye*, no matter what her story, no matter how trusted she had been. *So I can't not help him. I have to.* Yet if she sneaked back into camp, immediately gathered up Sova and the animals and got like stink out . . .

Swinging only slightly now, he didn't answer the threat, wanting to give nothing away by his voice, which was known, but kept his blades. His hands were ready, poised on guard, as if he always fought upside down; the stare was gone from his eyes now, replaced by calm, but she could see it underneath, biding its time, held back to be let out when the moment was right. Dead leaves itched her sooted ankles; they'd rattle if she moved.

"Very well, backstabber," the half-lordling said, boredom dripping in every word. "Have it your way. Illikren, stun him."

One of the other Arkans moved in, swung his spear-butt carefully. Chevenga's short sword came out for what looked like an easy parry, almost slowly, wood crack-ringing on metal, the blow setting him swinging. Blond brows rose, in surprise; the Arkan circled to get behind his back, swung again, into another casual block. And another, and another . . . The easy victory kept not happening, the Yeoli short sword or dagger or wristlet hidden under black shirt-sleeve somehow happening to be in the way each time, as if by astonishing luck. It didn't matter which way Chevenga was facing, or whether he was looking or not. *Weapon-sense.* The *solas* began to grunt with amazed frustration each time he was thwarted; he hawked, spat, tried harder, to no avail. "*Shen*, sir," he said finally, panting, "I can't hit the fikken guy! Can someone else take a crack at him, please? I'm getting tired."

"Certainly," the lordling said coldly. "But you stay. *Both* of you should have no trouble."

Koru. Chevenga could only defend; they made sure to keep their heads low, out of his steel's reach, though he took a vicious swipe whenever one came near. No matter how brilliant his moves—parrying, twisting, playing them against each other so they got in each other's way somehow; making another part of her think, *Koru I've never seen anything like this, what a story it would be*—it was a matter of time; no matter how great, he would tire. Like children at a Nayanta party, the Arhans were, striking blindfolded with sticks; but the children always hit in the end, and the treasure spilled on the ground.

He could only defend, waiting for her, trusting her . . .
He must be wondering why I haven't done anything yet.
One blow finally ended with a deep muffled thump
instead of a sharp one, a hit on flesh, not metal; she
heard his breath catch, saw them redouble, encouraged,
grinning; saw him pick up again as if nothing had happened, and go on fighting coolly, without desperation, in
what, without her, was a hopeless battle. *He could force
my hand, by calling me . . . but he's not.* He showed no
trace of doubt that she would help him, every move as
smooth and confident as if he had a whole company
hiding in the woods, and just had to hold out until they
arrived, thinking she was waiting for the perfect chance,
or preparing herself, or something. *Making my excuses
for me . . .*

Koru, such a fight. And only a handful of witnesses.
The watching Arkan faces had changed from sneering to
marvelling, except for the lordling, who through much
effort was maintaining his bored look. She swallowed;
another blow got through, Chevenga's breath catching
again. *It could all be over in a moment, my decision made
for me, if they find his head.* Then it came sickeningly
to her, what would happen then. They were trying to
take him alive; they'd truth-drug him, find out who he
was, and send him back—to Kurkas.

No. The thought was cold and pure and certain. *I
won't do that. I'll put my own steel through his heart
before I'll let him go to that. Lixand-mi—I can't. Not yet.
Lixand, forgive me.*

She reached for the metal in Chevenga's hands with
her thought, skimming part of her concentration off to
swim in the *manrauq*, shining motes locked in shimmering,
hard-edged form; for a moment she was almost sucked in,
losing herself in wonder, then steadied, centered. She set
a hook of power into the metal, as she had already with
her own knives, making them sensitive to her, and shoved
the thought into the back of her head where it could maintain without her effort, like breathing.

She drew a deep breath, and started the lowest hum she was capable of, filling the clearing with a sound like a kicked hive of bees, or the rumble after a distant lightning stroke. Directionless; but they were occupied, entertained, and didn't hear. She made it louder, lungs and diaphragm shaking to the sound. *Hold on, Chevenga.*

"Come on, come on," the half-lordling chided. "We haven't got all night; this *isn't* where we're all supposed to be, you know." *Nervous*, she thought. *Somewhere deep inside, Arkan, you can hear me.*

"We're trying, we're trying, *sir! Fikket*, this is *ridiculous*. Illikren keeps hitting *me*."

"*You've* hit *me* three times, shithead!"

Chevenga gave a dark cruel chuckle.

"*Fikket*," said the half-lordling. "Another, Imikas, get in there!"

"With all due respect, sir," said one of the watchers, with a little fear in his tone, "why don't we just kill him?" Two others had heard the hum, and knew it; they were glancing over their shoulders when they thought their commander wasn't looking, shifting grips on torches, making them dip and quiver. *This is only the beginning, Arkan rokatzk.*

"Are you out of your peasant mind, shit-for-brains?" She saw two square thumb-lengths of skin clear on the closest one, just under his jaw, and the strap of his helm. *Kill-target. Risk it.* "Have you ever seen a barbarian fight like that in your life? Do you know how much he'd fetch, if we can get anyone to believe this, in the *Mezem?*"

Something made her check the throw, and watch Chevenga's eyes. There it was: the stare.

"*Oh, no.*" His voice was like that of the Dark One, whispering life loose. "Forty-nine chains is quite enough, thank you."

They all froze, understanding, knowing who he was. In the stretching moment of stillness, it seemed he was the only one capable of motion, and knew it; he grinned, and winked, and carefully, leisurely, almost lazily, threw his dagger, a cast as if he'd played *cniffta* all his life, used to impossible throws. *And with his weak hand, too*, she thought, even the thought seeming slow. The dagger floated out, trailing her hook like a silken line, and buried itself in the half-lordling's eye. He went down like a wooden doll, crumpling to one knee, then falling sideways in a sweep of arms that waved life away like a bad bottle of wine.

"Celestialis-shit-fucking-dog-mother . . . !" Megan threw then, while her target stood flat-footed. She watched her hand point the path the dagger had followed, to stand up bright under the second man's ear until his head tilted sideways and he sank, torch falling to smolder in the damp loam. "Ohhhhhhh, fik!"

Two down. She sent power along the lines to all the hooks. Softly, gently, Chevenga's short sword and her own knives began to glow a yellow brighter than the torches. She drew in a few sobbing breaths, leaking them into the hum. It was like lifting her own weight straight up.

Don't be stupid, Megan, you've done more things with the manrauq. *Before you overstrained yourself fighting Karibal . . . Wrong thought, wrong thought*. She eased herself up again very gently on one knee so her hold on the glowing weapons wouldn't break, and split off another piece of herself, reaching for the second dagger Chevenga's left hand had drawn, so both his blades glowed.

His face gleamed with sweat, black headband solid as a tentacle wrapped across his brow. The crazy embarrassing position suddenly looked chosen, supernatural, a man inverted by choice like a bat, hanging for some greater purpose like the twelfth card in a Seer's deck. Laughing, gold teeth flashing in the unnatural yellow light, a cheery, rippling, tearing stream of it, crazing the air with terror, sending ice down even her spine.

"Who do you think you are fighting?" he said, voice death-low. "When you are fighting me, you are fighting all the world, and all its denizens." *The timing couldn't be better*, she thought, *if we'd rehearsed for a year*. They stood as if his laughter, his words, had driven nails through the top of their heads, the one supposedly helpless, holding four in terror. She felt a laugh inside and choked it back; *later*. Then, *no*. She giggled, shrill in the night, one short, high chuckle that wouldn't let them pinpoint where she was. Slowly, she cocked her next knife back. *I can't do anything difficult. Just nice, easy throws. Wait for them, juggle all the bits of self, concentrating on everything, and nothing. Watch him, stay in harmony with him. Save concentration for throwing.* It was still four to two, and one of the good side hung in a trap.

She floated in a sea of bits of herself, treading water, treading power, feeling it all around her. She could only use it in trickles. She reached and the warmth flowed in to fill all the spaces that people could not touch. She watched from a clear distance away in her mind, knew the next move would be perfect as if practiced a thousand thousand times. Her hand trembled no longer. She was at center at last, drawing in, drawing in to a tighter and tighter point, like the smooth scent of brandy, the calm of a shark swimming.

"Fuck it to Hayel!" One was brave. His voice sounded small and desperate against the hum, as against sea-waves crashing in an endless roar. "We've got Shefen-kas strung up for our taking! Think of the reward we'd get!" Two went on staring out into the woods; the other two spun their spears around to strike with the points, to kill.

"Come on, then." He grinned at them. "You'll have an easier time with me than with my . . . friends." One faltered, hung back, then stepped forward, reluctantly. Megan's hum felt somehow outside of her too, now, shaking the bones of her skull like the drone of a wasp caught and stinging in the eardrum.

Now they were stabbing, not clubbing, harder to turn for one without his feet on the ground. *Hang on. Hang on, Invincible, Immortal. Time, Koru, time . . .* "Ya-a-a-ahai!" An Arkan triumph-cry, as spear-head scraped across sword-edge, *off-line, angle wrong shit shit shit,* jabbed to a halt in flesh. *His left arm, near the armpit.* The dagger slipped out of Chevenga's fingers, to fall orange in the grass and fade out like an ember spat out of a fire. "Hah! Ya-hah!" The Arkan twisted the spear in the wound, hard, worked it back and forth a few times, then yanked it out tearing loose a spray of blood, and a gasp from between Chevenga's bared teeth. His eyes still stared, but had turned pain-frenzied; she saw him seize control of his breathing by will. *Do something. NOW.*

"See! He can bleed!" The Arkan spoke, turning, raising his head to look at his own bloodstained weapon. *His throat, clear*—her dagger was there, glowing like a chip of sun. He went down, not dead, but strangling around the metal in his throat, heels drumming with a dull, hollow sound. In the knife-glare his blood was like lava, brighter than Arkan red armor.

Chevenga spoke Megan's thought, deathly-hoarse even as she thought it; this was like the harmony she had with Shkai'ra, somehow. "And *you* can die." Despite his own blood half-coating his face, he smiled again, beckoning with his sword, gold-teeth flashing through crimson, a sight out of a nightmare. The two with torches stood, shifting, yearning to flee, afraid to flee; the third held his spear half-raised, country-boy Arkan face frozen in a flash-instant of terror. Her detachment was slipping, starting to tear like a too-often washed shirt. She struggled to hold onto bits and pieces as they were sucked out of her with the ebbing of the *manrauq.*

Chevenga's voice went on, a black gravelly droning in the soul, explaining as if to slow-witted children; in her weakness it seemed unreal, a voice in a bad dream. "Half of you are dead, without even knowing what you face. If all of you go, I get away. If one of you goes for help, he'll be alone in the dark woods. If two of you go then one will be left here, with me. If all three of you stay . . ." He let the words trail off.

My cue. Now, to make them break and run. She flung the knife and felt her control slip as it left her fingers, the blade clattering off the armor of the spearman, dull, dead metal. She wasted no strength making it glow. So natural a thing, to miss; only too human.

That's it, shit! They'll see through it all, stop being afraid, and he's rat-bait . . . It failed; I failed. First I decide to save him, then can't. She hissed air through her teeth, clung to what she still had—the bright, fierce glare of the knives. The bone-rattling hum, seemingly rising out of the ground itself, cut off, letting the silence of the woods around them crash on their ears.

But Chevenga flung his sword. The Arkan below him had turned his head toward Megan, trying to see where the knife had come from; now the short Yeoli blade blazed like the enchanted ones in ballads as it buried itself in his neck, a golden lightning bolt flung from the Hanged One.

The two remaining Arkans hesitated a moment longer, gripping their torches, mouths working, looked at each other, and then ran as if the Dark Lord himself drooled on their heels.

It's over. We did it. For a moment Megan couldn't believe. She leaped up, staggered, and let all her brightnesses die, leaving only the light of torches half-foundering in the brush. *My head feels peeled open. It wasn't much but lights, but for how long?* She wanted to throw up. *Why not?* She did, into the brush. As the Arkans' yells faded, silence thickened; she felt her blood thunder in her head. *Over,* she thought vaguely, bending to gather up the dagger lying in the grass.

"Megan." The same voice that had seemed to echo doom through her skull now came small and weak with fatigue and pain, human. *Koru, you fool, he's wounded.* "I can't cut myself down. I don't carry as many sharp edges as you . . ." *A short sword and two daggers, all he had . . .* he'd thrown his last blade. She heard distant alarm-yells. *Not over*. She felt near fainting, shook it off. *Find strength somehow* . . .

A sound came from him like a sob . . . *no*, she thought giddily, *it's too fast*. Slowly it came to her: he was laughing.

She looked up at him, still swinging gently, his face dripping with sweat and blood mixed, right fist pressed into left arm to stanch the flow, helplessly giggling, eyes closed and gold teeth bared, each panting gout of laughter louder than the one before.

You think this is funny, she hissed inwardly. *That it's a big joke that my head feels like Jade Button Third Rank is sticking his knitting needles into my temples, I'm so spent all I want to do is fall over but I still have to rescue you, Invincible, Imperturbable, Gold-bottom, up there dangling in the breeze bleeding like a stuck pig* . . . A chuckle burst up out of her chest, turned into a guffaw. *Madness is catching*. "I should leave you up there like a side of beef!" No help, it just made him laugh harder. She headed for the tree, feeling her second wind.

"Wait, there's rocks under me . . . forget it, there's no time, just cut me loose." Arkan yells grew more numerous; soon they'd come in crowds. She doused the torches on the ground—*too easy to find us that way*—hauled herself up the tree on her claws. Its bark was smooth enough to slide out on the limb without too much snagging; bowed by his weight, it bent more still under hers. She looked down at the soles of his boots in starlight, saw the faint gleam of his eyes and grinning teeth, as he bent his head to look up at her. "Shit. Those pig-sucking bastards are too cheap even to have a spare loop of rope to let you down easy. Hold on, Chevenga, I'll climb down."

She went hand over hand down the rope, hooked her legs around his body, while he hooked his free one around hers, then sawed through the rope until just a strand or two were intact. "We'd better not get caught," he chuckled, "in such a compromising position."

"If you won't tell I won't," she gasped. "Now shut the fuck up!" She caught the knife in her teeth, grabbed the rope with both hands, felt torn in two—*Koru!*—as it broke, slamming both their weights onto her arms. *Koru it's no heavier than wet sail but Koru shit I'm losing it* . . . He was still giggling as he slid down her body, curling to break his fall, but it cut off in a gasp of pain when he hit ground. Her own weight alone felt feather-light.

"I'm clear," he rasped. Praying she wouldn't break an ankle, she dropped, taking only bruises. The Arkans were coming fast now, breaking through the underbrush. *One of the dead, not so dead, still kicking, he'll tell* . . . She tore out the man's throat with her claws and grabbed up those of her knives she could find fast enough, while Chevenga staggered to his feet. *Claw up any corpse in my way, a bit, just to give them something else to talk about* . . . Leaning together the two fled.

He wouldn't let go his wound to lean an arm on her, probably wisely, she knew, so she steadied him by hanging onto his belt. And he started laughing again. Not that it mattered; they were making as much or more noise crashing through the bush. "Don't mind me," he chuckled. "I just have a seasoned appreciation for the basic ironies of life. Or else I'm going into shock, hee hee hee ha ha . . ." *Koru help me with this fish-gutted lunatic*, she thought. Talking too much; that was one of the signs of shock, she remembered.

The Arkan yells fell behind, stopping at the clearing. She pulled him to a halt by a rock. "Here, sit down," she said. "I'll bind it up. You lose strength to hold it shut, you're in trouble." He fought, weakly, saying, "No, dammit, I can run. Don't give me this shit that I'm incapacitated." That would mean she was in command. *Forestall me, will you?* "If I stand still I'll get cold and stiffen up, I might not be able to get up again, I *know*, dammit, I've been wounded a *few* times before!"

"Shut up, Gold-bottom!" She pinned him with her knee, grabbing a sash she'd tucked in her belt, felt him go still.

"Gold-bottom?" His voice broke into a giggle-fit. Under it he was trembling now, she could feel; she had his arm half-wrapped already, pulling the sash tight as she could under his other fist, knotting it. *"Gold-bottom?"* She hauled him up, half-carried him, laughter and shivers both growing worse. "I'd better go straight to Kaninjer," he managed to gasp, as they neared camp.

"Nooooo," she spat back. "Actually we're going dancing." *What did I say that for? He's going to drop dead on me,* she thought, *still killing himself.*

A snapping voice out of the dark: the sentry, a Lakan, was challenging them. "P-p-password?" Chevenga's teeth were chattering now. "Sh-shit, I c-can't remember the *ky-ky-kyashin* password, and *I* made it up—sentry, it's m-m-me! You know—G-g-gold-bottom! Let us in be-f-fore I *k-kyashin* freeze to d-death!" Megan dug the word up out of her memory, spoke it. Still suspicious, the guard let them show themselves, immediately changed to cringingly kowtowing.

At his tent a small crowd of guards and squires enveloped him, taking his weight—*thank Koru*—asking if she was all right as well. She heard Haian-accented Yeoli, giving orders: Kaninjer. "The report's up to *him*," she said, to the hard-faced command-council types who wanted answers. "He's superior officer." *It's chain-of-command policy, I have to pass the buck, ohhhh well.*

Shaking off their hands she staggered back to her tent, headache pounding from the base of her skull all the way up over the top of her head and around behind her eyes, and vaguely heard Sova's voice. "Zhymata, you've got blood on you, are you all right? Zhymata, lie down. You're *manrauqed* out, I can tell." She just let the Thane-girl tend her.

I've got stronger again, she thought. The *manrauq*-pain this morning was no worse than a medium hangover.

He'll count it strange—and suspicious—if I don't visit him, after that. Megan grunted, pushed up from her bedroll, paused, and tucked her seers' card case into her pouch.

As she and Sova ate breakfast, she waved down a passing Yeoli officer. "Are we still fighting today?"

"As far as I know," she answered, puzzled. "Why wouldn't we be?"

"Oh, rumors, you know." The woman shrugged and went. *I guess he's going to hill-top it,* Megan thought. The gong-signal to set ranks came just as she was heading to the *semanakraseye's* tent; he was long gone when she got there. From camp, alone, she watched the battle as best she could, seeing mostly a dustcloud.

It was over before noon, and word came back that the rest of the day was leisure time, but they'd march tomorrow. *We won,* Megan translated inwardly, *but bed down early.*

It took a good half-hour to talk and elbow her way through the scribes, messengers, officials, squires and hangers-on who always surrounded the *semanakraseye's* tent after a battle. Inside she heard the same Haian voice she remembered from last night, speaking in both Yeoli and Enchian, actually somewhat raised. "He's wounded, he nids quiet, can't this ell *wait?* Chivinga, lie *down!*" But someone obviously said something to someone, for suddenly people were actually being civil, even respectful, and ushered her in.

They'd set up a bed in the office portion of the tent, next to the desk; as soon as everyone else had left he sat up, folding back the covers at his waist, smiling. The wounded arm was in a sling; on the outside of the good one, that he extended to her, bruises showed purple-blue, from blocking spears. His cheeks were a little pale, and his eyes looked slightly groggy; now the battle was over they'd gotten a sedative into him, it seemed, though he was fighting it. She had a sudden memory-flash of his face in flickering flamelight, an upside-down death's head shrouded in blood, and could barely reconcile the two images.

"I don't know if I thanked you well enough last night," he said, reaching for her hand. "You saved my life." He kissed the backs of her fingers, and pressed them to his brow, for long enough to make her shift uneasily. Formal gratitude, Yeoli-style; the longer it lasted, the greater the degree.

His brow was warm on her knuckles. It gave her chicken-skin inside. *Don't thank me*, she wanted to say. *I might have to kill you.* Finally, after long enough that he'd take it for shyness, she pulled her hand away.

"You're welcome. It could just as easily have been the other way around. And I missed the most important knife cast. So forget it. I hope you don't think I meant half the things I said on the way back; my mouth runs away with me at times like that."

He waved it off. "Can't remember a thing. Well ... except something about something ... gold." Megan chuckled. "I hope *I* didn't say anything inappropriate."

"No, not at all. So tell me, O Infallible: what did your command council have to say about what transpired last night?"

There was something wonderfully satisfying in seeing someone who had all those use-names look so sheepish. "To be honest," he said, "I've kept them too busy this morning, and Kaninjer's kept them too far away ever since to say anything. I'm not nursing any hope that they'll forget, though." He shrugged, the typical Yeoli double-shrug, the shoulders and then the good arm. "What can I say? They'll tell me, 'You should be more careful.' I will say, 'Yes, I admit it. I will.' Some will leap on that and say, 'You young idiot, why didn't you listen to us sooner?' in the hope that will make me listen to them more next time. Others will keep an awkward silence, trying *not* to make me feel like an idiot. Others will worry that it'll shake my confidence, while still others will worry that I'll go haring off on some even more dangerous stunt just to prove my Infallibility. And I'll just keep going the same way I have all along, except I'll check for traps."

Megan raised one brow, drawing the leather card case out of her belt. "I'm glad I'm not in a position where I'd have to try to out-stubborn you." He laughed. "Let me show you something."

Megan unlaced the card case. She made no claims to be a seer—most such tended to cringe at the thought of handing their cards around—but carried them just to practice. She shuffled through the twelfth card, pulled it out and laid it in his hand.

"The Hanged One. A very powerful card. And very symbolic." In some witches' decks, the figure was shown hanged by his neck, as if being executed; with most, though, including Megan's, he was pictured hanging upside down by one ankle, from a tree-branch.

Chevenga burst out laughing. "What does *that* augur? Danger? A wound? Salvation by magic? A scolding command council?"

She grinned, and let her voice take on the cadence of the fortune-teller. "Fulfillment, moral or physical sacrifice, the period of respite between significant events. The approach of new life forces. A period of indecision. Change, if willing sacrifice is made."

"Well," he said, laughing, "I wasn't willing to step in the snare, if I'd had the choice. Here's the period of respite, whether I like it or not. I don't know where the indecision was . . ."

My face is stone, Megan intoned to herself. *Don't let him see where the indecision was.*

"Change," he went on, "that remains to be seen, I guess. Or maybe the meaning's different if instead of turning up the Hanged One, you *are* the Hanged One." He handed the card back, and she tucked it away. "Well, thank you again. I owe you."

Megan forced a natural smile. "Shit, Chevenga, you don't owe me. Like I said, it could have been the other way around, and *you* would have had to save *me*." He *would have,* she thought. "These things all come out even." *Yes,* a voice seemed to say in her mind. *They do.* "Nobody owes me anything."

He reached to kiss her hand again; she had to let him. This time there was something small and hard in his, that he slipped into hers as he opened his fingers. He winked, and put a finger over his lips. She looked; it was a Serpent Incarnadine. She'd won the second-highest award for actions of stealth already. This was the highest.

"Th-thank you, *kras.*" The honorific came without thought.

"I give it as Chevenga, not *chakrachaseye,*" he said. "Unofficially, I mean. I'd say thank you, but then we'd end up in a gratitude contest all day. When I should be letting you go, before Kaninjer gags me."

She got up. "Say hello to Sova," he added.

She put lightness back in her voice. "Right. Thanks, now hurry up and heal. Invulnerable. We need you." She tried not to walk out too fast, the Serpent hot in her palm.

The next night she overheard two of the *darya semanakraseyeni liyai,* the Elite Demarchic Guard, talking at a campfire, as she passed.

"It was on some secret mission, so no one knows how he got wounded."

"Aigh. I wonder how cursed close he came."

"I'll tell you one thing: whatever happened, he was ashamed enough to un-decorate himself for it."

"Un-decorate?"

" *'Tai.* He has two Serpent Incarnadines—right?"

"Right."

"Not anymore."

"Hah?"

"Take a look, next time he inspects us. He's only got one. No shit, I was there."

XIX

Like an eye glancing aside from heaven's gaze, Shkai'ra thought, as she walked down from the gate towards the City amidst the flood of refugees, imagining a bird's-eye view. Dark blue pupil, a lopsided rim of white buildings flecked with gardens, and the darker green of the woods and fields which the law preserved about the rim of the crater. The interior walls of the crater rose nearly two hundred meters, polished smooth as a politician's lies. The far wall of the crater was hidden in a haze of heat and moisture, trapped in this pocket in the earth. On the cliff-face above the Marble Palace was something impossible to ignore: the Imperial Eagle of Arko, stretched out rampant in bas-relief picked out with gold, four hundred meters across and three hundred high. Even now in mid-afternoon it glowed fiercely. At dawn, Shkai'ra thought, when the sun came over the eastern cliffs and caught it directly, it must blaze like an idea in the mind of a god.

The Imperial capital had started on the western shore of the lake; the Marble Palace was there, well back from the water, the gold leaf blinding from the pitched roofs and towers. A broad processional avenue, fringed by mansions and public buildings, and then lower structures in sickle-curves along the lake. Those would be the poorer quarters, where the *fessas* shopkeepers and artisans lived, and the free-poor *okas*. And it was *huge*, as big as Illizbuah on the far side of the Lannic. A million souls or more in times of peace; who knew how many hundred thousand more, since everyone in the provinces to the immediate east who had something worth stealing was running for the capital.

She studied their faces a little; Arkan women were shy before men, but one as wounded as she tended to be ignored. The *okas* were dumbly miserable, as at some natural disaster, flood or plague or rain at harvest. Most of the *Aitzas* seemed merely irritated, affronted at the disruption of their orderly lives; she even heard two daughters of minor nobility chattering about the unexpected chance to participate in the capital's social season and visit the Mezem. The *solas* were more quiet; a mixture of shame and fear, Shkai'ra supposed, since their Steel-Armed God, and Arko itself, charged them with its defense. The families of the warrior caste alone were likely to have an idea of what war and conquest meant, here, far from the Empire's borders. And it was less unimaginable to them that the Empire would lose the war.

Arko's streets were laid out on a grid, paved with granite blocks over concrete. Less filthy than most large cities, even with the extra numbers crowding in; there were stone grills at regular intervals, leading down to understreet sewers. Shkai'ra looked about at buildings gone seedygaudy, yellow tile along the edges a little chipped, many of the fountains at intersections dry and filled with litter; yet even in the poorer *fessas* district there was fine building and artwork enough for the rich of some lands she had seen. There were many shops, and the jewelers, trinket-sellers and tailors seemed to be doing a roaring trade.

Fewer food shops, and the prices—she could hear people haggling—were outrageous.

She grinned behind the bandages. Chevenga was making no effort to stop or molest the tens of thousands pouring ahead of his troops, so long as they took nothing useful to his army. They streamed in through the *lefaeti* and the great tunnel, thousands every day, thanking the appropriate god of their caste for the barbarian's inexplicable mercy. Then they went to the market to buy food. Meat and fresh greenstuffs seemed to be short already; fruit and flour were still plentiful, from the winter wheat harvest. But give it a little time . . .

The taverner looked up as Shkai'ra walked in, eyes widening slightly. She made a grating, bubbling noise at his question, and held up half a silver chain; he bowed, rubbing his hands at that.

"By all means, a room, bath, and dinner," he burbled, as she laboriously signed "Emmas Penaras, *solas*," in the register that Imperial law required all innkeepers to maintain; most of the rest of the column was simple symbols, with the innkeeper's handwriting beside them. "You honor our house, distinguished and heroic *solas*." There was pitying contempt in his eyes for the soldier who could not bear to show his face among his own.

"Eat . . . room," she rasped, deepening her voice. Her Arkan was weak, most of it things along the lines of "where is your unit" and "give me your gold or wear your intestines."

Shkai'ra took a seat as they readied the accommodations. The place was a mixture of strange and familiar; openwork arches on all sides, here where the weather rarely became more than chilly, an unlit charcoal brazier in the hearth. Tables, and a counter with covered jugs of wine, water and soup set into the stone flush with the surface. Some things were the same in this sort of dive anywhere there were big cities: the grubby, defeated-looking hangers-on playing chess in a corner, the dedicated soaks, the bitter-eyed youngsters with shoddy-bright clothes, and knives—here worn under the arm with the hilt down. Something bothered her for a moment or two before she realized. Arko, of course; the crowd was all-male, down to the tired-looking prostitutes on stools in the corner. The sweet-musky odor of Arkanherb drifted under the rafters.

Now, she thought, *a bath*—It was *very* fortunate that Arkans bathed and excreted in private wherever they could—*and tomorrow, I go to . . . it.* The Great Central Edifice of Post, to find out the relevant facts about Box 596, General Deposit, 5th Southwest Quarter, intersection of Delas Rii Crescent and Aesas-Berakalla Road.

The Edifice of Post was a large building even by Arkan standards, a square block of greenish stone four stories tall; the topmost story below the flat roof was streaked with pigeon dung from the forest of coops. Fast, light horse-drawn carriages drew up by the side entrances, to be unloaded by burly stevedores in loincloths and gloves under the direction of rabbity clerks. More crowds of people pushed in the row of glass doors on the bottom level, facing the court; long lines of them, in fact, in clothes ranging from rags to outfits that made her conservative dark-green long-sleeved tunic and brown cotton pants look extremely restrained.

Wouldn't mind mugging him, she thought, eyeing an *Aitzas* whose clothing positively shimmered, almost enough to dim the jewelled arm-rings, earrings and bracelets. The courtyard had an exaggerated version of what she was coming to think of as the Arko-city smell: charcoal smoke and alcohol fumes, since wood fires were forbidden, sweat, hot damp stone, soap, perfume and Arkanherb.

She craned her head as she elbowed her way into the courtyard; it was rather odd that the area around the near-identical building on her left—it even had the same noisome pigeon coops on the roof—was virtually abandoned. Except for the clerks, who were moving with a swift dispatch that seemed positively unnatural. *Oh, yes. That's the tax-collection headquarters. Getting all the money into Arko.* Governments facing defeat found all sorts of unexpected calls for cash, not counting that which stuck to the fingers of high officials heading for safer climes. *Rake it in, buckos, we want it all here when the Alliance army arrives. Good thing they haven't had time to debase the currency yet.*

It was a little strange not being one of tallest people around, too; Arkans were not as big as Kommanza, but nearly, which meant many of the men in the crowd were taller than she. She looked into the long room between the glass doors. Plenty of movement in the long chambers that opened out beyond the counter; plenty of milling about in front of the counter, but the clerks actually serving at it moved with a glacial slowness that raised indolence to the level of an art.

Civilization, she thought contemptuously. Back in the Zekz Kommanz, on the northern plains of Almerkun, if you had a message you sent a messenger with a couple of good horses. *Oh, well, it could be worse. I could still be working in Senlaw.* The ancient trading city at the confluence of the Maizap and Zaura rivers, south of her homeland; *there* aristocrats waged blood-feuds over kidnapped rosebushes, and the ministry of interior decoration drew more funds than the army.

The line in front of Shkai'ra moved more quickly than most, almost as swiftly as the one reserved for *Aitzas* business; she had let the chicken blood in her bandages age, and gobbled a little occasionally. Even the other solas present—some of them wounded as well—drew back. Finally she stalked up to the stone counter, littered with rubber stamps and pads of cotton soaked in inks of various colors.

"*Hrrrrrg,*" she said, and showed one of the cards Megan had had done up. *Pigeon Post Delivery Service.*

The clerk swallowed and recoiled slightly, rattling off

a string of Arkan too quickly for her to follow. She let her eyes roll and twitch, tapping the side of her head where the bandages covered the ears.

"Fifth floor, through there, nobleandheroic*solas*," he said, more slowly and carefully, pointing to a door to the right of the counter. "You'll need a pass to enter the nonpublic section."

He scribbled quickly and sealed it with half a dozen of the rubber stamps; they were in hardwood holders with a U handle on the back; some of them would have made passable bucklers. A watchman stood by the door, bristle-cropped *okas*-caste haircut. Up an open stairwell, ink and old tea smells. Floor after floor of corridors, open offices crowded with desks . . . clerks writing, or sleeping with their heads on their desks, or looking out the windows and whittling on sticks, once a group of younger men playing some throwing game with parcels wrapped in paper or burlap.

One of them looked at her pass on the fifth-floor landing, dropping his parcel; something crunched and tinkled as he kicked it aside. "Diras Tekis, third office on the left," he said quickly, not looking at her bandages, "nobleandheroic*solas*."

Shkai'ra felt fresh sweat break out on her upper lip, under the weight of stinking gauze. This was the moment of final commitment; once she passed through the clerk's office, nothing could go wrong. *I hate plans like that*, she thought, feeling her breakfast of creamed wheat sitting chill in her stomach. An oak door, walls done in murals showing heroic postal couriers fighting their way through hurricanes, snowstorms, wolves, bandits and tigers amid implausible mountains and jungles, painted by someone who had evidently never left the city, or waited for a letter.

Down another corridor; it was quieter here, but she could smell pigeons above. A middle-aged *fessas* looked up as she closed the door of his office behind her. *Stone walls*, she thought; still, best to be quiet about it.

A gabble of Arkan; she caught the word "help you," *miassiu*. She leaned across the desk, tapping at her ear. He frowned, swallowed, and forced himself not to draw back as he repeated the phrase, slowly as if to an imbecile. "How may I help you?"

"Like this," Shkai'ra said happily in her own tongue. Her hands shot forward; there was a moment of struggle, but she was clamping on the carotids, not strangling. It took a moment longer than she expected, difficult to find the veins in a neck so soft; then he slumped senseless across the paper-littered tile surface of the desk.

Work quickly, she told herself. There was another chair, a sturdy thing of glued wood; she whirled it around and propped it under the glass knob of the door, kicking it softly to drive it home.

The man stirred, murmuring. She went around the desk, tipped him back into his chair. It was another example of Arkan fancywork, swivel-mounted on springs. He slumped back bonelessly, and she had to fight the peculiar limp difficulty of an unconscious body as she rolled back the silky fabric of his sleeve and slapped the inside of his elbow sharply to bring up the vein. It had looked easy when the Haian did it back in camp—*Megan, how do you fare, my heart*—no, *no time for that*—but she frowned as she took out the hardwood case with the syringe.

"Yes, I speak Enchian," the man said dully, the drug having taken full effect. He spoke it better than she did, actually. *Gods, why can't everyone speak Kommanzanu?* Then again, that might be a little inconvenient. Her birth-tongue had scores of words for grass, horses, and various ways of killing, but she could not think of a way to say "post office" in it without taking fifteen minutes of circumlocutions.

"See this? What is it?" she said, holding out the pigeon's tag that Fishhook had brought in.

"A pigeon message," the man said dreamily. Shkai'ra

restrained an impulse to pound his face on the table; somebody under truth-drug felt little pain, and needed none to make them give the right answers. *Just ask the right questions, you stupid mare*, she told herself.

"If," she said, and stopped. *Organize it like a battlefield message, or a question to Sova in training.* "If, ah, you had this message, and wanted to find out who sent— no, who was going *to pick it up*, what would you do?"

"Look at the records."

Breathe in. Breathe out. "Look at this message, and tell me how I can spot the person who picks it up, and any others sent from the same person to the same person."

A long silence, while the Arkan's plump lips moved, as if he was talking to himself. "I can't."

"*Why not!?*"

"Because I can't remember all the incoming messages," he said, in the same dull, mildly amiable tone.

For a moment she tasted vomit at the back of her throat. *Think, think! How can he do his business if he doesn't know what messages come in?* "Ahhh." *I must get Megan to kick my ass. He* wrote it down, *of course.* Civilized people needed to do that, they had such terrible memories. How many times had she been astounded at a horse-trader who couldn't remember each individual in a herd by name and points, or recite their bloodstock's genealogies without cracking a book? She could still list her own ancestors back twenty-three generations without breaking stride, or identify every horse she had ever owned for longer than a day or so.

A half-dozen more questions brought the right file-ledger to light; for a heart-stopping moment she thought she would have to go out of the office to get it, but it turned up behind a reference volume on the desk. She had to turn the pages herself, maddeningly slowly when she could make nothing of the fine-lined Arkan script, and every question had to be utterly specific; half a dozen times she was forced to go back to the beginning.

"So," she said at last. "Two eight-days out of three, give or take a few, Box 596 and one of two others—at this delivery post over in the 3rd South-west *Fessas* Ward—get pigeon messages, and are collected by the same person. Then on the *third* eight-day, the *other* two boxes get a message, and the same person collects. Numbers 771 and 253."

Aren't we a clever little sheepraper? Shkai'ra thought vindictively of the Arban spy back at camp. *I'd love to have a long conversation with you, just yourself and me and a little sharp knife.* "And the next day is five days from now.

"Now," she continued, "if you looked as if you were sleeping, how likely would someone be to disturb you?"

"Not for a few hours, probably," the man said.

Shkai'ra took a small elongated leather sack out of the back pocket of the trousers liberated from a dead *solas*, and weighed it in her hand. *On the one hand, Megan's pretty squeamish about bystanders*, she thought. It was a little odd, if endearing and sweet—you did what you had to to get the job done, and anyway, who cared about strangers? *Zoweitzum, most of the people I've known had personalities that'd be improved by death.* But you had to be careful with Megan; just because you loved someone didn't make the differences of race and custom any less, and Shkai'ra had to live in her world. *On the other hand, he knows far too much, including where I have to be to follow the next lead to Lixand. Bad luck, clerk.*

She positioned the sap over her shoulder and struck with a whipping flex to the temple. The man's body jerked and slumped. This was one of the few ways of killing quickly that did not make the sphincters relax; nobody with a nose would miss *that*, even here one floor under the pigeon shit. Then she arranged his arms on the desk and laid his head down in the position she had seen other clerks in, arranging his shoulder-length *fessas* hair over the soft wet spot.

The next clerk gabbled in Arkan. Shkai'ra lolled and gargled and tapped her ear, but he was looking extremely suspicious, thrusting the sheaf of forms at her and offering a pen. She flicked her eyes right and left; a few of the others waiting in the outer room were glancing her way. *Shitshitshit, is that the word for* order *or is he saying* I order you ... *that's inferior-to-superior inflection, Zaik be with me now.* Of course he might not be; the Kommanz god of war—chief god of war, all their deities were involved in it—was notoriously fickle. *Glitch, godlet of fuckups, two more sheep.* She took the pen and scrawled her Arkan cover name on a convenient blank space near the bottom.

The clerk looked down, blinking in bewilderment, then his eyes narrowed. *When in doubt, act decisively,* she thought, and elbowed him aside with a grunted, slurred Arkan curse.

Fucked up again, you stupid mare, she thought; the clerk shouted to the porter, who grabbed her around the chest from behind. He was clumsy but had strength that would have done credit to a bear, as well as outweighing her by half again; and even an *okas* slughead knew what tits were when he had his hands on them. The mealy body-odor of someone who lived on cornbread and onions enveloped her.

Reaction was automatic. Bend the knees, hunch the shoulders to slip out of the clumsy hug, stamp one foot down on his instep and sway the hips aside as she snapped a fist backward into his groin. Use the momentum of that to spin, facing him. He was left in a half-crouch, hands halfway between the memory of his grip and the pain in his crotch that was bulging his eyes.

Kick, Straight up, to the chin. The heel of her boot punched into the man's jaw like a fist on the uppercut. There was a crackling sound; the bone shattered, and his head snapped back between his shoulders with convincing finality as he took a pace backward and fell. A mixture of shrieks came from the crowd waiting for service; they surged back from around her. Shkai'ra helped them along, drawing the long Imperial sword and whirling it in a series of smooth figure-eight cuts, trotting for the exit.

A *solas* shouted something; *foreigner*, she thought. Or *spy?* She cursed to herself, remembering; the Arkan unarmed-combat mode used kicks below the waist only, and handblows above; *you can tell it wasn't developed with women in mind*, she thought bitterly. In one move she had just identified herself as an outlander to any war-trained Arkan present.

Solas men were pushing toward her, faster than the frantic scramble of the others out of her way; heads were turning toward them from the street. She felt her heart speed, and pumped her breath deep, using the stomach muscles to draw air into the bottom of her lungs. Her eyes skittered, taking in the surroundings in flickering jumps, combat-detail leaping out diamond sharp against the blur of movement.

"*Eeeeeeeeiiiiiii!*" With the steel-edge on steel-edge Kommanza war-scream, she cut ruthlessly at the figures ahead of her, drawing her dagger with her left hand. X-cut, a *fessas* flew backward with a half-severed arm. The sword jarred in her hand but scarcely slowed, good steel. Her shoulder blades crawled, conscious of the vulnerability of cloth, bitterly remembering the fine suit of Arkan war-harness in her room at the inn; with that she could have plunged straight into the mass. Blood-stink filled the air.

Bull through: cut, stab into a belly, sudden shit-smell, cave in a ribcage with another kick. The crowd-screaming was loud now, and the bubble of space around her larger; she'd nearly reached the raised sidewalk beyond the courtyard. A shifty-looking *okas* drew a highly illegal fighting knife from under the back hem of his tunic and lunged; she swayed aside, clamped the knife arm under his with her forearm beneath the elbow, broke it with a sharp lift, used the broken arm to push his face down into her knee-strike. There was a brittle sensation, like striking a padded board that crumpled. Then she felt pain.

Shit. The back of her thigh: the man's dying reflex had stabbed the knife into it. *I'm dead*. The leg began to buckle; for an instant an invisible hand reached into her chest and squeezed with iron-rod fingers, as she thought the hamstring had been severed.

I'm dead -ead -ead -ead . . .

Megan, half-drowsing in the saddle, jolted up. The burst of feeling, too faint to be her own, flavored through and through with Shkai'ra-ness, like on the ice two winters ago . . . *The mind-link, it's her, SHKAI'RAAAAAHHH* . . . But the thought was Hotblood-toned too, as if it had come from him, *through* him. *She thought, he caught it, somehow sent it to me. SHKAI'RAAAHHH!* The pony half reared, crow-hopped and bucked her off, trotting off to one side, shaking its head, reins flapping; surprised at itself for bucking and surprised at her. The feeling wavered like a flame, then faded and winked out.

Someone smothered a laugh. Behind her one of the Demarchic Guard called, "You all right, Zak?" The column was hesitating behind her, then squeezing by, flowing around. With a wheeze, her breath came back, her lungs un-sticking. She clambered to her feet, nodding, limped out of the way. *Just shut up and let me listen for—*

"Form up when you can, then." She clenched her teeth, waved acknowledgement. *Shkai'ra!* Her leg hurt; her *good* leg, with a ghost-pain in the back of the thigh. *Is she wounded?* She strained, reached out, reached deeper in, to hear, to feel. *Hotblood!* Nothing from him.

"You need help catching the pony?" One of the outriders. *Shut up, damn you!* "*Nyata!* . . . I mean no. I'll be fine." She couldn't shout at them to go away, leave her to listen; it was like straining to understand a voice talking two floors down; she might miss something if *she* said anything. But there was no more. She had to get moving, form up, there was no time to concentrate, no silence.

No. Not over. You don't have me Zaik-damned yet, sheep-fuckers— Two *solas* barred Shkai'ra's way. Fear vanished as combat-mind took over; the leg bore her weight, the blood was only a trickle, a muscle wound. She could force strength out of it, tearing the sliced fibers wider, maybe—worry about that later.

Neither of them was armored; one was an older man, white-haired, holding a head-high staff as if he knew how to use it. The other was two meters of bad news; in his thirties and tanned brown, eyes slitted and cool, sapphires against the skin. There was a paler band across his forehead, from the inner padding rim of a helmet, worn for years. Some sort of light dress sword in his hand, *not* what he used normally, but it was steel and sharp and had a point. The two Arkans looked at each other, at her, then spread out on either side, old man to her left, young to her right. It had been about a full minute since she killed the porter, enough time for most of the spectators to flee, not *quite* enough for help to arrive.

Fast or nothing, she thought, her mind moving with crystalline speed. Feint left, toward the old *solas*. No fear in his face, only concentration; his shoulders looked thick enough to crack bones with the long oak staff. It hummed toward her, waist-high, as the younger man closed in on her right. She leaped; not straight up, that would have left her open to him when she landed. Forward, diving *over* it and to the old man's left. Jackknifing in mid-air, shoulder-high, landing on crossed forearms, tucking her head and curving her spine. Nothing for it but sheer speed, pulling her feet in to hasten the spin, coming up out of it and letting the point of the longsword draw her around in a blurring curve. The straight sword was less suited to the drawing slash than her saber, and she felt her hand adjust as at a distance, abstract.

Soft drag of muscle against the steel, the brief hard pop of taut tendons. The old *solas* toppled backward with a cry of shock. Shkai'ra surged forward, ramming the dagger in her left hand under his ribs through the kidney, expelling her breath in a *hunnhhh* of effort as she tossed him off the blade and into the other man's arms.

"*Pah!*" he screamed, face contorting. *Father!*

Shkai'ra lunged longline, right foot advanced behind her point, left back. Long limbs and a long sword, the young man would have been spitted through the neck if he had not dropped the dying man and whipped his blade around in a cross-parry. The longsword went *skringgg* along the length of it and the hilts locked; she stabbed up with the dagger, felt his hand slap down on her wrist, blocking. Their feet stamped as they strained chest-to-chest, open mouths snarling. There was a glazed ferocity to his, a hint of madness. More than that in the unnatural strength that squeezed her weapons in towards her body. Her knees tensed, preparing to leap back, wrestling a strong man gone berserk with rage was a *bad* idea. Then something locked around her thighs, iron-strong.

The old man. Dying, but she would have to hammer in his skull or sever the limbs that gripped her. Instead she threw herself backward. The younger *solas* came with her; she twisted as she fell on her back, but dodging the knee that would have driven the breath out of her body. His weight fell on her, pinning her arms, and she could feel him shift as their bodies grappled for advantage. Ready to shift his pinning grip to an elbow, freeing steel to kill her. There was a peculiar intimacy to the embrace, bodies seeking to make death rather than life.

Only one thing to do, she thought, working her lips; the bandages were thin there. She turned her head and thrust her mouth up onto his throat.

Tough, was her first thought. Thick neck, muscles like woven cable. She bit, trying to drive the teeth in, and felt the windpipe slide outward a bit. A gasping grunt from the man above her, and she screamed through the mouthful of tough rubbery flesh, pouring every ounce of herself into her clamping jaws. Both came up off the ground as her back curved, convulsing, the cords standing out in her neck; she jerked her head from side to side. Pain in her jaw, as if the big muscles that ran from the hinge to the temple were about to rip loose from the bone. Skin tore under her teeth, and her mouth was full of the salt and iron of blood. Suddenly he was trying to pull away, there was a shifting and turning of weights, then she was lying across him. The windpipe collapsed like a cylinder made of stiff paper, and one of the big veins beside it split open between her teeth.

The *solas* writhed, and the blood gushed fast enough that she breathed some in and had to spit and gag; more poured warm and stinging down over her face and neck and chest, soaking the cotton drill fabric of her tunic. With a grunt of disgust she reached down and hammered the pommel of her sword on the back of the old man's head, a *thock-thock-thock* sound until the leather-thong arms relaxed. Her lungs felt tight as she forced herself not to pant, and there was a ringing in her ears. It was almost enough to cover the pounding sound of hobnailed sandals and blowing whistles, as the Watch ran into the courtyard.

There were two of them, armed; barbed javelins, short swords, truncheons, and they had openface helmets and mail shirts enameled with the usual Imperial scarlet. Not as bright as the blood that coated Shkai'ra from sodden bandages to knees, nor as vivid red as the slick pool they skidded in as they braked to a stop, eyes blinking as they took in the carnage that littered the courtyard pavement. Some of the bodies were still thrashing and moaning as Shkai'ra rose, the sword dripping in her hand, the white snarl of her teeth the only thing not red. One of them jabbed with his spear, as much to fend her off as to strike. She uncoiled from the ground with the hilt in both hands, cut sideways, and the barbed spearhead fell

in one direction, backswung and took him across the side
of the neck. The man collapsed like a puppet with its
strings cut, and she lunged across him at the other. The
strike missed: he was running as fast as he could, away.

Shkai'ra turned and almost fell as the pain in her leg
struck again, then limped quickly across the courtyard.
There was a nest of tenements and alleys over *there*;
she'd cased the place before coming to the Edifice. She
spared a glance down at herself; the blood was beginning
to clot, sticky on the hilt of the longsword. *I'd better get
off the streets and get some new clothes*, she thought.
Even in a big city, this was a little much for a main
avenue.

XX

Just because she thought "I'm dead" doesn't mean she is. It happened all the time in fights; then one would find oneself saved by something that seemed miraculous at the time, but commonplace later. But the ghost-pain in Megan's leg could not have come from a fearful thought. *She must be wounded. How badly?*

She leaned back against her elbows, passing on the flask of beer, and stared into the fire. Even in the more regimented parts of camp, evening campfires evolved out of some unspoken group decision; some cook-fires would be doused and others brightened for people to gather around, without a word about whose turn it was to host. Her fire, in the secure section, seemed to be the one tonight.

Sova was with the Slaughterers, under oath to return at midnight sentry-change. This crowd was mostly Yeolis, with others, specializing in who knew what aspect of war, sprinkled throughout. A Yeoli woman had a harp, war-strung with expensive steel strings, and a dark, heavyset Brahvnikian with a mustache—what was his name?—had

brought . . . a *fahlut*, he called it, an instrument like a fife or a pipe but with bellows that he pumped under his arm.

Megan burped from the warmish beer, and fought down a sudden absurd craving for *kompot*, the sweet, mixed dried-fruit stew made with brandy, only in F'talezon. She hadn't had any for years; her mother had made it, just for name-days, in her childhood. There was a lull in the music and someone re-started the perpetual political argument. Megan listened half-heartedly, busy with her own thoughts.

Wounded . . . or worse, and I'm refusing to face the truth. Lixand-mi . . . It's been twenty-one days.

"Well, it's all very good, this power-to-the-people idealism," the Brahvnikian was saying—Wiktor, that was his name. "But you Yeolis have to admit, it has its problems. We've seen, passing through your country, everything publicly built is decrepit—bridges, roads, city walls, you name it, either falling to pieces—or there isn't one where there should be, and people still have to make herds ford rivers. All because there is no high authority to force what's good on the people when they're too blind or narrow-minded to see it."

"Come on, you're exaggerating, it's not *that* bad," a Yeoli rebutted. "And at what cost, high authority? The Arkans have high as high can get authority—"

"We can't use their example!" an Aenir cut in—Lin, her name was—her pale blond hair swinging. That was unwritten law: it gave too much offense to compare anyone's customs with those of the enemy.

"All right . . . no Lakans here?" The Yeoli took a quick glance around. "Good. Laka, then. The King is King, even if he's a complete moron; they have to knife him to get rid of him. And to enforce that authority, look what measures are taken: floggings, hangings, slavery, authority so strict it's *far* too easy for the evil to abuse."

"But you're using an extreme example, of a single, uncontested power." Wiktor. "At home we strike a bal-

ance between the Benaiat and the Pretroi . . ." An exposition on Brahvnikian politics followed, which by its sheer complexity was barely decipherable. "See, it's simple as that! None of this maundering with votes and petitions and percentages and . . . ah . . ." Wiktor's face froze, his mouth a wide stone-like oval under his mustache, the whites of his eyes shining ivory in the firelight. Megan had been dimly aware of an arrival a few seats down from her just now. "Ah, uh . . . greetings, Invincible."

Chevenga's practice was to visit campfires randomly, never announcing where he'd be, as a precaution against assassination attempts. Nor was it his style to make grand entrances; he'd just sit down, take the skin as it was passed around and join in the conversation, so that people sometimes didn't even notice it was him, and those who didn't know his face or happened not to ask his name would never be the wiser. He could never resist a debate on either strategy or politics, though, and would get ridiculously, arm-wavingly passionate, like any Yeoli, especially—like any Yeoli—when drunk. Though he'd wave only one arm tonight; his other was still in a sling.

"Um . . . er . . . ah . . . forgive me, Invincible," the Brahvnikian stammered. "I meant no offense to your irreproachable Yeoli customs." The *semanakraseye* did the classic Yeoli double-shrug, hand and shoulders, and said, "None taken; everyone's entitled to their opinion." Then added with a grin, "In Yeola-e, anyway."

"Well, it's no less so, in the *Free*-port of Brahvniki!" And the argument was at full boil again, as if nothing had happened.

Megan watched the fire fall and be replenished, each chunk of wood thrown in fresh to die brightly in flame, turn to coals and then feathery ash, light as nothing. The argument swirled around her, fading out of her thoughts, sometimes making sense, sometimes not, punctuated like all arguments with irritating stupidities, and every now and then held by the one voice that no others would interrupt, no matter how quietly it spoke.

Chiravesa. A Yeoli word; it meant playing something out, in your head, or with others; imagining, intensely, making it feel real. *Shkai'ra's wounded, at best. If I want to save Lixand, I'll have to kill him.*

She turned to watch his face, its sharp lines smoothed by firelight, the dark eyes one moment sincere and force-ful, the next creased with laughter, flamelight catching on a gold tooth. *When he laughs, his eyes dance with all the joy he was torn from before.* Other people at camp-fires wore some armor often, weapons usually; she did herself. Chevenga never wore so much as an eating-knife—he didn't need one, eating only odd-looking vege-table concoctions his Haian prepared, apparently, out of little bowls always brought by a younger brother or sis-ter—or wristlets, usually going bare-chested. To show he trusted his warriors to protect him, she guessed, or let people see Arko's marks on him; he was too calculating a person to be doing it just because of the heat.

She watched his good hand, bearing the white signet, gesturing ceaselessly in the Yeoli way, shaping this or that meaning with the grace of life-long practice. *I will kill him. I will touch him with a claw full of traceless poison, and he will die, as if from summer fever. One touch, and that will be the end of him, his name scattered to the wind, and my son back with me. His name scat-tered to the wind, so what? A year ago I'd never heard it . . .*

"In an autocracy there's no balance!" Some Yeoli woman declaimed. "No check, no give and take! So all its institutions are subject to corruption, to losing sight of their ostensible purpose of keeping order, and being abused for base urges against which there's no recourse. I mean—please, everyone, understand I'm comparing no one's customs to *theirs*, but I can't think of a better example. Look at the Arkans, and what they do to cap-tives, lower castes, women, children, dogs, trees, every-thing else that can't either run faster or hit them with something sharp . . ."

I will kill him. They'll have to figure out how to do without him.

"All to keep the social order, they say ... but, well, come on! It would be ridiculous, for instance, to look at our Chevenga here with a straight face and say, 'What they did to you while you were helpless, shit, they never did for *pleasure*, did they? I mean, you could feel it was all for sacred duty, couldn't you?'"

A sudden silence fell; everyone was looking at him for an answer, even though, by the sudden swallowed-a-peach-pit look on the Yeoli's face, she'd meant the question rhetorically. But the semanakraseye spread the fingers of his good hand, and answered, "They seemed to find their duty and their pleasure," the soft voice said, "by some lucky coincidence, happily allied."

Laughter broke out all around the fire; one man fell off the log, he laughed so hard—though he managed to keep the horn-cup in his hand upright—making Megan wonder what he'd seen or suffered, to make this so funny. "I'm putting it facetiously," Chevenga said, when the mirth quieted, "but it's true. By saying it is duty, they can excuse the pleasure, and so make it purer; by feeling the pleasure they can give themselves credit for enjoying duty. Virtue, either way; a very nice arrangement."

I will kill him, and have Lixand back. My rokatzk would be a fool to renege. And we will still win the war; it has enough momentum.

"Cheng." A drunken man. "When you learned that, when you got to feel that at *their* expense, it was a damned fine sight to see. A damned fine sight." He raised his cup; several others did likewise.

The Arkan general: Shkai'ra had told her. "Teik Sun-Shines-Out-Of-His-Ass isn't so driven-snow pure." Abatzas Kallen—she'd been struck by the similarity, to Sarngeld's true-name. "Neither he, nor his kind, sweet, gentle people, who voted for him to do it ... several have told me, how he milked every bit of ecstasy out of pronging that fat fuck-head. About time, I'd say; they had it coming, and no one deserved to give it to them more than him."

I'm going to kill you, she thought. *If you could do that to anyone, Arkan or not, for any reason . . .*

Chevenga ran a hand through his dark hair, and said, "*Semana kra,*" like an incantation. *The people wills. You mean it was duty. Just following orders. Your duty and your pleasure were happily allied?*

Megan wanted to be elsewhere, to continue; if it got intense enough, her face would show it. She yawned elaborately, stretched and got up, surrendering her place to the steadily contracting circle. Chevenga got up too, catching her eye.

Wanting to talk, it seemed; fine. Away from the fire, the darkness was full but for faint starlight, even in the open ground. She couldn't see more than his shape, naZak-tall beside her.

"I thought I'd walk you to your tent at least," he said pleasantly. "It's been all business lately, somehow, we haven't just talked . . . Unless you're tired, of course; don't let me impose."

In the dark, she knew, he couldn't see her face. "You're not imposing . . . ah, perhaps I should rephrase that." *A teacher's voice: "Smile, it can be heard even if not seen."* "Actually, you're very imposing."

He chuckled politely. "How go things with you?"

Fine, thanks, she answered inwardly. *Someone's using my son to blackmail me into killing you, how about you?* "Well enough. Except for some chosen problems . . . like my adopted daughter." He read people too well not to see her preoccupation with something, and it was true enough.

"Any of my business?" She had a sudden thought, of the Arkans he'd had drawn and quartered, how joyfully he had announced it. *Velvet smooth voice out of the dark,* she thought. *Habiku was equally charming.*

"If I choose to tell. I told you we adopted Sova a year ago and never mentioned why, or how. She and her

brother ... well, Shkai'ra took them away from their
father as a prize when we won a challenge when she was
twelve, and I didn't stop her. Her brother was killed in
my house war." She found herself worrying at the skin
around her claws again and made herself stop. "So she's
more than a little confused about who she is. I look at
her, try to help, but find myself looking at an angry
stranger, in part through my own action—or rather inac-
tion—then."

"Shkai'ra took her as a *prize?*" The soft voice took on
just the trace of an edge. "Yet you call it adoption. *Tzen
kel ...*" He cut himself off. "I can see why she's confused
about who she is. Whatever possessed Shkai'ra to take
children as prizes?"

Tzen kellin ripalin, he'd half-said: the Arkan ethic,
"Who kills becomes." Meaning who kills a lord takes his
position and property, who kills the Imperator becomes
the Imperator, who kills a child's parents becomes his
parents. She felt her calculated hardness against him flash
and roar into sincere anger. *Has he forgotten she's missing in action, how that must feel to me?* "She can be like
that." Her voice came out flat. "Or perhaps I should say,
could be."

For a moment there was silence. "Forgive me," he
said then, with formal sincerity. "I meant no ill of her.
You love her, and fear she's dead. I've spoken callously,
I'm sorry."

There was nothing to say to that, but "It's all right."
She felt the anger drain away.

They were standing before her tent. She didn't want
to talk to him, hear his questions, be near him. "Will you
sit for a while?"

"Sure," he answered, "if it's no trouble; as I say, don't
let me impose. You're sure? All right." They sat just
outside the flap. "You made things very interesting for
yourselves, acquiring a child that way ... though I guess
parents always do, even acquiring them the usual way.

Kids are the purest teachers. They'll delve out your imperfections, and shine them blinding in your face."

"Yes. We've found that. But we'll work things out."

"I'm sure you will. Megan, if there's anything I can do, you need only ask."

Die, she thought. *Go out and get killed in battle, so I don't have to have either your blood or my son's on my hands.* "Thank you. I'll keep that in mind."

For another moment they sat silent, listening to the crickets and watching the fire-flies blink all over the hill and field. It grew oppressive, his presence beside her, without words. She cut through it. "Shchevenga. What you said earlier, about Arkans . . . That general. Did you find it convenient then, that your duty and pleasure were happily allied?"

For a moment after it was out she regretted saying it; now he'd draw himself up, offended, snap back, wonder why, have her truth-drugged again. . . . But the motion she feared didn't come, and the silence lengthened. He was thinking.

"Convenient isn't the word," he said finally. "The sense of virtue either way . . . if I told you I didn't feel that, and relish it at the time, I'd be lying. Afterward, though, I closed myself in my tent, threw up and hit my head against the floor until someone stopped me."

That looks too good, Gold-bottom, she thought sharply. *Why did you leave out, to everyone but me, the part that does you most credit? You enjoyed what you did. You've admitted that.* "You didn't need to tell me that. It really is none of my business."

She felt his shrug as much as saw it. "It's no secret. Besides, it *is* your business, by what I agreed to before."

To lie with her, he meant, as she'd asked, to help her fight her fear of men. *Dark Lord curse you, you would remember that! Like any fish-gutted man would. You're all the same.*

"It reminds me of something someone else and I were chewing on," he said musingly. "Imagine this: you see a

rockslide starting, that will grow big enough to crush the
town below, where live ten thousand people—unless you
throw yourself in its path and stop it now, at the cost of
your own life. You have no obligation elsewhere except
what anyone has, to family, friends and so forth. No punishment will come your way if you don't do it, or accolades if you do, because no one will ever know. Those
ten thousand people are neither friends nor enemies to
you, just strangers; you've never even walked through the
town. Would you do it?"

Is this some kind of game? She'd play; anything else
would look suspicious. *Such a great moral dilemma,
whether to break my strength-oath, as if I haven't broken
it already.*

Chiravesa. She saw the scene in her mind, the mountain, the town hazy below, played it out.

"Yes," she said, finally. "Though Shkai'ra would be
angry at me for it, for leaving her."

"Would you want her ever to know?"

Megan thought for another long time. "Yes," she said
finally. "Even though she'd hate me. I'd want her to
know I was dead, instead of being uncertain for the rest
of her life . . . as I was with my son."

For whose life I would do anything, including kill you.

"Yes," he said, in understanding. "That makes sense.
I should let you sleep. Give my regards to Sova, and both
of you sleep well."

"Not so fast, Gold-bottom," she said, forcing the smile
again. "*Chiravesa* always goes both ways, I've heard.
Would *you* throw yourself under that rock?"

His answer came without hesitation. "Yes."

"You're saying that very easily. Convince me."

"I can't convince you, if you won't be convinced. I can
only try." He shrugged. "They are ten thousand, to my
one. *Semana kra.*"

Why can't you just be an asshole? she thought. *If you
were a child-raper or slave-seller or slough-kin, I
wouldn't have sent Shkai'ra off on a wild goose chase;*

I'd have just done it, easily, and we'd all be half way home by now, her and Lixand beside me, and no regrets, knowing the world was better off without you. Why do you have to make it so hard? "Sleep sound," he was saying.

"We will. You too." *Forever*, she wished.

In the cool darkness of the night, foul here in the standard meeting place, Matthas waited, watching two Yeolis, an Enchian and a Lakan visit. Different races did even *this* different ways, he'd noticed—the Enchian and Lakan quiet and furtive, the two Yeolis almost proud, with not a break or a change in their arm-waving yammering, aside from waving only one hand for a time.

Finally the Zak came, leaning on a stick, limping no less than she had last time. *Oh sure, the wound's that bad. And I'm a yak's brother.* "My leg got infected," she said in her high child-like whisper. "What you're asking isn't something I can possibly do unless I'm in perfect form. That's why I haven't done it, that's the only reason. Look, *please*, give me another eight-day, and I'll do it, I give you my word. I *swear* . . ."

"Another four days," he said, putting the usual ice into his voice. Like a strict father, then: "It had better be." Professionally brisk: "Enough said." She limped away. He prayed.

XXI

For a city as big as Arko, it was an unusually dark night. The *okas* women halted with weary nervousness, pulling the light handcart behind her. The clerks had said the campground for refugees was down at the end of the street, but she must have missed the turning. He had talked so fast, gabbling and biting off the ends of his words, like a city man; she sniffled, wishing her man was with her. The *solas* had taken him, just after they left their farm; him and her son, her only surviving child.

"*Yar, 'e war too yang,*" she mumbled. Only fifteen summers. Taken for the war. She shuddered again, remembering the horrible tales of what the black-haired barbarians would do, the columns of refugees past her village. Still, she might have stayed if the soldiers had left the men. The master's bailiff had run, but then he had all the master's beautiful things from the manor to protect; the villagers would have stayed, and run to the woods and hills until the enemy soldiers passed. But not without her man; a woman alone needed protection. Uncle Permas had been with them most of the way, on the Imperial highway that such as them would never set foot on in proper times, but he had died of the spotted raving-fever two days ago.

She shivered again, looking around at the deserted, darkened alleyways. It was *black*, the crescent moon sending only glimmers through between the tall buildings—most of them four stories, think of it!—and no lights showing in the windows. The cracked concrete of the pavement was nearly covered by the layers of solidified garbage, and there was a sour stink worse than any farmyard midden. There was a noise, a tall shape in the laneway to her right; where it ran off the street she followed.

"Who you?" a voice asked. The peasant woman cowered back against her handcart; the accent was even less comprehensible than most she had heard in the great City.

"Dilla, wife o' Kinnas Togas, *okas*, mayitpleaseyer," she babbled nervously.

"About fucking time," the voice said. Something struck the side of her head, and suddenly there were stars.

"Baiwun hammer me flat, *twenty* muggings before I get the right one," Shkai'ra muttered, pulling the handcart into the laneway beside the *okas* woman.

She had stuck carefully to refugees, looking for one whose bumpkin accent would be thick enough to disguise her own; *okas*, because they were not expected to be able to read. The fiasco at the Edifice of Post was fresh in her memory. Of course, once she had spoken to them she had to lay them out. Nobody was going to listen to a hysterical refugee *after* the fact, but it wouldn't do to have them raising the hue and cry immediately. Shkai'ra whistled through her teeth as she dragged the body further back and measured it roughly; not much difference in height, which was fortunate, since Arkans considered it lewd to show much ankle. Much of anything, on a woman. Stripping the limp bulk of the peasant woman was difficult; the clothing was filthy, but no more so than a soldier's after a week or so in the field.

Her sword and dagger went in the bottom of the hand-cart; she arranged it carefully, with the hilt easily available but not likely to be found unless they searched exhaustively. The clothing was simple, a long dress of coarse linen with several layers of petticoats and a thick hooded tunic, a cloak of the same material, and tattered gloves that looked like third-hand *fessas* castoffs worn for decency's sake among strangers. Shkai'ra shed her blood-stiffened *solas* suit and sliced it into rags, stuffing them past finding with a stick into various liquid puddles of offal. Something else for Megan's sake; she gripped the Arkan woman under the armpits and dragged her into the rear of the alley, behind a fall of crumbled brick. A tattered blanket from the cart went around her, and the Kommanza left a chain of silver resting on her chest, hidden under the blanket. More than compensation for the cart and all its possessions.

One last thing. She gathered her *solas*-style fighting braid and haggled it off, then began to crop her hair *okas*-short. *I'm going to be fucking bald by the time it's over, at this rate.*

Only for you, my heart, she thought, gritting her teeth at the tugging pull of the nicked blade.

"Move *along,* there, woman!" the watchman said.

Shkai'ra shuffled her bare feet in the dust of the sidewalk. *Remember,* she told herself. *Hands folded, eyes down, shoulders slumped, knees together.* Sweat trickled down her flanks, and ran stinging into her eyes from her stubbled scalp. The fine concrete of the avenue was blinding bright; the final layer had been mixed with crushed quartz and flung back the light like flecks of polished metal. There was color in plenty, gaudy cloth and the paste-and-ceramic jewelry that even poor Arkans wore, stone facings in a dozen colors, pavement-paintings in chalk done in the florid Imperial style. Heat radiated from the masses of stone and brick; the air was damp and heavy with an underlying smell of rot.

"Move! Your kind aren't wanted here. Understand?" The watchman prodded at Shkai'ra with the butt of his spear.

Only for you, my love, she thought, turning the instinctive snarl into a simper. Nothing and nobody was going to move her away from the marble-gilt-and-glass building at her back, the General Deposit Box Office, 5th Southwest Quarter, intersection of Delas Rii Crescent and Aesas-Berakalla Road. Not after four days of squatting here in these ridiculous clothes.

The watchman was not particularly impressive, well into middle age and with a broken-veined nose that had looked long and hard into many cups. His companion was younger, with the twitchy not-there look of an Arkanherb addict; doubtless the best of the capital police were out at the front, trading spear thrusts with the Lakan infantry levy, or getting their heads beaten in by Schvait war flails.

Bad luck to you and may your butts break out in boils, she thought, simpering ingratiatingly and drawing the side of her hood across her face for modesty. It was a relief not to have her breasts bound down, and the way they showed under the bodice was enough to convince anyone of her gender. Which made it *highly* unlikely she would be identified as the Postal Slasher.

The rumors had spread around the city quickly; she had even overheard a few expressions of sympathy for the mysterious bandaged figure, mostly accompanied by speculation about battles lost because of misplaced letters, historic battles, a century or two past, whose crucial missives still lay somewhere within the great building's walls.

"Arrr, sor," she drawled. The watchmen would be city born and bred, and probably contemptuous of all peasants anyway; the thing was to keep the vowels consistent. "Ta good man, promise m'two bonny yang lads a position, good wages, 'e say. I waits 'ere for 'em." That stretched her meager store of Arkan to its breaking point, so she let half a copper chain show on her palm.

The watchmen's eyes locked on it; the older man's hand swept across hers as he licked his lips, and the younger's hands shook a little more. They spoke among themselves for a moment; she caught *"position on their knees"* from one as they laughed and strolled on around their rounds, the iron ferrules of their javelins clinking on the hexagonal paving-stones of the sidewalk. This was a good neighborhood, three-story flats for shopkeepers and artisans above a row of stores and workshops spilling out onto the street. Or not; the jewelers and goldsmiths had wooden latticework over their portals. Despite the frenetic bustle, many of the shops were shuttered, and the menfolk were mostly old or young or crippled.

The plate-glass door swung open, and there was a puff of slightly cooler air from within. It *was* the man she had seen opening the boxes numbered 771 and 253. Youngish, lacking two fingers on his right hand, dressed flash-elegant seedy in saffron cotton tunic and gartered tights and a pleated kilt beneath. Shkai'ra bent to the handles of her pushcart; a vendor of candied figs blocked her way, crying his wares. She kicked him behind one knee.

"Much sorry!" she said, trotting past as the man picked himself up. She would abandon the cart if she must, but it was invaluable camouflage for now; her injured leg had stiffened, the wound swelling a little despite her washing it out with brandy and bandaging it. It sent a stab of pain up to the small of her back every time her bare foot struck the pavement. Her loincloth chafed in the damp heat, and her belly rumbled with hunger. *Sorry I didn't rip your fucking lungs out through your nose, cowbuggering Arkan,* she thought savagely. Shkai'ra wanted to kill someone, very, very badly.

With luck, there would not be much longer to wait.

The inn had no sign; Shkai'ra did her best to look terrified at the glares of the hangers-on as she limped down the street toward it. The man she was following hesitated for a moment, then turned in through the broad gate that lead to the outer courtyard.

Her adopted persona certainly would have been frightened, she reflected, slowing to a stop. The neighborhood looked run-down even by the standards of the one where she had mugged the *okas* woman. The inn had no sign, and for once there were none of the fancy Arkan plate-glass windows. Plain brick and wooden shutters for all the buildings along here; all the ones that had not been turned out and abandoned, that was. No refugees had set up housekeeping in the ruined ones, which said something. So did the youngsters who lounged at the corners, puffed kilts and knives openly worn, with the front of their heads shaved and the short hair trained up in spikes from ear to ear. Obviously of military age, especially now as military age descended with each day, but the pressgangs seemed to have avoided this area. There were more women about than in the other parts of the city, bare-faced and heavily made up. Two of them glanced up, pausing as they butchered the body of a dog that looked to have died of mange, a steady appraising stare from blue eyes ringed with black mascara.

Always wartime down here, Shkai'ra thought, and let some of the cringe out of her walk. Defending herself hereabouts could arouse too many questions; she let the cart tilt back with its pulling shafts in the air and stood with her arms crossed, scowling.

Another five minutes, she thought, letting her eyes flick across the open gate. The youngster with the missing fingers was even more nervous, for which she did not blame him. Whatever else he was, he was no spook; of course, a near-six-foot tall woman with a handcart was so conspicuous that even a professional might be forgiven for discounting it as a shadow-tail. He backed into a corner by a watering trough, smiling uneasily as the man watering a mule made conversation. The man had no nose. Her quarry's face took on a more genuine expression as another man came out of the inn and walked towards him over the courtyard. They spoke.

Shkai'ra watched him out of the corner of her eye, in snatches. This one looked uncomfortably alert. A *fessas*, by the haircut; silver-grey in the amber blond of his hair, perhaps forty fairly hard years. Slender, and still handsome in the boyish oval-faced way Arkans preferred, but he moved well. Conservatively dressed in plain forest green kilt and blue tunic; from the way the tunic was left open down the chest there was something underneath it. His hand met that of the other man's.

I'm going to follow this one more carefully, Shkai'ra thought. *He knows which end of a knife you pick up.*

"Amazing what whining, cringing and playing stupid can get you," Shkai'ra mused to herself as she pulled the handcart off to the gravel verge of the highway. "I should have tried it before."

The man had turned east after leaving through the tunnel-gate; none of the guards had seemed much inclined to do a thorough search of the belongings of a smelly peasant-woman *leaving* Arko; the incoming stream was being diverted to camps in the countryside, now. A bad moment when a spearhead had chinked on her sword, but the sentries had believed her when she began crying and begging them not to take the family's heir-loom iron stewpot; rubbing onion on her eyes was something Megan had advised her on. Then glacial-slow progress; the man she was following had fidgeted, but he was not impatient enough to force a quarrel on the roadway.

Then *everyone* had been pushed off the road for a military convoy; five rejin of cavalry, from the banners, a glitter of lances and a harsh cry to make way. Not more than three thousand of them, understrength, and the drooping necks of the horses showed why. You had to be very desperate to push heavy horse like that, they seemed to have ridden their remounts to foundering and been forced to use their chargers for the last stage of the route-march. The iron clamor of their shod hoofs on the stone-surfaced concrete of the highway overrode the endless weary shuffle of the foot traffic inching by to either side.

A good three weeks before they're *fit for duty,* Shkai'ra reflected, pitying the mounts if not the men.

Movement out of the corner of her eye; the *fessas* dodging off into the woods, west and to the right of the south-facing highway.

Naughty, she thought, pulling out a shapeless bundle that concealed sword and dagger and a small buckler she had liberated from a watchman who incautiously stopped to take a piss in an alley. *Very naughty,* she thought, skidding down the four meter side of the embankment; some conscientious soul had planted it with a prickly bush to keep the dirt from eroding. Doubtless anyone watching assumed she was going into the pinewoods that fringed the west side of the road to take a dump.

The closed canopy of the umbrella pines made left the tall trees pillars of a green-roofed hall; the air beneath was still and hot and smelled of resin baked free by the sun. It was drier than the closed bowl of the city. Duff crunched under her feet, and there was little undergrowth beneath that shade; she crouched and examined the wound in her thigh. The swelling had not gone down; the edges of the deep narrow puncture were more puffy than ever, reddish-purple, and it leaked clear puss. Shkai'ra swallowed experimentally and assessed herself; there was the slightest hint of fever-hum in her ears. *Not light-headed,* she thought grimly. *Yet.* There was still some brandy in the flask; she lay on her back and hauled the knee back to her ear so that she could pour liquor into the cut and let it stand for a moment. The pain was much worse than the initial wound, enough to make her swear softly under her breath.

Have to do, she thought, as she re-bandaged it and tested her weight. But it would slow her, and if there was going to be a fight it had better come in the next little while. She pulled the rear of the skirt up between her legs and tucked it into the belt at the front, and unwrapped her weapons with an unconscious sigh of relief. Having them out of reach made her feel considerably more naked than walking unclothed would have. She took the sheathed sword in her left hand, the one that held the buckler by its single central grip, and tucked the dagger into the folds of skirt that circled her waist.

Fifteen minutes, she estimated, squinting up at the flickers of morning sun that shone through the bird-clamorous branches of the pines. That would let the *fessas* get enough of a lead on her, and he was city-bred if she had ever seen such, used to pavement under his sandals. Shkai'ra had been a hunter from the time she could walk, mostly on horseback and on the steppe, but often enough in woods. Her bare feet made little sound on the needles. She ran stooping until she found the scuff-marks of her quarry's passage, then upright at a steady walk.

The pinewoods gave way to terraced fields planted with grapevines and fruit trees, and she followed cautiously through the fields as the man took to a secondary road, graveled and graded and good enough for a main highway outside the Empire. Cautiously around a village, and then past the hedges of *Aitzas* country-seats, a nerve-wracking half hour creeping through ditches while watchdogs barked and the *fessas* stopped and looked, suspicious.

Into oak woods at last, in a district even more rocky and tumbled than most of the land to the west of the great crater of Arko; slabs of porous volcanic rock reared up through the forest. The huge trees were shaggy with moss and laced with wild grapevines thicker than her thigh, tangled with masses of lilac bush and wild rhododendron. That forced her back onto the road, as it shrank to a rutted and overgrown carriage-track, one that had not seen wheeled traffic in years, from the look of it.

Horses much more recently, or mules—hoofprints and
dung both. Shod, but not too large, probably riding hack-
neys. Shkai'ra slowed to let the man get well ahead of
her, and because her leg was bad enough that she could
not do more than a hobbling limp. The sun was declin-
ing; a day's quick march, but they had covered only about
twenty kilometers.

She was sweating heavily; her ears buzzed, and her
breath came far more quickly than it should. She almost
walked into the yard of the stone house at the end of
the lane. Only the whisper of movement in the air as the
forest opened out warned her, and she sank to the
ground behind a topiary bush gone wild with neglect,
shivering as the sweat turned cold on her skin. She could
smell chimney-smoke, and a light gleamed through the
gathering dusk ahead.

Rasas gripped his five cards tighter and thrust a full
copper chain into an already heavy pot, with a poorly
repressed smirk.

"Look, boy of gold," Glikasonas scolded, taking a swig
of the harder gold-colored liquor he preferred over wine.
"Yeh keep your face still. Yeh don't show *anything*. That's
the first thing we told you. You're a pleasure-boy, yeh
must be able to stone up your face."

"Sorry, sirs," he said somberly, making the grin fall off
like a mask, blank underneath.

"Fold," said Moras.

"Same," said Akobas. Glikasonas and Patappas were
already out. "Whatcha got, kid?"

Rasas turned over his cards, giggling. "Pair o' threes!"

"Auggh!" they all cried at once. "Yeh little imp! Yeh
bluffed us *all!*" —"Hayel, what do we need Frenandias
for, we've got us a five!" —"Well, yeh beat us fair and
square, boy, go on, collect." Triumphantly he swept all
the money into his pile.

A footstep sounded on the front porch. Moras jumped
up to peek through the eye-slot, while Akobas gripped

the boy's arm, ready to rush him into the basement if it was a stranger. " 'T's Fren," said the first, and everyone relaxed.

" 'Transaction to be continued,' " Frenandias quoted, as he closed the door behind him. This happened about every eight-day, Rasas had learned; some kind of message from some other conspirator in this, that meant some kind of all clear. " 'Service lousy, natives smelly, wish you were here.' " Milisas snickered, clammed up when no one else did. "Him and his *fikken humor*," Patappas grated.

Shkai'ra crouched behind the bush; nausea seized her, and she bent over, struggling to keep her retching quiet. When the fit passed she sat back, spitting to clear the taste of bile from her mouth and waiting for the shimmering before her eyes to clear. It did, mostly, and she sat breathing deeply with her injured leg before her. There were dusky-purple streaks extending up from the wound toward her groin, and she hissed softly when she touched it. *Shit.*

The house looked like the sort a moderately prosperous merchant might have built for a refuge during the hottest of the summer months; the surrounding forest made it noticeably cooler, although the fits of shivering that were making her teeth rattle occassionaly made it hard to judge. Two stories, with a central chimney, everything of sawn blocks of grayish volcanic tufa. Windows shuttered, with light leaking around the edges; the second story extended to form a roof over the front veranda, resting on pillars. One oak door with a shuttered peephole.

I can't wait, Shkai'ra thought. *It doesn't matter how many of them there are. Much longer and I won't be able to walk well, much less fight.*

She drew the sword and laid it on the ground before her and her hands on her thighs, palm up and fingers slightly curled. A breath, and then another, counting the time. Sense heartbeat, air on skin, the minor tickle and itch of bugs. Shut down hearing, the awareness at the boundary of her own skin. Pull the mind in . . .

The sword. The Warmaster's voice echoed through her memory, so long ago. *Every other weapon has another use. An axe can cut wood, a knife skin a sheep. Spears and bows are tools of the hunt. The sword is made for one thing alone: killing. Take up the sword, take up death.*

A long breath, in, out. Let pain flow out, let anger flow out, let fear flow out.

"No one followed you, huh, Fren?" Cards slapped on the table, as Patappas dealt, the pack laid on the table for his one hand to deal from.

"Followed me? Why in Hayel would you think anyone would follow me?"

"Just asking."

"Maybe a stray dog. Or a werewolf." Outside it was getting dark.

Take up the death of your enemies.

Another breath. Let the awareness of the body return; accept the weakness, pain, torn muscle, joint-ache of fever. Accept, let them pass through. The body has its own reserves, the last horded strength for extremity. The trained will can summon it. She did, and felt her pupils flare wide. Her skin chilled and roughened as the capillaries under it squeezed, forcing her blood back toward the heart. A trickle of slaver ran down from one corner of her mouth as the lips ridged. The darkness went lighter, sharp-edged but distant.

Take up your own death.

She rose, almost smoothly, and stripped off the hampering skirt. Ripped the tunic down, a moment's distraction might mean the difference between killing and dying.

Killing and dying are one. Kill until you die.

Gravel crunched under her feet, and the feral scent of

flowers gone wild, overblown summer roses. Buckler and sword went behind her back. She halted before the door.

"_Hello_ in there," she called, standing two paces back.

The peephole opened, throwing light into her eyes.

"Go away, bitch," an Arkan voice said, halfway between anger and alarm. "No food, no shelter. Get lost."

You are the sword. Steel does nothing; it is the hard heart _that kills_.

"Death," she muttered, unconscious of the action. The point of the longsword slotted through the peephole, and the impact ran back up the steel to her wrist. A crunching feeling as the point punched through just above the nose, then a thud as the body hit the door when she jerked back on the sword to free it. Her good leg swung up, kicking flat-footed next to the latch; old dry-rotted wood shattered with a crack and a puff of brown dust, and the door gave. The stab of pain up her injured leg was nothing, something happening to someone else far away; she stopped it from buckling under her with brisk impatience. Through the door, shouldering it aside and stepping over the body of a man, eyes still wide in final surprise. Others around a table. One clutching the arm of a _blond boy whose eyes were kh'eeredo's_—

Shkai'ra screamed, blade arching back for a cut. Cards flew upward in a shower.

Good tactics, bad strategy. She found herself a dispassionate spectator, sitting behind her own eyes. Four men. One holding the boy. Middle-aged, some of them fat, one missing an arm; old warriors, or street-fighters. Balding man holding Lixand by the arm, reaching across to drag out a long knife with the other. She'd given them no way to run and no time to be afraid.

The _fessas_ she had followed snatched up a javelin from the wall, threw himself backward with a shriek as the tip of her sword drew a line of red across his chest. He backflipped, came to his feet and threw, screamed again as her sword blurred and the barbed head went _ktang_ off the guard, to sink quivering into the inside of a shut-

ter. Shkai'ra shrieked back at him; he threw up his hands
as the return slash opened his belly.

Everything went clear, like the air on a crisp day, rare
in Arko, like cold air that Rasas knew from somewhere,
his childish made-up stories of imaginary places; nowhere
could air be that cold. Some nights here he'd imagined
being rescued by a knight on a white charger, whose
armor shone, and who would gallantly yet kindly over-
power Patappas and friends, turning them over to the
authorities to be thrown in the dungeons; then the
knight, learning Nuninibas was no less evil, rather more
so, would take Rasas away and adopt him. . . .

But *this,* this huge female-gargoyle-faced . . . *creature*
with blurring sword and rotting leg, did *not* fit the part.
There were splashes of blood flying everywhere, everyone
was screaming, and Rasas knew only one thing: *I've got
to get out of here.*

Out of sight, out of mind, he knew, with a slave's
instincts. When *it* (it couldn't be a *she*) had its back
turned, he scurried under the card table. Next, the
door—if a chance came when there weren't legs or blurring spattering weapons in the way, before it was over
. . . he waited. Or the stairs; there were broken windows,
maybe he could crawl out over the roof . . . he waited.
The witch-demon, what else could it be, was hacking up
his kidnappers *fast. There goes Frenandias . . . Akobas
. . . I can't wait much longer . . .* His chance for the door
never came.

Shkai'ra batted the thrown chair aside with the buckler
and stabbed down at the knife-arm swiping for her
ankles; the point of her sword slammed between the
bones of the man's forearm—his only forearm, it was the
amputee—into the hardwood blocks of the floor, and
stuck. A third man lunged, barbed javelin thrusting for
her belly. She began to quarter, and her leg gave. *Ah!*
Down on one knee; the javelin-head banged off the boss

of her buckler with an iron clamor and shower of sparks, and the man tripped and fell full-length over her out-stretched other leg. She pulled herself up on the hilt of the sword, and the next man was on her, a knife in either hand.

Turn-step-sweep-parry, her empty hand grabbing the wrist of the leading knifehand, other driving the edge of the shield into his temple. Turn-twist-hips and *throw*, flowing with and speeding his motion so his weight never really fell on her bad leg; his flight ended with the top of his head thudding into the stone block wall with an ugly cracking sound. Somewhere she could feel pain alarms, more than one, sounding in the depths of her mind.

A man on his knees, nose mashed flat to his face, bleeding, whites showing all around his faded blue eyes—but grabbing up a loaded crossbow, the four edges of the pyramid-shaped head of the quarrel glittering . . . Shkai'ra slipped the shield-thong off her arm, twisting her body as she flung, the shield spinning like a giant discus. It struck his throat; he pitched back to lie against the wall, biting for air as his crushed windpipe refused to pass the air his chest heaved to draw. The crossbow twanged, the bolt knocking a chip out of the stone wall across the room.

Shkai'ra turned, staggered. *No more. Over.* Except for the one with no left arm to free his pinned right arm with; quiet now, he stared up at her. She wrenched the sword loose, finished him. Grey edged the corners of her vision, a grey-red mist that faded in across the icy clarity of the battlemind; the hysterical strength that had worn her like a cloak vanished. She toppled forward like a cut tree and lay, gasping and straining not to faint, tears and mucus streaming across her face as pain hit.

The boy. Silence had fallen, the strangled man passed out and soon to die; the hanging lamp over the card table swinging was the only motion, though by making every shadow sway and shift it filled the whole room with false motion. *I did come here and do this all for the* zteafakaz *boy. Where did he go?*

She moaned, forcing her hands underneath herself and levering her torso up. A ragged breath, and she rolled onto one side. *Damn.* The cut along her ribs—*when did I get that?*—was shallow, but too deep to clot, making a sheet of red down her side. Blood was flowing from the leg-wound, mixed with oily yellow matter. She ripped off the remains of her tunic and clamped it against the cut with an elbow, and crawled sidewinder fashion with one elbow and one knee over to the table, which still bore tall clay tumblers and an opened bottle; she hooked an elbow over the table edge and came to a knee, grabbed the bottle and poured half a dozen swallows down her throat. It was wine, cut with brandy, cloying sweet and strong. The grey receded a little and she half-fell into one of the chairs. Bending over, snarling at the pain, she managed to rip off enough of a dead man's shirt to bind the bandage crudely to her ribs.

She glared around. "He couldn't have gotten out the door," she said; her voice startled her for a moment, a breathy rasp. She drank more of the wine. "Trapdoor to the cellar's closed. Door to the other room's still closed." Most of the first floor was this single large dining hall. "Upstairs, then." There was a spiral stair at one end of the room, curling around a post of carved and inlaid oak; the stairs were beautifully inlaid parquetry.

She heaved herself to her feet; the room swayed, then steadied. "Lixand!" The name sounded strange in her ears. *Shit, what language am I talking?* The bad leg nearly turned under her, unable to bear any but the slightest weight; she swore long and savagely in the ripping, clicking gutturals of Kommanzanu. There seemed to be a plate of Arkan-glass between her brain and her tongue, as if she was moving it like a puppet through a glove. "Lixand, it's—" She stopped. *He's not likely to think of me as his mother.* "Lixand, I've come from

Megan, to take you home." *Come down those stairs, you little shit.*

No answer. She switched the sword to her left hand, to use as a crutch; a terrible thing to do to a good weapon, but devils drove. *Thump*-drag-wheeze, over to the base of the stairs. Prop the point against the lowest one.

"Lixand! Come out, boy!" *Thump*, up a step. She gasped through clenched teeth, leaned panting on the stair-rail. Another step. Another. Faster, and the black square of the opening to the upper floor was just above her.

She stopped just below it, bellows-panting. *Maybe he got out one of the doors and I didn't notice!* she thought. *Better take a look here. City boy, he won't go far in the dark outside anyway.* Shkai'ra put the point of the sword on the next step, inched her head up through the opening.

A whistle of cloven air warned her; but she was slow, slow. Too slow to do more than begin to drop, before the icy sensation of the blow struck the back of her skull.

There was one more, she thought, in the moment before her body went boneless. *Forgive me, Megan. I failed.*

The witch-demon's head flopped back, lax, and dropped away out of the rectangle of light; he saw the gray eyes, clenching shut, falling through a shaft of lamplight, the too-muscular-for-a-woman body with the purple spider-wound on one leg tumbled limply, thump *thump thump* down the stairs, turn over, lie still. The almost painful tingling in his hands gripping the oaken chair-leg, that he'd quietly unscrewed from a cob-webbed dining-room chair, seemed to linger.

I never thought I could kill a witch-demon, Rasas thought.

XXII

Redfurherdmareleadernononononono!

Megan sat bolt upright in the dark of the tent, claws out, rags of sleep tearing away to leave the echoes of Hotblood's thought-scream.

She opened her mind up as far as she could, like spreading open a clenched fist, till the fingers and the webs between them burned with stretching, wide open, wider.

HOTBLOOD! Through him, again, somehow, came Shkai'ra's sensations. *Knife-edge clear, fighting, the leg-pain so bad* now Megan heard a whimper slip through her own teeth. The blow, *blast of ice-needle pain through the back of my head there was one more Megan kh'eeredo* . . .

The last thought, etched with weakening anguish, as the power to think sank into darkness: *Forgive me, Megan. I failed.*

SHHHKKKKAAAAAIIII'RRRRAAAAA! Megan curled into a ball on her bed, hands clasped to her head, points of pain where her claws dug, unnoticed, into her scalp, her whole body shaking with the force of the thought-scream. Nothing.

*Redfurherdmareleader*dead*moanwhimperwhimper* . . .

HOTBLOOD! She sent the call out so hard she reeled sitting. Nothing. Again, again, almost to passing out. No thought-answer came. *Without her,* she thought dully, *nothing, not even annoyance, binds him to me.*

She huddled on the bed, curled around nothing, absolutely still. The thought came dully. *She thought "I'm dead," before, when it wasn't certain—idly, just out of fear. She would never, unless it were certain, unless she knew she'd drawn her last breath, think: "I failed."*

"It's been twenty-eight fikken days, Whitlock," the icy urbane voice said, that night. "You said you'd do it. Gave your word, renounced your hesitations. It's not a matter of my tried patience, Whitlock, not anymore, though it's been tried to the bones. Any longer and it gets academic whether Shefen-kas dies, as you and I both know. And I'll snuff your boy, though it makes no difference, just for failing me.

"I'll snuff your boy if *he* isn't dead or well on the way in another four days, and that's *it*, final. You've known damn well how long you could play games with me; and you must know now that the time for games is over, Arko has nothing to lose, and I *have* to play my last card, though it be my last. No, don't answer. I know you've heard me. Just get the *fik* out of here and *do* it, if you're any kind of mother."

I must do this, so she will not have died in vain.
The glow of manrauq was small, hardly more than a bright yellowish-green aureole around each claw, so that she could see in the dimness of the tent. *Careful.* Megan touched the tiny brush to the tips of the claws of her left hand. *Dangerous.* She hadn't done this for years, too much a risk that she might scratch herself or someone she loved, but she'd brought it, just in case. A slow blood-

poison, colorless, untraceable, that killed in three days, acting like flux. The sort of thing her aunt would have enjoyed. *No. I am not Marte.*

I must do this, so my akribhan will not have died in vain.

She took her unbound hair back out of her face, used to being careful with her hands. Outside cook-fires were being doused and consolidated into night-fires. With unhurried, controlled motions she screwed on the cap of the tiny jar. It looked like an ordinary bottle of nail-paint, but she always hid it in the secret pocket in her leather case.

She'd tell him she wanted him, she wanted his help. In the bushes. "Like sleeping with a rabid wolverine!" Shkai'ra's words, when they'd awakened, loud and vivid in her ear as yesterday—grief stabbed without warning, like an assassin's knife, gushed suddenly like blood. *No.* She pushed it away into a corner of her mind, before tears could come. *Not yet.* Ten bleeding pits in Shkai'ra's muscle-smooth back . . . In a twitch of passion or fear, she would scratch him. Slightly. Men had used her; she would use a man, to get back her son. In three days, four if he were strong . . . *Lixand-mi.*

I must do this so she will not have died in vain. She stood, pulled the mass of her hair to the nape of her neck, and let it fall over her shoulder, as night fell.

Calm. He's better than good at reading people. As she searched from fire to fire, she forced it, blank, wide, dulling like snow-blindness.

At the second A-niah fire, three men and a woman danced to the music of a bamboo flute, a Hyerne dance linking arms across her shoulders. Brown limbs swung, black hair bounced slick. Flash of white, on a gesturing hand: the signet. Those dark shining eyes, spark of gold between grinning lips. *Here.*

They shuffled a place for her, waves and smiles even from familiar hands and faces seeming distant as trees across a bay. Five people away from him. She accepted the wine-flask as it came her way, took one draught.

Take up the death of your enemies.

She caught his eye, and raised an eyebrow at him. He raised both his back at her, smiling, making the gesture for unbound hair. He'd never seen her with it down. She smiled back.

As people got up to dance or visit the latrine or leave, she worked her way next to him. Even her slight drunkenness was fish-bowl distant, like in a fight. She passed the wine-skin to him, careful not to puncture it with the claws of either hand. His wounded arm was out of the sling, but he moved it carefully.

Not yet, take your time. It wouldn't be so soon. Through song and talk she sat, waiting, feeling his warmth on her side. Then when the time was right, an hour or so having passed, she laid her right hand on his arm, half-casual, half-tentative, feeling the soft fuzz; he wasn't a hirsute man. "I was thinking about a talk we had a while ago," she said quietly, under the sound of the harp and flute tuning to each other. "I thought I'd take you up on your offer." She tossed her head, sending ripples down the fall of her hair.

His eyes remembered, understood, smiled a smile deeper than greeting. He touched three fingertips to the back of her hand, feather-gentle.

She leaned her head into his shoulder. She'd seen others do it, friends, even strangers, wanting comfort against the stress of war. He never denied them. Someone else called him into conversation. The wine-skin came around again; she noticed he took only a short draught. She caught his eye, tilted her head toward the woods. She slipped her right hand in his left, feeling its gentle grip, large and warm, as they stepped away from the fire.

"I have a daughter in my tent," she whispered.

"So do I. There's my office-cart: it's stuffier than the woods, but more private and better guarded." They threaded their way through trees and fires, talk and song in a score of tongues. He needed no password, knowing all the sentries' names.

He gave her the usual hand up to the door. Their feet drummed softly on the boards. She heard him grope for the light, the rasp of a tinder box; a flame leapt up and he lit a taper to a stone lamp, alabaster, carved in the shape of a leaping dolphin. He set it on the floor next to the bed, and sat on its edge at her feet.

"I knew your hair was long." His accent gave his words a silvery sound in the dimness. "I didn't know it was *so* long." She looked down at the ends brushing just below her knees, then at him, the lamplight from below and to one side making his scarred face faintly sinister.

Now? She could half-trip and scratch him when he moved to steady her. It would be done, she could leave . . . *No.* It would seem suspicious, he'd have it checked. *For one so subtle, only the subtlest plan I have in me will do.* "I swore I'd never cut it again. That was eight years ago." She smiled and sat to his right—her left hand, the poisoned one, flat on the bed.

"It's beautiful," he said. She leaned toward him, laid her right hand softly on his chest. Warm, muscles hard like Shkai'ra's, but in the more massive masculine form, under a small patch of black hair. The new scar on the inside of his left upper arm, still an angry red, with stitch marks. She remembered her thought: *better I kill you myself than send you to that.* He would never fight again.

She brought her lips close. His came to hers, but slowly, waiting, letting her lead. His eyes were closed, showing delicate black lashes. "All through this," he breathed, "I'm yours. You choose. You rule."

Yes. Lixand-mi. Akribhan.

She slid her arms around him. "Hold me first, please." He did it as if she were fragile; as she kissed his neck, tasting the slight trace of salt on her lip, she felt shivers shoot through his body, from head to toes in a wave. Yet he didn't clench her. She felt the heaviness in her loins, the solid weight of her own passion, twined with the

man-fear at the back of her throat, lurking at the roots
of her muscles, waiting to lock her in its grip. All distant.

She pulled at his belt buckle, *right hand* . . . "You want
me naked," he whispered. He slid off the bed to
unbuckle his kilt, then waited, kneeling, for her to
beckon him, his eyes shining in the lamp-light, warm
brown. She saw his hardness, standing up from black
curls, stirring.

She skinned out of her boots and trousers. *Why be
afraid? I carry the power of life and death, on my claws.*
She wiggled out of her tunic. She turned to him, held
out her hand, *left hand*; he slid his fingers into hers,
closing his eyes, making her guide him by touch. She
drew him onto the bed.

He was so large, even kneeling he loomed . . . The
wrong thought crept in like a thief, *ship-berth, him
between me and the door, naZak-big, me child-small, him
male-smelling* . . . She stiffened, froze, hands up in front
of her, trembling. *Natural enough,* the flat cold part of
her thought. *Good act, illusionist. Shit,* another part
thought. *I should have clawed him.*

Chevenga spread his hands, away from her, leaving himself open, the motions all old-fashioned Yeoli, straight,
formal. "Megan, I'd die before I hurt you." She took a
deep, slow, controlled breath, stilling the pounding of
her heart by will. *Yes. You will. I don't need to fear you;
I will kill you.*

"I . . ." she stammered. "I need to be on the same
side the door is." He shifted back to let her change places
with him. "*He* used to like to give me just so much
running room, and then catch me."

She saw a line of muscle near his temple flex, as his
jaw clenched. "Tell me how not to be like him," he said.
"Forbid me to be like him. Tonight, here, I am yours."

"Mine?" She let out a laugh, plausibly nervous. "*He*
used to say 'you are mine.' Whatever your power-stingy
people say, Fourth Chevenga, you're a king; you can't
know what that means."

"Oh?" His brows rose, challenged. "You think Kurkas didn't say 'you are mine' to me? Do you think I was a king in the Mezem, killing some other wretch every eight-day so they wouldn't kill me, with the Mahid hauling me off every month to drug Yeola-e's secrets out of me?" He drew up, kneeling straight, formal Yeoli warrior-style; imposing, but not frightening, somehow, every line full of the bounds of discipline. His voice softened. "What I mean is: I will do and be what you will, for this one night. Nothing you have to take; I give it. All my life I have been my people's, doing their will, as I was born and bred to." His words checked then, his eyes searching hers. "Look, Megan, if it seems I'm urging you, if it's too fast, we can hold off till another night, or forget about it entirely. Whatever you choose."

Almost irresistibly came the urge to put it off, to be out of this too-hot walled place, to be gone and forget. *No.* The pain of Arkan steel again, pinning her wrists, no different than if it were real. *Lixand-mi. I might not get another chance. And she will have died in vain.* She calmed, made herself claw-steel, to match steel. Easily. *So easily. What innocence did I miss, am I missing, having learned to be so hard so young? As your life shaped you, Gold-bottom, so did mine shape me.*

"I'm tired of being afraid. It's been long enough. Kiss me?" She heard her own voice, even in the darkness, steady, alluring. His lips touched hers, softly, open. She reached with her tongue for his, holding his curly head in her clawed hands. A familiar awe, through everything else: *I'm kissing Chevenga, the Invincible, the Immortal, the Gold-bottom* . . . Bitter inward laughter. *Kissing, killing. Duty and pleasure allied. I am the Immortal's mortality.*

He smiled—*I lend you my strength*, it said—and lay back on the bed. She slid down in his arms. What frightened her most, because it was what Sarngeld had most often forced from her, what she could do only very rarely for Shyll, she would do. *Then in fear I'll jump and nick*

*him. I might not even know when I'm doing it. All I need
to do is stop being so careful.*

Man-fear swelled, stifling; she choked it down, fought
not to gag. His scent was a vegetarian's, sweet on other
parts of him, but *here . . . All men are the same.* His only
touch was three fingertips air-light on her shoulder.

"Megan, are you sure?" He slid upwards, drawing
away.

"This is the hardest. Don't make it harder!" She
clasped his hips and laid her cheek against his belly for
a moment, clinging, eyes closed, some part of her like a
baby taking comfort from his warmth.

"Megan. You need what will make you feel safe.
Here." He took her right hand up, laid it across his own
throat, claws spread. Under her fingertips she felt his
pulse-beat, quick and steady. "If I do what you don't
want, if I become *him* somehow, give me just a clench,
the first time, a warning. If I do the same thing *again*—
kill me."

She tore her hand away, raised her head to stare. A
moment of panic: *Would I do that? Yes, I would. In
shock.* His eyes were serious. *I trust you,* they said. *And
myself.* "It's only my own hands my fate would be in,"
he said. "I'd have none but myself to blame."

What she should say came easily enough. "Kill you,
and fight my way out through your army, leaving what's
left of my family to the mercy of those who loved you?"
She heard her voice, dry, cynical. "Do you think I'm an
idiot?"

He slid out from her arms, picked a sheet of paper
and an Arkan pen out of the cupboard. Crouching in the
circle of lamplight, he wrote three lines in his quick firm
hand, Yeoli and Enchian, signed, sealed it with a daub
of seal-wax and the *semanakraseye*'s signet, and handed
it to her.

*I, Fourth Chevenga Shae-Arano-e, semanakraseye na
chakrachaseye, absolve Megan Whitlock of my own death*

this seventh night in the moon of the Corn. There was reason; she knows.

The words, as she read them, four times, seemed to shift and swim; the dark air had currents, like water, that moved her, became hard to breathe, the cart-floor rippling. *No. Shake it off, but without motion. You should feel just amazement.*

His eyes gazed at her, black reflecting two tiny dark flames, one gold tooth reflecting a brighter one. "They'd truth-drug you, you'd tell the truth, and they'd know it as the sort of thing I'd do. If they even caught you." He shrugged, naked shoulders lifting. "Who would say anything to Megan Whitlock strolling by night, with her adopted daughter?"

Don't show him the world's spinning. She kept the impassive merchant's face, with a mask of lesser surprise. *I know what I'd say now.* "How can you trust me so? I was truth-drugged three months ago, you don't know I haven't been compromised since then, somehow." *Subtle, witch.*

He lay back on the bedding, tucking his hands behind his head, shrugged again, smiling. "I know who to trust."

You idiot. You fish-gutted over-reckless, Gold-bottomed idiot.

She laid the note on the cabinet, and he reached for her hand again, guided it to his throat, throwing his head back slightly. "You're mad," she said.

He just chuckled, the muscle under her fingers vibrating with it. "I suppose so, if it's madness to do what one believes in *kyan'mon* ... entirely, that means. Wholly."

She made herself steel again, except for what she carefully chose to let through the screen. *Emotions: cards to play.* He closed his eyes, as if savoring her touch with its sword-keen threat, not knowing his true danger lay on his hip, her left hand. She lowered her head, took him in her mouth. He'd softened in the pause; now he surged hard again, with a gasp, and threw his head further back, trembling to her touch like a leaf to the wind's.

His hand, its warmth, naZak big, was comforting on her shoulder; then it tenderly stroked her hair and flung her into the past. *Huge calloused naZak man-hands, holding her head in place, pressing on the hinges of her jaws to make sure she wouldn't bite, fear and bile and the taste of semen*—She bit her scream into a choking squeak at the back of her throat, pulled away, remembered, clenched her hand on his neck. He froze, stone-still. The quiet voice was like a healer's over the operating table. "What did I do?"

She knelt panting, heart hammer-banging. *I don't need to be afraid.* She struggled, mouth working, for words, glanced at his hip. *No blood. I didn't. I didn't. Shit, why didn't I? Both hands at once, spasming, he wouldn't even have noticed! Shit, shit, shit, Shkai'ra, Lixand, next time, next time* . . . "Your hand. Your hand on my head. *Don't*—" Unreality: she was commanding the Invincible. "*Don't* do that."

He drew his hand away, spread his arms wide, far from her. She forced her breathing and her thoughts steady. *I killed Sarngeld. He's dead and no one will ever do that to me again. I'm here to kill another. I don't need to fear him. She won't die in vain, akribhan, Lixand-mi* . . .

On his throat lay three drops of red, almost black in the dim light, growing; *there*, she'd done it properly. But his eyes were closed and his head back again; his member still stood, his passion unbroken.

Koru, she thought, *he isn't even afraid.* In her mind came a sound like the slamming of a great iron gate. *This, I cannot kill.*

Nooooooooo . . . A scream from within, echoing through her bones. *Lixaaaaaaaand!* "Megan?" She tore her hand away, both hands, her head, choking not on him, on herself. "Megan." Bile pushed up onto the back of her tongue, made her cough. "Megan!" His command-voice cut through the spinning of the world. She blinked, found his face, many images blurring. He was sitting up, bed-clothes hiding him from the waist down. Carefully and clearly, as if to a madwoman: "Can you hear me?" She wasn't sure whether she was crying or not, couldn't feel it, didn't care.

The world needs you. As Imperator of Arko, as whatever you will become, in your life. How many other people have died, to put you there? Whose deaths would be in vain?

"I'll be back." Her voice clanged to her own ears like a coin rolling around an iron pot. *Still acting. Still subtle.* Crazed laughter, death-laughter. *Oh, subtle Zak!* She staggered past, took the stairs in one leap. "Don't follow me! Just a moment, please, let me have just a moment, alone." Yes, she was crying; she felt tear-streaks on cheek and side of nose turn cold in the night wind.

You do know who to trust, Chevenga. It's I who is the idiot. She plunged her left hand into the bucket of water next to the wheel, drove her claws into the earth, scrubbed with the sandy mud, rinsed in the water again, tipped the bucket out so no one could drink from it. She staggered back into the cart, where he knelt, waiting, eyes utterly gentle. She seized his note from the cabinet, burned it in the lamp, down to the last blank corner in her left-hand claws.

"I will finish you, your pleasure," she whispered. "Just hold me, for now, please ..."

His arms were tender at first, then, as the sobs strengthened, and began to feel as if they'd tear her in two like paper, his embrace gently tightened, as if to hold her together. "Never mind finishing me. That would be too much. You've gone through enough tonight. Agh, Megan, poor Megan, strength, there'll be an end to your pain, there *will* ..." She curled her hands into fists so that the claws rested on the pads of callus, and wept harder.

Night broke off chips of dark, rained crashing on her head like broken glass, thoughts dropping dully from her mind into her heart. *Lixand-mi.* His baby curls under her hand, his toothless smile as he grabbed for the rattle; baby trust, entire. *Lixand. Someone else killed Shkai'ra, but I have killed you. You will never know it was me. You'll just die. I am worse than slough-kin: kin-killer.*

I should have clawed myself, the thought came, dead and cold as an assassin's thoughts. *I still can.*

"Zhymata?" Sova's whisper out of the dark, from inside the tent.

Koru—no. She'd be orphaned, twice-*orphaned, by my hand.*

"What's wrong? Are you all right? *Zhymata?*" The Thane-girl unhooded the small *kraumak,* the light-stone.

"I've lied to you, Sova." The words came out, unthinking. *What am I saying?* She heard her own voice, dull, deadened, tell the whole story, as her hands mindlessly stripped off her clothes again, her body crawled under the covers, lay curled tight around her pain. *Let there be only truth between us. I won't be slough-kin with her, too.* "I can't kill him. The world needs him too much. I've thrown away my son's life, Shkai'ra's death." She was finished telling; the pain loosened enough to let her cry again, open, unrestrained, wailing like a child.

For a long time Sova stared, her mouth slightly open. Then she snapped it closed, and blinked, playing back the words in her mind, several times.

"*Zhymata . . . No.* You didn't throw away anyone's life, or death. You did what you had to." The girl's strong arms wrapped around Megan, hugged crushing tight. "*Zhymata. Zhymata.* You don't know for *sure* Shkai'ra's dead, you still don't know absolutely for sure! Oh, *Zhymata,* poor *Zhymata,* it's all right, you had to lie to me, don't worry, you did what you had to, *Zhymata,* you threw nothing away, you did what you had to. You did what you had to. You did what you had to."

XXIII

The silence was absolute but for the pounding of his heart and the hissing of his breath, which slowed and quieted. The swinging of the lamp faded to nothing, stilling the shadows, filling the lower room with stillness. All that moved was blood, dripping everywhere, on the walls, even on the ceiling; the air was warm with fresh butcher-shop stinks. Rasas was alone, in a falling-apart house full of corpses and new-made ghosts.

"Tikas." His voice in the dark seemed unreal, insect-small. "Ardas." Tears sprang to his eyes, left over from the fight, the death-screams, louder than he would have believed out of men who usually moved so slowly, the blood. Clutching the chair-leg, he let the tears run, and splash on his knees.

After a while his whimpering sounded stupid and weak to him; calmer, his inner voice sounded pleasingly sensible. *I've got to do something.*

He put down the chair-leg and lowered himself onto the spiral stairs. *No, wait—I don't want to be down there.* But he'd have to, eventually, to get out of there. *Tomorrow, when it's light. I'll stay up here till then.*

Then out the corner of his eye he saw the witch-demon move. His heart froze.

I didn't hit hard enough. Celestialis, I didn't hit hard enough and now she'll wake up and kill me. Sprawled with one leg still trailing up the bottom-most stairs, the creature moaned, turned her head, moaned louder. He groped for the chair-leg. *I've got to hit her again, keep hitting her until she stops breathing.* But the slit grey eyes were looking at him, watching even if the long limbs weren't moving.

Then the lips worked, and in a croaking whisper said a magic word out of his ancient stories, his mythic memories, a word he thought only he knew, a word he'd thought no one in the world would ever speak.

"*Lixand.*"

A feeble bloodied hand fumbled at the red-stained shirt, groped a pouch inside, over the witch-demon's heart, fished out something long and black and white. Suddenly he remembered something out of the lore of witch-demons: they didn't bleed. "*Chi mata, Lixand.*" Hair: a lock of the hair of the fairy-mother of his dreams, black except for one white streak.

The chair-leg slipped out of his hand, rolled. "You're . . . you're my *rescuer?*" Those eyes, inhuman with blood-madness before, held only pain now; and recognition. *Witch-demons don't cry* . . . a tear streaked down one hawk-thin cheek.

"Oops," he said; the largest, most sincere, most moved, most moving "oops" possible. Witch-demons, he remembered, didn't smile, either.

Then her grey eyes closed again, and her head sank back. *Dead?* He scrabbled down the stairs, trying to remember everything about healing he'd ever been taught. Her heart was still beating, he could feel; but barely and she was hot, much too hot. *Little Humble God,* he prayed. *Help me save her.*

This is the last time, Matthas thought, waiting. The meeting place was dark, even in the moonlight, downwind of the Yeoli picket lines. *Thirty-two days. I will tell her she will never see me again; just if he isn't dead in another four, I'll send the order* . . .

There: the familiar child-sized silhouette moved among the black trunks of the trees, still limping a little, slow and careful to not trip in the dark.

"Stop there, Zak." No dry wit now; he didn't have it in him. He was tired. She froze. He couldn't see her face, just a feathering of moonlight through shadows of branches, catching the lock of silver in her hair. She turned to face him.

"What is it now—you've poisoned him and it has yet to take effect? Is that it?" Underneath the demand in his voice, he heard his own desperate hope. *Shit . . . maybe I just gave away the whole game.* She just stood still, three paces in front of him. Wind touched the trees, momentarily shone a patch of moonlight on her face.

She was smiling, moon-glint on teeth and eyes giving them a dull cruel sheen, like sword-steel. Slowly he realized he could see a lighter patch of meadow between two tree-trunks, *through* her. Then she vanished.

Oh shit. Almost imperceptible from such a small person, the sense of warmth, of presence, *behind him to his left, close* . . . He whirled, his face turning straight into the dark flash of a small arm reaching up, a blow, slashing, snagging dully, across his cheek.

"*Shen!*" The shriek tore out of him, almost breathless; involuntarily he did a standing leap two paces straight backwards, clutching his face. Wet, warm, his blood trickled.

"Some things are more important than kin, Arkan." The high small female voice was as cold and edged as steel claws. "Like seeing a corrupt Empire die. Ask yourself how long the poison will take to kill you. Then go to Hayel, for failing." She turned, and was gone into the dark.

Matthas staggered to the stream, thrust his face under, icy cold seizing his skin, knowing he was muddying the water as his hands slipped on the stones, scrubbed his face with one palm trying to drive dirty water into the claw-gouges, draw blood out; better the chance of infection than the certainty of poison. The wounds stung, but perhaps no more than they would anyway; he couldn't tell.

"Shen shen shen . . ." He pulled himself up from the stream, struggled to his feet. The cold flowing on his face went warm again; he pressed his kerchief to it. *I need a healer.* But if he went to a Haian here, they'd take records of his wounds, he'd be asked how he'd got them, leave a paper trail for them to follow. *God, why did Manajas have to get killed?* His good contact with the Arkans gone, he had only the replacement, a dour old fart who was suspicious of anything underhanded. How to explain? *Shen . . .* Truth impinged. *I've failed. Even if I send a note to snuff the little bastard, snuff him slowly, one fikken sinew at a time the little son of a worm and a witch, I've still failed.* A tread in the underbrush; he froze behind a tree, while the other passed. Urges without reason came, desperately strong, to be in a warm bed, with his mother sitting next to it stroking his brow. *That dwarfish bitch calls herself a mother, throwing away her son's life like that, that's unnatural.*

He'd hired two men to guard his tent, northern mercenaries drawing a little extra pay for a little extra sentry-duty. "Kras FrahhnsssohhndeNuubohhn, you all right?" The bumpkin accent grated on his ears. "Get healer?" He just mumbled a no thank you, the Thanish accent coming naturally. *Good thing I kept the habit of thinking in it.*

As if it matters now. All that was left was to do what a good Irefas man did before he died: remove himself from where the enemy could get knowledge out of him while he was helpless. He'd go to the old fart, throw himself on flatulent mercy. *He can stretch my neck; fine, I'll have done my duty.* Strangely, there was an intoxicating sense of liberation in being doomed.

Failed. He quickly packed his merchant's papers and seals, a change of clothing—he didn't even have a pair of gloves—to cross to the Arkan camp. *How am I going to word this letter to Patappas and Frenandias?* "*You risked everything for nothing, my old friends . . .*" He could kiss his elevation good-bye, his triumph good-bye . . . but that was nothing, really, that was just *his* problem. *Because I've failed,* he thought, *the whole fikken great lumbering elephant of an Empire's fikked.*

Liberation brought clarity, and revelation; in a lightning burst, Matthas's vision extended for a moment across the whole known world, and he understood why Arko would fall. He'd lived with the answer all his career.

Arko's fall was in *Aitzas* spy-runners who got assassinated because they hadn't bothered to learn the ways of a place. In mud-slow bureaucracies that kept back funds needed to maintain a spy office for six months. In blockhead Mahid who didn't believe two women could exist who took ten strong-arms to bring down, then blamed Matthas-types for the result and sent them off on desperation missions with no support. In *Aitzas* who cared more about throwing gold and oysters around at their parties than the health of their country, and . . . the last thought came, brutal, laughable. *An Imperator whose head is so far up his butt he isn't even fikken weaned.* Of course it all came from the top; it always did. The seeds of Arko's fall were in Kurkas's birth, or his father's, or his grandfather's. It wasn't *quite* all the fault of Matthas Bennas, *fessas.*

Who presently threw himself backwards across his pallet, and did what he felt like: laughed, until he cried.

Book III: Fulfillment

XXIV

Headline on the front page of the Pages, *Machine-Scribed News-Chronicle of the City of Arko, 20th Day of the First Month Autumnal, 55th to the Last Year of the Present Age:*

STRATEGY OF ATTRITION SUCCEEDING: BRILLIANT GENERALSHIP LURES BARBARIANS DEEP INTO TRAP

In the plains of Finpollendias, just above and east of Arko the City Itself, the corn had turned gold; the wood-lots around wore the deep but faintly tattered green of late summer. On a slope a little way above, the alliance army rested.

The next battle would be the last; though the Empire had fielded an army not much smaller, it was made up of the dregs of Arkan manpower, and no one much doubted what the result would be. Poised over Arko like a sword for the grace-stroke, the Alliance waited for the hand that held it to bring it down. Across the fire, Megan watched its light on the planes of his face, as he spoke.

It had been more than a month since she'd decided not to kill him, since Shkai'ra's—she still couldn't bring herself to say the word. *Death*. Her dark-work had been less necessary lately, and she'd avoided him as well. *Why am I more afraid of showing something now than when I really did have something to hide?*

The days immediately after had been a shapeless blackness. So much practice mourning; she knew its every stage, its every line and crack. *I'm still denying. Because I didn't see her die, I guess, the way I did Mama and Papa*. Then she'd realized, what Sova said was true: she couldn't know for certain Shkai'ra was dead until she saw her corpse. Which meant . . . *uncertainty, again. I'm practiced at that, too. Maybe forever, I'll live not knowing. About the two people I love most, instead of one of them. Koru, why did I send her* . . . She cut that thought off. *No. It's no use. We had to try something. We had to.*

Whatever happened, she could cling to what she still had. These days, some people would kill to sit at Chevenga's right hand; now it was one of his command council, but Sova was only three down, her eyes shining. *Daughter*. Every battle, she'd had to fight down sickness at the thought of the girl—whom her mind *knew* was not as fragile as her thread-bare emotions felt—facing Arkan steel. *Sometimes you don't care if you break my heart, but I'd rather hear a hundred times as many cruel words from you, than lose you.*

At Chevenga's left sat Niku, his A-niah lover who'd been the subject of such controversy, when they'd wanted to marry. Their toddling daughter Vriah, bright blond curls shining against warm brown skin, crawled between her parents' laps until she fell asleep in his. *Another child, I would have harmed*, Megan thought, *saving my own.*

Imperator. In a day or two, what she had once created

as an image by *manrauq* would be real. She watched his hands, the one curled shielding around the child, the other gesturing expansively, and imagined the golden seals flashing on them. *I guess I have you, too.* He only still existed by her choice, though he didn't know it; by not killing him, she'd made him, in a way, one of her own.

The topic turned to revenge, and he let everyone else do the talking. *Ever quiet,* she thought, *about your grudge. Are you hiding something from yourself?* She wet her lips with wine, and said, "I had an experience of vengeance," she said. Faces turned to her, attentive.

"My second in command drugged me, sold me off— he thought he'd sent me off for an underling to kill— and took over my House and my business. He'd almost ruined me by the time I came home. But I had the backing to fight him, then. He'd hurt so many of my friends, to hurt me, that I was determined to lock him in a cage too small for him to either sit, stand or lie, hang him in my hall-garden and torment him for the rest of his life."

The silence deepened. She looked down at her claws, shining in the firelight, and thought of Habiku's loving/hating amber gaze in Ranion's arena where he'd died, almost at her feet. "The rage, the need for vengeance, almost ate me alive."

"Almost?" someone else asked.

"I didn't let it," she said softly. "I didn't cage him, or even kill him, after all. I'd have tied myself to his memory, if I'd done it, driven everyone else away from me and been alone and a little bug-fikken crazy by now."

She gazed across the fire at Chevenga.

His brows rose. "You're worried I might do the same with Kurkas." She felt a strained smile form on her own lips, confirming.

Peyepallo of Hyerne was there; she snorted. "Kill him and be done; that's the best way. Death ends all disputes."

Chevenga signed chalk to the Hyerne, more in ac-
knowledgement than agreement, but addressed Megan.
"I can't spare my tormentor, for one reason: his position.
It's political necessity."

There was a round of affirmative noises. "But have you
decided *how* you're going to kill him, lad?" That was his
shadow-father, Esora-e, grinning cruelly; she'd heard
tales of their quarrels.

"No." Just that. *You never answer such serious questions so shortly*, Megan thought.

"Then vengeance doesn't obsess you," said someone
else. "No one need worry." Another Yeoli asked whether
he would feel at Kurkas's mercy forever if someone else
killed him, which he waved off. Then a Lakan—the general, Megan guessed by the elaborateness of his dress
and the length of his hair-earrings, Arzaktaj—spoke.

"We've all heard the tales, of what he did to you,
Shaikakdan. It's not natural for a man, even a kind one,
who is going to have in his mercy one who has done to
him what Kurkas did to you, to have no thought at all
of what he plans to do to him."

Chevenga held up the wine-skin for quiet. "Listen,"
he said, in a voice that could only have been heard in
total silence. "However it goes, *I* will not come away
feeling the victim. Believe me." He raised his wine-skin
for punctuation, and laughter rocked the fire.

"Am I a barbarian?" he went on. "I look at myself in
the mirror and ask, because I'd be a fool not to. War
makes barbarians of all of us; the pain and fear we all
suffer turns to anger and hate. I will say what my father
told me: in war, barbarities are neither to do for their
own sake, nor not to do because they are barbarities,
only to do when necessary. At the same time, one must
never forget they are barbarities, else how can one
remember how to conduct oneself in peacetime?

"I picked a flower on the mountain, when I was a
child. 'You killed it,' he said. 'Here, so high, where they
take twenty years to grow back . . .' I felt awful. His point

was, whatever you do, you must always know what it is
you do, no matter how much pain that brings. That pain
is the price of power . . ."

He went on in that vein, while Megan waited for a
straight answer. *A snake in the grass, Chevenga. You
usually chew things over with these people, now you're
hiding behind philosophy.* In truth, she'd never heard
him get so preachy. It was increasingly irritating.

Of course, in a day or two, when it was over, her oath
would be fulfilled and he would release her; then she
would do whatever she had to, to trace the fates of
Shkai'ra, and Lixand. *Your problem, Gold-bottom,* she
thought. *And Kurkas's. Go with Koru.*

She stood on a hill overlooking Finpollendias, and
scanned the ranged armies with Shkai'ra's far-lookers.
The lines faced each other waiting for the order to
charge, like black caterpillars with tens of thousands of
legs, standards poking upwards like spines, spearpoints
and lanceheads winking like innumerable fireflies. As
many Arkans as Alliance, but a good three-quarters were
boys and old men; Megan could imagine the faces under
the helmets, wrinkled or childish. Only some of them
had armor.

Nothing moved in the thousand meters of open space
between the forces, land that had been manicured garden before war came to the inviolate heart of the
Empire; it was dreamlike, seeing the armies arrayed
among lawns and flowers and clipped trees. The buzzing
noise of two hundred thousand voices was like distant
heavy surf.

The Lakans were on the left flank, with their banner
of a fire-horse on black, the dark-faced knights wearing
animal crests on their helmets. Backed by the Enchians
with their two overlapping diamonds balanced on the one
point, infantry next to them, the Schvait with their black
bear on yellow and all the division standards; all the motley mercenary flags and figurines. The Yeolis with town

standards—*Where's the blue and green? I don't see it,
that's strange. Chevenga can't be taking today off*. The
few Yeoli horse and the mercenary cavalry on the far
right, with their lance-butts resting on the toes of their
boots; *Sovee*. She would be carrying the Slaughterer's
standard—everyone had steadfastly refused to let the unit
be renamed, until Shkai'ra's corpse was brought in—and
the Minztan saber.

Everybody stood waiting; it seemed all the world stood
waiting. She wanted to worry at the skin around her claws
but kept the far-lookers steady. *What are we waiting for?*

Then from straight up she heard tight cloth flapping,
like kites, and a distant A-niah voice. She looked,
expecting to see a single-wing, and swore to herself.
Koru, my Lady Goddess. Ho-o-o-o-ly shit.

The sky was full of them. There had to be a thousand.
Black, blue, green, in a pattern like one huge wing, or
bird, with torches, each one leaving a trail of smoke. The
one at the tip of the formation, the bird's head, was blue
and green with the mountain and stars, the Yeoli standard in wing shape. *No, Chevenga isn't taking today off.*

They were out of arrow-range but not out of hearing;
she heard his cracking voice yell "Sing!" Then a creepy
off-pitch shrilling, like nails on slate, tore out of a thousand throats and bellies.

She swung the lookers back to the Arkans. Their helms
were all turned to the sky, some even dropping their
weapons; the neat boxes and lines of their formations
rippled. When the wings were right over them, and just
starting to drop for the cliff-edge behind them, the Alliance gongs crashed, "*charge.*"

Like a wave cresting, cavalry lances lowered into place,
misty sun sparking off the tips, the horses starting at
a walk/fast walk/trot/canter, a crescendo like thunder.
Behind them the infantry started forward at a measured
trot, fifty thousand strong, an earthquake sound. A howl
shook the field, exultant from the Alliance troops,
despairing from the Arkan. Flights of arrows preceded

the charge, thick enough to cast a moving shadow like a cloud; the crossbows replied, flatter trajectories and visible only because the sun shone on the occasional head or cock-feather. The long whistling ended in a sound like manyfold hail on a metal plate, as the heads struck steel; the duller sound of points driving home in flesh was lost in the half-kilometer of distance. The Arkan cavalry had gotten up to speed, those were the professionals; where they met the Lakan chivalry the impact threw broken lance-shafts twenty meters into the air, and horses pinwheeled head-over-heels. Enchians and Mogh-iur rode around their flank, shooting point-blank with their horn-backed bows.

The Arkan shieldwall stood fast for a moment, sending a ripple like a wave through the sea down the Alliance line; archers were running behind the pikes, loosing a continuous rain over the long polearms. The kilometer-long front bristled like a hedgehog with linked shafts, and swayed back and forth; the sound of it struck her chest like a blow. But too many Arkans were looking backwards, or up, watching a thousand wings make their stand futile.

She could hear the frantic shrilling of the Arkan's command whistles, *"Stand. Hold. Stand."* The line tore like a sail in a Lannic storm, one moment whole, the next, useless fluttering rags. Alliance cavalry rolled over them, throwing them back left and right; Arkans ran pellmell, flinging away shields and helms to run faster, back toward the city, as if that could help their homes, their families. Here and there a knot eddied around a group standing fast, circled back to back, shields up; but they were few.

The Slaughterers would go to the Great Gate, the tunneled one, when they were finished here; there, she saw them thunder away to the west, striking down stray Arkans all the way. *Go with Koru, daughter . . .* Under the lookers her mouth curved in a smile. There wouldn't even be many Alliance casualties. Just mopping up, then the usual orderly distribution of loot . . . if Chevenga

stuck to his word that there would be no sacking, that
was. She hadn't heard any particularly strong orders
against it. *Is it that you're hiding?*

Her lips thinned, as she pinched them shut against
fear. *That won't help my search, Chevenga. That won't
help at* all. *You gave your word; don't fik me up.* A ribbon
of smoke rose from beyond the cliff; not surprising, since
the flyers had all had torches. *Intimidating as Halya*, she
thought, *making the Arkans all think you're going to do
it, but there were bound to be some accidents.*

Around the upper entrance to the spiral tunnel that
was the Great Gate of Arko, bodies lay in windrows,
bristling with arrows or scorched by clingfire. A burning
springald rested on its side, one wheel spinning in the
flames, the Arkans who'd taken it out resting around it
heroic and futile and dead; the inside end of the tunnel
had fallen to A-niah and Yeoli flyers coming from the
city. But Arkans still held, between.

"Bows forward!" Bukangkt shouted. "Second battalion
in reserve." They rode into the great tunnel, the arching
rock ceiling four stories above Sova's head, the sound
like being inside a bucket with someone beating on the
outside with an iron bar. Even with wall-lamps burning,
the darkness was thick after sunlight. Smoke and heat
pressed in from above and below, burning her throat and
chest, heating her armor like a roasting pot. Two turns
down, past scattered bodies of a dozen nationalities, an
Arkan shieldwall held the twenty-meter width of the tunnel, against Aenir footfighters from the riverside towns
along the Brezhan with great two-handed axes and long
spears, locked in a snarling, screaming, grunting knot.
Blood ran down the smooth paving in a continuous thin
sheet; the horses' hooves scrabbled at it, wet clattering.
As Sova watched, the whole mass took a single lurching
step backward down the slope.

"*In line!*" Bukangkt screamed. A trumpet called, thin
and reedy through the huge clamor; the Aenir seemed

to slow at the second call, backed a few steps and then dashed upslope to either side. Between the slope and the height of her mounts, Sova could see past the Arkan line to the exhausted ranks snatching rest before being sent in again. *"Draw shaft! Pick target!"*

Five hundred horn-backed compound bows rose. The Arkans were less than twenty meters away; at this range armor-piercing arrows would drill right through a shield. Sova could see their faces as she drew to the ear, saw one in the third rank close his eyes and move his lips in prayer. But none broke ranks.

"Loose!"

"Aaaahhhhhghgh—"

The Arkan with the mace reeled away, face slashed across. Sova felt Shkai'ra's saber wobble slightly in her hand. The Slaughterers had kept true to their name, here at the tunnel's inward end; it was hand-to-hand now, but the dead from their archery stretched back scores of meters, where Arko's last stand had been crushed from both sides. Yeolis and A-niah came laughing and leaping to meet them, arms outstretched, the cry echoing through the tunnel: *"Victory!"*

Then came the impact on her thigh: so hard it didn't hurt at first, only made spots of grey form like clouds before her eyes. *The moment's slip of awareness . . .* the Arkan with the mace had just been reeling, not down, maybe blinded, but not weakened enough not to make one last blundering but death-throe-strong blow. She looked at her leg, saw nothing—Zak chain-mail didn't dent—and wondered whether she'd imagined it. Then the pain came, dizzying. Her leg wouldn't move. Someone cut the Arkan down.

She wiped and sheathed the sword, her hands shaking, taking a little time to find the scabbard. *What do I do? I'm wounded. This is what it feels like. I'm wounded, but it doesn't show. No one will believe me. Where do I go?* Bukangkt was smiling, cold and unpleasant, as they rode out of the archway over a carpet of Arkan bodies, some still moving; the horses placed their feet cautiously, the riders looked down and stabbed with lance or swordpoint to make sure the Arkan dead stayed that way. The Lakan threw his hands up and his head back in exultation as they came into the clear, sun so bright she had to half-close her eyes. The inside gate was flanked by two marble wing-lions, each big as a house.

It was over; not just the battle, the whole war. Sova dragged off her helmet. Every instant of her horse's lurching became agony. She swilled water around her mouth, spitting before she drank, felt sick as she swallowed. The view ahead was breathtaking; from this angle at least, the huge marble-white mass of Arko was beautiful, the most beautiful city she'd ever seen. But fires sprouted all over it; from here she could see little figures ant-tiny with distance running through the streets.

Bukangkt turned in his saddle. "*We won!*" It was quiet here, compared to the tunnel, and his voice carried to them all. "Here, the richest city in world, waiting for us with legs spread! Plunder and burn! *Forward!*" Sova wanted to throw up.

Megan watched the battle on the plain push closer and closer to the cliff-edge; in spots the first climbers had already reached it and were lowering ropes. The Arkans facing them had either fled sideways or been forced over the edge.

She lowered the far-lookers and took a swig of water. Even if the battle were in effect over, it would still be a while. Out of the corner of her eye she noticed more smoke starting to rise in the City. She peered through the lookers.

Another thin column of smoke rose to join the first two, thickening black instead of thinning . . . then panning she found a fourth in a wildly different spot. She pulled the glasses away from her face as if she could see better without them; the scene shrank to flickers of light and ant-crawlings; she snapped them up again. It made no difference, even these lenses couldn't look down into a city, through ground. More smoke.

The City's on fire. The fish-gutted City's on fire. You were hiding that. It was what you were hiding, damn you, Chevenga! If Lixand is there . . . She checked her pouch, felt the crinkling of her map. *I've got no armor, just my knives; I'm crazy to go down there.* But she did, at a dead sprint, leaping over hedges and ditches, thinking only: *Lixand.*

Near the cliff-edge was madness; the Alliance had seized the *lefaeti*, the lifts, and dropped hawsers, whooping, to slide down them like spiders to a helpless prey. Scattered skirmishes were still going on. A unit of Arkans, about fifty, threw down their weapons; the Yeoli commander made them strip, marched them to the cliff-edge, and let his people drive them off. Other Arkans flung themselves over of their own will.

She ran to the crowd around the head of one hawser, cutting her way through with vicious elbows. Everyone around her was screaming and laughing, throwing around gouts of wine—*how in fishguts did they get that onto the battlefield? Koru, shit, I thought we'd be fighting all day, and it's already over, so fast* . . . She couldn't see, for taller people, until she found a fencepost to stand on.

Arko. There it lay, like a dream in the haze. A ring of forest, a sickle of lake, houses, houses, row upon row of houses, spreading over *chiliois*, shining white buildings sprawling, towers, so many towers.

A dream, burning. More plumes of smoke grew and billowed upward. *No sack, you said. No sack. My thread of hope could be burning in that. And if it does I will never know. Never, ever.*

She saw a building explode into flames: a sawmill . . . *the whole pit will go up, forest and all.* She had to get down, fast.

Lady Koru. Chevenga. I trusted you. I didn't kill you, because I trusted you.

She pulled her climbing gloves on, hands trembling.

The cliff was two hundred naZak-long paces down, maybe a fifth of a *chiliois*. She adjusted the harness; the feel of it, pressure on the shackle at her buckle and over her shoulder was familiar from rope-climbing in F'ta-lezon, as a child. She pushed off with her bootsoles, gently, watched the grey and black mirror rock-face glide up past her, controlled her fall with her hands. It was straight down, as smooth as polishing over centuries could make it, no worse than scaling down a building, unclimbable any other way. Mirror image of herself shining in smooth rock, almost glass-smooth, and black billows darkening the sky behind. Longer and longer bounds, *if I burn the palms out of my gloves I don't care*.

At the bottom she pushed off over loose rock, and was down. She unclipped; the smoke of houses, sweet wood-fire smell mixed with fouler odors of more precious things burning, blew across her face, making her choke and cough.

If Shkai'ra had found Lixand, but not in time to come back to the army, they'd be at one or the other meeting place—now, not tomorrow noon, she knew. Shkai'rn wouldn't wait. The Marble Palace steps began at the head of the Avenue of Statuary, according to the map.

There was fighting in the woods, screaming, but not much; a stream of warriors flowed into the city itself, whooping, howling, faces twisted with loot-hunger. She'd memorized the route; past the Arboretum Gate, along Charity Road, right, then left, all the way along the Avenue of Statuary.

The fires were thickest to the south; she angled north, out of the trees into underbrush. Trampled dirt with the sickening odor of blood gave way to cobblestones. She dodged a group of Tor Enchians tossing a small girl from one to another, laughing, while a man, her father perhaps, watched, struggling against their blows, shouting, crying, going down on his knees. Another child ran, though no one was chasing her, screaming "Mother! Father!", her formality strange in the chaos. *It's always the children who suffer most.* Megan knew. For an instant she was five years old again, in the riots in F'talezon, breathing furnace-hot air. The smell was the same; what race the residents were made no difference, it seemed, to that.

The smoke was thick enough now to make the streets dark as at dusk. Flames cut the old brick of a wall like knives, only a few houses and yards away; the air singed, full of sparks and burning flakes of ash. She pulled her tunic up over her head, covering her nose and mouth against the rancid smoke, and ran. Someone screamed close by—long, long shrieks one after the other, high over the thunder of fire.

An Arkan boy Lixand's age with a toy sword stood in the door of a house, the picture of defiance, with a Yeoli woman in front of him; his stand was useless, the house already on fire from behind. He lunged with both hands, trying to hold the sword straight; the Yeoli stepped aside, hit him in the back of the head with the edge of her shield, kicked him out of the way and stepped into the house.

Right, then left—then a blank wall where the street should continue, a building in the way. *A bloody building*—in more ways than one; smears of grey mixed with the blood, the stink of bile, piss, shit and blood cutting even the smoke; a body lay with blond head broken open in a splatter pattern.

She hesitated, thinking she'd got turned around. The fire was *there*, she couldn't go back or get trapped by it. *Up. Look from the fikken roof.* She yanked out her climbing claws rather than take the gloves off, clambered up the new brick wall, over the circles carved under the eaves and over the edge. *My map's out of date, dammit. This was just built, and now it's burning.* The tiles were warm through her gloves and she could hear them cracking in the heat, the sound like bones in a dog's teeth. She felt the hairs on the inside of her nose crinkle as she breathed. Four or five houses down a roof fell in, loosing whip-tongues of flame to roar up into the sky.

No sack, you said, Chevenga. I remember your eyes, so honest. No sack.

The house behind her, blazing curtains waving out of broken upper windows, bricks bulging outward, crumbling, ready to fall at any moment. She slid over the peak of the roof to the other side, snatched at the map, the roaring fire-wind trying to tug her off the roof, into the fire, or pull the breath out of her lungs. *Stopping to read a map in the middle of the bottom furnace of Halya, shit, shit, shit . . .*

The street twisted the other way from what her map showed, but the one beyond looked right. Wind tore the paper almost in half; she grabbed it and flattened against the tiles. There—the Avenue of Statuary.

Fishguts. Everyone's here. Of course, where else? This was where the good stuff was. Yeolis and Lakans and Enchians ran back and forth carrying gold-leafed chairs, paintings, bundles of bright satin clothing, jewel boxes. They danced in the fountains with gold chains and baubles and sparkly stones dangling over their grimed oily armor, carried huge glass vases out of the houses just to smash them, made bonfires of books just to see something valuable destroyed, *stupid assholes*, waving their arms in the air like savages at a fire altar. A crowd of warriors laughed and danced and sang around a cart with a huge cask on it, filling cups from the casks. A dozen Arkans, *Aitzas* by the few waist-long strands of their hair not hacked off, were harnessed to the cart like horses, with blinders and bits in their mouths even, their faces dead with shock. The cobbles shone red with wine and blood.

Statues. A bronze horse being pulled down by a motley group of mercenaries, beating on it just to hear the hollow boom, a marble form hacked off at the ankles, leaving sandalled feet on the plinth amidst scattered shards. Glass everywhere, not enough left to tell what it was, jagged shelled pieces sparkling in the flames. Another

bronze, a winged lion rampant, holding a sun-disk, too
big to shift . . .

There—the head of the street lay in line with the great
Eagle. The buildings marked as the University seemed
to huddle behind the statues and chestnut trees on either
side. Avoiding the fighting, dancing, fucking crowd in the
middle of the street, Megan slipped around a hedge and
across a trampled lawn. Almost in its middle, an Arkan
scholar lay face-down as if to pray to the Eagle, a book
under one hand, shattered spectacles lying in a puddle
of blood.

At the head of the avenue, a building on the left set
back from the street, in a garden, seemed untouched,
grey columns rising to where the glass dome reflected
the fire across the street. On the right a colonnade ran
to a small round bell-tower; a tall bearded Aenir beat
the oak door in with an axe. The bell-tower blazed, dark
sooty limestone starting to glow and crack, flames biting
out of the windows, mortar flung out like ballista shot as
stones shifted and cracked.

Megan had time to scan the square and the steps to
the Marble Palace, as the tower started to lean as if
bowing to the opposite building. No sign of Shkai'ra, or
anyone who could be Lixand. The tower screamed as it
teetered, like a person dying. She dived for shelter
against the bronze lion, crouched and heard what seemed
like the sky falling.

The impact jolted her up, dropped her again, like an
earthquake; she raised her ringing head out of her arms
and blinked at the mound of rubble, smashed burning
trees, the dust almost burning too, across the meeting-
place.

Second, her mind thought dully. *Also, the place he'd
go if he got free from the kidnappers in the confusion.
The Temonen manor.* Megan kneeled behind the statue,
wiped soot and dust out of her eyes, read the map again.
*Left from the square, left again onto Faith street, right
onto Fidelity* . . .

Left. A row of pines blazed; one cracked in half with a noise like Shkai'ra's shot-pistol, spraying burning tar and needles across the street, boiling oily turpentine strong enough to make her eyes water. *Faith Street*. A crowd in the way, someone still able to fight back; three or four ancient *solas*, helmetless, their beautifully-kept antique weapons unsteady in liver-spotted hands, trying to defend what their sons couldn't.

Fidelity Street. A white marble wall with painted scenes of domestic tranquility, the paint bubbling and peeling in the heat. *The Temonen family seal*; her agent had included it in his letter. It hung from broken open gates, banging against the wall. A lace-gloved hand trailed out of the fountain. A closed carriage lay on its side. Formal gardens, perfectly manicured, now trampled, the geraniums broken, a sprawled body by the carriage. *Koru . . . how can so much destruction be done in so little time?*

The manor house wasn't burning, yet.

"Shkai'ra! Lixand!"

From one of the thick-grown flowerbeds came the sound of someone making love or raping, cries of pain or pleasure, she couldn't tell. The heat was enough to dry the tears on her face. *Tears. Koru-forsaken, Goddess-damned tears*. One of the walls of a manor down the street started to fall outward, stately-slow. Her ears were too full to hear. Bricks didn't burn but it smelled as if they did, fire-wind blowing the smell across her face.

She stepped through the manor's huge fancy-carven door, hearing things smash upstairs. She ducked back as an inner door burst open to the sound of screams and a keening laugh.

Two blue-painted barbarians from Goddess knew where dragged a *fessas* by his ankles, pulling as if he were a wishbone. They held him head-down over the balcony for a moment before letting him drop onto the pavement, brain splattering. She waited until they went back in to where their fellows were still looting and drinking, crossed the hall and through the door on the other side.

Glass doors led into the private gardens, flanked by the lesser wings of the house. Over a yew hedge she could see a sudden crest of flame spring up: the stable.

She trotted along the wing. *"Rasas! Lixand! Rasas! Shkai'ra!"* It was almost quiet, the fire-roar muffled by the estate wall and the brown searing trees between. Ashes choked the fish-pool, golden and spotted carp gulping at a surface slimed with black. Beyond that a sunken, walled patch of lawn lay smooth and green-clipped as if waiting for a game of *krukat*, surrounded by overturned chairs and satin-clad corpses, wine-glasses smashed, a harp rammed over one lord's long-haired head, steel bass strings driven into the face, rose-petals scattered under it. *A last battle of two hundred thousand's being fought on the plains around their Empire's heart*, she thought, *and they throw a party*.

Two or three black and gold dressed boys lay strewn on the lawn, a youth of sixteen or so cradling another in his arms.

"Rasas!" she bellowed in her ship-captain's voice. She'd check the dead ones after she'd called; even the thought brought sickness. *"Rasas!"* A child's yelp of recognition came from behind a stone bench carved with griffin arms, across the sunken lawn.

"Rasas?" She stepped forward, sudden hope bringing blood pounding into her head.

A dancing boy with a thin strip of blond mane on a shaven head scrambled out from behind the stone bench, ran toward her. Behind him there was a shout and three of the blue savages came running from the stable, after him, pointing. They were all red-haired, two carrying bundles of javelins, one a squat giant two meters tall with a mace as thick as her leg, topped with what looked like a small boat's stone anchor. Their leather kilts flapped against their thighs as they ran; they were naked other-wise, except for the wolves' teeth wound into their shaggy manes. Clotted grey dripped from the giant's mace. "Yi-yi-yiyiyiyi," they shrilled in exhilaration, as if they'd started a grouse up out of underbrush.

The kneeling youth didn't move, as if he didn't care to save his own life. A spear thumped through his back, was yanked out, a blue foot braced on his neck. He slowly slumped forward, across the child's corpse he'd been cradling, and both lay still.

"Rasas!" She vaulted down into the dance area and ran toward the fleeing boy. No wonder they were after him: he was covered in jewelry. One of the blue-skins raised her javelin to throw, checked, flipped the weapon around. "*Down!*" The blue-skin loosed the spear, butt first—*not to soil her goods with blood, grub-eating bitch, that satin's worth ten silver claws*—"*DOWN!*" The boy looked back over his shoulder instead; her heart clenched but he tucked, rolled on his shoulder as the spear thudded into the grass next to him, ashwood gouging a handspan deep.

He dove behind her. "Help me, please, you know him, help me too!" The blue-skins stood at the rim of the dance lawn, standing, looking at her, considering. She lifted her gloved hands, shook her head, felt the boy grip her ankle with a shaking hand. "No," she said. "This one's mine."

They said something she didn't understand, except for the gestures, the levelled spear. *Koru, I can't fight off all three of them.* "Don't be afraid of what you see," she hissed to the boy in Arkan, quickly. "It's just to scare them." She took a quick breath, summoned her *manrauq*-demon. The boy tore his hand away from her ankle, shrieked and curled into a ball. *One breath, two . . . hold . . . hold . . .* tearing pain and a green flare behind her eyes. The image steadied, giggled and pawed. They cringed back a step; the spearman threw, saw his spear go through the thing and into the grass behind, heard it hiss. They ran screaming.

Megan let the image go, tested her headache, her fatigue. *I have to sit down. Now.*

The boy was still curled up, whimpering, "Tikas, matron, Tikas, Rasas—it's Hayel, it's Hayel. Tikas." Megan knelt beside him, put a gloved hand on his shoulder.

"Rasas? Lixand?"

He jerked away from her, blue eyes staring—*blue eyes!?*

"Where'd it go? Where is *it?*"

"Gone," she said. "You aren't Rasas! I saved you because I thought you were him. Is he one of these dead ones?"

"No! He's gone, he got kidnapped, ages ago! I'm his best friend, we pretended we were brothers! Who are you?"

"His mother. You mean he's not in the house?" The boy shook his head. "He never came back?" He nodded. *In the city. Somewhere. What will I do, run through the streets of a city of a million dying people, shouting my son's and my love's names? I haven't a hope in Halya of finding him. Or outside? I'll never know. Chevenga. You said no sack. I should have killed you. Maybe I still will.*

"Strip off the satin and jewels, they make you a prize. Hide. This should settle in a day or two." She rubbed her hands across her face, looked up at the sky, darkened with smoke, as if it were evening. No; it *was* getting on to evening. *If Shkai'ra is alive, with Lixand, they'll come here. Sova would, too. Uncertainty; always, uncertainty. Best I stay.*

The boy stared, mouth wide open. "His mother!?"

She looked down to where he sat on the grass. "Dah, his mother. He was taken from me by an Arkan, eight years ago." Several screams came from the main house. "Look, if you want you can hang around with me for a bit. I'll make sure nobody parts your . . . hair or decides to rape you to death." *He may be Arkan, but he's just a*

boy, a little younger than my Lixand. And his best friend.
Grief and fear came back roaring; she shook them away.
The child needed her. "And you can tell me about my
son, sometime."

The boy stood up, and pressed closer, as if sheltering
behind her. "He's my best friend and I'm his. He's the
nicest person in the world, except maybe Tikas, but then
Tikas uses the whip. He has black eyes like onyxes and
a profile like a line of clear flame." *Some poet's line*, she
thought. *Poet child-raper*. "He's really good at dancing,
he does solos now. Master's thinking of entering him in
the City Diadem boys' dance . . ."

As if that will ever happen, now. "What's your name?"
she said, putting an arm around his shoulders, steering
him away from the slaughtered party-goers. She had the
urge to save someone.

"Ardas," he whispered. "Slave of House Temonen.
They're all dead. I hope he isn't. He's the nicest person
in all Arko and I miss him."

"Well, Ardas, you aren't a slave anymore, and I hope
my son isn't dead as well. I miss him, too." With effort
she smiled at the boy. "I think we'd better find an
unburned outbuilding, the gardener's or groom's house,
and defend it from all comers, hey? I have a daughter
who'll be showing up here, soon as the fighting's done."
The boy silently nodded, eyes wide with fear, and followed, sticking close, as if to a parent.

They camped in the gardener's house, a cottage with
a false tower built onto one corner. When Sova came,
bone-bruised so badly she couldn't walk, only ride,
Megan left the two of them to see that the cottage didn't
get torched, and went up-cliff to collect all their things
back at the camp. The *lefaeti* were all held by Alliance,
now; saying briskly it was official business got her
winched up, and back down. Her headache faded, hunger grew.

It was pitch dark by the time she got back to the
cottage, seeing her way by firelight. *Even with the lake*

right there, flinging buckets would be like spitting into a furnace. Yet the fires stayed scattered, the whole City had not gone up, so far; in the great pit, there was little wind. The pony walked docilely with her. *Thirstyliedown,* like all animals, accepting things as they came. Sova had got a blackrock fire going, brewing tea and re-heating stew from yesterday, filling the room with mouth-watering smells. *Though she should be lying down.*

"Zhymata, part of a century of Yeolis took over the main house. We should be pretty safe."

"All right. Thank you, Sovee."

You said no sack, Chevenga, Imperturbable, Infallible. I want to see you again. Tomorrow, Gold-bottom. Maybe I'll kill you, and let your minions kill me. Maybe I'll just tear some gold off you with my claws, you lying bastard . . . She stored away the anger.

The boy was wearing one of her tunics now, belted in at the waist, his jewels all hidden inside somewhere. She turned to him. "Well, Ardas, my son's best friend, what are we going to do with you?"

His blue eyes went wide, blinking, white all around. "I . . . I thought I was yours now."

"I don't keep slaves. As far as I'm concerned, everything you had, jewels and all, is yours." That didn't make the boy's eyes any less wide.

"Zhymata." Sova's voice, switching to Zak, held a touch of reproach. "He's only, what, eight, nine? And cut loose, everyone responsible for him dead. He's never been anything but a slave. He told me. We can't just send him out onto the street."

Megan looked up from where she'd sat to pull off her boots. *What kind of person does she think I am?* "Of course not." She switched back to Arkan, turned to the boy. "I was thinking of finding a good orphanage, once things settle down."

"No!" The boy's cry was full of terror. "No. Please." He gripped the edge of the chair, leaning forward as if to run, but with nowhere to run to, blue eyes huge.

"Orphanage not a good idea? Why?"

He hesitated, biting the inside of his cheek. "I was already in one. They sold me *here*."

Megan just blinked at him, feeling anger pop like a lava-bubble inside her. *Isn't there one decent person in this whole maggot-ridden place?* "Well then, not an orphanage. Until things are settled down, we won't decide. You can be part of our household until then, all right?"

The boy flung himself on his face, hugging her ankles. "Don't do that." She bent over, hauled him up away from her, by the shoulders, careful not to claw. "You're not a slave. Don't grovel." Megan caught a glimpse of Sova's eyes, fixed on the boy with the mix of sympathy and irony, and knew she was thinking of a past moment, on a dais in Brahvniki, nearly two years ago.

"What do you mean no one is allowed in to see him? He was wounded, you say; fine, don't friends visit the convalescent?"

The Yeoli guard shifted, frowning down at Megan. "I'm sorry, *kere ranya*." *Sister foreigner*, that meant. They'd never called her that before. "Orders."

"Let me speak to your superior." The guard called a squire from inside the building. She was at the first door off the main square, away from the main steps of the Marble Palace and the three-story-high gates; the one wing of the University building whose tower she'd seen fall, was a long block behind her, still smoldering. The chestnuts and cherry trees along the Avenue of Statuary stood charred and withered.

It was morning. The City had quieted down. Yeoli patrols stopped arsonists at least, and the looting had tailed off as the more obvious targets were stripped bare. She had seen plenty of troops camped here and there, mostly sodden-drunk or sleeping it off; the better-organized units were busy. Here, a Schvait wagon-train, heaped with bulgy loads under businesslike tarpaulins; there, Hyerne kicking burdened prisoners along to add to an enormous heap of fabrics and weapons and chests and whatnot, with Peyepallo standing on top of it dressed in an Imperial high-priest's robe, directing. There, a huge column of prisoners under Enchian guards, women and children mostly, ready to be hustled out of the City before the Yeolis collected their wits and remembered their emancipationist convictions. *So where are you to save them, people-wills-one,* Megan thought, *who was going to make them your citizens?*

She tapped her foot impatiently, looking the other way, along the wall. It was covered in carvings, from the base right up to the top, gilded around the Imperial speaking balcony. At the far end of the square there was a small public park, and where the wall turned away from the square an ornamental tower rose over the flowering bougainvillaea, the fist-sized cut crystal at its peak still catching the sun though the gilding on the roof was sooted. The smoke from the fires hung like eye-stinging fog, making it hard to see across the marbled square.

A patter of feet, and the squire was back with a piece of paper which he passed to the guard. "*Kere ranya,* the *semanakraseye*-Imperator is seeing no one," he rattled off. "Healer's orders as per Emao-e Lazaila, signed, Estennunga Shae-Fiyara for Krero Saranyera, Guard Captain." *Semanakraseye-Imperator; what a mouthful.* It was odd, though; Chevenga's policy was not to let people in no matter how badly he was hurt—if he was conscious—one at the very least to carry his message to everyone else, in which case she should have heard it being announced. Dead? No; they'd announce that, and make Arko his funeral pyre. No announcements had come out of the Marble Palace at all, in fact; that was stranger still. Under her anger, she saw it clear. For some reason . . . *he's not in control. What's going on?*

"All right," she snapped to the guard. "I guess you'd better keep that for everyone else who shows up. He *was* friends with a lot of people." She stamped away.

The ornate carvings on the palace wall offered her more than enough handholds. The smoke in the night air, and the fact that the moon hadn't risen over the cliff's edge yet, helped her too. Near the roof-edge she waited, frozen like a bug on the face of the highest god of the Arkan pantheon, Muunas, hands clawed around a stylized lock of hair, one foot on his bottom lip, the other a toe-hold on his mustache.

Not too different from sneaking around the Arkan camps, only the guards are even less familiar with the holes for mice to creep through. I suppose that person thought he was going to stop me from seeing Chevenga. However badly hurt he is, whatever's going on.

The beat of the sentry's spear-butt on the roof grew closer, overhead, then passed. She counted under her breath. . . . *fifty-nine, sixty*, before the next walked by. *Same as during the day, a good enough gap* . . . twenty-four running paces, soft boots noiseless on the tiles; then up the next wall—*twenty-nine, thirty, thirty-one*—each sentry's line of sight was almost overlapping—*thirty-five. Freeze, no movement to draw their eye.* The sentry paced by, scanning, keeping up the light, occasional whistle that was the Yeoli contact. The second sentry round, another tiny heartbeat of time to slip through; the third, and she had to pretend to be a large marble tile flat on the roof; none of the sentries stepped on her, so it worked.

Now, the rising moon was just showing its light over the cliff, sparking a faint glint from a distant tower crystal, giving the golden eagle on the cliff over the palace an eerie cool glow. No one had stripped *that* yet, she realized, because that would take organization. Below to her left, a courtyard; next to that, a glass dome enclosing a garden. She darted down over the edge. *Time to go inside. That looks pretty Imperial to me.*

She had to go almost all the way to the ground to find an open window. "Yowp!" *Strangerstrangerhelpmaster-alarm!* "Yowp, rowf!" *Damn, what is it with me and enemy dogs?* Megan let out a cat's screech. A Yeoli voice:

"Stupid beast, stop chasing cats! Temila, *come!*" Megan needed no *manrauq* to hear the question in the next bark. *Really, boss, with that intruder here?* "Come!" She ghosted through the window, into an office with a gilded floor-to-ceiling mirror and a huge desk whose edges and corners sparkled with gold.

Outside the room's door, the alcohol wall lamps were blinding to her dark-adapted eyes. The corridor was twenty meters across, nearly that high, its floor glossy-polished squares of white marble, separated by thin lines of metal . . . a quick fingernail test showed it was elec-trum, silver-gold alloy. *Koru. This place is out of a fairy tale.* The walls were tessellated mosaic, tiny squares of iridescent glass and gold and semiprecious stone set right into the marble; gods and goddesses and warriors, gold-haired and sapphire-eyed, looked down with regal calm; the coffered ceiling held alternating skylights of glass so flawless it was invisible, with gold-leaf sunbursts between. Every ten meters down the center of the hall was a stat-ue-column: giant ivory-robed maidens with baskets on their heads supporting the ceiling, their eyes shining tourmaline and emerald.

Megan had to force herself not to gasp. *Has no one found this hallway to strip yet—or was there just too much?* A guard paced across where another hallway intersected. She worked her way closer from column to column, fast and silent. *Wait. I know him.* Elite, she'd seen his face in the secure section of camp. More to the point, he'd seen hers. She pulled off her black hood and gloves, sauntered out briskly. "Hi, Ka . . . Kar . . ." She knew his name started with a "k." " . . . Halya, I can't pronounce it, sorry. Which way to Emao-e's office?"

He stared at her for a moment. *I guess near midnight is a bit late to have an appointment.* But he said, "Sure. Thataway. You got pretty close to him, I hope you can help."

Act like I know what's going on. "Dah, I hope so too, thanks." She saluted, and strolled down the corridor.

Down yellow marble stairs, across a floor patterned with alternating gold and silver tiles—some missing—hide inside an urn, pink alabaster, as two guards passed . . . a servant's corridor went the right way toward the domed garden. The first and second doors opened on gardening tools and a closet, the third door down was locked tight. She pulled the lock-pick out of her belt buckle, was through in a moment.

The fountain, five jets of water bubbling into a glass basin with a gentle plashing, covered her noise. She clawed her way up the wall-ivy. The floor of the balcony and the room beyond was another flame pattern in rubies and yellow tourmaline. A row of glass doors, bordered in polished brass with flame patterns edged in copper and gold, heavy cloth-of-gold curtains hung inside. . . .

The centermost two doors were open. She heard Yeoli voices, sharp, arguing.

"*Yen' dyanai.*" *Young fool.* The words were fast, hard for her to follow, the voice one she didn't know, only distinct when it was raised. "*Kya krenanirae . . .*" The best translation of that, really, was *everything goes tits up.* " *. . . tetyuyae . . .*" *Kill, kill someone, which fishgutted pronoun was that, starting with "t" . . . ? You. Kill yourself.*

The answering voice was Chevenga's. Though hoarser than usual, it was clearer to her than the others, being familiar. "I've explained to you, I've explained to everyone ten times, and no one will listen to reason—"

"Reason! You call it *reason?*"

"I've talked enough—get out of here!"

A slithery, high clashing was followed by the sound of a slamming door, then by the echo of both. The room sounded big as a banquet hall. He would know she was there, she realized, know it was her, by his sense for weapons; but nothing happened. She shaded in.

The room was lit by two candelabra as tall as she was, with twenty candles in each, set inside a shimmering curtain of gold chains that surrounded the bed, which was huge, three of her height long and just as wide. The headboard was an obsidian column that reached up into the dark beyond the candlelight to where the ceiling glittered indistinctly far above; against its black the Aan sunburst blazed gold. Almost lost in the middle of it all, his skin pale white against the black of his hair and the gold-embroidered black quilt, both arms in Haian plasters and tied down, lay Chevenga.

She walked over, checked her step; the gold chains had slivers of glass set into the links to cut anyone who tried to burst through. She used one of her knives to swing them aside—someone else doing the same had made the slithery sound—sat down on the edge of the bed. His head was turned away.

She could kill him, easily; she had a naked knife in her hand and he was bound. Kill him, and leave Sova an orphan twice over. *Why isn't he saying anything, calling guards? Does he think because it's me he's safe?*

"Well." She kept her voice low; no point drawing the guards herself. "Here we have the *semanakraseye*-Imperator, the Invincible, the Infallible, the Irreproachable Fourth Chevenga, most Noble Liar, who said he wasn't planning on sacking Arko. And the fool here, who believed him."

His head turned to her, black tendrils of hair pasted to his cheeks and forehead. Changed: instead of looking the usual ten years older than he was, he looked twenty. His voice was barely audible. "Megan."

She made her whisper cut. "You realize I didn't make any plans to find my son if the place was sacked? Should I have known not to believe you? I suppose I can turn over every piece of burning rubble calling his name, but it won't do me much good, will it?"

He gazed at her, dark eyes frozen, answerless.

" 'If there's anything you can think of that I can help with, tell me and I'll do it,' you said," she went on. "*Pfah!* Should I toast the Imperator god of Arko who is so *just?* Makes this mess and leaves me to find one helpless little

boy in it?" She spat full in his face then. Most landed
on his nose, some in one eye, that he tried to blink clear.

He didn't call guards; the furrow between his brows
deepened, but not with anger. "I can do one thing," he
whispered. "Chinis—" He cut the summoning call off,
flinching more than when she'd spat. "*Kyash*. Scribe!
Emao-e, I need you too."

Chinisa bought it? A scribe? Megan hadn't known the
old woman well; her face had faded from notice, being
there always, like furniture, and, she'd thought, safe from
harm.

Footsteps came quickly; Emao-e knife-opened the
golden curtain for the scribe, a man, and froze staring at
Megan. The general's use-name was Steel-eyes; now
Megan truly saw why. "What are *you* doing in here?"

"It doesn't matter," Chevenga cut in, rasping. "Scribe,
write a letter, authorizing whatever means necessary to
aid Megan Whitlock in learning the whereabouts of her
son Lixand, as promised and sworn by me . . ." The pen
flew; Emao-e's grey stare didn't waver.

Whatever means necessary . . . he hadn't added the
usual qualifier, "within reason." A breath of the familiar
warmth she felt near him brushed through her anger.
She shook it off; *no. Don't be charmed, again. Even if
this makes it possible to find Lixand, it doesn't make his
lie any less a lie.*

His voice stopped, the scratching of the pen continued
in quiet. "I repeat, Whitlock," Emao-e said, her voice
deadly-edged. "What are you doing here, without authorization? Perhaps you don't understand the concern
behind my question, though having the skills you do, you
should."

"It doesn't *kyashin* matter!" Chevenga again, as if his
own security was a trivial detail. "Let's get the thing
signed and done." Lying on his naked chest was a tangle
of gold: the Imperial seals, slung around his neck on a
chain.

"Emao-e, I would be glad to tell you how I got in,

though I don't think anyone but a Zak could. I'll go through it with you point by point." She'd say she'd made herself invisible to the sentry who had let her by; he didn't deserve trouble for it. *What did that one mean, saying I was close to him, perhaps I could help?* The scribe was holding the letter to Chevenga's half-encased hand so that, moving only his fingers, he could sign.

The general's eyes softened. "Well enough." The scribe was doing the sealing now; four separate stamps with the Imperial seals, one with the Yeoli signet. Chevenga had made no attempt to get the spit off his face; Emao-e and the scribe, it seemed, were pretending not to notice. "I leave this in your hands, Emao-e," he said, prompting the scribe to hand the letter to the general, who took it civilly enough. The scribe scurried out. "Megan, if this isn't keeping my word well enough, I'm sorry."

Sorry. As if that makes any difference. Then the signs fell together, so obvious she wondered how she'd missed them. Leaving it in Emao-e's hands, no one being let in, no announcements, his carelessness about security, his bonds, the sentry's words, *tetyuyae* . . .

"You're trying to kill yourself," she said, amazement breaking through anger. "You're trying to fish-gutted *kill* yourself!"

His dark eyes met hers. "Weep or spit on my pyre, as you choose."

As if I haven't already shown what I'd be inclined to do, she thought. *Why isn't Emao-e calling the guards to give me the heave?* She studied the casts, the linen bandages used as bonds, wrapped carefully so as to be comfortable. "Mind you, I don't see how you're going to do it," she said tartly.

"Refusing water," he answered, as casually as if she'd asked the time of day.

She glanced up at Emao-e, and read her grim face. *Another voice to persuade him to change his mind*, it said; *I'm not about to stop you.*

"Another small, piddling, trivial question, if I may. *Why?* You've won. You're Imperator. You've killed Kurkas, obviously, no doubt in some appropriately unpleasant way—and he wasn't your Habiku, you said. You've burned down the city and danced on the ashes. You should be happy! You're making no fish-gutted *sense*. Gold-bottom."

"I know," he said.

"Besides—are you going to leave this mess to everyone else to shovel up? There's going to be war all around the edges of Arko *and* all through the middle for centuries, if *someone* doesn't take it in hand—and who else in Halya can? I thought you gave a shit about that kind of thing!"

"The hand that bore the scythe can't give the ivy branch." That old-school Yeoli formality again; but under it was pain beyond tears.

"He's sentencing himself to death for the child-raping sack," said Emao-e. "If he dies Arko's hate will be purged, he keeps arguing. You'd think he'd forgotten his own people exist!"

Megan gazed down at him. *The scythe*, she thought. *Not the sword; the scythe. Chevenga. You don't do anything in half-measures, or without utter conviction, or without it creating its own truth and convincing everyone around you. Not even madness. You're bug-fuck, Imperturbable Chevenga.* The first time she'd ever seen him, she'd thought so. How many times after? *Crazy from whatever they did to you. Come back to where it happened, and it's too much. Shit, I should have known, by how tight-lipped you were, by how you wouldn't face it. Two nights ago; seems like an iron-cycle. We all should have known it. For all I know maybe some did. What could they have done about it? No one was in a position to do anything. Your brilliance will ensure your madness leaves its mark across the whole world.*

She leaned close to him, took his chin in her hand. "Always know what you're doing, you said. You didn't, did you?"

"No," he answered, in a half-whisper. "That's why, this." *The ultimate wrong, to his mind,* she thought, *so he wants the ultimate punishment. Still.*

"And I'm supposed to think you know what you're doing *now?*"

"Aigh, *mamaiyana!*" He clenched his eyes shut. "I've been arguing this all day with everybody and his sister, do I have to with you, too?"

All through, his expression hadn't really changed, stone-hard, a closed book. If he hadn't turned away, it was only out of politeness. *You are in a different world,* she thought, *a place I don't know, and can't understand.* Suddenly her anger came apart like wet bread in her claws, and she just felt tired and vaguely sick. *I know what you are, for all you make a good show of not being it: human. Fallible. The moral of the story: I shouldn't have expected any better.* Against her hand, his cheek was warm. He lay quiet, eyes closed.

I won't tear your throat out but I won't stand in the Dark Lord's way, either. I don't feel like lifting a finger either way. Why should I? You wouldn't let me anyway. She let go, and stood up.

"Farewell," said Chevenga. She looked: however wanly, he was smiling. "I'll pray you find him. Live well."

The sickness suddenly swelled, and tears, *Koru-forsaken Dark-Lord-damned tears!* were burning behind her eyes. *Damn you! Damn me if I show you anything! Like everyone else, everyone else you've fish-gutted betrayed, and are betraying now, I love you.*

"I just hope they find someone stubborner, or crazier, than you," she said, forcing the pain in her throat not to pinch her voice and show her heart. "Faint chance though that is. And I won't say farewell, or mourn you, until you're stiff." She stalked away, Emao-e following.

XXV

It was the third day. The fires were all but out now, leaving whole neighborhoods of ash, only humped fragments left of their walls. Getting rid of the thousands of fast-swelling corpses had been the first priority of whoever was in charge now, so they were mostly gone, leaving only their stains; but rubble-heaps still slumped across roads, and burst water mains had made puddles of filthy ash-mud deeper than a man could stand.

Noon; somehow, through the pall of smoke that hung trapped in the great pit, and the aging sick smell of burned living-places, the temple bells still rang each day. *If the other's not there in, say, an eight-day, we'll know for sure.* Megan remembered Shkai'ra's acknowledging nod faintly, like a ghost's face.

She was just waiting for the eight days to pass; it was only for the sake of sticking to the plan she came to the Marble Palace steps. Every time hope tempted her, she reminded herself of Hotblood's last thought-cry. Hope would be nothing but a hindrance to her mourning, she knew from experience, and delay her final acceptance.

On the ninth day, she would make use of Chevenga's note: *full* use, price no object. He owed her that. As he had admitted, dictating it.

Though just showing at noon would do, she had been on the gleaming marble steps, wide as a field, most of today, sitting back against a sun-globe clasped by the familiar eagle, that had once had gilding, and a head. They'd cleared away the broken tower, and there was a small crowd here, all looking as if they were waiting for someone. *We weren't the only ones who thought this was a good meeting place.*

The great palace gates stood open. She absently looked that way. Tiny in their yawning hugeness, a Yeoli warrior staggered out into the light, slid to his knees, and threw back his head with his hands raised. *"Aiiiiiigggh!"* The scream froze and silenced everyone; hands clasped hilts. *"Naaaaiiggh! Amiyaseye mya!"* He drew his sword, and smashed it down on the marble, breaking the layer-forged blade in two. The silence deepened. *"We've lost him! He's dead!"*

Megan hissed in a breath. *As usual*, she thought. *He got his way.* Then: *oh, shit.* After an instance's stunned quiet, the people on the steps took up the cry, some dashing away. She heard it spread out into the City like a circular ripple, its tone anguished, then enraged. *They'll go nuts.* Whenever Chevenga had got wounded badly enough in this war that his life was in danger, the army, especially the Yeolis, had gone on a rampage. She'd heard tales of fleeing Arkans being chased for days, prisoners by the thousand tortured, babies flung into fires . . .

She jumped down and dashed flat out to the manor, outrunning the news. Biting back her panting, she sauntered shaking her head into the main hall, where some of the Yeolis loitered. "I tell you, some *rumors!* I don't know who could be stupid enough to believe the one I just heard."

"What's that?" a stocky woman doing stretches turned her head to ask.

"Oh, some dumb thing that the Invincible's dead. They started that one the _last_ three times he was wounded. I've never heard anyone with a decent healer die of broken arms."

"_Dead?_" the woman gasped. The rest all started, froze blinking; fast Yeoli words flew back and forth, and then they were all yelling, "_Boru! Boru! Amiyaseye-mya-sema-nakraseye-mya-boru-boru-boru-naaiiiiiggh!_"

Well, that answers my question, who could be stupid enough. "No, no, _no!_" she yelled in her ship-captain's voice. "He's not dead, dammit, it's just a stupid rumor, didn't you _listen_ to me?!" The roar outside was distant, but audible. Then the centurion came running in, snapping orders angrily, making them all freeze in place. By the time the first keening warriors had reached the manor, the rumors that Chevenga was dead and that he wasn't were being bellowed in equal amounts, as far as she could tell. But the centurion, having got warning enough, managed to hold his people in check.

Chevenga, she thought. _Your people catch whatever you throw them. When you were fearless for them, they were fearless; when you were angry, they were angry. Now you are insane, so are they, the whole fish-gutted city-full._ From the garden house, with Sova and Ardas trembling near, she watched the plumes of black smoke rise thick and fresh, heard the screams and the mad laughter, as Arko was sacked again.

The great Yeoli war-gong, newly set up on top of the Marble Palace, began its crashing roar; the code alternated between "stay arms" and "assemble," and went on for most of the afternoon before things quieted. The centurion kept his unit here, sending a squire; she came back with the news that Chevenga was still alive, the whole thing a misunderstanding. "I saw him," the girl said, clutching her crystal, swearing. "Second Fire come if I lie, he came to the window, alive."

A faint roaring chant came from the main square,

where the assembly was. *Three syllables; his name, what else? Someone convinced him it was a dumb idea.* She felt her heart lift, then thought angrily, *your charm still casts its spell, you bastard. Or . . .* Thirst might just not have killed him yet, and his minions had dragged him out to stop the chaos. *So . . . it could happen again. Your life-force is too strong to extinguish without taking a lot around you with it. What are you going to do to us all before you're finished?*

Another day, the city waited.

In the manor-yard, Sova stood with Ardas, at the grave they'd dug for his trainer, Tikas; she could walk now, but it was difficult, even with a cane they'd found in the manor. Megan watched from the now-cleaned-up fountain, wanting to be alone with her thoughts.

She adjusted her seat on the edge of its bowl, filed a snag out of the third claw of her right hand.

Smallsharpsnippydisagreeable

Megan froze. Cautiously she sent out a thought. *Hotblood?*

Hmph. Hotboredtired. Concentrating, she paid little heed to the shape of a mount and rider coming up to the gate that she saw in the corner of her eye. A quick glance towards the rider's face; for a moment she wondered who the gaunt-cheeked crop-haired warrior was on Hotblood's back where her akribhan should be, and the boy peeking around behind her—then dropped the file, *splash*, into the water, stood up, stopped, hand outstretched, afraid to move, afraid to wake up from the dream she'd had so many times before.

"*Kh'eeredo.* You do such a lovely gaffed fish imitation."

"*Shkai'ra!*" Megan staggered a step forward. "And . . ." Blond hair, short but for the central strip, which was long in a dancing-boy's cut, black eyes, the face lengthened and strengthened with years but *the same, the same* . . . "Lixand?" She'd spoken in a whisper.

o   o

All through her month-long convalescence, as Rasas had nursed her, the witch-demon turned sword-fairy had told him the same thing, in broken Arkan. *They weren't dreams. It was only the whip made you think they were dreams. She's your real mother. It's Rasas that's your pretend name . . . Lixand is your real name, the name she gave you, after her father.* They'd had plenty of time to talk, and she'd told him how *mata* had killed the man who'd stolen him, taken his ship, built the merchant house, battled against the Thanes, crossed the Lannic, met *her,* taken the house back from Habiku, fought in this war. Rasas—*No, it's Lixand, I've got to think of myself as* him *again, now*—had taught Shkai'ra more Arkan just to hear what happened next.

It all seemed like a story. The black and silver green-eyed horse-wolf-thing that had materialized out of the dark one night, and would do what the sword-lady wanted without her saying anything, the stringless blue kite with a person hanging under it, circling over the ruins of Arko—*the Yeolis' flying-machine, it's real.* As they had come into the city: familiar sights horribly changed, brightness turned to darkness everywhere, marble soot-blackened, gold stripped . . . The streets near the Temonen Manor, Banatammas, Morroa, Rarneras, all were nothing but littered spaces between double rows of smoldering rubble; the marble and glass trees of House Arboretus were all felled, fragments of craven branches, green glass leaves strewn across the pavement; only by a miracle had Boulevard Jibaennen been spared.

And now . . . the swooping orange tabby *bat?* No, *cat,* cat, with orange tabby *wings,* where else could such a thing be, but in a story? He kept waiting to wake up in the boys' barracks, to find it had all been a dream. In Master's manor . . . he saw the smashed windows, and the rooms beyond them empty, felt in his pocket, a brown-stained pack of cards.

The woman sitting on the edge of the fountain, the

small woman with a silver-white fall of hair amidst jet black, was real. She was *mata*.

"Lixand!" Two steps and she was next to him. *My son*. She touched his shoulder, still afraid he wasn't real, felt its firm warmth, swung him down from the Ri's back into her arms. He threw himself into her hug and they clung, laughing, crying. His smile was the spitting image of hers. "Lixand-mi, my son, my beautiful son. You're not my baby anymore but grown so big, Lixand!"

She was world-big back then, he thought . . . *because I was small!* "Mata . . ." She was real; so, in a way he'd never known before, *he* was, as real as his true name.

Shkai'ra swung down off Hotblood's back, while Fishhook mewed protestingly; on a closer look at the Kommanza's face, Megan's joy faded, in concern. "Love, are you all right? Koru, I heard thoughts, I thought you were dead . . ."

"Bad wound," she said, smiling gently. "Lixand was my healer. After he belted me over the head with a chair-leg—that was before we were introduced." She seized Megan in a bear-hug; they kissed, long and hard and deep. *These tears I don't mind*, Megan thought. "Oh, gods, love, it's good to see you again. How's the daughter?" Lixand glanced from one to the other through tearful grinning eyes.

"*Khyd-hird!*" Sova limped up the laneway. "Oooh! We've *both* been wounded!"

"*Rasas!*" Beside her the other boy, the blue-eyed one, broke into a run.

"*Ardas!*" The two boys flung themselves into each others' arms so hard they knocked themselves over. "I thought you were *dead!* I thought you were *dead!*"

"*Mata* . . ." Lixand's voice, already more familiar with the word, held a hint of pride. The two boys hadn't let go of each other, even as they picked themselves up off the ornamental gravel. "*Mata*, this is my best friend and, umm . . . pretend brother, Ardas." His eyes shone with optimism.

Megan looked down at the two clinging together, over at Sova leaning on her stick, at Shkai'ra's wry smile. *I keep thinking all my problems are over*, she thought, *and new ones just keep ripping holes in my nets*.

XXVI

Five days after the Sack—people were already speaking of it as a historical event—Assembly was called again, in the square. None of the family went; whatever it announced would be Arkan politics, about which they didn't care. If it announced Chevenga's death, they'd find out soon enough without being there.

But the sound of the crowd was joy, clear even from a distance. The news came: Chevenga had not only shown, with the Imperial robe on his shoulders, but spoken; the gist of it being that the war and all grudges against Arko were ended, that he would rebuild the City and maintain the Empire. In barely a day, soot-darkened ruins here and there were giving way to the bright lumber of rebuilding.

"You know, love," Megan said, lying on the grass of the Temonen manor's gardens next to Shkai'ra, watching the boys show Sova some of their dance moves, the wing-cat flitting overhead as they tumbled. "It's amazing how sanity can rear its ugly head, when you least expect it. I thought he'd crazy himself to death." She lay back, one hand stroking Shkai'ra's hair. "I imagine his innate heroness will carry the day from now on, not that I mind."

"*Ia*, having an ass of gold keeps your balance well," Shkai'ra said. "Besides, that one's life is nailed tight to his backbone, he'd be dead ten times and a day, else. Whoever kills him had best shoot him asleep, in the back." She grinned. "Ah, well, he's a good general and a good lay, that's all you can ask of a man, *nia?*"

The next day was as bright as it got in the lingering smoke, warm but with a first hint of fall. Sentries stood at the Marble Palace steps: Yeolis, the circle-sword insignia of the Demarchic Guard on their breastplates, leaning on their spears with relaxed alertness. The caravan was parked in a corner of the square, since they would probably not be in audience for more than an hour or so. All it had taken was a note passed into the Palace with their names on it, and they were in, same day; things were back to normal. Shkai'ra swung down from Hotblood; the Haian had said her leg would be good as new by next year. She grinned and looked over her shoulder at the half-dozen horse-drawn wagons waiting. "Didn't think we'd pick up so much junk," she said, taking Megan's hand.

"Well, when in Arko, shop," the Zak replied, looking up at her with a slight smile and squeezing back. There had been a number of very nice things left in the Temonen manor, and a quit-claim to the property which the Yeolis stationed there had paid out of *their* share of the loot. One of the wagons below was solidly packed with books from the library, for example, that no one else had been interested in; Shkai'ra's long gold-buttoned scarlet silk coat was another, and the silver and turquoise studs on her sword belt, and the rings . . .

"Lixand! Ardas! Stop fidgeting!" Megan snapped, though fondly. The boys were pulling at the hems of their tunics; nervousness at the thought of meeting the Imperator, she supposed. Sova was elaborately nonchalant; the plundered clothing she wore were at least as expensive as Shkai'ra's, but understated, as if in deliberate contrast.

A Marble Palace flunky, an Arkan, came down the steps to meet them, excruciatingly polite but standing a little away as if dreading proximity to these unclean foreign females. That meant he had to hold the heavy ceremonial umbrella at arm's length, quite a strain.

"After you, old son," Shkai'ra said, with a cheerful wave to the guards as they passed; several of them stamped their spears on the steps in reply, grinning. Megan and she followed the functionary, walking hand in hand, herding the boys in front while Sova limped beside.

They were ushered through courtyard after courtyard, gradually rising, in splendor as well, till the very marble tiles were edged with electrum. Down a hall with chryselephantine statues of ancient Imperators; someone had stripped the golden hair and eye-jewels, leaving blind white sockets, and gone down the line with a war-hammer breaking off the noses. Then into the one where sculpted maidens upbore a ceiling half crystal skylight and half golden sunbursts; Megan hadn't noticed that, in the dark. "Zaik Mother of Death," Shkai'ra said, fingering the hilt of her saber. "I had to miss the sack of *this*?"

"Shut up," Megan said *sotto voce*, as they passed a knot of deliberately unintimidated but harassed-looking Yeoli bureaucrats, their wool ponchos looking rough and primitive against this decor. Then into a smaller series of rooms, still sumptuously appointed. More guards outside the final inlaid door; Yeolis, and—astonishingly—an Arkan with the stone face of a Mahid.

"Under new management," Megan muttered in Zak. A rebirth, perhaps, but still one had the sense that something grand if wicked had died here.

They were ushered into a relatively plain office. Relatively: the desk and wall-mirror were edged with gold filigree. *Yes . . .* Megan remembered. *I did sneak through here the night I came to see him.* Chevenga waited, face looking harried, wearing a half-poncho in the Yeoli style, a *marya*, they called it, but made of white Arkan sun-cotton, feather-light and translucent so the casts on his arms showed only faintly, the seals still slung around his neck. He smiled.

Suddenly Lixand's shoulders were gone from under Megan's hands; both boys in unison were dropping to the floor. *Arkans—they prostrate themselves in front of the Imperator.* In a single motion, she and Shkai'ra grabbed one each by the collar. "No, no. You don't have to do that. He's a *friend*, not the Imperator. Well, he *is* the Imperator." A sudden thought came: *maybe he is standing on ceremony . . .* then, *nyata. Not him.* She was right: Chevenga just chuckled, gold teeth flashing.

"You're free citizens of F'talezon," Shkai'ra added. "Bow, like this." She did, one hand on her chest and the other resting in its usual place on her sword-hilt; as the Imperator-by-conquest's eyes met hers, she winked. The boy's repeated the motion, but without the wink, with dance-trained elegance.

"You found him," said the familiar soft voice.

"*Ia,*" Shkai'ra said. "Them, actually." She looked around. "You and your Killer Mountain Boys and Girls seem to have found new jobs, too, changed wool and water for silk and wine, hmm? Your Imperatorness."

"So it seems," he said, in that impossibly ingenuous way. "Though you know that wasn't the purpose. Everyone have a seat and say what you want to drink. Lixand— I am very pleased indeed to meet you."

I bet, Megan thought. "I'm very pleased indeed to meet you too, You-Whose-Mind-is-the-Fortress-of-the-World," Lixand said, with annoying obsequiousness. *We'll train him out of that. Still, the polish is good . . .*

"Where'd you find him? Them, I should say. And what happened"—he was looking at Shkai'ra—"to *you?*"

"Well . . ." Megan said fast. *Let's get the omissions right.* "We found out—through an agent of mine—that Lixand had been spirited out of House Temonen. Shkai'ra went after him; she got cut up rescuing him. He didn't know who she was, hid in an attic and wielded a table leg against her when she put her head up to look for him. That's it, in a fingernail's worth of script."

Shkai'ra grinned. "When I woke up at the bottom of the stairs, I knew he must be Megan's."

"You ... *faked* going missing?" The *semanakraseye*-Imperator's black brows flew up. "*That's* why Mad Cow Whatsername came clean! I thought that would stay an unsolved mystery." *You and your fish-gutted attention to detail*, Megan thought. "I suppose"—his grin turned a touch contrite—"you wanted to get him out of the City before *we* got here?"

Thank you for giving me an out. Better a friend in a high place thought her cynical or prescient, than almost his assassin. "Well ... yes." She waved it away magnanimously.

His dark eyes flicked to Shkai'ra. "You might have *said* something, though; we all thought you were dead. You were designated successor for Brigadier-General First, you know."

Sheepshit! I was?! "Well, to be honest," she lied, "we heard the hands the boy was in ... weren't kind, shall we say. It had to be quick. And we thought ... well ... if we asked permission, you might deny us. Wanting to keep me for cavalry commanding, and such."

"They weren't *that* bad," Lixand piped up. "They taught me how to play cards."

Lixand, my precious long-lost son whom I love like life itself, Megan thought, *shut your trap.*

Chevenga's brows rose, but his smile stayed. "I might have denied you. I might also have sent in my best to do the task for you. I'm a parent too, remember? Strictly speaking, it was acting without orders; you forswore your strength-oath."

Megan looked sheepish for all she was worth, found enough sincerity in it to redden her face. *Come on, Shkai'ra, squirm, dammit; he'll stop asking questions that way.*

"Well . . ." He shoulder-shrugged. "Stroke of the past. If it had done us harm, heads would roll, but it didn't." *He means that literally*, Megan thought; by Shkai'ra's glance, she was thinking the same. *Oh, Invincible, if you only knew.* "Where to for you, now?"

"Back to F'talezon," said Megan, wiping sweat from her brow with a looted kerchief.

"Which has lousy winters and that noxious little shit Ranion running it . . . sorry, love," Shkai'ra added. "I'll be glad to see snow again. Not to mention the rest of the family." Megan smiled. *You'll never make a courtier.*

"How are *you?*" Megan looked Chevenga in the eyes. *So I'll be a undiplomatic indiscreet, too.* "Better than last time we talked?"

The *semanakraseye*-Imperator suddenly found his desk-top fascinating. "Oh, yes, much better, thank you," he said, looking up after a bit. "Then, I was . . . shall we say . . . under *stress.*"

"As long as you've got over it." Megan looked significantly around the opulent office. "One wants the Imperator of Arko rowing with all oars, as it were."

"Ordinary people go mad; Imperators become . . . eccentric," Shkai'ra said drily.

"I'm as un-stressed as a person can be," Chevenga shot back, "when nine of every ten people coming up to him tell him his Mind is the Fortress of the World. I've *always* been eccentric; you *know that.* Seriously, Megan, you might say they found someone more stubborn, or perhaps I should say arguing a better case, than myself. Amazing, I know, but true. Several people, really. Now . . . I'm working. I should say: conquering Arko was easy, compared to *running* it."

You're working too hard, she thought. *Trying to make good. As you said you should; as Ivahn predicted, too.* Looking at him across the desk, she reined in an impulse, then . . . *Why not?* "Do you trust me enough to let me close enough for a good-bye hug?" They hadn't been searched on the way in, she'd noticed.

He smiled. "Of course. *Kahara*, Megan—how can you keep doubting I should trust you?" *I wish*, she thought as her heart predictably lurched, *you'd damn well stop saying things like that*. She stepped around the desk, put both hands on his shoulders, leaned forward and kissed him. "For lessons learned," she said as she straightened and ran a gentle claw tickling down the scar on his cheek. *I forgive you*, the touch said. "And a good teacher. You're always welcome in my house, if you visit F'talezon."

"Thank you," he answered, and his eyes said, *for your forgiveness*. "I hope I've done good that will last. As a friend does, I love you." He stood up, for the final fare-wells. As Shkai'ra hugged him she pinched his rear. "I can't get you back," he hissed frustratedly—and simultaneously put most of his weight on her toes. "With my arms, anyway," he grinned.

Sova took her turn. *I can't hug his casts because I might hurt him, so I'll just have to put my arms around his neck. Ohhhhh . . .* "Imperators don't bite, or at least *this* one doesn't," he said, crouching so that Lixand and Ardas, who were shy at first, could reach him. *They'll remember this all their lives*, Megan thought.

As they left, a clerk was already clearing her throat, try-ing to get Chevenga's attention for a pile of documents.

As they came out into the vast hall of the maidens, Shkai'ra dropped behind the others, and bent far down to whisper in Megan's ear.

"An agent of yours, I love it. If only our *rokatzk* could have heard you call him that." They shared a snicker. "But," the Kommanza said more loudly then, mischief dancing in her eyes, "it seems I'm not the only one in this family to wrap my legs about the *semanakraseye*-ish, Imperatorial, golden butt."

"Shush!" Megan snapped, swatting. "*Honestly*."

"Shyll will be happy. Look." The Kommanza tilted her head back and threw her arms wide for a moment, in perfect mimicry of Chevenga.

"*Stifle yourself!*"

XXVII

Echera-e Lemana,
Village of Voryaseretanai,
Yeola-e

Dear Echera-e:

I'm really, really sorry, I swear I am, but it's not
my fault. I can't come visit you, at least not now.
My adopted mothers decided that the best way
home would be by ship from Fispur, and I don't
have any say in the matter. I protested and
yelled and told them I promised you and did all
I could, but they just called it a tantrum and
wouldn't listen. They say I can visit some other
time. As if they could stop me, ha ha ha.

Shkai'ra didn't get killed, just like I told you she
probably wouldn't. Turns out she kind of faked
going missing, to find Lixand. Which she did. I

know more but I can't tell you because it's a secret, highly classified, eyes only, for reasons of national security. I guess you know how the war finished, though. That is, we won. I fought in some more battles, and then there was the sack, mine goodness, which I'll tell you all about when I do visit.

I still love you and will forever and ever and ever and ever and ever ...

Love and a million kisses.
Sova.

"Have you thought about the choice before you?" Shkai'ra asked the girl.

They leaned on the ship's rail in the pale light of dawn, the sky a deep pink bordered with flame-orange in the east, the water of the Mitvald a restless purple. To the east, the long forested coast of the Diradic Tongue, taken back from Arko by Laka in this war, lay dark. The wind was just enough to keep the sails full; except for waves lapping the planks, and the cries of seagulls as Fishhook chased them, skimming the water like a huge bat, there was quiet.

"Of course I have," the Thane-girl said.

"Care to enlighten your mother on your decision?"

"I would if I could. But I have no idea whether she's dead or alive. Here, Hooky-hooky-hooky!"

Shkai'ra spat into the sea. *One of* those *moods*, she thought. "Your training is too important a matter for word games, girl."

"So's my ancestry. It's 'adopted mother.' I've thought. I haven't decided."

I'd have fewer wrinkles, Shkai'ra thought, *If I'd* left *those two with their Glitch-taken pigs of parents.* Her fingers drummed her sword-hilt. "I think I gave you all the necessary advice before I left—shall I run over it again?"

"I remember. The better trained you are the better you can deal with what comes up. But ..." Under ash-blond brows, the hazel eyes rose to meet Shkai'ra's. "It all depends so much more on whether you happen to be on the winning side than how well-trained you are." Those eyes fixed on hers, with a twisted smile. "I should know that, shouldn't I, *khyd-hird*?"

"Point taken. Though forgive me if I point out you're not exactly working in a mine, right now."

"No, but I wasn't just thinking of myself—the only one of my blood, probably, who's alive."

Shkai'ra turned to face her, brows furrowing. "Sova, I've been in many, many fights. But it's a *long* time since I *picked* one. If people *insist* on fighting me, the consequences are on their own heads, *nia*? Neither Megan nor I went out of our way to pick that fight in Brahvniki; we'd have been more than content to pass on our way—"

Sova shrugged, looked out to sea again. "That's *your* story."

"It's the truth as far as I know it."

"You think you know everything, but you don't!" Sova's eyes flashed.

"I *do* know what my own motivations were, *nia*?" She slid a little of the saber free and touched the steel. "I swear it and I do not lie: that fight was none of our choosing. Further, I'll tell you so under that fucking truth-drug, if you insist. I think I can liberate a little of it."

"There's a reason we don't talk about this around the dinner table," Sova said coolly. "Something to do with language, perhaps." The sort of thing Megan would say; even the tone reminded Shkai'ra of Megan. *But it was her who brought it up*, she thought. Then the girl went on to say that which could not be left unanswered. "Only *zhymata* knows everything that was going on."

"You picked up this Yeoli custom, what do they call it, *chiravesa*?" Shkai'ra snapped. "Pretending to be the other side? Right, be us for a moment. We're passing through Brahvniki. Megan—entirely within the law— takes back her property, the agency for the Sleeping Dragon, *paying* for it to boot. She took no other action against a man who had been hired to kill her, and *had* sold her for a slave—ask her about that sometime. He challenged her, and then *cheated* on the challenge. Maybe he needed the money real bad; was that *our* responsibility? Should we let him kill us—and all the other people who depended on Megan—because he'd dug himself a hole too deep to climb out of? Everything I've said is true as the word of the gods, and can be proved. Who started it, then?"

The girl's face had gone livid, the cheeks, always pale, now bone-white. The eyes bore the same flatness they had looking at Francosz's killer. "No one who loved me," she said quietly, the Thanish accent strong, "vould say dis."

"Unless they respected you too much to lie to you," Shkai'ra replied. "You're not a child who rages because the world isn't as she would have it; I'm telling you my mind, as one adult to another. Return the favor, please."

"You say you do not lie, and zo call *me* and *him* liar. Like everybody who doesn't see your way. Dat's not respect. *Chiravesa*." She saw the girl bite the inside of her cheek, and take a long deep breath, to muster control. "Always *both* vays.

"My Fater vass no saint; I know. I've only had that rammed down my zhroat, a lot by perfect strangers, all my life. But when Habiku ordered him to kill *zhymata,* he didn't. Else you never would have met and loved her. Some say it was greed; maybe it was mercy, you ever think of dat? Zo she came back, and he was ruined either vay. Because of deir hate, her und Habiku, which you saw for yourself; he got caught between, he got betrayed himself by Habiku.

"Zo be *me!* He had to feed us all. If you can't win, *cheat*, you say yourself! How vere the rest of us at fault, my mother, my brother, and I, and the servants, who all lost deir places? Be *me*. Be me and Francosz. Fater pushed us away, ven you took us as your prizes, ya; if he'd clung, you vould have torn us out of his arms. Und *den* you cut our hair, und made us strip, *right dere in front owf a crowd owf Zak*"—the lividness had turned red, now, and the eyes were bright with the beginnings of tears—"*made us strip und leered at us und made everyone laugh und den chased und beat us naked all de vay to the Knochtet Voorm . . . zight.* You don't understand *zight.* No, you do—you chust vanted to ruin it. It was the vorst blow to his *zight,* and mine, if I may be permitted to have some, O *khyd-hird* who says only you give me *zight,* the very worst that could be in the vorld, that you took me into your house, and made me *your* daughter. Und it burns my *zight* further still now, dat you say these things.

"And my brother, Francosz! I don't know vether anyone else is left alive in my family, but I *do* know *he* issn't. Maybe he vould haf died, if you had left us—*but maybe not!* Definitely not, if you vould haf left my family alone! He died in *your, your* and *zhymata's,* feud!

"You took us to get your own back, for the rotten vay *your* parents treated *you*—as if dat vass *our* fault! Of *course* I agreed to let you adopt me—think about it! Vat else vould I, *could* I, have done? In your own words: scutwork somewhere! You don't and never did treat me like a mother does—more like a slave-driver! And you call yourself Mother. How dare you! How *dare you!"*

The girl was trembling from head to foot. *Maybe some of it's fear,* Shkai'ra thought, *but more than half is anger.* "So: *chiravesa,"* Sova said, evening her voice. "Be me and imagine all that, if you want to be my mother."

Shkai'ra took a deep breath, and stared out to sea frowning. "Don't know how the woolheads do this all the time," she muttered under her breath to herself. "Makes my brain hurt." *It's sort of like meditation.* She was suddenly aware of Megan standing near, drawn by Sova's raised voice, but didn't let it interrupt her imagining.

"Well," she said, after several minutes. "You're quite right, Schotter's deeds were no fault of yours or Francosz's or the others." She inclined her head toward the distant coast, in the direction of Arko. "Kurkas made a mistake, and peasants get their houses burned down by warriors from nowhere; that's the way the world works. I took you two on impulse, red-angry-drunk-on-rage, because he'd tried to kill me and my love and I wanted to make him suffer; about the consequences to you, I just didn't think, that was sheer stupidity. Not that I'd wish it undone; it can't be. *A-hia*, what's more common or futile than the wish to be able to do it over?

"Making you strip and run through the streets was, umm, crueler than I intended. I'd been told Thanes didn't like to be seen naked, but didn't realize how seriously they took it. Strange . . . another point to my stupid impulsiveness and lack of empathy, as Megan told me at the time. So you're quite rightly angry at me for that; I apologize. I was raised a savage, what can I say? No harm to your *zight* was intended, to my people a child that age doesn't have any to begin with." A thin smile. "I don't think anyone will treat you so again and come off harmless from it, eh?"

"Sometimes, *khyd-hird*, some places, it doesn't matter *how* vell you *vedam* fight!"

"*Ultimately*, it does."

"Not ven it's a matter of finding somewhere you belong! Dat's life and death, too!"

"Because you ask it," Shkai'ra went on, "I'll try seeing selling Megan rather than killing her as a mercy. I'd rather be dead myself, but he may truly have seen it otherwise, and you knew him better than me. Your brother—we didn't kill him, Habiku's minions did. Treacherously. We couldn't know what would happen."

"You made him a warrior. You ordered him to watch, to fight if someone attacked. Else he would have swum away and lived."

"But he was part of the crew, part of the family, in spirit, by then."

"*Tzen kellin ripalin*," Megan muttered. "Who kills becomes. Yes, we did that."

"On my honor," Shkai'ra went on, "adopting you was done purely from regard and a desire to do well by you, from all four of us. I thought . . ." She looked slightly wistful. "I thought you understood that at the marriage."

"Oh, I understood that. And a lot of other things."

Shkai'ra looked aside, out to the open water, her

mouth twisted with an old bitterness. "The way *I* was raised, I remember hiding in a corner of the upper castle when the adults, parents included, had been at the drink again and wanted to rape someone small and tight. We'd hear their boots on the stairs; they knew where we were. *They'd* hid in the same corners."

"Oh, well, yes!" Sova broke in, voice cutting-high again, but this time in a startlingly accurate imitation of Shkai'ra's accent. "It was so rough and I'm so tough and no way a weak honey-pastry wimp like *you* could ever survive *that*, little silver-spoon-born Thane-brat. And I'm doing you *such* a favor by *just* taking a belt or gauntlet or boot to you, I must be going soft in my old age!" From Megan came a snort of barely repressed laughter, which drew a furious look from Shkai'ra. "It was *so* horrible," the Thane-girl went on, "you wanted to get your own back. That's what you *said.*"

Her eyes stayed on Shkai'ra's, but her pale face went suddenly red. "So I thought . . . I'd hear *your* boots on the stairs one day."

Shkai'ra's jaw dropped. "*What!? Baiwun* Thunderer, dip me in *shit!*"

"You *looked* at me like dat!"

"I've never done it with anyone under sixteen, since I was sixteen myself!"

The Thane-girl's face was colder than the moon, even as her teeth pinched her lip. "Vell, you said I was too young."

"Sova, I wouldn't touch you with a lancebutt if you got down on your knees and begged me! First, I never wanted to; I'd rather juggle skunks. Second, I'm happily married, three times, and not so ugly I can't get more if I've a mind to, and besides . . ." She jerked a thumb towards Megan. "Don't you think *this* one would claw my intestines out through my nose if I did?"

Sova and Megan exchanged a remembering look, which Shkai'ra didn't miss. For a moment the Kommanza's teeth clenched, words failing her. "Listen! Until I was exiled, I thought the way of Stonefort was the way of the world. The Warmasters said that a child taught to hate all that lived was the better killer ... warrior, most peoples say. When I saw the ways of some other peoples, where parent and child could ... feel for each other, it was as if they walked with their heads held under their arms, it was so strange. For a time, I doubted everything I'd been taught, down to how to latch my boots, because so much seemed to be lies." A softening. "Then I met Megan ... She's always telling me I'm sensitive as a stone shithouse, and occasionally it's true, I know."

"Occasionally?" Sova said, blinking. That went past Shkai'ra, but Megan smirked, then shook her head scoldingly.

The Kommanza raised her hands in a gesture of helplessness. "How good a parent I can be, I don't know. I know what *not* to do, mostly: the way I was raised was shit." Sova's thin brows rose in surprise. "Administered by people who were shits, and all it taught me was to turn out *more* shits, if you take my meaning. I'm still learning else."

"I don't want to be a shit," said Sova. "*Khyd-hird*, you molded me no less than my parents. They would have said it was a *man's* mold. I wanted to marry a nice Thanish man, and live in a nice house in Brahvniki. I can't now, never will. You say that's only because I was raised to want nothing else; but maybe, underneath that, I really *did* want it. I'll never know now. I never would have known had things been left as they were, either; I wouldn't have known either way."

Shkai'ra paced. "You've got choices, girl. More than most: peasants grow to be peasants, because their lord'll lop their heads if they try otherwise, or else they get dragged off to the levy and filled full of arrows. Crafters count themselves lucky to get apprenticeship ... You have half a dozen callings you could take. You're getting a good general lessoning—I can hardly write more than my name, you know—"

"Emmas Penaras, *solas*," Megan cut in. Shkai'ra's words were lost in laughter, even Sova's.

The Kommanza went on, "So if you want to shake the dust of the House of the Sleeping Dragon off your feet, you can, easily enough."

"I didn't think you cared what I wanted," said the girl. "You certainly didn't, at first."

"Well—true. But that changed. Don't you remember the words: 'Sova, do you consent to be the child of these, *as of their blood*'? We *wanted* you to be our daughter, by then; we *felt* like you were our daughter. You'd fought at our side, shed blood with us; we knew you and ... hmmm. A lot of reasons. Megan saw something of herself in you, I think, and wanted to make the story come out better this time." Sova looked; the Zak nodded, confirming. "Shyll has a loving heart, and you appealed to it. Rilla likewise, and ... well, you'll have to ask them for the details.

"Me ... had I a daughter born of my blood, I couldn't ask for better. You're as brave as any youngker I've met, you've learned fast, you're smart, and you've got a loyal heart, when push comes to shove." She grinned. "Don't get a swelled head, girl, but I'm actually quite proud of you. Besides, having you around makes life ... more alive, *ia?* Of course, you're sullen and flighty and give me grief, at times, but I said you were a daughter to be proud of, not a god. Gods know, *I'm* no vessel of sweetness and light. ...

"It was for honor, too. Once we had you, we had to do *something* for you, and would have—fosterage, an apprenticeship, something. Less would be acting like a shit to someone who'd done me no wrong; that's ... injurious to the self, if nothing else, I've learned that. I was under obligation; I'd taken you from your home, such as it was, and for your brother's sake, who died like a *zolda*, a hero—he was in my care, so it *was* in a way, as you said, my fault.

"Sova called Far-Traveller." The girl blinked, to hear herself named so formally. "If you feel I still owe your honor a debt, I will pay any sum within reason, if that will settle accounts; you can break my sword or strike me in public, if you wish."

Sova's jaw dropped, her eyes showing white all around the pupils; the red on her cheeks deepened. "Break your sword? Break your *sword?*"

Always in excess, my love, Megan thought. *Fighting, making love, paying for goods, honoring debts.*

Shkai'ra inclined her head. "Whatever you wish. When you decide, I will abide by it."

The girl went on staring, anger and amazement and shame and fear fighting it out in her eyes. "I . . . I have to think about this. Excuse me." She sprang up, whirled, and darted away to the other side of the ship.

She lay in her berth, her mind a storm of thoughts, but her insides full of a strange, huge peace. *I can't believe I said all that,* she thought, for the hundredth time. *I can't believe I did it.* Then it came to her. *That's what I chased them to the war for. I chased them to say that.*

Papa hits Mooti, Mooti hits 'Talia, Franc and I hit Piatr, khyd-hird *hits me . . .*

She'd had one big brother before—never two little ones. At first, on the trip, they'd been unnaturally well-behaved, fearing, it turned out, that Ardas would get put off at some port if they were bad. But they'd slowly come to realize—partly from Sova's own reassurances—that no such thing would happen, that the full-Arkan boy would be publicly adopted as she had been.

So now, she thought, *they run like little hellions all over the ship, pestering the crew, talking back, playing pranks. It's because they have nothing to do.* It hadn't escaped her notice, that they weren't being made to do pushups or sword-drill or fetch and carry much for Shkai'ra. *I know why,* she thought. *Because Lixand really is a child of the blood, and* zhymata's *figuring it wouldn't be fair to make Ardas do it as well.* Though whenever

Shkai'ra *did* make one of them fetch and carry, it was always Ardas, she'd noticed. He was always happily willing. *Ya. He knows where his bread's buttered, too.*

Impact, low, from behind. Shrieking little-boy laughter. She whirled around. They were playing tag, and Ardas had blundered into her. She grabbed him by the collar, drew back her hand. *Maybe you don't know quite well enough where you're bread's buttered, Arkan brat, and you need to learn some more. I'll get some of my own back . . .*

She froze. The boy had flinched and thrown his hands over his head; now his bright blue eyes peeked between tiny shielding fingers, terror-stricken. She saw tears brimming, caught in the sunlight.

Papa hits Mooti, Mooti hits 'Talia, Franc and I hit Piatr, khyd-hird *hits me . . .*

But I don't have to. I don't. He's just a little kid playing tag. He didn't mean to hurt me. Why hit him?

"I'm sorry! I'm sorry, Sovee! I didn't mean to! Please forgive me, *please?*" *Someone hit him a lot*, she thought. *Too much. And other things . . . he was a pleasure-boy. Gotthumml curse me, if I make that go on.* "I forgive you," she said, letting go. "Of course I do—I'm your *sister!* But be careful. It's rude to run into people, it makes them mad." With another apology, Ardas ran off, Lixand with him.

I can choose, she thought then. It hit her like a lightning flash, but a lightning flash of sunlight: warm and dazzling instead of grey and cold. *I do have choices. I can be anything I want, do anything I want.*

"I've thought about it," Sova announced, "and I've decided what I want to do to collect my honor-debt, *khyd-hird*."

They had just put into port in Brahvniki, and were arranging the transfer of the spoils to a ship of the Slaf Hikarmé. The early fall sun shone bright on the white onion domes and brilliant blue walls of the Benaiat across the river, the duller grey of the *kreml* wall on this side, above.

Shkai'ra walked to her, stood straight, facing her. "As I said, I'll abide by it."

Megan came to stand at one side, with the boys. The crew, sensing something was afoot, went on with their work but with one eye over their shoulders. Except for those who were off-shift; they gathered openly. On the piers, people nudged each other, curious, recognizing some of the players in this scene.

"You said I could break your sword, demand any sum, or strike you in public," said Sova, in a tone not unlike a politician's making a speech. "Well . . .

"As far as your sword goes, it's far too valuable to break. And since I'm the only one in the family with the heft for it, as you said, you're going to bequeath it to me. So it seems to me breaking it would be quite against my own interests.

"As for paying compensation: since your money is the family's money, and mine is too, our financial affairs all bound up in each other's, it would seem somewhat superfluous to demand such." *It must be Megan taught her those big words,* thought Shkai'ra. *I sure didn't.* "That leaves only one alternative."

Zaik-damned, thought Shkai'ra. *That's why she's been doing strength-exercises so hard and long ever since we had that talk. This could hurt. If she remembers half of what I taught her, she should lay me out. . . .*

But in the silence, as they faced each other, the Thane-girl seemed to lose some of her nerve, her look of pride and triumph fading some. "Maybe I should do this where no one's watching," she said.

"No." Shkai'ra chopped with her hand. *Tempting; but honor is honor.* "I said public, and I meant it."

"All right then," said Sova. "Turn around."

"Turn around?" But she did as the girl asked, and understood as soon as the first kick came. *A loose definition of the word "strike." Oof! That did hurt. Close enough, oww! Glitch, I didn't specify strike "once," did I? Dip me in shit, ouch!, damn . . .*

EPILOGUE

From somewhere in the dungeon came a steady dripping. Sometimes it seemed near, sometimes far. What liquid, he wondered as he lay on the cold stone with its thin layer of straw; while half-asleep, he was convinced it was blood.

Clanging. Calling. The officious Yeoli-accented voices, butchering an Arkan name. Making a man choose. He'd learned, from listening: they were giving everyone the choice. Swear allegiance to Shefen-kas, or die. Imperator, he was calling himself now; Imperator and you better believe it.

I wondered ... The old fart general had had him truth-drugged, learned the whole thing from end to end. And taken pity on him, of all things, admiring his plan. "To Hayel with Eforas Mahid," he'd said. "Eforas Mahid matters less than rotted shit in mud, *now.*" And sent for his best healer.

My clawed cheek ... In the infirmary of an Arkan camp, being driven further back into Arkan territory every battle, Matthas had waited, for fever, for sickness, aware of every tiny twinge inside . . . and waited, wondering just how slow acting a poison those demonic claws had carried . . . and waited, while the four gashes healed, into scabs, then scars—spectacular scars, he'd be able to tell a wonderful story of a bear or lion, if he lived—and waited, and realized the Zak had put no poison on the claws at all, but had only said she had, to torment him.

I wondered, he thought now. Why she hadn't turned him in to Shefen-kas, he knew: she'd have been incriminated herself, not having done it sooner. *But why didn't she kill me, when she could have, and hated me so?*

Now he knew. She'd let him live to witness the result of his failure: to see the Empire fall.

To see the City sacked; not knowing what else to do, he'd gone there, one of thousands of refugees. Irefas credentials had been enough to explain his *Aitzas*-long hair to the gate guards; but that would gain him no mercy, he knew when the fires and screams started, with the conquerors. He could likely get away from the random killing by hiding in the woods, he decided—*lucky I have no home here to try in vain to defend, like all these poor bastards*—but when it was over and he had to come out, he'd more likely be left alone if he were *fessas*, not *Aitzas*.

So he'd knelt in a thicket under the cliff, breathing deep to keep the knife steady, and was half-done cutting his hair, struggling to keep it even—when a bunch of shrieking Yeolis had stumbled into him. *Sheer chance. Sheer fikken chance, they were the type honorable enough not to kill an Arkan who threw himself on their mercy, as long as I showed them the way to the Marble Palace dungeon, so they could throw me in.*

He heard rustling on the stone. Something slithered away from his hand. Torchlight flickered, making a square of firelight through the tiny barred window, moving like water on the wall. He was thirsty. The boots slowed down instead of passing, tread lightening as he'd noticed it did when they were about to stop.

A key turned in the lock. The door swung creaking, thumped against the wall; torchlight filled the cell, blinding.

"You."

They had truth-drug. He knew that. He'd heard men struggle, cry "No!"; then the same voice flat and mindless, revealing secret intentions, treasons against the Yeolis, dully spilling its own death. Sometimes they'd scrape someone, and he'd hear personal things, things so trivial he couldn't see why they were such terrible secrets, or things that made him flinch.

"Name."

He couldn't see the Yeoli's face in the dark, the light behind him placed to shine on his noteboard.

"Matthas Bennas. *Fessas.*"

"You got hair long." Even holding a pen, the hand waved. "Half-long. Like hurry-cut. *'Tai,* note here says you caught cutting it."

"I am *fessas.* Truth-drug me if you like. Send for the birth register of Karoseth, son of Mantalas Bennas, born Month of the Pipe, 106. Why my hair's half-long . . . is a story longer than it ever was."

They didn't believe him, of course. Out came the box, the syringe. Naked Yeoli fingers handled it quite deftly. *Tricks we taught them,* he thought. "You swear to Chevenga or die—choose," said the first man.

I'll swear if you like. But I'm fessas. What's it matter?

After all those years, he thought with an inward laugh, *of cursing that I was* fessas.

"Well, swear anyway. Or die."

What choice do I have, realistically? It wasn't as if there was still an "our side" left to work for, to struggle to maintain his loyalty to, to get paid by. An old memory came, a childhood memory, of Karoseth, the wind with its sea-taste through the spread-hand palm trees, playing Don't Step on the Crack on the boardwalk. Then rain pattering on the clear glass pane of his office in Brahvniki, the smell of thick Brahvnikian tea in the samovar, a finger-cup of Saekrberk. *I'll be a merchant for the rest of my life,* he thought. *Most people in the world would fall on their faces to their gods for such good fortune as that.*

He cupped his hands on his temples. "On my hope of Celestialis, Second Fire come if I forswear ..." As he forced his tongue to shape those obscene syllables, he thought, *it's a simple matter of this: do I ever want to see the sun again?* He did.

"Fourth Shefen-kas Shae-ra-noi. Imperator." Three times they made him say it, as if to make his tongue keep it ringing in his brain so it sank deep into his heart, like a slow knife.

Then they made him lie down in the filthy straw, and extend his arm. *Celestialis. Too suspicious. Too suspicious. They're going to truth-drug me anyway. I'm dead. It's done. I swore, and I'm dead anyway.*

Even descending into it feels different, in enemy hands, he thought, when the drug had worn off enough that he could think again.

His will could only watch from far away while his mouth dug his grave. They knew everything. The more he'd told, the more intrigued they'd got. "Now you know how Shkai'ra felt when you truth-drugged her," they'd laughed.

Now they pulled him up by his arms, and led him out of the cell. He didn't resist, his limbs numb. Suddenly he became too aware of everything, flames too bright, noise too loud; he could feel every hair at the back of his neck, all of a sudden, where the blade of the axe would first touch as it blurred down. He found himself imagining it, heavy black steel, the edge shining, whetted razor-keen—or dull, depending on how many people it had eaten since it was last sharpened—the block with its curved neck-rest and old blackened gore. He swallowed,

felt his throat close; that would soon be parted, the blood
that now throbbed in the arteries spraying out free.

His legs were water, his guts felt as if they wanted to
fall out. *No, I won't feel the sharpness or dullness of the
edge,* he thought; *they say wounds that severe don't hurt.
It will just be a strange, blunt impact. Will I see the block
spin for a moment as my head tips off? And then . . .* A
too-vividly written passage from an old book came to
him, of a kindly executioner asking the condemned
whether he cared how he looked; if so, he should relieve
himself first, for the body voids at the moment of
beheading. He didn't care, he decided, whether he
sprayed the heathen whoresons all over with shit. But
the thought brought no relief. *I guess I didn't want to
die for my country,* he thought. *I guess in the end I'm a
coward. Probably most people are.*

They took him upstairs, the corridors turning brighter
and more ornate as they rose. A public execution? He
marveled at the richness that had been before, clear from
what was left. *All theirs now,* he thought. They led him
through doors that had been glass but were now only
frames or hinges, with pairs of curly-haired sentries
whose dark eyes followed him.

They took him to a room with a thick oaken door,
pulled it open, led him through an anteroom, another
door. An office; an ebony and gold filigree desk open at
both ends for two to work across it, with some Yeoli
behind it; the wool of his *marya* looked rough and
upcountry in this place, the shape under it too rugged
for an office. Yet there was something in the man's presence . . . he looked at his face.

He'd seen engravings in the *Pages,* before that in the
Watcher, the posters, paintings, mosaics. Strange, to see
a sight so familiar looking more alive than his remembrance of it, because his remembrance came only from
its images. Now those hard, scarred features framed by
the famous halo of black curls faced him, those notorious
piercing dark eyes with their touch of sadness fixed on

his—living, seeing. He recognized the gleaming swatch of gold hanging against the rough-knit wool: the Imperial seals, fastened to a neck-chain.

He threw himself into the prostration, trying to do it as gracefully as he'd imagined it could be done. *No one instructed me*, he thought. *No one even searched me. They never did; I could be carrying a knife.* "Rise." He felt too weak to lift himself, but did, and tip-toed to the chair offered him, keeping his eyes lowered.

Silence stretched to what seemed a day. Shefen-kas called in Yeoli, and rattled off orders to the servant who appeared—or squire, by his manner; there was no obsequiousness in it at all. He caught only the word "Saekrberk." A glass appeared before him, was filled, the green liquid swirling. Its scent haunted him with memories. "Drink up, Matthas." Shefen-kas spoke Arken, superior-to-inferior but only one step down. *Poison? No, he wouldn't waste it on me. Does he mean to torture me with hope?* "You need it, I can see. Go on. *Korukai.*" He'd never imagined a conquering king could have such a quiet voice.

As per Brahvnikian tradition, he downed the whole glass in one draught. As he felt color burn out into his cheeks, the servant filled the glass again.

It's not fair, he thought, glancing up at Shefen-kas for a moment and then down again. *It's not fair that he, whom all the might and stealth of the greatest Empire in the world broke itself against, is sitting here in front of me disguised as a mortal, looking exactly like a plain medium-sized man whom I could reach across and strangle with my bare hands. . . .*

"I only skimmed the transcript," the Yeoli Imperator said. "There were things there I don't want to know, and things not there that I do. How long did you work for Irefas?"

I am recounting my career, Matthas thought with a sense of unreality as he spoke, *to the one who's about to cut it and me off*. He told no lies, even by omission,

seeing no point. When he came to times the old state had
made his life difficult, Shefen-kas seemed, of all things,
sympathetic, as if its incompetence somehow saddened
him. *I don't know why*, Matthas thought drily. *You'd be
worm-meat ten times over if not for it.*

"Well," Shefen-kas said when he was done, "you
worked for Arko under Kurkas. Would you work for Arko
under me?"

It was like feeling his heart miss a beat, or expecting
floor at the bottom of a darkened flight of stairs, to feel
his foot find only air just as he put his weight on it. He
stared; Shefen-kas's eyes stared back, no lie or game in
them. "I mean it," he said. "At the same rate of pay you
were earning before, but with better consideration of
your requirements, and respect of your opinions, from
above."

Matthas took refuge in his cup of Saekrberk, staring
down into it, lifting it to his lips. The muscles of his
middle hurt; he realized it was with being so terrified,
so long. Now that he was merely stunned speechless,
they'd relaxed.

"Tell me honestly," Shefen-kas urged. "Do I strike you
as one who would hinder his own underlings through
incompetence or neglect?"

"No," Matthas said, glad to be asked a question easily
answered. "You certainly don't." *Gods curse you forever.*

"Perhaps you need time to think on it?"

Words burst out. He couldn't stop them. "I tried—
didn't you read that part in the transcript?" He wanted
to swallow his tongue; perhaps he'd given away what
hadn't been given away yet. He knew the words were
too familiar as well; he should have started with the
proper title and obeisance, it should be a further degree
of inferior-to-superior, he should never speak such a
direct question . . . *I'm not used to talking to Imperators*,
he inwardly whined.

"You tried to arrange my assassination. Yes, I read
that." Matthas stared; Shefen-kas shrugged with his

shoulders. Matthas noticed the white through the stitching of the *marya*: casts. The only possible reason a Yeoli wouldn't wave his arms; he'd wondered what hadn't seemed quite right when Shefen-kas spoke.

"A hundred thousand Arkans have tried to kill me. Should I fear or resent one more? I can't blame you; I'd have done the same. It was your duty."

"But ..." Matthas tried to blink away amazement. "How can you ... I swore, but they didn't make me repeat it under truth-drug. You didn't even have me searched coming in here. I was the enemy, I tried to kill you, and now you want me to work for you. How can you trust me so much?"

"They'll swear you in again, drugged. Policy." Shefen-kas shrugged again, and gave a smile that was almost childishly ingenuous, with a flash of gold teeth. "But I know who to trust."

Lixand put his hand into his mother's as they walked up Flutterwing Lane, at the head of the wagon-train, to the House of the Sleeping Dragon. It was cold here, the cold of his fantasy cities. *F'talezon*. Ardas couldn't pronounce it to save his life, but it was easy for Lixand; his tongue somehow remembered. He made a plume of steam in the air with his breath. "Mata, are we ... are we really *Aitzas*?"

"Ya, and far too dignified for snowball fights," said Sova, shoving a fistful of snow down the back of Ardas's coat, to his squeal. "Ow! That white stuff is *cold!*" The manor was no smaller nor less rich than House Temonen, but in an utterly different style.

Megan smiled and put an arm each around the boys. "It's not the same, but we're wealthy enough—oh, *no.*"

From the gates ahead came a thunderous chorus of barking. Dee and Dah barked, puppy-shrill no longer, but close to the belling tone of full-grown greathounds. Inu led the pack.

Megan put her hands up, as always. "*Inu, sit!*" As

always, he gently knocked her over and washed her face with a dinner-plate-sized tongue.

"Inu! Back, you son-of-a-bitch!" Shyll's clear shout and Rilla's laugh rose through the noise. Over it all, they could hear the baby crying.

Shyll gave Megan a hand up, and the hugging started—Shkai'ra picking up Rilla, then Shyll as well, then Shyll having to prove he could pick *her* up, and Sova rushing to hug Rilla . . .

Ardas dropped back beside Lixand. "We sure have a lot of family now, don't we, Ra—I-mean-Lixand," he whispered.

"Yeah. But I think I could get used to it."

The Arkan boy's grin split his face. "Yeah. Me too."

wounded-cart, even on roads this smooth. It was stuffy in there, and people kept groaning. *Never thought I'd wish I were riding.* But the Haians weren't going to let her up yet; when she did try standing, just to see what would happen, she instantly felt why they didn't—her head going light, and her whole body insisting on lying down again.

The only bright moment today had been when Chevenga had come into the cart, to squeeze hands, stroke brows and present everyone with the decoration all wounded got, the Saint Mother's Bloodstone, slipping it under their pillows if they were sleeping. *Good thing he can't read Zak,* she'd thought as they exchanged pleasantries.

It was an old habit, laying out her thoughts on paper to see in black and white whether an idea was viable. Most times she had to burn the paper once the decision was made, this time no exception.

Shkai'ra would have to count on the fact that no one would challenge the wound—on both head and throat— and her limited Arkan vocabulary could be garbled enough that no one would notice the accent. Scribbled in one corner of the list was the notation "Emmas Penaras, *solas*"; Shkai'ra could learn to write that. For the rest, a few cards that Megan could easily forge, along with travel papers ... If she could stall the *rokatzk* for an iron-cycle, and Shkai'ra were both lucky and careful, it was possible.

"I'll wrap my head in bandages stained with chicken blood." Shkai'ra, lying back by the fire with one ankle over her knee and fingers laced behind her head, grinned raffishly. In two days, Megan had healed enough to be let out of the wounded-cart at night. "Poor valiant ... umm ... Emmas Penaras, *solas*, head-wounded fighting the benighted barbarian invaders. Can't speak very well, forgetful, lost his letters mostly, hands shaky anyway ... it's perfect! We can get Imperial harness easily enough."

Megan appraised her. "You'll have to trim your hair some, dear. It's too long for a *solas.*"

Shkai'ra winced. "My hair! I guess I couldn't pass for an *Aitzas* ... Damn, I haven't done more than trim the ends since I got warrior-braids." She brought the plaits, shining in the lamplight, around in her hands. "Well, that should wait until I go missing, of course. So, love, think you could make a convincing widow?"

Megan scanned the dark tents around them, idly wondering if the blackmailer was near, or whether people were starting to wonder why she and her wife had started speaking Fehinnan so much. "Or at least the worried wife of someone gone missing in action," she answered. "I'll stall things for an iron-cycle, the length of time I told him first. I think I can do that."

"That should be enough time," Shkai'ra said.

"Then you bring Lixand back to the army ... or if the army takes the City first, we'll meet on the steps of the Marble Palace. Or, barring that, the Temonen manor. At noon. And if the other's not there in, say, an eight-day after the army arrives, we'll know for sure." The Kommanza nodded wordlessly. "Hotblood would have to stay here."

"He will, if I tell him to, even though he doesn't like it," Shkai'ra said. "You can trust me, my heart. I'll win for both of us."

"*Three* of us," Megan corrected. "Lixand, too."

I trust you, love, she thought later, when sleep would not come. Shkai'ra snored peacefully. *Chevenga will have to as well, though he doesn't know it.* She tried to feel as determined as she could make her voice sound. *You always come through in the crunch. You're your best when things are worst.*

The next morning, well enough to walk a little, she was summoned to the office-cart. *Koru ... It couldn't be to plan; she was wounded. Lady grant he doesn't suspect something. He can't, how can he know anything?* She swallowed back nervousness as the *semanakraseye* spotted her, and handed off the blue and green standard, smiling.

In the cart, a few words of small talk, then he came to the point. "However much one might deserve the army's accolades," he said, "there's an award one is always presented in privacy." His stern scarred face cracked into a grin like a boy's, waiting to see the look on the receiver's face when he gave a present. In his hand lay an award-pendant, a white one: Megan recognized the Nephrite Serpent. Not quite the Incarnadine, which required very spectacular results, but still, the second highest award there was, for actions of stealth.

She felt her face go burning hot. *Don't think it. Don't remember, I've forsworn my strength-oath. Don't think it, now.* "I was just doing what you're already paying me for," she sputtered. *I'm blushing; Koru, don't let him see it's more than I would for just modesty.* "You didn't decorate me the other times."

"Look," he said, his dark eyes fixing hers, in emphasis. "If you had fallen out of that tree when the arrow hit, if you had given up, they'd have truth-drugged you, and taken all you *have* done away from us. Then they'd have killed you, and taken all you *will* do. That's what you're getting it for. Now stop wasting my time arguing."

"You'll win, Shkai'ra," she whispered to herself, as she limped back to the wounded-cart, fingering the prize in her belt-pouch. "Not for three of us—for four."

Shkai'ra backed carefully, taking the blows of the practice sword alternately on shield and the wood of her own blade. The brown-gold dust of the impromptu field scuffed up around their feet, mixed with bits of dry grass. Or a crop, before? Possibly; it was unrecognizable now. The harsh sound of their breathing sounded under the clack-*bang* of the field, shouts, clatter from half a hundred sparring pairs, lost in a universe of concentration that narrowed down to the bright slit bisected by the nasal of her helmet.

Now, she thought, and began to back more quickly. The man followed, hard and fast, cut-thrust-backhand cut-thrust-thrust-thrust, shield up and point keeping line with his rear foot, stamping into each blow. Shkai'ra let him fall into the rhythm of parry and stop-thrust, then *squatted* under the next, releasing the outer grip of her shield with her left hand, letting her knees relax and gravity carry her down. Instinctively he slashed, dropping his shield to cover the exposed thigh; her legs shot out, one hooking behind his knee and the other around his ankle. Curling erect, braced on the man's leg, she chopped two-handed at his exposed shoulder. The heavy curved oak of the *boka* thudded flat and heavy on the steel and leather of his armor, and the shield-arm went limp.

Eeeeeeeeeeeeeeee! she shrieked, a sound like a file on stone, and attacked with a berserker flurry that banged off shield, blade, helmet, shoulder, midriff, finishing him with a footsweep and a precisely controlled overhead cut that would have sliced halfway down from his shoulder.

"You Enchians get too fucking academic," she rasped, to him and the other defeated sparring partners who sat nursing their bruises along the edge of the trampled ground. "A battle's more like a bar brawl than fencing in the *salle d'armes,* remember it. Dismissed from foot drill: report to your centurion for formation riding." She turned her head. "Sova! Water!"

The girl brought the wooden bucket to the edge of the commander's tent. The sides were rolled up along the guy ropes, leaving an awning from the bright morning sun. Shkai'ra unlaced her armor and the sweat-soaked gambeson, pulled her shirt off while the girl put the equipment on its stand, drank thirstily and wiped herself down with a wet towel. She glanced around; nobody near, and nothing she need do urgently for the next little while.

"Thanks," she said, pouring a final dipper over her